Bourbon Breakaway

A Small Town, Brother's Best Friend Romance

Starlight Canyon

Sienna Judd

BOURBON
Breakaway
STARLIGHT CANYON SERIES
SIENNA JUDD

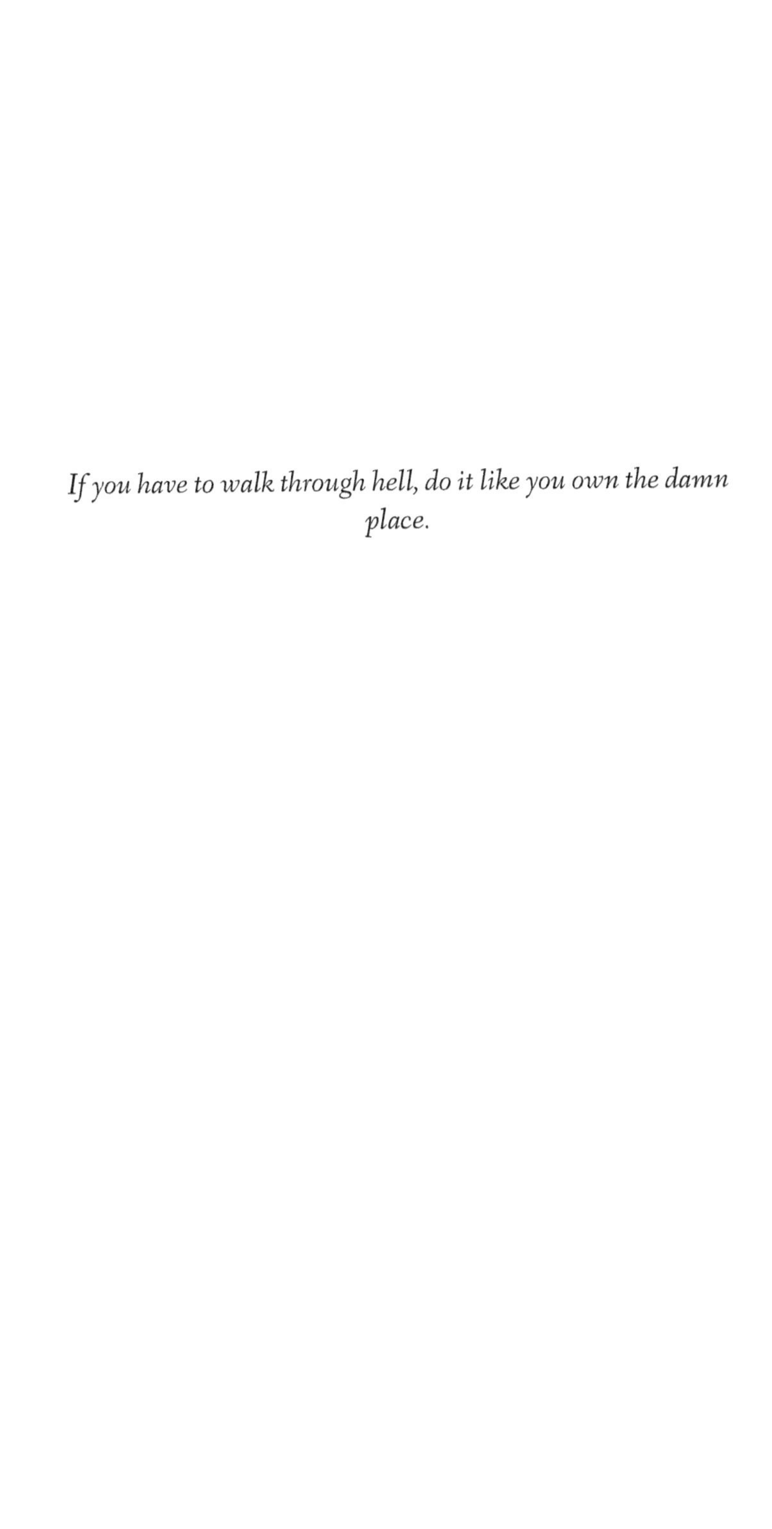

If you have to walk through hell, do it like you own the damn place.

Prologue

Ashton

THIRTEEN YEARS AGO

I NARROW my eyes at the teenaged guy ogling the small of Jolie's bare ivory back, exposed by her low-cut prom dress. We're slow dancing, if you can call it that. It's more me holding her at arm's length and at a perfect distance to see perverted guys like the one behind her, letting their gazes roam where they don't belong.

"You need something?" I growl.

The senior attempts bravery. It's a stiff, uncertain stare down—or stare up in his case because at my height that's how I glare at most people, from the top down. His gaze slips quickly when I flare my nostrils. He thinks he can look at this girl? *Wrong*.

Like a dance twirl, I swing Jolie's body around one-eighty in my arms. I make an opaque human wall with the cheap polyester of my blazer as a barrier between Joey and this loser.

My surrogate little sister lets out a long, exasperated sigh that blows curly tendrils off the side of her forehead. "I thought you'd be more... fun."

Her eyes are round and lined lightly with eyeliner, not a severe black like a lot of the other girls have going but the color of eggplant. She has a glittery shadow of a similar shade on her eyelids, and the makeup makes her green eyes pop. She's pretty tonight. Logan was right to send me as her date. That pimply twat was the first of many who would have her, I'm sure.

Jolie deserves better, which means she'll end up alone, because after going to college I realize all men are fuckwits. Or maybe it's being in the hockey world. Since discovering puck bunnies in college and the way my teammates treat them, I've become pretty disgusted by how we're led around by our cocks.

Sadly, I'm not immune to these male genes. I count myself among the fuckwits, but Logan knows I'd never be one with Jolie.

I hold my hands steady, floating just above putting any pressure on her hips. I balance between being polite enough to perform my duty as a stand-in big brother, and touching her enough so she doesn't feel ugly, because she's anything but. It's a fine line I walk, as tough as keeping the steps to this slow dance. I have no rhythm.

She tips her head sideways. Long blonde curls drip down her bare shoulder, and she casts flirty eyes upward. "Come on." She reaches up and fists my shirt. "Loosen up."

I gaze down at her. In heels, she's a good five or six inches shorter. She's a tall girl. Even just this last year of me being away in college she sprouted up a couple inches.

Inches. The flutter of her eyelashes that tease and urge me to be more fun reminds me of the shameless sass of her invitation. She sure is getting a mouth on her. Jolie texted me when the prom invitations hit email inboxes...

JOEY

Hey- The hall of fame quarterback asked me to prom but I was hoping you and your extra five inches would come with me.

I'm tall. Taller than most men I meet and apparently five inches taller than that guy. But I knew what she was really saying. And her vocal advances have made their way to her hands tonight. She fists my shirt again like it's bedsheets and yanks me hard enough to pull me one breath closer.

I said no to being her prom date when she asked. Her innuendo has snuck into nearly every conversation and brush of a shoulder since she turned fifteen. The last thing I want to do is lead her on. Besides her basically being my little sister, losing my best friend is not something I can handle. Especially after what I found out tonight—the universe-shifting lie tucked in the most obvious hiding spot, under my dad's ties.

If I'd said no to prom with Joey, I would have never found that piece of paper.

It would have never fucked my entire sense of reality.

But here I am. Logan urged me to say yes; to come back to Starlight Canyon tonight and escort his sister to prom. He'd said he'd rather it be a fucker he knows than a douchebag he doesn't. I came back from college for the weekend to do him a favor. That's it. And I'll be damn sure not to enjoy it the way she's suggesting and allow my best friend to demote me from fucker to douchebag.

Jolie sways her body, dancing herself through the last bit of personal space holding us apart. "Earth to Ashton. You're... far away... again. You've been a total space cadet tonight. What's up with you? Do you have something to talk about? I'm not Lo but I'll listen."

"Nothing to talk about, Joey. I'm just being your brother's soldier. Keeping an eye out for trouble. What I came here to do."

She tuts then releases a sassy scoff. "What? You actually think any of these losers would try something with me while you're here? You could fall asleep and they wouldn't dare. Or maybe you already know that because you've been hazed half the night."

I have a lot on my mind, but I won't be a downer. It's my shit to handle, and I won't stink up her evening. I half-smile. "You want entertainment, do you? How about I do the running man to the next song?"

She giggles and tugs my shirt's fabric back and forth frisky as always. Her strength isn't enough to jostle me, but I move under her spirited touch anyway and the corner of my mouth tilts upward, playing along to lighten the mood the best I can. She's a good girl. I want her to have fun tonight. And I'm being pretty crap at giving her a prom to remember.

But it seems her idea of a good time and mine are very different.

She releases the fabric from her grip. It's crinkled now. She smooths it and stares at the spot where her hand was. As she strokes my chest, her cheerfulness washes away, and it's replaced by pure mischief. "I have an idea that could spice up the night." She eases herself up and into me as if she wants to drop a secret in my ear, and the top of her hip skims my dick in the process.

I'm pretty sure Logan wouldn't like this.

"Yeah? What's the idea?" I hope it has more to do with finding some spiked punch than the suggestion her bony pelvis is making against my cock. "Shoot."

She rocks herself back and forth over the sensitive area of my zipper. These aren't jeans. The fabric is thin, and her movement offers dangerous pleasure. I have a bad feeling about this... and it only gets worse.

"I'm ready to lose my virginity..." Her voice is almost husky, but nerves interlace her words. "...to you."

I can't help but let out a laugh. "Did you have a drink when you went to the bathroom?"

She rolls her eyes. "I wish." Her purple-lined emerald eyes glimmer wickedly. "Even if I did, I've been thinking about this for the past three years."

A strangled laugh escapes me, sounding a little too flattered, and it falls down between us.

Joey slaps my chest. She's a live wire. It's hard to tell if she's serious or trying to get a rise out of me. She does that sometimes. The girl is going to be top-notch banter for a man some day. "Ashton, I'm leaving for college. I'm eighteen. You'll have graduated Golden Sierra when I get there in the fall, and I can't think of a better dick to open my legs for."

Holy hell... "You've definitely been drinking..."

She presses her tits into me. They're small but fiercely sharp. "You know I've tried with you before tonight. You blew me off. And over the years, it became painfully clear—because I tried and tried—that you won't date me. That your bond with Logan is too important to risk. Or maybe you just aren't attracted to me?"

She pauses, waiting for me to correct her, fishing for my compliment.

She's attractive. Still all gangly limbs like a baby giraffe, but the high school boys are all over her. She knows she's pretty without me saying it, and I don't want to because the words would be taking part in this charade. This is absolutely absurd. Beyond it.

How the hell did she sneak a drink without me knowing?

I eye the crowd behind her suspiciously.

"Fine," she breaks the silence. "You don't like me. But I like you. And I know when I go off to college I'll start drinking and probably fuck some guy and do a walk of shame home. I'll lose my virginity in a way that matters to nobody."

What kind of statement is that? "Are you trying to guilt me into having sex with you? A one-night stand isn't your style, is it? You're not that stupid."

"One-night stands aren't stupid."

"No, but with drunk college boys, they're reckless." I think about her at Golden Sierra next semester without me and Logan to watch out for her. The frat boys, the jocks. I shudder imagining their greasy palms and drool all over this girl. She's hardly a delicate flower, but she deserves... more.

"I am reckless. Veeeery reckless. Don't underestimate what it's been like for me, especially since Dad died. I've been under the thumb of my watchful mom and three protective brothers. Damn right I'm going to get a fake ID and blow off some steam."

She wraps her hands around my back, and even through my shirt and blazer, her fingernails scratch my skin. She digs in with them, strong and sensual. Aggressive. Assertive. Quite the tiger for a virgin.

This is ridiculous and has already gone too far. This is not going to go down well if Logan hears about it.

I put my hands on her arms to ease her away, then slide my palms down her skin to take her hands in mine. I don't even know if she's serious, but the conversation is off-limits. Even if she's kidding. Which she must be. "No. I'm flattered. But no."

"No?" Her chin drops, and she peers at me from under her perfectly groomed eyebrows.

I bring my head down in one swift nod, like a gavel.

Her jaw goes slack. "You're playing hard to get? Are you seriously going to make me beg? You know I won't say anything to Logan. I wouldn't want him knowing either..."

Wait. Is she for real? "No. Not just for Lo. I'm saying no *for me.* You're like... family. I promised myself I'd look out for the Hunters like I look out for the Danes..."

Rejection smears down her face, leaving her normally round, sunny cheeks crestfallen. "Wow." She takes a long pause, processing inward thoughts as if a first-time revelation and one she is devastated to discover. "You really don't like me." She says it more to herself than to me.

"Joey, I'm saying no because I *do* like you. You should find a guy who commits to you. An actual boyfriend. And..."

"You don't like me..." she repeats it, confronting some reality she never knew existed, as if she was holding on to a hope for us I never saw before. Her shoulders slump, and her hands slide out of my palms, leaving a stain of regret.

"Joey..." I plead. I've hurt her. Not that there was another option apart from no, but... I hate this. In all the years of knowing Jolie Hunter, I've never seen her this way —eyes glassed over and glistening with the threat of tears.

The tip of her nose blushes. "This is... embarrassing. I thought you'd say yes." An almost hysterical laugh leaves her lips, but she sucks it back with a sharp breath. "I actually thought you'd say yes."

"Really?" As soon as the disbelief leaves my mouth, I regret it. She doesn't need to hear I haven't spent the past three years dreaming of this the way she has. It's a cruel reality I should have held back.

And it's this reality that finally releases a tear down her cheek. "Yes, Ashton. I thought you'd say yes."

My chest is tight. Flames crawl up my neck. I can't let her hurt. Over me? Convincing her this isn't real seems like the only thing that will help. "It's not right, though... you don't mean it, Jo... you liking me is like... some game."

"Game?" She says it as if it's the most offensive word in the English language.

But it's true. Her crush on me is an age-old cliché. "Yeah, as in, I'm the first guy you've trusted in your life besides your dad and brothers and it's just natural to think you have feelings for me, but it's not real..."

Her gaze is equal parts fire and pain. She grits her teeth. "I know the difference between fantasy and reality, Ashton."

"Hey..." I pull her head into my chest. I won't fight with her, but besides a hug, I don't know how else to fix this.

"Just..." She plants her hand on my chest and eases

herself out of my embrace. "Just take me home. I don't want to be here anymore."

***

Jolie says little in the car on the way home. Her head rests against the glass of her window, her once strong, sure posture deflated in her dress. By the time I get her home, she slips out of the car like a puddle. When her mom, Joy, opens the door, she has her arms in a welcoming semicircle and a warm smile ready for her daughter. Jolie pours into her embrace. Her mom's expression quickly morphs, and her gaze shoots down at me over Jolie's vulnerable bare back, like Joy thinks something worse happened than it did.

Then again, can anything worse happen than a broken heart?

Joy waves me off without a word and escorts her daughter into the house.

That night, I lie in bed for hours with her lively, sassy expression on my mind. I still see the cute arch of her eyebrow when she said we didn't have to tell anyone; the brazen innocence in her crooked smile, her not having the first clue how losing her virginity to me would have caused bigger heartache than me saying no.

Though no is the final and *only* answer, an ache to make her feel better rattles my bones. I've known Jolie since I was eight and she was four. Joey was the little shadow following me and Logan around. Colt was always too mature for her. Dash, too aloof. So, the little tomboy had us. Even knowing her all those years of skinned knees, a broken arm, bruised from puck after puck under goalie gear and layers of pillows... I never once saw her cry.

This is the worst fucking night of my life on so many levels.

After hours awake, I decide I can change the course of at least one thing.

I rush to get dressed and leave a note for my mom before sneaking out of the house. Half an hour later, I tread quietly up the Hunters' driveway, having left my car at the end and hoping like hell I don't wake their shepherds. Her mom is alone now, and I don't want to scare her.

Jolie's cell is off, so throwing pebbles at her window is my only option. I throw, and throw, and wonder why my aim isn't better when I'm so good at putting a biscuit in the back of the net.

Tink.

Tink.

Tink.

Finally, the curtain peels aside, and a flash of long, golden hair mimics its motion.

"Joey!" I whisper-shout. Thankfully, the bedroom next to hers is Logan's, and he's gone.

The sash slides up, and Jolie's head pops out. Golden hair tumbles down as if I summoned Rapunzel into the cool mountain air. Her body is halfway out the window, and she holds a dumbbell in her hand. "Ashton? What the hell?"

I can't help but ask, "Why are you holding a dumbbell?"

"In case you were an intruder or something."

I press my fingers into my eye sockets. *This girl.* "Come down."

She glances at her pajamas. "Wait. Did you change your mind?"

It's a question full of hope which might have made me laugh, except I have to say, "No."

"Why are you here, then?"

"I can't leave you like this. I care about you. Come on. I leave tomorrow and I'm not going knowing I made you cry."

A sigh leaves her lips. "It's fine."

"Shut up with that. It's not fine. You were crying. Come here before your mom wakes up. Meet me on the bench."

She shakes her head, and her moonbeam hair dances in the midnight breeze. "Fine."

I snake myself around the house in the shadows to their backyard. It's a garden I know like my own. I spent as many hours here as Logan has at mine over the years, and there's only one bench. It sits in the middle of Joy's flower garden, a place that even I can appreciate.

I pad my feet along the stepping stones from the grass to its middle where the bench is. The scent of honeysuckle fills the air. Crickets sing, and the trees blow with a rustling breeze that almost relaxes me. But then the crunch of gravel rounds the bend of the house, and there is Jolie, in her pajama pants and a winter coat snuggled around her body. It might be near summer, but the temperature drops here in the mountains.

She approaches with her arms wrapped protectively around herself. I tap the wood next to me, and she sits. Words aren't my forte, but the best ones are typically simple.

"I'm sorry. I can't do what you asked. It's not because you aren't pretty. You're the coolest girl I've ever met. I don't want you thinking you're not... worthy. You mean a lot to me, Joey. We're family."

"Stop saying that. We're not related." She hugs herself more securely.

"No. But... I want to be your friend forever. Doesn't that mean more than a fucked-up night that confuses everything we know about each other?"

She considers my words while staring at the ground in front of her. She hasn't looked me in the face yet. A beat passes, but she's not ready to let it go. "It wouldn't confuse anything. It's just sex."

I let out a tight laugh. "You don't mean that. And it isn't just sex. What I do with girls at college is just sex."

She bumps into my side. "Ew. Dude. Come on. Are you here to make me feel better or worse?"

"See?"

"See what?" She finally raises her chin to gaze at me.

I tuck fallen hair behind her ear and caress my finger along her jaw. "You're jealous."

She rolls her eyes. "I'm not jealous."

"You are. And that's why it won't be *just sex*. It's more than sex when two people care about each other. And I care about you."

She flops her head to the side and purses her lips, still resisting me.

"Hold out your pinky."

She narrows her eyes. "Why?"

"Just do it."

She extends her tiny feminine finger, and I curl my own around hers.

"I promise I'll always be your friend. You can count on me to help you. To protect you." I lean my forehead against hers. "Even though I know you don't need it."

She blows a laugh out of her nose and takes her forehead off mine, her round eyes beaming stronger than the moonlight. God, I hope I make her feel better.

"Joey, I want to be your friend. I know it isn't what you asked tonight, but I promise it to you anyway."

A smile tugs at the corner of her mouth. "I guess it's better than nothing."

I yank on her pinky. "Friendship isn't better than nothing. It's better than most things. Trust me. It's the basis for all things worthwhile in life. I'm offering you my best."

She lowers her eyes, but we still hold hands. Though I can't see her face well, her cheeks round the way I'm used to.

"I bet you're not that good in bed anyway."

I laugh. "Exactly. I'm terrible." I let go of her hand and wrap my arm around her, pulling her into me because it's cold out here and I don't want the chill to reach her.

She puts her head on my shoulder. "I'm still a little sad."

"Me, too," I say, thinking about my dad's tie drawer again. I squeeze her to hang on to the present instead. "But when I pinky promise, it's ironclad. You need me, I'll come running. All you have to do is ask."

"Same."

Her words have a surprising effect on me. They wrap around my heart like a layer of protection I didn't know I needed.

I kiss the top of her head. "I can't think of a better crazy-ass woman to have on my side."

Chapter One

Ashton

PRESENT DAY

I NEVER THOUGHT it possible to consider moving back into my childhood room at thirty-five years old a success story. But today, when I roll my things into the biggest room with the smallest closet at Moon Ridge Ranch, it feels like a goddamn victory. And the first thing I want to do now that I'm officially back in Starlight Canyon is get some comfort food.

I walk through the door at Creme de la Creme's. Some

things never change because the tinkle of the bell is just as welcoming and friendly as it's always been. I've missed that sound. And I've missed what will follow. The simple pleasure of dessert and a strong brew to wash it down.

It doesn't even cost a fucking fortune either like it did in LA. Eyeing the drinks board, I remark on everything being normal-people prices. That's what I've missed about home. Salt-of-the-earth folks with nothing to prove. Just loving what they have. Being who they are.

Here, I can melt into the backdrop again. Sure, the women at the bars won't treat me like your average cowboy, even though in my mind, I still very much am. But there are enough Tom, Dick, and Harrys that think I'm nothing special. To them, I'm just the Danes' kid. And that's plenty good enough for me. I sampled fame. I chewed on Hollywood attention. It doesn't taste as good as home.

Sitting down at a two-top table, I take the laminated menu with today's soup and sandwich specials in my hand, look at it but don't read it. I tap it on the counter.

The doorbell jingles again, and I twist. No Logan yet. I check my watch, and it's five minutes past the time we agreed to meet, so he'll be another ten. I pull out my cell to check the news for my brother's pro-football team.

Sometimes it sucks that our sports are on during the same season. But he's a star. A fucking superstar. He's getting amazing press as usual. I swipe over to a new screen to see how my fantasy football team is doing. *Ah, crap. Can't start with Schafer this week, he's injured.*

The restaurant door chimes in the background.

Hansen has a bye week.

Tinkle.

Damn... my players are dropping like flies...

Tinkle.

I'm deep in thought over how to rearrange my team this week when a gust of cold autumn air puffs at me along with the scent of a woman. An earthy, natural perfume. Roses and... patchouli? What's that shit the hippie chicks wear? I've always hated heavy perfumes; all that artificial stuff isn't for me, but this? It's an invasive, provocative breeze going past me, and it piques my interest...

Keeping my head down, I dart my eyes up to see who the scent belongs to. I only catch her from the back side, and what a backside she has. Long, blonde hair reaches to nearly the small of her back. Her spine curves in sensually, her round ass stretches her back pockets, and her ass is so luscious I'd like to smack it like that Wrangler stamp she's wearing. This woman is a sinful sight and should be against the law. She has her shapely, lean legs stuffed into a pair of cowboy boots. This tasty combination of a horse-riding cowgirl and the apple bottom of a pinup model has my cock swelling in my jeans.

Who. Is. She? Seems I've been away from this small town long enough for some serious eye candy to move in. I keep my head low, with my gaze fastened to her ass so tightly it's going to hurt to pull it off.

Moving back to Starlight Canyon will not be good for my dating game. Not that I want it to be. Since splitting with my ex a year ago, I'm not ready for any level of commitment. And there won't be a lot of women in this town I don't already know. But maybe this peachy vixen is one of them... I shouldn't be thinking this way. Getting involved with someone in the Canyon right now is a bad idea. The rumor mill will grind hard on it, and I've had enough of being featured on the front of tabloids.

The blonde bends down when she gets to the counter, leans on her elbows, and her hair falls down and hides her face with a veil of sunshine. She chats with the barista. It's an innocent hello between two women who obviously know each other, but to me, it's like she's bent over to enhance my view. Her hips hitch upward invitingly, and her ass spreads just enough to keep me watching, every curve on full display. I imagine my hands hooking under the cradle of those immaculate hips and holding them steady...

"Can I help you?" A man's voice pinches me.

I nearly flinch. If I was a flincher, I would have. My gaze climbs from a pair of well-used leather boots, traces dusty jeans and a Henley all the way up to Dashiell Hunter's face. His expression is unmoving, but his eyes are expressive, darting from me to the ass I've been perving on and back again.

Shit. Has Dash actually gone and got a girlfriend? I've been ogling his woman?

I stand. "Fancy seeing you here."

"I was thinking the same." He offers his hand casually.

Maybe he didn't catch me staring.

He takes it in his grip, grasps me with the appropriate level of firm, nothing threatening in the pressure. But he shakes my hand slowly and stares at me bone-deep. I swallow hard, considering maybe he noticed my shady activity after all. That's the thing about Dash. He's hard to read, and his gaze makes you feel very, very exposed.

Damn. Of all the women to get my blood racing, I only had to fantasize about the ass that belongs to my brother from another mother.

"You're back for good now?" His voice is low and tempered.

"Yeah, I moved back in with the folks this morning until I find something for myself. Divorce is final."

"Mmm." Dash nods. He spins his head. "Hey, Jolie. Look what the cat dragged in."

Joey is here? I dart my eyes around the tables. How did I miss her?

That's when, as if I'm watching a shampoo commercial, the long blonde locks fold over on themselves in bolts of golden satin. Soft honey melts over her shoulder and the back I've been admiring...

I glance quickly at Dash to see if he's looking at the same woman I am.

He is.

My perfect peach stands, turns fully, and there, all grown up like a goddamn signet to a swan, is Jolie Hunter. I haven't been peeping at Dash's woman. I've been devouring his sister. It's been a mighty long time. Long enough for her to grow luscious breasts and a round ass that can fill out a pair of jeans like... well... a woman.

She smiles and pushes some of that glossy hair behind her ear. "Ashton!"

She steps toward me. Her hips sway and switch. Her swollen breasts, so full they must have taken every day of all these years to get like that, lead the way. "Sorry. I didn't notice you when I came in."

She holds out her arms for a hug. We've hugged before. A million times. Birthdays. Holidays. Any time she was down in the dumps I'd pull her into my arms and try to comfort her. We're friends, and friends hug.

I haven't been much of one of those over the years, and my body rages with a heat that tells me I don't want to be one now. Fuck. I'll cool down. I will. But when she smashes her tits into me, arms wrapped around my body, giving me her signature bear hug, her breasts do not convince me this is the girl I left behind. And now, the sensual scent that had me groping her with my eyes in the first place, encircles me like some sort of spell. The fairy godmother has definitely paid her a visit.

I peel myself away from her breasts as soon as I can without being rude. "Joey..."

We stare at each other. Or maybe I stare at her. Smiles are plastered across our faces, and I wonder if her toothy grin is as surprised as mine is. Probably not. She follows hockey. And probably the odd tabloid or two. A sour taste lines my tongue, when I think of Jolie seeing me with Chloe in the news. I don't know why, but it does.

When did she become so goddamn beautiful? I've seen pictures of her, too, over the years. The occasional blog of Jolie with her fuckwit ex. Eric Larose from the New York Huskies. Chloe would occasionally share gossip news with me when Jolie and her ex were mentioned. But truth be told, Jolie always appeared to be miserable in those photos. I figured the paps caught her on a bad day. Or in between smiles. There was nothing in those photos like the glow I see in front of me. And I certainly never noticed her hourglass figure.

I had no fucking clue.

The sound of her voice is as delighted and youthful as I remembered. It's full of warm energy. I anchor myself to that to stop my gaze from floating back down her body.

"Logan told me you moved back to the Canyon in May," I say.

"Yeah." She punches my arm. "Thanks for never coming to see me, Pup."

Jolie started referring to me as Pup in my junior year of high school as a response to everyone else starting to call me Great Dane. It was cute then. It feels like some sort of pet name for the bedroom now, coming from those glossy strawberry lips of hers.

I clear my throat. "Sorry. I was busy having a stiletto shoved up my ass in LA."

"Sounds kinky," she says out of puffy lips. Were her lips like that before?

"I wish."

"It's been a long time." She shoves her hands into her back pockets, and her tits push out into the space between us, stealing my oxygen.

I keep my eyes where they belong, but I have to work hard to avoid her perked nipples, pebbled and highly alert under a thin, unbuttoned polo shirt. The chill in the air. That's all that is. Or maybe she's happy to see me, too. Goddamn, her cleavage taunts me.

"So..." She rocks on her heels, and her breasts sway enticingly. "Is it good to be back in the Canyon? Or is it going to be too slow here for Hollywood's hockey boy?" She bats her eyelashes because she just made a cute little dig, but it feels like she's flirting with me.

She's not. I know she isn't. Thirteen years ago, we agreed to be friends. This is just Jolie being... well, Jolie. Sassy. Says whatever comes into her head. And why shouldn't she be friendly? We're... friends. Well, if that's what you can call two people who haven't seen each other in over a decade. Maybe more like family. Yes. Long-lost family.

Family. Cold showers. Chicken fertilizer. I think of all the things that have the opposite effect on my dick than her luscious frame does.

"Hollywood's hockey boy?" I chuckle lightly at her comment. If she only knew how much I craved for the simple life of the Canyon so many times while out in California. "I know you are not accusing me of being a city boy, are you?"

"You've been called worse things," she teases.

"Not possible." I tilt my head. "Though some have been close."

Just then, a burly arm wraps around me, and Logan slides into the picture.

"It's like a reunion here." He points back and forth between Dash and Jolie. "You guys want to grab a table with us?"

"Too busy," Dash says. "Just getting a drink to take back to the stables."

"Me, too," Jolie says. "We'll leave you to it."

Logan and I take the table I bagged and sit. He snatches the menu to check the specials. "Man, it feels good for us to all be back here." He's reading the menu and doesn't glance up at me when he asks, "Have you gone through the plays Coach sent yet?"

I wouldn't remember a play right now if someone etched it onto my brain with a tattoo gun. All I can think about is how different Jolie looks. Different doesn't begin to describe it. "Nope. Not yet. I literally took in my shit from the movers at the ranch this morning and came here."

Logan puts the menu down. "Cool, we'll check out plays over grub." He stands. "Are you having anything? I'll order for us."

"I was just waiting for you. Get me some of that carrot cake. And a black coffee."

"Got it. Be right back." Logan shuffles up to the counter and catches up on a word with Dash and Jolie. Well, Jolie really, since Dash doesn't talk much.

I lower my eyes because I need to adjust before looking

again. Reconciling Jolie's ass in my mind as one to firmly *not* think of sexually is going to take a second.

She's a stunner. I should have known she'd become one. Her mom was the MILF in high school.

I stare at my phone. When suddenly, crouched next to me, is a set of tits with a crease deep enough to suffocate a man. Jolie stares up at me, her green eyes sparkling. How did I never notice they were so damn alluring? How they're hooded and sexual and make her invitation seem like it's just for me?

"Hey, do you and Logan want to come out to Sly's sometime?" She loses her balance and puts her hand on my thigh to catch herself, but when she regains composure, she doesn't move it.

Logan sits back down across from me. I have to fight the heat creeping into my neck at his sister's face being so close to my crotch. Especially with me thinking her mouth is so pretty.

Logan repeats the offer as if she already mentioned it to him earlier. "You up for it, bro?"

"What?" My mind is numb with Jolie's hand still on my thigh, inches from my cock. You'd think I've never been touched before.

"Sly's," he repeats.

"Oh, yeah. Course. Count me in."

Jolie taps my leg, this time feeling more friendly. She stands and wiggles her pants back fully up over her curves. "See you later." She puts her hand on my shoulder. "It's really great to have you back."

She saunters away, hair shining like liquid gold, dripping right above that glorious ass of hers.

I move my attention back to Logan, and he has an

eyebrow quirked. "You okay? You seem all... I dunno... out of it."

There are a million easy excuses to use besides his sister. "Just been a lot getting movers here this morning. The storage company dropped everything at like five-thirty. Guess they did an overnight drive from Cali."

"Ah, yeah, early starts are tough."

"Tougher when you drink too much."

"What?" He feigns innocence. "You talking about me? Because in my opinion, Coach is overreacting." Logan flaps his hand in the air and sits back, lacing his fingers behind his head. Life always looks so easy on him.

"Your drink ban officially ends in a month," I remind him.

"You wouldn't tell on little ol' me, would you? What harm could I do at Sly's?" The glint in his eye does nothing to hide he's perfectly capable of doing harm anywhere and everywhere.

Logan finds mayhem wherever he goes. Usually, it's the wild-child variety. Puck bunnies. Last call at clubs... But lately, he's been in Vegas more than usual, and Coach thinks he's getting tired on the ice. At our age, playing a good game means we can either be tired or hungover. Not both.

"You know I have your back," I reassure him. "But we don't have much time to win you a cup." I've already been part of a Stanley cup win in my years on the LA Cougars. But Logan hasn't.

My friend started his career off strong playing for some solid teams, but the Scorpions, being such a new team in New Mexico, have struggled to get the talent. Logan and I were hopeful last season that the dream team being back together would send us to the finals, but we only reached the semis. And much as I hate to say it, I think my best friend could use a few more nights of sleep.

But it won't be starting at Sly's.

And if I can't erase the pinup-girl image of Jolie Hunter in my mind's eye, I won't be getting any either.

Chapter Two

Jolie

I HIT the back of the metal rails when a cow dancing her rear end smacks me out of a daydream. I've been breathing shallow since the minute I saw Ashton in CCs. Now the wind is completely gone from my chest.

"Shit, you all right?" Luis Mendez peeks over the cow chute, concern tugging at his brow.

His daughter, Shay, is just like him when she's all serious.

"Yeah." God, he's going to think I'm such an amateur.

How is it possible that after all these years, Ashton has

the same effect on me as he did when I was a little girl? I don't know the answer, but seeing him this morning stole my concentration. Why didn't Logan mention he'd be back today? And in CCs? And be so damn sexy at that time in the morning?

I've seen him on social media over the years, of course, but... the way he smelled. The way his chest felt when I hugged him... fuck, the girl crush came rushing back again. But that's all it is. A crush. A crush just like millions of other women have on the specimen of a man fit for a wet dream.

My head needs to focus back on the game or I'm going to get hurt out here. I wish I could say I'm not the easily distracted type but I am. I have to recenter. The last thing I need right now is a broken foot. "Don't worry about me, Lou. Got the steel-toed boots on today."

"You're gonna need more than that if this one steps on you."

He's right. *Focus, Jolie.* I stick the ultrasound wand inside to check if this cow is a mama. "Got another one," I tell Luis to mark the girl is with calf.

I'm more careful when the next cow comes into the chute. In goes the wand, and after some jiggling, a bovine fetus appears on my screen. Discovering a life always fills my chest with warmth before the chill of its fate freezes my lungs. I cough to try and forget it. "Got another one."

Luis lets the cow out. "A lot of good news today. Get two more and we'll have an eighty-percent success rate. Higher than we've ever had. I'll owe you a bonus or something for your turkey-basting skills."

I laugh and arch a brow. "Yeah? What are we talking? What's that worth to you?"

"Oh, I don't know... a drink at Sly's?"

Another cow comes in the chute. "Foolish offer, Señor Mendez," I tease. "You think that's getting off cheap, but I can shut that place down. Don't forget I have three brothers and used to hold my own with the rodeo crowd."

He laughs. "And hockey players..."

Hockey players.

I slide the probe in the cow and think of how I once asked Ashton to put his probe in me because my mind works in gross ways like that.

He looked mighty fine this morning. He's even better now than at twenty-two. He's all man. Filled into that six-foot-five frame of his. His thigh under my hand was like... titanium. Forget steel or whatever, it was Superman shit. *What years of skating does to a man's legs...*

The cow coming in the chute lets off a loud moo, startling me from my millionth daydream.

I get back to my job, inspecting Bessie, and my second highly inappropriate thought races to my mind considering my long, ultrasound wand. I wonder if Ashton is proportional?

I do my job deciphering a screen of what mostly looks like television static. Wow. Another babe. I've never had a success rate this high. The Mendez ranch has fertile stock. "Mark that as a plus sign, Luis."

A ranch hand scuttles around the corral, trying to get the last cow to me.

I stand on my tiptoes to spy on Luis. "One more to go and we got that eighty percent. You know, I don't want a drink... but I can think of something else you might be willing to shake on."

"What's that?" He leans over the metal bars.

"A chicken." I passed his ginormous free-range chicken yard on the way to the cattle fields. The hens pecked and waddled so happily. And what better pet than one that gives you a gift every day?

"A chicken?" He's perplexed.

"Yeah. There's a coop over at my house, and it's been empty for years." It's time to bring more life to my home. Pets do that, and I have yet to take the time to get a rescue dog. Chickens are probably just the thing. Especially with my unpredictable work schedule."

"All right. You got a deal, but you have to take at least two, three would be better. They don't like living alone."

"Perfect."

The ranch hand behind me finally urges the last cow into the chute, and I pat her rump.

"Come on, girl. I got hens on the line here…"

I examine the screen intently but I'm already stoked with such a high success rate. I know it has nothing to do with me and everything to do with the cows themselves but I'd love those chickens.

I hate to admit it, but I've been lonely.

After years of all that shit in New York, I was elated to live on the ranch with my brother, Dash. He's grumpy sometimes, and not exactly the life of the party, but he's also the kind of man who knows when you need a little extra TLC. And I do. But he moved out days after I came back, not wanting company as much as I do.

I tried not to let it hurt my feelings when he said he needed to be closer to the horses at the resort stables, because there's a lot of truth in that. I'm not going to hunt him down. He has enough going on with the new horses we all decided to bring on for the dude ranch business. All my brothers have a lot going on.

I thought it would be good to come back to the Canyon. But both of my best friends from high school moved away, so I truly feel like I'm starting fresh. It isn't exactly the cozy feeling I thought I'd have at home. Thankfully, I've already made some new friends. My brother's new wife, Sam, is incredible, and two women from the resort stables are fab—Georgie, a local gal much younger than I, and Molly, a seasonal worker who just turned permanent. I'm so excited she's staying.

But she's awfully busy, and much as it isn't fair, she'll have to work her tits off to keep Dash off her back.

My mind wanders to Ashton again, and his ancient words echo in my memory. *I promise I'll always be your friend.*

Thirteen years ago, the man uttered words I never wanted. I wanted more then. But a lot has passed in both our lives since Ashton said he'd be my friend forever in the dark and cold summer air. My curled hair still smelled like hairspray and tears when he promised me that. It was heartbreaking. But I believed him. I believed he valued me and wanted to be my friend. Even though after that night, I never once saw him again in the flesh.

I left and lived my life, our times visiting home never aligned, and he got married. I had Eric. I still wonder what the hell happened all those years he was away in Los Angeles, him galivanting around with A-listers, married to that disrespectful, gold-digging bitch...

"Well, what have we got over there, Jolie?" Luis asks.

Though I've been staring at the screen, I wasn't really reading it, I never really saw anything. When my eyes adjust and it comes nice and clear, I know it's a good day indeed. "Well, Mr. Mendez, get those cluckers ready. You got another calf on the way."

With a box of three hens in the back of my Land Rover, I start the ignition when my cell bleeps.

MOLLY

DASH APPROVED OPERATION SANTA. I
TEXTED MONICA DANE, AND SHE SAID
WE COULD LOOK AT THE DRAFT
HORSES TODAY! I DON'T KNOW WHAT
I'M LOOKING FOR, THOUGH. CAN YOU
HELP?

Nice to hear my crabby brother isn't standing in the way of change. When Molly told me about all her ideas for the dude ranch business, I was duly impressed. But I did worry Dash would be a sourpuss. He hates change. He hates people.

Operation Santa—getting a snow sleigh and draft horses to bring in winter business rather than lose money with an offseason—is a great idea. If not to bring more money to the ranch, then selfishly because I'd love a sleigh ride.

ME

OF COURSE! DO YOU WANT ME TO GO
WITH YOU?

MOLLY

THINGS ARE STILL FRESH HERE. IT
MIGHT BE BETTER IF DASH GOES WITH
YOU FOR THIS ONE.

She's probably right. It'll go down better that way. I know my brother. One look at those horses and he'll never change his mind about Operation Santa.

ME

COOL. I HAVE A FEW HOURS THIS
AFTERNOON.

MOLLY

celebration emoji

I start the car, and no sooner than getting a few minutes down the road, my hands-free rings. "Jolie Hunter," I answer.

Logan's voice pounds through my car. "So formal."

"I didn't know it was you. I'm driving."

"But why do you answer your personal cell that way?"

"I give a lot of clients this number."

"Really? Geez, that's dedication."

"Yeah, well, not all of us need a burner phone to keep work and play separate."

His suggestive, boyish laugh fills my car.

"Why did you call?"

"Ashton's mom asked him to help her bring out the Belgians for Molly to see? Who's Molly?" He says her name with sexual curiosity. It doesn't take much more than two syllables to pique my playboy brother's interest.

"She's the new stable manager Dash hired. Off-limits because she works for the resort. No fraternizing."

Technically, Logan doesn't have anything to do with the dude ranch business, though it is owned by all us Hunters, and the last thing I want is for Logan to be near a nice girl like Molly. He's very charming. Very convincing. And very emotionally unavailable.

"So are you calling about Molly or the horses? Or just to bother me?"

"I thought since I have a day off, I'd go over with Ashton and help out Monica. Maybe I'll drive us over. Meet this Molly first? I need something to do."

"It's amazing how much day there is when you're not sleeping it away, hey?" I taunt him.

His voice is full of sarcasm. "Yeah, I've been doing it for a whole week already and I can't believe how many episodes of *Judge Judy* I missed. What was I thinking?"

I laugh. "Well, I just promised Molly I'd examine the horses. I'll text Dash and let him know you're fetching us from the stables but I'll need half an hour because I have to drop off my chickens."

"You got chickens?"

"Yeah. Luis Mendez gave them to me as a tip for my high insemination rate." I turn the corner off the main road and up the private drive leading into our family-owned land.

"You're weird. Like, zero other people would ask for chickens instead of money."

"Hey, you'll be eating your words when my free-range chicken business is killing it."

"Maybe I will. See you in a bit."

"Bye."

I press the button on the steering wheel to end the call. I glance in the rearview mirror at my windswept hair. I have a little panda thing going on because my eyes always water in the wind. Shit. I won't have time to change or get clean before going over to the Danes'. But why should I care?

I know exactly why I care. *Because Ashton will be there.*

This time I won't hug him. I won't get close enough to smell his cologne or think about which superhero to compare his muscles to. I'll be his friend. And he can be mine.

Because it's possible we both need one after the decade we've each experienced.

Chapter Three

Ashton

"IF THIS IS JUST the first of many jobs you're roping me into, Mom, I need to remind you of my contract," I joke, leading two seventeen-hand Belgian draft horses out to the arena.

"Your contract says you can't *ride*," Mom challenges me with a cocked brow.

"That means you have a list of chores for me?"

"I pay good rates."

"Lord knows I need the money," I quip. Well, it's a joke but isn't. I haven't run on such low accounts since I was a rookie. Thank God I made my final payment to Chloe last month. I'll be fine when my rental property in Manhattan Beach sells and I get another paycheck. I can't believe I'm even thinking about money after so many years of having more than I could spend.

My mom mumbles something, and I'm guessing it's a litany of expletives because she never liked my ex-wife, even when I used to. "You need to keep yourself busy."

"Trust me, I'm not grieving." I wanted a divorce from Chloe for a long, long time. I was just too lazy to approach what I knew would be a traumatic, drawn-out process. And maybe it's weird to some, but I didn't give a shit that our marriage was lame in terms of love. She had her focus in trying to climb Hollywood hill, and I had mine trying to win a cup. We weren't the worst partners. Mostly because we stayed out of each other's way.

That is until she crossed the line. I was loyal to our unspoken arrangement, she was not. Humiliation can be a serious ignition switch for action, and now that I'm back in Starlight Canyon, I'm trying to look at the silver lining.

I won't be able to handle living at my parents' for too much longer, but for now, it's nice to be around my mom and dad, the horses, Shay's carrot cake, and... Jolie's ass flashes in my mind again.

"The press doesn't bother you?" my mom asks, stopping my imagination from sliding up Jolie's curves and around those luscious breasts she grew while we were apart.

We tie the horses onto o-rings on one side of the arena where six other horses await. I'm silent and not quite ready to answer Mom's question.

Does the press suggesting *I* was the one who did something wrong since I gave my ex a huge-ass settlement bother me? Sure as hell it does. But I know I shouldn't tell my mom that. I don't want anyone prying. Especially not those close to me. "I just want to move on with my life. We've been split for over a year. And before the split, I was already wasting time with someone I knew wasn't right. It is what it is."

We walk toward the edge of the arena where the enormous doors are open to the autumn afternoon.

Mom takes my crumbs and tries to make a cookie out of this conversation. "She sure was a waste of time. You're in your mid-thirties. Time to crack out some kids."

Here we go... "Are grandchildren all you and Joy Hunter think about?" I shake my head.

"That and our pelvic floors."

"Too much information, Mom."

I smear my hand down my face, but she does draw a smile. And a laugh. I missed Mom's jokes. Dad's jokes. The fresh mountain air...

I lean against the door of the barn when Logan's fancy-ass rhinestone cowboy RAM truck pulls up. The back door opens, and Dash's dog, Memphis, hops onto the dust followed by his owner's well-worn cowboy boots. And then, the other door opens, and out comes Jolie Hunter.

She's less put together than she was this morning at CCs, and thankfully her hourglass is covered by a wax jacket, smoothing out the brain blip I had when I first saw her. Blonde hair pulled back into a ponytail. Her coat and jeans are dirty. She must have been out on a call somewhere. In many ways, she looks even better now to me. It reminds me of good times like when it was my brother's turn to groom the horses—me, Jolie, and Logan used to bareback ride as many of them as we could if it was a muddy day. We'd get them, and ourselves, dirty as hell. Dirty like my mind is watching her enter the arena.

Logan comes over and fist bumps me, followed by Dash.

Jolie approaches, but she's less enthusiastic than earlier today, bumps fists with me, then quickly joins my mom who would never settle for a fist bump from Jolie Hunter. Mom never had a daughter and scoops Jolie into her arms and plants a pink lipstick kiss on her cheek that Jolie quickly rubs away.

Dash and my mom get to talking, Jolie starts inspecting the horses for health issues, and Logan and I wander deep into the arena, our feet moving mindlessly until we reach the last horse in the line. We do what we do. Talk hockey.

"Did you hear Sutten is hanging up his skates?" Logan asks. "The Barracudas just did the press release. Another one bites the dust."

Logan and I are ancient in the NHL. The foot speed even in the last five years has been remarkable, new players come in with athleticism that didn't exist in our day. We used to, at best, have chicken for protein; now kids start whey at thirteen and know more about training than we did in high school. Rookies are more developed than they used to be. And guys in their thirties are goddamn geriatrics.

"Yup. Saw that." I wanted to retire a few years ago. I have a shoulder that hates me, a knee in constant need of icing, and an ankle that is more like an Achilles heel. I know I should get out before my body is useless and I can't get up off the floor anymore. "Sutten did the right thing. Better to quit than be let go."

Logan strokes his hand along the back of Fred, the chestnut horse to our side. "True," he says, his voice far away.

His mind is elsewhere and yet, I know exactly where it is. Retirement. It's all about striking the perfect balance. You don't want to leave when you can keep making money doing what you love but you sure as hell don't want to be forced out.

Fred noses my pocket. I slip my hand inside and give him the horse treats he was sniffing around for. His velvety lips tickle my palm. I missed this. The simple feeling of caring for an animal that is happy with so little. All this... it's the polar opposite of Los Angeles.

Logan's thick eyebrows are knitted together.

"What's up? Sutten has you second-guessing next season?" I ask. "You need to be focused on the one at hand."

"Just thinking about how you've been with PT a lot lately," he says.

"You're thinking about me?" I wipe my hand off on my jeans. "You should be worried about yourself, old-timer. I'm a month younger than you."

"Yeah, but I'm younger at heart."

"But I have a cup win. You'll be more relaxed about retiring if you feel you left it all on the ice." Sometimes I think I want this more for Logan than he wants it for himself.

"Are you going to bust my balls again about living my life? Work hard, play hard."

"You want a cup, you need to play hard, play hard. Especially at our age."

"Can Tweedledee and Tweedledum let the professional through?" Jolie's voice snaps our heads toward her.

She has her hands on her hips. Those hips... she's taken her coat off, and the polo shirt from CCs is on full display again, stretched to the max with a Starlight Vets logo beaming right at me from where a nipple would be. One button is undone, but it looks as though it could have fallen open under force of pressure. Damn, the girl can fill out a polo now.

Logan teases, "Okay, *Dr.* Hunter. We'll just step aside like we didn't teach you everything you know about horses."

She rolls her eyes. "Yeah. I didn't learn anything in eight years of college. But you know what? I'm not even being paid for this vetting."

She leans against the wall of the arena, crossing her arms just under her breasts, and I swear they push up, cleavage growing along with the gesture.

"Go ahead then, boys. Just let me know if you see any signs of corneal ulcers, heart murmurs, sarcoids..."

She rests her head on the back wall and closes her eyes. "I'll just be here when you're done."

"Show-off." Logan sweeps a foot under hers and knocks her off balance.

She catches herself just shy of hitting the ground and lets off the same wild laugh she had when we were kids. When *she* was a kid. Except now it's coming out of a set of full lips. Jolie Hunter grew into her body, but she didn't grow out of her sense of humor. The corner of my mouth lifts upward.

Joey takes a pair of gloves out of her pocket and slips them on, then pries open one of Fred's eyes. "So what were you two talking about over here? You guys were all serious."

Logan and I glance at each other. We know the minute either one of us mentions retirement, a family member won't let the topic go for weeks after. Every professional athlete knows this woe. No sister, wife, mother, or father wants the one they love to be hurt for life. They always think about it money-wise. And Logan and I are set with our finances. True, I just lost a huge amount of my money but I still have enough left for anything I care about. People don't understand the fear of retirement is what to do with yourself when your identity disappears. Money isn't the problem.

"Nothing," I say.

"Training," Logan lies.

"Hmm. Seems to me you were discussing something you don't want me hearing." Satisfied with Fred's right eye, she examines the left. "So, that has to be women."

I scoff. "Not sure you'll hear me talking about women anytime soon."

Joey releases Fred's eye and glances at me. "That bad?"

I nod. "That bad."

She works her way down Fred's body, checking his legs and hooves, his ligaments and every inch of his body. She's serious. Professional. Thorough. I've never seen her in this light. All... capable. Her nimble fingers glide along Fred's spine. She listens through her stethoscope, staring into the air in front of her, concerned with the inside of the horse's belly.

And then I have the strangest feeling watching my childhood friend go about her work. A sense of home races through me from the most unlikely sight. Jolie lifts Fred's tail to have a look at his behind. Like she just stares right at his ass as if it's the most normal thing in the world. The women I've been around for the past ten years—namely my ex-wife—wouldn't dream of staring at a horse's asshole.

And I know I've been too far from home for far too long when my chest loosens up remembering there are down-to-earth women out there. People. My people. People who don't think horse manure stinks.

Satisfied with his backside, Jolie lets his tail down. "Are you guys in for Sly's tonight? To celebrate?"

"What are we celebrating?" I ask.

"Molly. Dash's new manager at the stables. We've

become really friendly since she got here in May, and she just got the new position. I mean, any woman who gets past the beast and into the lair deserves a toast."

"She's cute, too." Logan slaps my arm with the back of his hand.

Jolie's eyes drop momentarily but meet mine again quickly, and in them is that same old mischievous shimmer they had when she was eighteen.

I know I said yes at CCs this morning to going out sometime at Sly's, but will me going only encourage Logan? He needs a better influence.

Jolie misunderstands my hesitation. "Is Sly Bull's too spit and sawdust for you now? You're not one of these men who drinks martinis, are you?" She challenges my ego.

I gaze at Logan and narrow my eyes. Has he told his family he's on a drinking ban? It's not really about the drinking, though, it's about the rest. He needs to sleep at night like a normal human being. I really should tell him not to go. Then again, knowing Logan, he'll do what he wants, and if I don't go, I won't be able to make sure he doesn't have more than one. "Logan, we need to get home by ten, though. Yeah?"

Jolie is confused. "Really? Why?"

Logan tips his chin at me then glances at Jolie. "We're cursed. We'll turn into pumpkins."

She laughs. "Yeah. More like rats. A fat one and a dumb one."

"It was mice in *Cinderella*," Logan corrects her. "And I'm not fat."

She rolls her eyes.

I punch Logan's arm. "Guess that means you're the dumbass."

Jolie giggles. She always loved it when I messed with

Lo. "Look at my brother. All polished up on the Disney characters."

"Eve taught me well," he says with no shame.

My gaze connects with Joey's, and we share a moment of amusement at Logan's expense. Logan doesn't need us to insult him. He often does it inadvertently to himself. It's the smallest crack in an otherwise perfect facade that makes him so likable. But our shared moment goes from focusing on Logan to me thinking about how beautiful she is now, and I'm not sure if she sees the shift in my eyes, but hers flutter to the ground before too long.

"We're meeting at seven. To be honest, I have a lot of early starts these days anyway." She pats Fred's rump, bends down to grab her vet kit off the ground and hoists it over her shoulder. "And Logan?"

He tips his chin up, listening.

She lowers her head and peers out of two hypnotic emeralds. "I know why you can't stay out late. If you think you're having more than one drink tonight, I'll have you cut off."

His eyes widen at being caught out. "Ball buster."

Jolie turns on her heel and waves her hand in the air, owning it. It always was hard to pull a fast one on her. She's been around boys all her life, and anyway, men only ever hide two things. Too many women and too much booze.

Her ass swishes and sways as she walks away in the sand of the arena. Her voice echoes in the open space, an invitation I didn't realize I'd been waiting for.

"See you boys later."

Everything was so hectic in LA, I never had time to imagine what it would be like living back here again. But something about this scene—me, Lo, and Joey around the horses, messing around... it's normal in the best possible way. It's one of those moments where you think you had to experience all the bad to have the epiphany. I belong here. Maybe not in my old bedroom still sporting a Wayne Gretzky poster from the nineties, but most definitely in Starlight Canyon.

Chapter Four

Jolie

"I'll take a Chimayo Blondie, Izzy."

The handsome bartender tips his chin to acknowledge my order and snatches a bottle from the ice buckets under the counter. He snaps the lid off with a fizzle. "You're alone tonight?" He pours the drink into a pint glass. "Haven't seen you in a while."

It's true. The combination of not knowing a lot of available people in Starlight Canyon and working ungodly hours doesn't leave a lot of time for Sly's. Not that I care about going out as much as I used to. At thirty-one, and after all those crazy years with Eric Larose, NHL party animal, I'd rather Netflix and chill. Though I always imagined when that day came, it would be under a blanket with a special someone.

"I'm waiting for my brother and some friends."

"Ah, going to be a big one tonight?" Izzy asks. "Scorpions have a day off tomorrow?"

Everyone knows Logan likes to shut a place down. The comment sends a wave of guilt sloshing through my stomach. I know Ashton imposed a curfew earlier because Logan must have another drinking ban by his coach. And I should have disinvited them. If there's such a thing. Lo doesn't have a problem with liquor. He has a problem with being alone.

"I'll have one of those," a manly voice booms behind me. Very close behind me.

Izzy's eyes slide upward, practically to the ceiling, so I know the voice can only belong to the Great Dane.

I turn and he's gazing down at me but mostly I only see that crooked, half-smile of his. A baseball cap casts a shadow over the top half of his face like he's a man of mystery. I know he wears it because he doesn't want the attention he gets as a celebrity. He never liked attention, but even when he just played for Golden Sierra, he got a lot of it.

I wonder how he coped with Los Angeles. I wonder how he coped with a social media whore like Chloe. The amount of photos I had to endure of those two over the years could stack up and reach farther than Mount Everest. I guess I could have not looked. But it was hard.

"You're here early." Ashton slides into the seat next to me. His body, a pure wall of man, fills my view. He peels off his jacket, and two biceps stretch the sleeves of his t-shirt.

"Yeah... Now that the nights are creeping in a little earlier, I'd rather sit here than watching the clock at home."

He pauses and considers what I just said. Ashton hasn't changed. He's a rare man who thinks before he speaks. "You should have told me you were driving yourself. I would have picked you up."

Izzy sets another bottle and half-poured pint glass of amber liquid in front of Ashton. He salutes me and tends to another patron at the far end of the bar.

"I grabbed a cab. I'm not a kid anymore."

His eyebrows dance almost imperceptibly, and I don't know what he's thinking, but it seems my comments amuse him.

"But you live alone now?"

"Yeah."

"Someone needs to get you home safe."

"Ashton. That someone is me. You might have missed the memo, but I'm a grown woman now."

He takes his cap off and smooths his hair and pops the cap on backwards. His brown eyes flicker. "I did not miss the memo."

His words are simple but loaded, and I have to remind myself to keep breathing. I sit up taller, thinking about what I wouldn't have given for him to say something like that when I was younger.

He leans on his elbow, chiseled jaw on his fist. "You're on my way to town, and I always made sure you got home safe just like your brothers did. Courtesy."

"Well, Logan will be here tonight." As soon as I say it, I realize how stupid it probably sounds.

"Pfft."

I chuckle. "Hey, he might be the last man standing but

he's a chivalrous one. He often has the same trusted driver take me home if we're out together."

He nods. "Well, that's something."

"It is." I drink. "But anyway, I lived halfway across the country taking care of myself for a decade without any help from any of you. So like I said"—I peer over my glass flirtatiously as I take another sip—"I'm all grown up now."

He throws his head back with a silent laugh, and his half smile deepens. "Yeah?"

He licks his lips and gives me the most devilish amused dimple I've ever seen. Why is he staring at me like that? He takes his thumb and swipes it along my top lip in a long, delicate movement. His touch sends a shiver down my spine, gripping me hot between my thighs.

He draws his thumb back. It has beer foam on it and he licks it off. *Holy shit.*

"All grown up?" He asks, as if he didn't just provide me with the most seductive moment of my life.

I want to narrow my eyes, but his thumb on my lips paralyzed me. Normally, I'd bite back with some sort of insult and let him know how lame he is, too. That's the kind of relationship we always had. But then he never ran a thumb along my lip line and lapped up my seconds like he just did.

We're adults now, but some things never change. One, Ashton Dane can still turn me to jelly in an instant. And two, we'll never be closer than friends. I send the thought around all the cells of my body, refuting their ulterior motives. He's teasing me. Not flirting. There's a difference. Even if it's hard to tell.

"For your information Molly is only having one and driving us girls home." I wipe the back of my fingers along my mouth in case he missed a spot. "And Chimayos are mega frothy."

"They are." He says it most politely, but with a shit-eating grin.

I punch his arm. His very steely, completely solid arm. A chortle escapes him, and he rubs it as though it smarts.

"Oh, I'm funny, am I?"

I punch him again, and this time he seizes my hand to stop me because he knows I usually dish out at least three in a row when the guys make fun of me.

"You're stronger than you used to be, Joey. It almost hurts now." His eyes dance with humor.

His hand envelops mine firmly and sends the exact same crushing emotion it always did when his skin was on mine. When he restrained me. It often happened this way. Him stopping me from laying into him. I started to lay my hands on him in elementary school and never grew out of it because when he'd get a hold of my sides, or my wrist to stop me from coming at him, his touch radiated right to the core in a way that was so desirable, I punched the guy a lot.

I refuse myself the same giddy pleasure and yank it away, but my appendage misses the warmth. I've been in the elements most of the day, and even my hot bath didn't seem to relieve my hands of the rigid cold in their bones the way his skin does.

I slide both of my hands under my thighs to feel something on them other than his skin still lingering there. "It's not my fault they're so foamy." I tilt my head toward my glass. "Look at that. There's hardly any beer in there."

He tips his chin. "Well then, you can help me with my beer mustache when I get one."

"I will." I think of what it would be like to skim his lip

with my thumb. His lip so soft. His stubble tiny, sensual pinpricks.

He takes a sip, but his boyish smirk comes away from the glass without anything to wipe. Damn. "Okay then. We'll look out for each other. Like spinach in teeth kind of thing."

I smirk. "Deal."

We stare at each other for a while. I take another drink, careful to lick my top lip, and he doesn't take his eyes off me. He's always been an intense stare kind of guy, considering, searching your face for breadcrumbs that lead him to the places you're hiding.

He always used to find me. Logan would never see when a joke went too far or I held back tears from a graze, but Ashton did. He always knew. And I wonder if he'll see any of the things I have buried now.

The beat of silence that passes makes me wonder if I should punch him again. It's more comfortable than sitting under his gaze feeling naked.

Finally, he drops his gaze to his beer and runs a finger along the rim of his pint glass. "How is being a vet going?"

It's probably small talk or catching up on time; or did he see something just then? "Yeah." I swipe some suddenly annoying hair behind my ear. "Fine."

"Fine?"

Curiosity I would have rather avoided seeps into the space between us.

"You always wanted to be a vet. Is fine really the best it is? It would have been a huge bummer for me if the NHL turned out fine."

I shrug. "Just like any job, it has good days and bad days. I'm sure you don't love hockey every single day now that you do it for work."

He resists the knee-jerk reaction most people would have to tell me I'm wrong or I'm right and considers what I just said. He presses his thumb to his index finger and then follows it down the pads of the rest of them, a habit he's had since high school, or at least the one I noticed he started then.

"Fine still wouldn't be a word I'd use. Even the bad days are better than fine. Plus, I'd never expect such a boring word from you." He lifts his dark eyebrows.

A thin-lipped smile spreads across my face, and I change the subject. "Are you glad to be in the Canyon again?"

He narrows his eyes long enough for me to wonder if he's not letting me off the hook. But he does, saying his words with a gaze that dives right down to my soul.

"I wish I never left."

It should be a happy sentiment, but it's laced with something melancholy. I understand. Sometimes I wish I never left, too.

Just then, a group near the door erupts with noise, and my brother, Logan, fist bumps two of the guys who pat his back and shower him with jubilation at his entrance fit for a Roman emperor.

My eyes track back to Ashton's face that's turned to watch the commotion. His jawline is sharper than the last time I saw it up close. His cheekbones are more defined. His stubble is thicker, and he has a small scar now that cuts through one of those enviable manly brows. It wasn't there when we were younger. He's always been a tough defender and he gets in fights in the rink. Big ones. But I never thought anyone would be tall enough to reach his face when helmets get thrown down. The fact that he wasn't able to dodge that one tells me he didn't think his opponent could reach him either.

My brother approaches, and Ashton messes with him.

"Your minions forgot their trumpets."

I snatch my eyes from Ashton's face and glance to my brother instead. I hope Logan didn't catch me staring at his best friend like I did when I was fifteen. Because I'm over that now, and the last thing I need is a man, and Logan knows that, too. Even one as good as Ashton.

The guys fist bump, and Logan gives me a hug.

"Jojo, you made an effort. First time you haven't smelled like cow shit in days."

"Better than I can say for you," I retort.

He pulls his shirt from his chest, puffing it in and out as if wafting his scent upward. "Smells expensive to me. It's all about taste, little girl."

"It actually explains a lot. The kind of women you attract do match your cologne."

"What's that supposed to mean?" He bites his bottom lip, bracing for an insult.

"Come on strong. Fade quickly."

Ashton chuckles behind his hand. "She has a point."

"Whatever, Old Spice. You've been wearing the same shit since high school."

He shrugs. "If it isn't broken, don't fix it. And it's Cool Water, not Old Spice."

"It's old now."

Logan does love the finer things in life and trend-chasing. He's still a country boy somewhere underneath it all, but he's the only person at Sly's tonight wearing dress shoes instead of sneakers or cowboy boots.

I point to Logan's wrist. "Guess your fancy watch actually tells the right time now, too? You're early." I'm only slightly disappointed I don't have more time to catch up with Ashton alone.

Logan wiggles his wrist. "I actually didn't know what time it was. I forgot to put this one on the watch winder." He lifts his hand, and a shiny Rolex blings.

I have no idea why such an expensive watch can't just have a battery in it.

Ashton stands and takes his beer off the counter. "Why don't you just reset it? Or did your butler not show up today?"

I bump into Ashton. "You're on a roll."

Logan brushes invisible dust from his shoulder. "You two are so jealous."

Ashton takes out his wallet and pulls out his credit card, holds it in the air for Izzy. "Can you start a tab?"

"Sure thing." Izzy grabs the card.

I lean on my elbow over the bar. "No. Iz, I'll pay for mine."

"Like hell you will," Ashton says.

"I thought you were broke now that you got your divorce?" I taunt him.

His features are more serious.

"Fine," I concede. "Thank you. But we have the other girls here too in a bit, so we can split it."

Logan searches around for a suitable table and points. We follow him in the direction.

"We don't need to split the bill, Jo. I'm sure Ashton and I can manage a few rounds at Sly's. Besides, I'm on rations so I'm sure it will be seriously less than I'm used to."

"It's a wonder you have anything left for your watches and gaudy cologne." I will *never* let the cologne comment go because even though he's sparing me now, he's called me *tree-hugger* because of mine more times than I can remember.

As I follow two broad-shouldered men, the familiarity of being with this pair, the comfort of knowing I can be myself for the first time in years, makes Logan's digs feel like bear hugs. I never thought my heart could smile after being told I smell like cow shit, but it's doing it right now.

Sly's isn't too busy tonight. It's offseason, the summer crowds have gone home, so we snag a big round table with no problem. Ashton pulls out a chair for me and takes the one next to me. Logan next to him. We shoot the breeze for ten more minutes and order a round of shots ready for when Molly and Georgie arrive.

It's a whole lot of pleasantries when they do. We tease Molly about conquering our dragon brother, which makes her squirm for some strange reason, and when she says Dash is "nice," I suspect it's because she's a glutton for punishment.

It's all fun and games, and I'm very relaxed, apart from making sure Logan isn't eyeing Molly too closely or even thinking of having more than this one shot to cheers for Molly's new job. The evening goes on, giving me warm and fuzzies like I stepped inside a *Friends* episode. That is, until the conversation turns to Ashton and Chloe which gets me fidgeting.

Molly asks Ashton about his move back. "So where do you live?"

It's an innocent question, but heat rises next to me.

A not-so-proud scoff escapes him. "With my parents. I'm cool like that."

Logan punches him in the shoulder. "You'll find something soon."

"I better," Ashton says. "The closet in my high school bedroom is only a few sweatshirts wide."

I can't help myself. Why on earth would a woman who owes her career to Ashton's fame, his generosity in putting himself in the limelight, something I constantly couldn't understand... "Fucking bitch. She better not ever step a foot in this town or I'll cram *her* in that closet. She owes every fucking ounce of her career to you."

I stop myself, but "bitch" slips out under my breath one more time because I've been drinking.

Logan cocks his eyebrows. "Tell us how you really feel."

"You don't agree?" I poise myself for an argument.

"You know I do." He nods.

Ashton shoves his fingers in his eye sockets, but in the shadow of his hand, his half-smile is there. Good. It might have been a very long time since Ashton and I were last together, but once an ally, always an ally. I have this man's corner and I don't care what the blogs and gossip mill suggest.

Now Molly is curious, and unfortunately, keeps the conversation rolling. "So, your ex is still in LA?"

"Thank God, yeah," Logan answers for him.

Georgie piles in. I should have given the girls a memo of off-limits discussions. I'm not enjoying this one and I suspect Ashton isn't either.

"Why did you only just now move back for real? You played last season with the Scorpions and you and Chloe broke up like a year ago?"

The shot must have gone straight to her head or she doesn't pay attention to tabloids, because the question couldn't put Ashton on the spot more. But truly, it's a question I want the answer to myself.

An image of Chloe and Ashton holding hands on a

spread in *Snowed* magazine appears in my mind. It was the first one I saw of them when I still carried a torch for him. It took years to get over my childhood crush. Loving him felt like something fundamental.

I examined it so hard way back when that ink stained my mind. And often when I'd think of him, he wasn't there in my memories on his own. He was with her. Slowly, but surely, my heart caught up with that tattoo on my brain. He wasn't mine.

My heel bobs up and down, tapping at the floor like somehow my foot is trying to signal danger to my reptilian flight response. I fidget, and questions flood my mind.

Was he hanging on to their relationship all that time? Trying to save it? Did he have a mistress back in LA? I never could believe that. For a while, those questions ran through my mind as much as they did the general public's, but not so long ago, they stopped. Something in my heart cut off the outside and remembered the man I know. Ashton has always been a loyal guy. I couldn't believe he'd cheat. Though I knew in my heart what he *didn't* do, I still couldn't figure out what *did* keep him away from Starlight Canyon all those months when he played for the Scorpions and it would have been a hell of a lot easier to move home or to Santa Fe.

Ashton tips his empty drink to the side. "I'm going to need a lot more of these to get into that. And for the doors to stay open past closing."

The alcohol evaporates the decade between us, and I instinctively rub his back for a moment but yank my hand away almost as fast as it got there. Nervous energy continues to feed down my body, and my leg jitters back and forth until the ticktock motion of my leg hits Ashton's. Oops. He gives my leg a restrained shove back, not realizing

I did it by accident, and his deliberate touch sends a puff of butterflies out of my belly.

And a real desire to make him touch me again.

I let my leg flop back on his, and he nudges mine again, and somehow, this playful game calms me. We bang thighs against each other gently under the table like a game of footsie, and I think our legs will move in perpetual motion until I feel Logan's eyes on us.

And it's the same look he'd give us when we'd play football in the snow and I'd tackle Ashton to the ground and he'd pretend I got him good. It's the same look Logan would give when I'd jump on Ashton's back and tell him to giddy up when the boys took me out too long but I didn't want to admit I couldn't walk another step. Ashton, of course, always carried me home.

And Logan had that same exact look he does now. It's hard to read. Maybe he thinks I'm being annoying to Ashton. Maybe he thinks we shouldn't touch each other. Maybe he just doesn't know what to think, but in any scenario, his features aren't approving.

I pull my leg away for good, but it doesn't matter that I stopped. I already feel filled with everything I needed and wanted to take away from this night. After months of being back in Starlight Canyon, somehow only now do I feel like I belong here. Now with my brother, and Ashton, playing like we're still in elementary school under the table.

And then, the most unlikely thing that could make me feel like I'm back in Starlight Canyon happens. A cowboy asshole decides he's welcome at our table.

"Well, if it isn't Miss Manager herself," he sneers at Molly.

Who the fuck does this guy think he's messing with?

"Hey, Bobby. You know everyone at the table?" Molly is ever-polite.

When I first met Molly, I wondered if she was a pushover. But the longer I knew her, the more I understood she has a strength I don't. It's actually easy to stand up for yourself. To get mad. It's harder to let people think what they think and still go about your business with confidence.

When I realized Molly was said woman, I developed endless respect for her.

Bobby—who I know from the stables—nods at Logan and Ashton. "Course I do. Climbing that Starlight Canyon social ladder one rung at a time?"

I can't tell if it's a question or a statement, but either way, this man is treading a fine line. Unlike Molly, I haven't outgrown my temper.

He scoffs. "Shame I don't have all the skills you do." He trails his judgmental gaze along her body, allowing a brief stop at Molly's chest. "Guess Dash just doesn't think I have your assets."

I'm ready to land a punch on his smug little jaw and stand up so fast my chair pushes back with a screech. "I think it's time for you to leave, because I'm a few drinks deep and I'm starting to hear things."

Ashton chimes in behind me, "Man, don't make me stand up, too."

Bobby glances behind me at Ashton and Logan, and his body language changes. He's a dumbass but he knows better than to tempt a man who shreds ice and beats bodies into plexiglass for a living.

Bobby tips his hat. "Enjoy the rest of your night."

He ushers his date away to the far end of the bar, but she glances over her shoulder with an apologetic look.

I sit.

"Thanks, guys. Bobby is going to be... a challenge. I can stick up for myself, but I'll have to figure out how to pick my battles with that one," Molly says, her integrity intact.

Georgie is already tipsy from the one shot. "Just fire his ass. You can find someone else. He's such a prick."

Molly shakes her head. "Yeah. But he's a prick who knows what he's doing. And he does care about the horses. And even though he doesn't respect me, he does respect Dash. So what if he doesn't like me? We don't have to be friends to work together."

Logan pipes up. "Good attitude, Molly. Assholes are part of the territory in ranch life. Contrary to popular opinion, not all cowboys are gentlemen."

I dart my eyes to my brother and Ashton who I know would have stood and thrown Bobby out by the scruff of his neck to back me and Molly up. Something about them being there for me, behind me like they did those times when we were kids, it's... it's a gesture that utters three words. Ones I expected my soul to say back in May when I returned, but it never did. She's saying it now, though.

Welcome home, Jolie.

Chapter Five

Ashton

I ALWAYS DID THINK Jolie was cute when she'd stick up to anyone she thought was trying to double-cross her. Or even to us. She'd always stand up straight and tall and tighten her lips like she meant business. And I knew she always did. Sure, Joey had me and Lo behind her most of the time, just like now, and we would never let anything happen to her, but her feisty, scrappy nature was adorable back then.

And it's downright sexy now. I should not be thinking about it, but goddamn it, I am.

The cowboy she's up against, though he's been a total

dick to Molly, doesn't have the posture of a man who'd go toe to toe with a woman, but I still make sure he knows I'm here. "Man, don't make me stand up, too."

The guy doesn't overstay his welcome, and Jolie sits her feisty little butt back down. I've learned better than to let some small fry like him get me ruffled, but Jolie steams for another minute or two until she realizes Molly isn't too bothered. I'm sure the cowboy's comments did get to Molly, but she's tempered. Mature. I'm impressed by her outlook because rising to every occasion like Jolie isn't always the best thing for your mental health. Or physical health. I would know.

We end up changing the subject to horses, something all of us have in common. I can't remember the last time I had something in common with every person out for a round of drinks. It's a feeling of ease I haven't felt for so damn long. For years, the only time I felt comfortable was playing hockey. The rest of the time in LA, it was as if my bones were made of glass and I had to tread carefully. Being back in the Canyon is the feeling of slipping on an old pair of well-worn boots and ambling like I don't give a damn.

When I get to the bottom of my beer, I recognize the telltale body language of Logan considering a second drink. I know much as I could talk ponies all night, I need to get my teammate home. We're the only ones on the team who live in Starlight Canyon, so it's unlikely this would ever get out, but pissing Coach off isn't worth the risk. I pat his shoulder. "Time to get home, bro?"

Logan pretends to read his fancy watch. "It's not even ten like we agreed."

I let my head flop into my palm.

Jolie says what I don't. "Is that what your broken watch says? It's not time to leave?"

"It's not broken," he protests with a shit-eating grin.

I glance up. "Time to go."

Logan isn't big on taking instruction, but thankfully, he's sensible, calls a cab and when the alert comes, he's a good boy and leaves. The rest of us seem ready to make a move apart from Georgie whose expression is decidedly disappointed the night is over at ten p.m. Molly tosses Jolie her keys and asks her to warm the car up while she and Georgie go to the bathroom.

Before I call my own cab, I'll make sure the ladies are safe. It's not like Starlight Canyon is dangerous; it's courtesy. Manners, I reason. But as I walk Jolie to Molly's car, side by side, I know it's more than that.

I've always had a soft spot for Joey. I can see her time away from the Canyon didn't change her ability to speak her mind or defend her corner, and I know she's capable of getting to the car alone. But I've always thought, even when she was just a little tomboy telling us she didn't need help, the ones who say they need it least, often need it most, and I'm still thinking about how she changed the conversation when I asked her about her job.

We reach Molly's car, and she fumbles around with the key fob that doesn't want to unlock the doors.

I prop myself against the vehicle. "Are you coming to the game next week?"

She peers up from under her eyebrows. "I've been at all your games, Ashton. Every single one of them."

She sounds... disappointed. I should've known she'd be there. "Course. You wouldn't miss Lo."

She presses the plastic remote harder as if that will make it work. "I wouldn't miss *you* either. I've roped my sister-in-law into all the games, too. It's a full house in the box when you boys play at home."

I flip my cap around so I can see her better in the dim light. "Maybe that's why I couldn't see your face."

She stares at me for a moment, completely unreadable, then shrugs, turning her attention back to the clearly broken key and picks at its edge to get the manual one out from within its plastic shell. "Or you didn't look."

I'm partly bummed she thinks I don't care and partly flattered she gives a shit what I think after all this time... After dating another famous pro-hockey player, after graduating from vet school, after growing into a goddess... a lot of time has passed, but I still care what she thinks, too.

"I had my head up my ass, I guess. Anyway, it'll be nice to see your wild banshee face up there screaming for the Scorpions."

Her head is still lowered, but her cheeks round. And she finally pulls the silver key out, lifts it, and wiggles it between us. "Well, you know I'm a die-hard fan. I'll be there screaming 'til I'm hoarse." She unlocks the car.

"Good." I open the door for her but not wide enough for her to get in. Not yet. I find myself hanging on to the evening. Drawing out the goodbye. Being here tonight with Joey has been the most *me* I've felt since leaving all those years ago. "Your cheerleading makes all the difference."

The low light of the lamp and the moon illuminate her face in an ethereal way. "I'm not a cheerleader."

"Mascot? You still got the sting." I flick my head in the direction of the bar.

"Bobby's an idiot."

"Seems like one."

I lean on the car door, still blocking the way for her to get in. But it's not like she's making a move. "It's nice to see that fire never went out, Joey."

Her eyes lower again, gazing into the distance but

focusing on nothing in particular. Still, there's something. Her body tells me she's ready to get in the car, but I don't budge.

"Everything all right?"

"Yeah. Why wouldn't it be?" She smooths hair behind her ear.

"You just disappeared for a second there."

She places her hand on the doorframe and pries it open farther, indicating it's time for me to let her pass. "I'd rather not catch up on the last ten years and just... try to live for today. You know?"

Forgetting the past sounds like the most luxurious thing in the world to me right now. "I get that."

"Good. Let's just do that. Pick up where we left off. It was really nice being with you and Logan again like the good ol' days."

"Yeah, for me, too." *She has no idea.*

She sits in Molly's SUV, and I bend down to check the backseat. "Molly's dropping you and Georgie off?"

She nods.

I tap the top of her car. "Text me when you're home safe."

"I don't have your number anymore."

"You do."

She pinches one eye shut. "You never changed your number after going pro? That's the first thing Logan did."

"Well, I kept mine."

She shakes her head. "You must have had a million and one nutters and stalker fans on the line."

"Yup." I think of all the times it was a total pain. I think of the headaches I had with Chloe when she wouldn't believe the puck bunny begging to suck my dick was some 'friend of a friend' from high school who I'd never even met.

Pain didn't begin to describe it. But, keeping the number all seemed part of a promise I intended to honor.

Genuine confusion paints her features. "Why didn't you just change it?"

I lean in farther, and for some strange reason, I feel like kissing her cheek goodnight but I ruffle her hair instead. "In case you needed it."

I ease the car door shut, but she slams her hand against it.

"Wait. Seriously?"

"I promised I'd always be there for you. How was I supposed to help if you couldn't get a hold of me?"

"You could have sent me your new number."

That would have been the logical thing. But it hadn't taken long after being with Chloe that her incredibly jealous nature was apparent. I figured I would deal with the unsolicited calls or deal with Chloe's drama. She would have gone ballistic if I went out of my way to make sure Jolie Hunter, a woman from my past, who Chloe always seemed to hate hearing about, just had to have my new number.

But Jolie doesn't need to know all that, so I let her think I'm an idiot and shrug.

She's in disbelief. "Are you serious?" She narrows her eyes, still thinking it's some prank.

"I promised you I'd always be there, didn't I?" Bringing up the night she asked me to take her virginity sends waves of memories crashing through me. I wonder if I would have had the willpower to say no to the woman in front of me now.

She chews the inside of her lip, thinking, nostalgia ablaze in her eyes. That prom night promise isn't any farther from her mind than it is from mine. She nods.

"All right then." I let go of her car door and step backward. "You drop me that text when you're home."

"Okay."

She starts the car, but the door is still open, and I get the impression she still hasn't recuperated from my confession. The pause is an opportunity for me to drive it home how much I still care.

"Joey?"

"Yeah?" She glances up.

"I'm happy to pretend the last ten years didn't happen, but if you ever want to talk about it, I'm all ears."

As if I melted something heavy on her shoulders, liquid tension rolls down her arms, and her body relaxes. *What is Jolie hiding?*

"Thanks." She closes the door.

I walk away backwards, away from the old feelings and the new. Saying all that out loud, that I saved my nuisance of a high school cell phone number all this time just to keep a promise I made in college... I wonder if it sounded like more than it is.

I wonder if it *is* more than it is.

Because to my mind, keeping that number protected a girl. But now, it protects a woman.

Jolie's house, Bird's Eye, is closer to town than mine is. So only a few minutes after stepping through my front door, my cell buzzes.

UNKNOWN NUMBER

HEY. MADE IT HOME, CAVEMAN.

I chuckle to myself. Jolie always said she hated me and

Logan fussing. All the time she wanted to be treated like an equal. Guess some things never change.

I quickly tap her number to save her contact. *Joey.* She changed her number. I wonder why. Maybe it's nothing. It's been over a decade. Still, when it comes to cell phones, most people I know have the same one as when they got their first.

ME

WOMAN HOME. MAN HAPPY.

JOEY

WOMAN HAPPY, TOO. NICE TO HAVE
YOU BACK.

ME

NICE TO BE BACK.

JOEY

WE SHOULDN'T WAIT SO LONG BEFORE
CATCHING UP AGAIN.

My mind goes to places it shouldn't... *with or without Logan?*

"What are you smiling like a goon at?"

My mom is still awake and catches me, still standing in the hallway with my neck scrunched, my cell in hand, and only now do I realize, yes, I'm smiling like a goon.

I slip my cell into my pocket. "Just a funny text."

Mom side-eyes me. "Yeah?" Her senses are going as well as they should.

The text wasn't funny *haha.* It was funny, *my stomach going fluttery on a roller coaster* funny. And Monica Dane knows it.

"Good night with Jolie and Logan? Good to have the gang back together?"

I follow her into the kitchen where she puts the teapot on the burner.

"Yeah. And then some. Jolie has some nice friends."

"Pretty?" Mom asks hopefully.

I didn't even notice. How could I when I'm still floored by the change in Jolie? But Mom doesn't mean my childhood friend and best friend's sister. She means Molly and Georgie. Who, rude as it might sound, I couldn't tell you what color hair they have.

"They're nice. It was easy."

I sit at the breakfast bar, waiting for my mom to prepare her chamomile and a hot chocolate I know is coming for me. Might as well enjoy the few perks that come with staying at home again.

"So that's a no-go?" Mom goes for the jugular.

"I'm not really looking."

"Well, when you do, will you please look at home?" She rubs my arm. "It's so good having you back. With your brother living away, it's an empty nest."

"Are you mom-guilting me?"

She kisses my cheek. "Begging more like it."

I shake my head, take my cap off, and rake my fingers through my hair. Somehow, her comments have me thinking about Jolie because the woman is as *home* as it gets.

Mom scoops some cocoa powder into a cup and mixes a drink for me, sliding the mug across the counter. "Sweet dreams, handsome."

I take the mug up to my room, pop it on the nightstand, and throw myself onto the quilt my aunt made out of spare blankets and my high school jersey. Propping three pillows behind my back, I take a load off and wrap my hands around the warm ceramic. I wasn't feeling so sure about my choices that led me back to this room.

I used to live in a mansion. This room isn't even as big as my walk-in closet was. No matter how much money my brother and I offered our parents, they never took it. They said this house was saturated with memories they can't pack up in boxes. Even though I've definitely outgrown some of the style choices, it still feels quintessentially me. *Me.* A person I lost in years of doing shit for other people. Having my head so far gone with winning and the next big game, I didn't see the one my ex-wife was playing.

Tracing the walls with my gaze, I blow steam from the top of my mug and consider the room. Trophies. Plaques. Certificates pinned to a corkboard. And there's a crumpled piece of paper there, too. Shockingly, my mom never put her hand on anything. It's like I just walked inside a time capsule.

I squint. *What is that piece of paper?*

Placing my mug on the bedside table, I get up to inspect the corkboard, and there is my last handwritten note to self before leaving home for good. Senior year of college.

TO DO:

Frozen Tide Podcast

Gym key return

Thank you note to Mrs. Ikande

Wyatt to J

Wyatt to J. When I left Golden Sierra for the pros, Jolie entered her first year. I laugh at myself. Back then, a stuffed animal had significance. It was a great birthday gift or something to make a woman smile that little more on Valentine's Day. That's not the kind of relationship Joey and I have now or back then, but I still worried about her and thought a lot about her well-being. I left Golden Sierra only a month after she asked me to take her virginity so I guess I was thinking about her more than usual.

Before I left, I asked a second-year student to somehow make sure that Wyatt the Wolverine was left in her dorm, on her bed, to welcome her to her first year of college. I wonder about my motives... were they pure? Or did I want to leave that stuffed animal there to give an evil eye to whoever it was who did crawl in her bed instead of me?

I got busy after that. Fast. My first year in the pros with all the attention I got was manic, and I never followed up to see if she got Wyatt. She probably assumed it was from Logan. I think back on tonight and I know she said not to talk about the past, a welcome invitation, but I wonder...

Throwing myself back on my bed, I grab my cell to ask what's now a burning question.

ME

> HEY, STRANGE QUESTION, BUT DID YOU
> EVER GET WYATT...

Buzz.

I nearly jump out of my skin at the interruption of another text coming in. It's Logan.

PUCK BOY

> HEY, DID YOU SEE BRYANT IS INJURED?
> GOOD NEWS TO HAVE A KEEPER LIKE
> BRYANT OUT FOR OUR NEXT GAME

I stare at Logan's text, a timely interruption. I shouldn't be texting Joey like this—with wonder in my heart and curiosity on my mind. I abandon my text to her and write back to Logan. We talk about moves that would work with Bryant out of play and how we need to play a more offensive game, how maybe it's time for our rookies, Mahmoud and Rosario, to step up into the second line.

When I finally settle into bed, though, I'm still thinking

about Wyatt. And as I drift off into that space between fantasy and reality, melatonin oozing into my brain, on the backs of my eyelids that stuffed animal is nestled comfortably right between Jolie Hunter's insanely alluring breasts. I fall asleep and dream of being that goddamn wolverine and sinking my teeth right into her.

Chapter Six

Jolie

Ashton and I don't see each other again, even though we said we should meet up. He's been at away games. And when we crossed paths on the couple of days he was in town, it was in the darkness of the Danes' Fright Night haunted house. The moment I smelled his signature cologne, I moved out of there as fast as I could. I'm glad he and Logan have been busy. It was nice seeing him, but the minute he swept away to Boston for games, my heart started doing that pining, obsession thing it did when I was younger.

Ashton saved his cell number for me.

Ashton could still see something was wrong before I told him.

Ashton said I could call him and talk anytime.

Ashton wanted to know I got home safe.

Every thought I had in the days that followed Sly's started with his name. It's too easy to fall into patterns where him being nice to me confuses me into thinking he has feelings bigger than friendship. He sees me as his little sister. I have to remember that. Anyway, I have no desire for a man at the moment. I really don't. I have bigger problems than stupid twenty-year unrequited crushes.

I sit in my car, forearms draped over my steering wheel, and stare out at a sea of yellow trees and mountains. I wonder how Mother Nature can die so gracefully. I wish I had the capability of becoming more beautiful and colorful as life drains out of me like the autumn leaves. I went straight to brown when shit hit the fan, and spring never really came around again.

I've been sitting in my car outside my brother's office for half an hour. I'm going in. I have to this time. I resist that voice in my head telling me I'm being a coward and remind myself that the truth is braver than lies. I need help. And there's no one better for advice and a guiding hand than my big brother, Colton.

I get out of my car and bound up the stairs at his office. Not bothering to knock, I barge in. My boots are still muddy from my second visit to the Mendez ranch, and when Colt's gaze leaves his screen to greet me, it tracks immediately down to where I drag mud in on his rug.

"Finished with the preg-checks?" he asks, not too bothered about my boots.

Knowing Dash, he comes in here the same way.

I plop down on his sofa. "Yeah." I had my wand in the rest of Luis' heifers this morning.

"You look like you didn't enjoy yourself." Colt sits back and folds his hands over his lap. "Don't tell me there isn't some advantage to having your hand up a cow's ass on a cold day?"

A weak, uncommitted laugh leaves my lips. When I became a vet, I expected cow ass and crusty horse dicks and oozing injuries. And there, at the Mendez ranch today, it was a pleasure to check if the cows were pregnant. It was much better, and the total opposite of what I had to do afterward.

I let my head fall on the back of the sofa and stare at the ceiling. A spider hangs out in the corner. *Easy life.* "I don't think I can do this anymore, Colt." There's no use lying to my big brother or beating around the bush. He's a flipping mind reader anyway. "I'm not cut out for this career. I..." Saying these words out loud, ones I've only had in my head, whirling around in rumination for about two years, haunting me at least once a week, often more, it's a lot. It makes it real. And my eyes glass over because of it. I concentrate on the tiny movement of the spider to stop me spinning.

"Hey... what's going on?" Colt gets up and joins me on the sofa. "Whatever it is we can handle it."

"No..." I melt into the cushions farther. I wish they would gobble me up. "It's not really something we can change. I've been trying for two years—more probably—and it's just..."

Colt leans against the back of the couch, props his leg up, settling in to listen to me.

"Colt... I can't... " *Shit.* My eyes sting. I blink hard. I clear my throat of all the mucus and tears building up in my sinuses and swallow to push them down. I don't cry. "I can't keep putting animals down. I... hate it, Colt. It kills me, and I have to do it and then go to my next call where I have to pretend to be smiles and butterflies for the next animal and client. It's even worse in the clinic than on the farms. I feel like I have a goddamn personality disorder. It's not healthy. It's not human what I do."

Colt puts a hand on my shoulder.

The spider uses its dexterous legs to wind out some thread, and I want to shrink right down to its size and hide out in a corner. But I can't. I'm human. A shitty fucking human.

"Are you going to tell me what happened?" Colt interrupts my moment of escape into the world of that little arachnid.

I swallow thickly, take in a deep breath, and let the story out with a sigh. "After the exams today, Luis asked me to come around to his stables, as a favor, to look at his horse. He wanted me to make the call. To tell him it was all right." I try to erase the memory of the dim soul in his horse's eyes. "He asked me to play God. I'm no God, Colt."

My brother rubs my arm reassuringly. He's a cowboy, a veritable ranch man, and I don't need to say any more for him to understand. But I still say the words that have played through my mind so many times anyway. "I'm a killer."

"Jolie. No... I can't let you think like that. It's merciful..."

He says the words I've tried as self-soothing many times before. They don't work. I keep telling the story as though he said nothing. "Luis asked if I could help him for a discount because times have been tight..."

I think about standing there, Luis' eyes misted over. If times were tight, he could have done the deed himself with a shotgun. But people pay vets anyway. They pay us because making the decision is fucking hard. They pay us so they don't go to Hell. Instead, we do.

I became a vet because I love animals. I knew this was part of the job. And I've spoken with enough other people in the industry to know it's mentally tough. I thought I was tough. I reasoned that euthanasia was always a merciful thing. But when a half-ton animal, graceful and powerful on its feet as any on God's green earth, falls to the floor in a loud, sad heap of thunder... I can hear that haunting sound in my sleep sometimes.

Luis' dappled, gray companion wasn't the first I sent to the rainbow bridge. I don't know why this time has me running, heart racing, needing to escape straight to my brother. Hoping he'll let me quit. Hoping he'll give me another option.

I just can't ever do that again. I don't have it in me.

I stare out into space, speechless. There's nothing more to say.

Colt puts an arm around me. "How long have you been feeling like this? Two years? Why didn't you talk to me sooner?"

Because I hate letting you down. Because you already think I'm fickle and don't know how to stay the course. And because you didn't get into vet school so it's the one thing I'm better than you at. I'm not sure if my face says any of this, but my mouth doesn't. I just smash my lips into each other.

He continues. "When you say you want to quit... have you actually given this real thought? You've been to school and spent a lot of time getting to where you are now."

"I don't need your lecture, Colt. I know. I was there for every all-nighter and I got the tuition checks in the mail myself, so I know." I sigh. "I know." I hang my head. "That's why I waited so long. I've been trying to manage my mind over this since the very first time I did it. But every time, I just break a little more. And to top it off, clients are so demanding there's no space to gather up my bootstraps in between."

"You've waited two years to talk to me about this. Have you opened up with anyone else? I'm sure this is a standard thing in the vet community. Maybe you can get some support?"

I shake my head and finally face him. "Do you know what I did two weeks ago? The virtual miracle of a horse being pregnant with twins happened here in Starlight Canyon. One in ten fucking thousand chance, Colt. I thought I'd never see the day. And I won't. Because the owner asked me to ablate one. And I know, I goddamn know this is best for the mare and the remaining foal... but shit... these hands are fucking dirty, Colt, and I can't get over it. Two weeks ago I told myself to hang on by the shred of decency I had left, but Luis and his gray, Daisy, came around before I could stitch myself back together, and I'm falling. Spiraling... I can't anymore. I came running to you. *Running.* I hate to admit it but I'm fucked up."

"You ran all the way from the Mendez place?" He lifts an eyebrow.

"Shut up. Figuratively." His stupid dad joke almost deserves a smile.

He tries to boost my confidence. "Jo, you've saved a hell of a lot of lives, too. You give life every day..."

"I know. I confirmed forty-eight pregnancies today."

"Did you wash your hands?" Colt will never stop trying to make me smile.

I smooth one of mine across his cheek, pretending to

slather cow crap all over him. "No." I puff a laugh out of my nose.

He pushes me on the arm, and I tumble over. I feel a little better because messing around with my big brother like this reminds me of when life was easy. When I was just a pony-crazy girl with a plastic stethoscope and a reflex hammer.

"Maybe you just need a breather. A break. Don't make any knee-jerk decisions about what you can and can't handle, or about your identity. Just take a break. You only moved back home six months ago and have dealt with some serious relationship shit in recent years. Sometimes people just need a change of focus. We'll figure it out."

"I still need to work. I can't just sit around on my ass all day. That will be the opposite of good for me. It's offseason in the Canyon. I probably can't even wait tables this time of year."

He gets up and holds his hand out to help me. "I got you. I'll set something up so you're not mulling around. In fact, why don't we get you working over with Monica again for a while? She always needs more help."

The Danes? "With the pony school? God, that would be two steps forward, a thousand back."

"You used to love working there. Doing roping and barrel racing with the kids? It'll definitely take your mind off things."

"Yeah…" I agree half-heartedly. I'm not sure. It seems to me like the solution will just replace one obsessive thought with another because Ashton in his backward baseball cap is just about the best and worst distraction a messed-up girl could have.

But just like so many other times in my life, I dive right

in. I never did give a damn choosing what's unhealthy. "Sure," I drawl.

"I'll call Monica when you leave and drop you a text. Get washed up. Hang out with the girls after school lets out. Sam, Eve, and Mom are making a pink-themed dinner." He scratches his head. "Can't seem to escape the Barbie era my ladies are in."

He sits back at his desk and eyes me seriously. "Jo. Don't you dare wait two years to tell me something so big again. It's bad for you to keep it inside. And just to say as well, there's no shame in therapy."

But is there shame in quitting? "Okay. Let me know about Monica."

"Just assume it's on. You know how she is."

I nod. I don't feel any better about what happened with Daisy, but it does feel better to know tomorrow the possibility of doing that again won't be looming over me. "Who will take over my schedule...?"

Colt lifts his hand to stop me. "I got it. Just leave it with me. Shower up and go over to Big Sky with the girls. You need some company. I don't want you hanging out alone when you're feeling like this."

My brother is all man. All very busy man, but he always finds the time to come to the rescue.

"Thank you."

I leave, and when I get back to my car, I mostly feel lighter. I guess the saying is true. A problem shared is a problem halved. And that's exactly what I've done. I've only halved my problem. Because now, when I go to work at the Danes', a new one might come back. It took years to get over Ashton Dane, and the bubbles in my stomach, the flutter between my legs at the sight of his scruffy hair and thick neck, the feel of his thigh on mine were way too reminiscent of that lovesick teenage nausea I had lasting well into my twenties.

At least tomorrow is the last Scorpions' game for a while. Then he'll be away and I'll have a week or so to get my head on straight.

Chapter Seven

Ashton

I CHECK the box again between periods. Never, in the history of playing hockey, have I glanced at the crowd so many times. But it's like I'm a marionette and something out there is pulling the strings. We only have sixty minutes to win a game, and I've always been good at concentrating, especially since in the first line I'm still only in twenty minutes. But today, I can't swat away the distraction.

Finally, between the second and third period, it's impossible to ignore the satisfaction of seeing a long blonde mane come into view at the front of the box. Jolie stands next to my mom, and suddenly I'm hot in my pads. I squint. She wears a Scorpions jersey, and I know it isn't my number because it's a single digit I can't make out. I'm number eleven. I narrow my eyes farther, trying to focus; it must be Logan's. Coach is talking, but I'm tuned out, searching around for players with single digits, wondering if they've ever crossed paths with her. I glance back up again... *It looks like Logan's. Is it a seven?*

"Dane! You fucking listening?" Coach snaps me back to the rink side.

I tip my chin.

He gets back in it. "Like I said, just keep playing clean. We got this one in the can with Bryant out. This keeper is intimidated by quick drives, so no time-wasting at face-off."

The buzzer goes, and it's first line out on the ice. Usually, with us being so far ahead score-wise, I wouldn't be so motivated, but something lights a fire under my ass, and I decide it's my turn to put it in. I glide out onto the pristine canvas beneath my skates. The ice glistens in the artificial light of the cold arena, and I skate out to my defense position, my eyes, hard as I try, have a mind of their own and work their way back up to the box.

I slap my helmet, reminding myself to be present. Here. Now. Puck. Ice. Skate. Slap. Before the puck drops, I imagine my moves. I imagine a breakaway. I play it out in my mind's eye...

Chill seeps through my gear, and I crouch low for the face-off, and with the Steamrollers being behind, their morale is low, and me and my teammates make plays as if performing well-rehearsed choreography. I get a pass, and with a sudden burst of speed, I weave through their defenders who might as well not be there today. My skates float, it's like there's no resistance, I'm so damn determined to score. My heart pounds when I approach the net.

The second-rate goalie braces himself for the challenge, intently focused on me barreling down. When I reach the high slot, the puck has a presence of its own, weighty on my stick. I don't have the best opening. My teammate calls for the pass, but I'm greedy for it... There's a small opening, a sliver of light between the goalie's shin pads...

With a crack, I smash the puck. It sails off my stick, a blur of black and white, but years of experience tell me it's in. I turn before the rookie keeper realizes I nutmegged him and the home crowd erupts.

"WOOF, WOOF, WOOF. GREAT DAAAAANE!"

My eyes flick back up to the box, and Joey jumps up and down with my mom in her arms. Her hair bounces in golden ribbons up and down her back, and I can only imagine how her tits dance like that.

But before my fantasy takes me any farther, a shoulder comes flying into me. Unprepared, I lose my footing and fall to the ice. My ankle cranks with a searing pain. Fuck. A veteran from the Steamrollers stands over me, ready to fight. It's not even a clever brawl. He's seeing red, bright like the humiliating score. But if he wants a fight? I'll never back down.

I push myself back to my feet, but my ankle turns inward, and I barely make it to one skate. My ankle is weak... shit. I grit my teeth... I'm going to fuck this guy up... But I can hardly plow into him on one skate. My teammates pile onto the ice in my stead because they all know. This isn't the first injury I've had, and if I was all right, this guy would be in row Z right now.

I don't even know what happens next because several Scorpions form a shield of fighting soldiers and physio comes onto the ice to fetch me. Goddamn it. I took my eyes off the game for one fucking second and didn't see it coming.

I. Am. Screwed.

By the time I return to my bedroom that night, I've been told I need a couple of weeks' rest. It's total bullshit because my ankle already feels better after icing, but seeing as this isn't the first time I twisted it, and as my blunt PT likes to point out *at my age,* better safe than sorry.

A string of away games means this is it. A twelve-by-twelve bedroom will be my fate for at least the away games, possibly more. I take another look at the space and wonder if it's worth getting a TV mounted in here while I'm around. Or maybe during the next week or so I should hit the ground running, finding me somewhere to live in Starlight Canyon. I should focus on the silver lining, I could use the time to get my shit together, but none of it seems to be as important as being useful to my team.

I fall onto the mattress. It's still pretty damn bouncy after all these years but not nearly big enough. I settle myself into the queen-sized bed. Truly, my California King is the only thing I miss from my mansion.

Buzz.

I let my head fall against the back of the headboard. It's probably Logan. But when I flip my phone over, it's another Hunter.

JOEY

IF IT'S ANY CONSOLATION, I'M PRETTY
SURE YOU KNOCKED THE DICK OFF
THEIR GOALIE WITH THAT SLAPSHOT.

A genuine smile tugs at my lips.

ME

MAKES ME FEEL SO MUCH BETTER. I
BET THE ZAMBONI BARELY NOTICED
THAT COCKTAIL SAUSAGE.

The Steamrollers are a team made of small-dick men relying on sucker punches. Fuckers.

ME

IT'S NOT EVEN A BIG DEAL. I COULD
PLAY, BUT THE MEDICAL TEAM ARE A
BUNCH OF CAUTIOUS WIMPS. I'M FINE.

JOEY

YOU WOULD SAY THAT. ALL YOU CARE
ABOUT IS HOCKEY.

And there it is. It's the "you'll poke your eye out" comment. It's what a lot of us professional athletes view as someone trying to take away our fun before it's over. But coming from Jolie, a woman I know likes to take a risk or two herself, I know she understands on some level that life isn't worth living without a little danger.

ME

ISN'T IT YOU WHO SAID THE BEST VIEW
IS FROM THE EDGE?

I expect her quick-witted return but all I get are those three dots, appearing, disappearing. I reread her last text and think maybe it deserved less of a smart-ass response because hockey isn't all I care about.

I care a whole lot about getting a text back from her for one.

The bubbles dance one more time before she finally writes:

I push myself up, her words bringing me to attention. Why would she work with the western sport school instead of her vet business? Her expression and words from the bar come flooding back. *Fine.* She said it was all fine. It's hard to believe it, but it's pretty obvious she doesn't like being a vet. Or maybe it's work stress. All jobs come with it. My ankle is a case in point.

But a sickening memory emerges from the past and makes it seem a lot worse than being off with a twisted ankle.

My heart beats harder, my veins stiffen... is Jolie okay?

I remember when she went off to vet school, Logan tried to talk her out of it. He'd read the data around mental health in that profession. Honestly, it shocked me when he quoted stats on suicide, therapy... We were in the dorms our last year when he read an article to me out loud, and I still remember one of the heartbreaking thoughts about the highs and lows of being a vet. One minute you're euthanizing an animal, the next, helping a family welcome a new puppy into their home. Logan, protective as always, confronted Jolie about it. She brushed him off saying it's worse for small animal vets. She said that kind of thing isn't as prevalent with large animals and that's mostly what she wanted to do. But still...

I can't think of a single other reason why Joey would need a break.

She texts again before I have time to respond.

JOEY

IT WAS DECIDED BEFORE YOUR INJURY, SO DON'T THINK I'M FOLLOWING YOU AROUND OR ANYTHING. YOU'RE NOT THAT GREAT ANYMORE.

I bite my cheek. Whatever is going on, Jolie Hunter is still all sass and wild words. If she still has her humor, that's something. And know she'll appreciate mine.

ME

I CAME BACK TO THE CANYON TO FIND MY PLACE NOT BE PUT IN MY PLACE.

JOEY

LUCKY BOY. YOU CAN HAVE BOTH NOW. HAVE YOUR CARROT CAKE AND EAT IT, TOO.

This woman has always had a way of making me smile. And maybe I'm here for these two weeks for a reason. Maybe it was all meant to be, because even though Jolie and I haven't talked properly for over a decade, I know I can get through to her.

Chapter Eight

Jolie

I shouldn't have mentioned I'd be working with his mom for the next few weeks, but the last thing I want is for Ashton Dane to think I'm going to start chasing him around again or that me being here has anything to do with seeing him. He still might be a tasty snack, but I won't let myself get caught in that orbit again. His gravity was impossible to escape the first time around.

But since I mentioned I'd be at Moon Ridge Ranch, of course, he showed up. To bother me. To get in my hair.

My belly flutters at the sight of him walking in, limping

slightly, with a thin, well-worn t-shirt as a mere silhouette over his broad chest. He wears a jacket with a hoodie sticking out the back and has that goddamn backward baseball cap on. And he doesn't look like he shaved today. Why am I a sucker for stubble? It's the pain-pleasure dynamic. And that's exactly what Ashton Dane is. Pain and pleasure at the same time.

I let my eyes linger on the sexy country boy hobbling across the sand of the indoor arena toward the small grandstands along one side. That boy totally broke my heart. I let him. And I never once got mad at him for it. That's the thing about him. No matter how hard I try, he's just too well-meaning to push away. Even now. Even the other night at Sly's...

Thankfully, five eight-to-ten-year-olds command my attention because they all start to try to lasso one another while waiting for me to snap out of my daydream. I'd better do that right quick because one of these youngsters might get hurt, and Monica—thinking I'm a responsible adult—said she'd leave me to it. She taught me well when I was as small as these kiddos, and knows I can handle the basics.

I give one last glance. He's sitting now and catches my eye, salutes me. I send one back and turn my attention to the youngsters, but it's not easy pulling my eyes off him. "So the first thing we need to talk about is, we will not be trying to wrangle each other. That's rule number one."

"Hey," a red-headed boy pipes up. "I thought this was supposed to be fun."

A soft laugh reaches me from the stands. Ashton leans on the front of the grandstand, one arm draped over the front row barricade, and his fingers trace his upper lip like he eagerly awaits my showdown with these kids.

"Rules are fun"—I search my mind for the boy's name—

"Gareth. At least that one is because I don't want anyone getting hurt."

"When do we get to do this on horses? I don't want to rope a dummy calf," Gareth moans again. "That's for babies."

Another snigger wafts over my shoulder from Ashton's direction, but I don't show him I heard it. In fact, if Ashton thinks this boy's defiance bothers me one bit, he's wrong. Gareth and his copper hair might come off a bit bratty for some, but I kind of like it. He has the *jump right into it* nature that I always thought a kid of my own would have, and lots of gusto.

I bend down to face the ten-year-old eye to eye. "I assure you, a baby can't rope a dummy calf."

He rolls his eyes, and the challenging gesture ignites a part of me I haven't felt in a while. I love a cheeky kid.

I speak quietly to him so Ashton can't hear. "Listen, if you focus and do as I say all lesson, and concentrate really well, I'll let you try to lasso that guy over there." I point to the stands.

Ashton has no idea what I just said, but he sees me and Gareth watching him and waves at us.

Gareth grins. "Okay. Deal."

It's a little unfair, potentially letting Ashton get walloped a few times by the nylon rope when he's injured. But he's obviously well enough to make the walk over to the yard and has enough energy left to heckle me. He thought he was coming here for me to entertain him? He's mistaken.

I teach the children about the parts of the lasso, this is supposed to be a 101 course after all. I tell them all the things Monica Dane taught me. How to flick the wrist in circles, how to throw the rope like a baseball.

Then, we begin by simply trying to make a circular

motion overhead. It's harder than any of them thought it would be. I jet from kid to kid, trying to help them move their wrists around, helping them out when they pretty much rope themselves. One girl keeps hitting her own head, and I never thought we'd need a helmet for lassoing. The back of her head is a nest of tangles.

Ashton runs his mouth from behind me. "Tell her to put her elbow higher."

I spin around, and he's pointing to the one who keeps hitting herself.

Oh, lucky me. I have a teaching assistant and unsolicited help today. I ignore him but position the girl's arm higher. She must just be tired because she can't keep it up. She is only eight with bird's arms but she purses her lips like she's trying.

The next thing I know, Ashton is making his way over the sand to us and standing next to me and the young girl.

He speaks to her. "You want me to help you?"

"We don't need your help." I step in between him and my student. "We're doing just fine. Don't you need to rest up?" I ask in such a way he knows I want him to get the hell out of here.

"Not really."

"Well, just now you were walking like you have fins for legs."

He laughs that magnetic laugh that makes it harder for me to push him away. But I need to establish boundaries. At least until I get used to his alluring smell and vampire's feast of a neck. Damn, there's something about his neck.

I give him another proverbial shove. "Go bother someone else. I'm not your babysitter, Ashton."

Gareth decides now is a good time to listen and be a class clown. "Ooooh. She told you off, mister."

Ashton isn't the least put off by either of us. He cocks that crooked smile of his and wipes the corner of his eye. "I kind of like it here." Then he speaks to the kids. "Who wants to watch a rope off?"

The kids drop their lariats and jump up and down, excited to stop the required repetition to actually learn how to rope.

I cross my arms. "This is supposed to be a roping club. Their parents brought them to *learn* not to watch."

But the kids are in a full-on mutiny already. After a long day of school, they're probably hangry. All of them have dropped their lassos to the ground and are pounding their feet, dust kicking up beneath them. They chant, "Rope off! Rope off! Rope off!"

I shake my head slowly, knowing I'm not getting out of this, but neither is he. "You're done, Dane. There's no way you have better tricks than I have."

He licks his lips, sinking his teeth into the bottom one. "Let's see whose cowboy blood runs deeper, Hunter. Did mine survive California or did yours survive New York?"

"*Upstate* New York," I correct him.

"Not here anyway."

I narrow my eyes ready for our Western duel. In the past, Ashton would beat me in anything and everything he put his hand to. But as far as I know, he never really did much trick roping. Then again, his mom and dad do own the most well-known Western skills school in New Mexico. But I learned here, too.

We both pick up our loops, and he keeps his small. I know immediately he doesn't have much in him, and every last nerve inside is smirking.

"All right then..." He concentrates, furrowing his brow, a guy trying to remember which side is up. Finally, he takes the end and twirls, getting a good motion going, and he starts by circling it in front of him, like a flat spinning plate. It's not a bad flat loop trick, but it's something I plan on getting these youngsters doing within several lessons.

"That's all you got?" I taunt.

He concentrates hard. "Hang on. Just getting back into it. Like riding a bike..."

He darts the tiniest bit of tongue out between his lips. I have to admit he looks cute this way, all intently focused. Eventually, he manages to turn the rope sideways and do the butterfly. The lasso moves vertically in a smooth motion in front of him, then in a figure of eight, he crosses his body and the rope emulates butterfly wings.

The kids all clap. Egged on, he gets cocky and tries to have the butterfly fly around his body, but when it gets behind him, it hits his cap and knocks it to the ground.

I clap politely. "Not bad. I didn't think you'd even get the loop going."

"Never underestimate me." He takes his hat off and smooths his hair, then replaces the cap.

He stares at me with a challenge, all square jaw and intense brown eyes that remind me of when life was just fun and games as a kid. And it feels amazing to not be so serious after so many years of pressure and negativity. Ashton's presence reaches down inside me and draws out the girl I've been stamping down for years. The fun one with not a care in the world, a bit too much courage for her own good, and... a massive crush on this boy.

It's all too familiar. But I have twenty eyeballs waiting for my performance. I pick up a rope and contemplate the size of the loop; I hope it's about the right size or I won't pull off my first win in anything against Ashton Dane.

Ashton glances at the kids. "She looks nervous. Who else thinks she looks nervous?"

They laugh, and two put their hands up.

I ignore him trying to throw me off my game. Even though there's nothing tangible at stake here, Ashton, me, and Logan have egos the size of dump trucks, and I don't want to lose. Especially since I have to teach these kids again next week and a loss could ruin my street cred.

I back up pretty far away from the kids so I don't hit anybody and hope like hell I don't embarrass myself. I used to love trick roping and spent long hours in my backyard practicing. But like Ashton, when I get the lasso working to my side, I have to give it a few extra spins to allow my muscle memory to come back.

But it does. I spin it at first in a low, flat loop to my side. I circle and circle until I feel the rhythm in my bones; until it becomes a dance and the next step comes naturally.

Gareth heckles me. "We've already seen this one."

"I guarantee you have not..." It feels right in my hand, the weight is where it needs to be... I flick my wrist and pop the loop off the ground and right over my head, then slide the big hoop down over my body and soar it back up and off again like a yo-yo.

"Woo-hoo!" One of the girls shouts, inciting applause from the rest of the children.

I show them I'm not a one-trick pony. I twirl the lasso overhead in a wedding ring and yo-yo it back up and down my body one more time before giving my final hurrah. Twirling it high overhead, I know my aim won't be great without my hand on the loop itself, but I'm about to show these kids I'm the winner, hands down.

I send the lasso out and away from me and catch it

around Ashton's shoulders. His mouth drops open in surprise, and he buries his face in his hand, defeated.

My students erupt with laughter and squeals of delight and give me a round of applause to which I take a deep, shit-eating curtsey.

Ashton peeks out between two fingers. "You got me."

I stride over to one of the abandoned lassos on the arena floor, swipe it up, and head straight to Gareth. "You've been such a good boy today. Have a go at a live calf."

The last of the students have been picked up, and Ashton sticks around to help me put things away. We wind up the ropes and hang them in a tack room to the side of the arena. I think Ashton will leave after that but when I go inside to start rolling the dummy calves away, he follows me. I could get this done a lot faster if he wasn't here, but night has fallen, and I'm already thinking about going home alone. So I just push my dummy calf at his pace, and we work slowly, seamlessly, and silently.

Two more calves and we'll be done.

"Are you sure you should be walking around with your ankle like that?"

He moves the calf and makes it look like an easy job even with his injury. "I've been through this before. An old injury rearing its head."

I feel a little guilty letting him help, letting him stay just to keep my loneliness away for another second longer. Ashton has been told to rest, he's not even allowed on the road with his team, and here he is, teaching lasso with me and tidying equipment.

"Just saying you should rest. And I don't need your

help." I don't mean for it to come out as petulant, but it does. Especially after I know as well as he does the class ended up being a lot more fun for the kids once he came in the picture. "Sorry. That sounds ungrateful. Just. I'm fine."

He scoffs. *"Fine..."*

We line up the last two dummies into their bays, and I lean against the wall.

"You're going to bust my chops again over my vocab?"

He perches himself on a plastic calf and crosses his arms. He's taken off his jacket now, and his forearms bulge with muscle and veins. "Why are you here?"

"I told you, I'm taking a break."

"From what?"

I stare out into the dim-lit arena at nothing in particular. I'm not ready to tell anyone else what's going on. It was hard enough to pour my heart out to Colt. And I only did that because I needed his help. "Just life." I drop my gaze back to his. "Don't you ever just want a break from life?"

"No, Joey. A break from life is actually the opposite of what I'd ever want. Is that what *you* want?" Concern blazes from his eyes like I said something I didn't.

"You know what I mean." I suggest he's overreacting. "I'm not suicidal."

He braces his arms to his sides and leans forward. "I didn't know what you meant, and you can't fault me for checking. Something is going on with you, and people don't ask enough about that kind of shit. If you're here, something is wrong."

His comment steals my next breath. He's right. He's absolutely right. People see the signs all the time and don't say shit. It's hard to ask a question like that, and I respect Ashton more than ever for it.

I laugh, but nothing is funny. "So you came to check on me?"

"Course not. I just need a babysitter, right?" The corner of his mouth quirks.

A burst of something like happiness goes off in my belly like firecrackers. In all my life, I've never met someone quite like Ashton. I have a loving family. Logan is protective almost in spite of my best interests. Colt goes straight to solution mode if I ever have a problem. My mom is an infinite supply of words of wisdom, and Dash is like a secret weapon I could deploy at any time if I needed to.

I walk over to the calf opposite Ashton—the one who has always been comfortable enough to sit through my pains. He was protective but also nurturing. And it's the exact reason why my heart yearned for this special balm when I was at my lowest.

I outline my finger along the plastic ear of the calf. "You're so annoying."

"Why?"

"The way you just... " God, he has no idea. It's the first time I've felt seen in ages, and a genuine smile spreads across my heated face.

He uses his good foot to kick the toe of my boot. "The way I don't just accept *fine*? Nobody worth a damn in your life will, I can tell you that. You don't have to talk to me, but what kind of friend would I be if I didn't ask?"

I draw a line in the sand between our feet, and the symbolism crashes through me. I should build a strong wall between us. Opening up to Ashton has always made me feel better but also fall harder.

I stare at the sand. "You are a solid friend for asking. And I appreciate it."

When I glance up, his eyebrows are pulled together in concern.

"But I don't feel like talking about it. I'm not sure I really even know what I want or how I feel, so I just want to take a break from thinking about it."

Ashton stands. "Understood."

We stare at each other for a moment, his eyes flicker with a thousand more questions.

His gaze searches my face. "So... you need a break?"

I nod.

He pops himself up to standing. "Okay then. Let's get the fuck out of here."

I slide my hands into my back pockets. "Yeah? Where?"

"Sly's?"

I'm still not over that backward hat and the way being this close to him still makes me feel funny. But what am I going to do? Head home and watch reruns of *Grey's Anatomy*? Logan is out of town. Sam and Colt are at parents' evening—as a teacher and parent respectively. Molly is working her ass off night and day trying to get that sleigh ready, and Mom has her book club...

I shrug. "That actually sounds great. And for once I don't have to get up early tomorrow morning. So don't even think for a second you're getting off cheap."

"Shit, girl. You're going to wring me dry?"

"And I'm asking for the top shelf tonight," I tease.

He heads toward the exit. "Come on, then. Sounds like we should leave the cars and catch a cab. Or I can ask my mom to drive us?"

"How high school prom. Like I ever want to live that night again." I'm joking, but he stops in his tracks and tilts his head.

I tilt mine in return. "Hey, it didn't exactly go to plan for me."

He flares his nostrils and shakes his head. "Not going there." He points to the barn doors of the arena. "Go on and git with that sassy mouth."

A giant ray of sun beams from my chest. It's going to be a good night.

Chapter Nine

Ashton

"What's your poison?" I ask as I watch Joey slide out of her wax jacket and take down her ponytail.

She's been wearing that jacket for the past few hours. On our way over, I thought to myself how nice it is to be around a woman who can just hit up the bar without having to go home and freshen up. But I guess when you have a rack like hers and hair that tumbles out of a ponytail like a silken waterfall, what improvements are worth making to impress a childhood friend?

Friend.

I haven't been around a woman I cared about more than a friend for a very long time. And I'm pretty sure if Joey is one, I shouldn't be staring the way I am and thinking about how one of her nipples is pebbled.

Suddenly, it occurs to me that Joey and I have never been out like this. As many times as we'd been together when we were younger, we never once hung out since she turned twenty-one. The other night with her friends was tame. She leans her elbows on the bar, considering the options, and her tits nest in the space between her biceps. Nothing about Jolie Hunter looks tame right now.

The bartender—the same one from the other night, Izzy, I think—comes over immediately. Course he would, her boobs are bait.

"Hey, Hunter," he says, obviously familiar with my Joey. "Fancy seeing you here on a Tuesday."

"Iz. Me and my friend here need to take the edge off."

Izzy holds his hand out to fist bump me. "Hey, bro. Saw the game highlights. That was a fucking dick move."

I bump him back. "I blame myself. Shouldn't have taken my head out of it."

This Izzy puts his hands up like he kind of agrees with me. At least he's not a people pleaser. "What can I get you two?"

Joey wiggles herself into a comfortable position on her stool, and her jeans spread out like voluptuous blue frosting over a cupcake. "You have to ask?" She cocks her eyebrow. "You know I only shoot bourbon."

I raise my eyebrows. "Oh, we're going straight to shots, are we?" And bourbon at that. We are definitely not in LA anymore. "Bourbon?"

"Yeah. And since you're paying, I want the good stuff."

Izzy smirks. He thinks her attitude is cute, and now I

just want that bourbon here fast and him gone even faster. I order, keeping my eyes on Izzy's, watching to see if he lets them wander where they don't belong. "Two Whitetail doubles and two Chimayos."

"Coming up."

We're not staying at this counter with a good-looking guy she knows. I spot a small booth and point. "Can you have someone bring them over there?"

"Sure thing."

I grab Jolie's jacket and tote bag from the hook under the bar. My instinct is to take her by the hand to lead her over, but I settle for a more subtle hand on the small of her back until we reach the booth. It's a one-sided semicircle facing out into the room with a table. She slides in on one side, and I shuffle into the other. We both keep a small distance, like bookends.

It's not busy tonight. Tuesday during offseason means there is a small group of cowboys in one corner—they're actually playing cards at a table, and a couple is sharing some French fries and beers. A few people I assume are regulars are dotted along the bar. Before long, Izzy brings our drinks over on a tray and thankfully fucks off right away. He seems like the only one working tonight. Maybe I was a dick asking him to play server, too.

But I want to be alone with Joey. Or at least with our conversation. I don't want Izzy and his regulars listening in on years of catching up. And there's no chance of her opening up if we're on display.

I take my shot glass between three fingers and lift it. "Well, here's to a break."

She smiles. "And breakaways." She corrects her language. "I don't mean hockey breakaways. I mean, breakaways. As in us making it back. You know... home?" Her typically sassy gaze fades, replaced by a question.

I did break away from something. And her words tell me she did, too. What has Joey been through these past thirteen odd years?

Her wide eyes wait for an answer. She wants to know if I'm happy to be back. I feel happier now on a Tuesday night in Sly's with Jolie than I ever felt in California. But I still don't have the same sense of calm I had before I left. When it comes to my ex-wife, I stay on my toes. I don't know if I'm in the aftermath of a hurricane or the eye of the storm.

"Yeah. Home. It's good to be back."

I search her face, asking the same question she just did, but don't find the answer. Maybe it's confusing for both of us. Especially now that I know Joey questions her career.

We clink our tiny glass shooters together. Blonde hair tumbles down her back and shoulders as she tips her head and brings that drink to her puffy pink lips. Her neck is exposed and milky white, vulnerable almost. I watch her throat bob as the liquid slides down and I wonder what it would be like to slip my dick down in there.

Before she catches me staring, I throw my shot back, and goddamn, did she make taking it look effortless. My body, on the other hand, sears like I just swallowed a snake of acid.

"The hell? This shit is strong."

"You acted like you knew Whitehall. It's a hundred and thirty proof."

"I've only ever had it neat." I try not to pull a face.

She shimmies her shoulders and giggles. "Oooh. So fancy." She wraps her fingers around her beer and draws it closer but doesn't take a drink. "What was it like in LA? Was it all espresso martinis and whiskey *neat?*"

"A little bit. But actually, even though there's this image of everyday stilettos and shit, it's pretty chill, too. It wasn't all bad. I liked that I had a heated outdoor pool and I could use it year-round."

"Yeah, that would be cool."

"And I lived in the mountains."

"Really? I imagined you hanging out on the beach all the time."

She imagined where I lived? "Not for me. Chloe wanted it, but I needed more privacy. Too many tourists down there."

Jolie's body language changes when I say Chloe's name, and she doesn't keep her feelings a secret, her words are simple but hostile. "Chloe seemed to want a lot of things."

She signals her fingers toward Izzy like they have some secret code. A secret code I can't exactly read and I don't like not being a part of.

I'm guessing she's asked for two more bourbons. I already see the first one settling into Jolie. Her shoulders are relaxed, her eyes, too.

"How the hell does a guy like you end up with a woman like her?"

"You sound like you know her."

"Are you defending the woman who put you through a public divorce and wrung you dry?"

"No. I meant what I said. You sound like you know her. That the two of us couldn't be any more different."

"Was it opposites attract or something?"

Izzy is table side now, and he did indeed bring another round of doubles. How do Izzy and Joey know each other? From here? Or more? I try not to eye the bartender with suspicion but I do make sure not to let my gaze linger long enough for him to feel invited.

"Thanks, Iz," she says.

He nods and doesn't stay. He's better at his job than I gave him credit for.

"Opposites attract?" I think about it. What drew Chloe and I together back then? The alcohol works through my veins, and my body loosens. The gentle lighting, the smell of stale beer, and the country music in the background gets me talking.

And Jolie. She gazes at me like she wants to know. Like she needs to know. And I feel like I want someone to know. No. Not someone. *Her.* A person who has cared about me since before I became famous. Before I became a hundred-thousand-dollar news story.

"Chloe was ambitious and had her own thing going on. She wasn't needy but seemed to support me when I was pretty lonely. It was hard after so many years in a small town, then going to Golden Sierra with my best friend, then all of a sudden, I'm in one of the most transient places in the world with no one."

"You had your team."

"Yeah." It's hard to say out loud to Jolie that a bunch of jock straps aren't exactly the same thing as female company.

She considers what I said, circling the rim of her pint glass, thinking. When she raises her gaze, I can't read it but I know she's more serious than she's ever been.

"We always end up with the wrong person when we don't like something about ourselves."

I'm taken aback by the depth and intimacy of her words and move closer, intrigued. Opposing emotions swirl inside, I'm exposed and seen all at the same time. No man wants to admit weakness. No man wants to be told they are anything less than confident. But I'm too old to pretend I'm invincible now. And it never got me anywhere anyway. There's no use pretending with Jolie. We were both homegrown in the same dirt.

My words still come out laced with a bit of denial. "Are you saying I got with Chloe because I didn't like myself?"

Her eyes search mine. "Maybe. I saw the change at prom. There was something new inside you that night that wasn't there before. Something sad. Unsure. Far away and way too close at the same time."

I thought I was the one who could stare into Jolie and see most everything, but now she's boring right through. Soul-deep. Because that night? It shifted my universe. It still continues to be the stain on my existence. And Jolie saw it?

Jolie runs her fingers through her hair, shifting it off her neck like she's getting hot. We probably both are. The bourbon. This conversation.

She lets her hair tumble back down, and a few strands fall over her breasts. "Chloe? She was the pretty thing you thought would hide the ugly inside." She shuffles a little closer, leans into me with her hand on my thigh, bracing herself, preparing to drop a secret in my ear. "If I was pretty enough back then I could have told you"—she gets closer, not a sliver of space is between us now, her breath hot and moist on my earlobe—"there isn't one goddamn ugly thing about you."

This woman just murmured raw facts through spicy alcohol whispers like she's just tasted a truth serum. Like I've just tasted it, too. Because she's right. Chloe was a cover. A shelter from the prom night discovery that my family wasn't what I thought it was.

When Jolie finally eases herself back, she's never looked more confident in herself, and if I didn't already know Jolie Hunter grew up into a goddess, the power in her eyes right now would have convinced me. She's sure of what she just said. And so am I. But I'm not prepared to talk about all that. Hell, I'll never be prepared.

I'm stiff. Speechless. She flutters her gaze to our shot glasses, and we pick them up to drink again. She wipes the corner of her lip with her fingertip and puts her knee up casually on the booth. Her legs are splayed open, and I'm drawn to the seam of her jeans tracing down between her middle. Her other knee rests on my thigh.

She leans on her elbow, and the action somehow shifts her another inch closer. Her beautiful hair pools on the table. "Well? Am I right?"

I brush her hair off her shoulder and instantly wonder why I didn't keep my hands to myself, but the brown liquor whispers *it's all fine*. Better than fine. Something inside tells me this is why I came back to Starlight Canyon—for the soles of my feet to connect with something real again.

The moment is meaningful, but my senses are getting less sharp. *Should we be talking like this?* I shouldn't let her lips ever come that close to my ear again. So I lighten the mood. "When did you become so wise, Joey Hunter?"

Her laugh is deep, throaty, and to everything waist down, sensual. "Oh, Pup, I went through shit, too. I probably ended up with Eric for the same type of reason you were with Chloe."

Logan never had a nice word to say about Eric Larose. And now that Jolie brings up her ex, also a pro hockey player I've heard about over the years, everything fed back to me was the complete opposite of Jolie's character.

He's painted as hockey's party animal. A city-hopping, bling-wearing, pap-hunting fame-chaser. Then again, maybe people said the same about me. When you get a chance to make a few million from an underwear ad, you do it.

"You were with Eric for a long time." I don't want to talk about her ex but I force myself. To remind the increasing charge of electricity as I sit here with my lifelong friend that it is just that—*friendship.*

"On and off." She peers at me from under her eyebrows. "Mostly off. Even when we were on. If you know what I mean."

I think I know what she means and I don't like it. "His reputation is warranted?"

She shrugs.

My blood simmers close to a boil. Did Eric mistreat her? I rub my thumb in circles around the delicate bone of her wrist. "You should tell me what happened."

"Right." She scoffs. "I won't tell you for the same reason I'll never tell Logan."

She's already said enough to put me in the sin bin next time we play the Huskies.

"Anyway." She gazes out into the empty expanse of the bar. "I thought we were going to focus on the present."

She sips her beer and doesn't take her eyes off me while she drinks. When she pulls away the glass, she has a tiny Chimayo mustache.

I can't help but smirk.

"What?" It hits her. "Foam?"

I say yes with my eyebrows.

She makes no move to clear it off herself. "I thought we promised to help each other?"

It feels like a dare. Maybe if I hadn't had those shots. Maybe if it didn't feel so goddamn good to be around someone who likes me for me, maybe if she didn't look so enticing with her leg hitched up and her thighs spread open and her tits stretching her polo to the limit... I might have done the right thing and found her a napkin. But instead, I wipe my thumb in slow motion over her lips, along the smooth wet surface, over her cupid's bow and dip into the sensual corner of her mouth and peel away my foamy finger, dripping with bad intentions.

Hers.

And mine.

I lick my thumb, and her eyes blaze through me. I should be concerned by the pressure against my jean's zipper. I should take my eyes off her glistening lip and back away to allow some cooler air to fan between us. But I don't. Because together, those shots are two hundred and sixty proof of madness and sanity at the same time. Madness because this is my best friend's little sister. And sanity because any lucid man would be doing just as I do.

Joey knows exactly what she's doing, staring at me like a vixen through bedroom eyes. This isn't the first time she's flirted with me. But it's the first time it feels as though I'm playing with fire.

I shift the conversation away from her lips and the way the foam tasted of beer and woman at the same time. "Seems like a lot has changed since we last saw each other."

"And yet nothing at all." The way she considers me is just how she did when we were kids but better. Because it's now coming from a woman who seems to know more about me than me. Maybe she actually always did.

We gaze at each other, almost starstruck, and in any other world I might lean in, lace my fingers through the back of her hair, and sink my tongue inside her mouth. It's the kind of moment that is so palatable I could slice through it.

I should go home, but I can't make myself say it, because even though the tiny moral compass in my mind is pointing in the right direction, my dick is pointing the opposite way, and it paralyzes me.

"Why are you staring at me like that?" she asks as if she already knows the answer.

I hope she doesn't. "Like what?"

"Like you regret not having sex with me when you had the chance." It's half a joke and half a question she really wants the answer to.

The bold statement both turns me on and flushes me with a smile. "I thought we were focusing on the present?"

She ignores what I just said, her voice full of a tipsy rasp. "Are you sure you don't want to sleep with me? The last time a man looked at me the way you are, they were trying to get in my pants." Her teeth sink into her pouty bottom lip, her smile is cheeky.

"How about we don't talk about other men around me?"

"And why shouldn't I?"

She comes close again, or at least I think it's her and not me.

"I don't want to hear about your men. Logan wouldn't either."

"Oh... you're pretending to be family again?" Her gaze drops to my crotch and slides back up my torso. "Whatever you say."

I want to drop my gaze and see if my half-erection is showing in my pants. It's pathetic I can't control myself, but it's been a while since I've been this turned on, this bourbon must be laced with something.

"Should we go home?" she asks. "All that's left here for us is trouble."

I don't know what she means by that, but it's probably true. "If that was enough of a break for you, I'll get you home."

"Do *you* think we should go?"

"If we don't want two wicked hangovers tomorrow, yeah. But I'll stay here all night if you want to." I recall the whole reason I brought her out in the first place so I repeat my question. "Is that enough of a break for you?"

She slumps into the back of the booth, and for the first time in a while, there's oxygen between us. Goddamn, it was getting hot.

"You okay?" I ask.

"Yeah. Even though I don't have an early start, I probably shouldn't have any more drinks." She shoots me another flirty glance. "Or any more of those sex looks you're giving me either."

I laugh, but it's a weak one. "Beer goggles."

"Now that you say it, you're decent tonight." She giggles and hiccups. "Shit. Yeah. I don't need any more. And I have to shut up my chickens, so I should probably jet."

And just like that, somehow, we're back to something like normal.

We catch a cab to hers so I can see her through her front door, and it's not even that late, but she falls asleep on my shoulder. Her hair smells like mangos and sawdust, and I think it must be the best smell in the entire world. I practically hyperventilate breathing it in. Finally, we pull up to the front of Bird's Eye which sensibly has a light on the porch. I tell the cab to wait while I escort her up the stairs. Jolie holds my arm, but I don't think she needs it. Still, it just kind of feels right.

She unlocks the door and reaches inside to flick on a light. Her kitchen appears through a window. "Thanks for going out tonight. It was nice." She seems a bit more sober now.

"Nice? Or *fine*?" I tease.

She slaps my chest, leaving a trail of goosebumps under my thin t-shirt.

"All right." I take a step back, but it's hard to peel away from her. "Cab's waiting. Maybe see you tomorrow?"

"Yeah, definitely. Stop by. I could use an assistant. It's barrels tomorrow."

I rub my hands together. "Count me in, then."

I make my way down the stairs back to the cab.

"Ashton?"

I turn. "Yeah?"

"Just to make it clear. You had your chance."

I throw my head back and tense my muscles not to go into a full-on grin. "Understood. Night, Joey."

"Night, Pup."

Chapter Ten

Jolie

I woke up realizing maybe now that I'm thirty-two I can't shoot two double shots and feel totally normal. Especially after tossing and turning all night, thinking for the first time in my life, Ashton Dane flirted back. I think. I'm pretty sure...

Falling back into old patterns was something I told myself to avoid, but then... doesn't a person deserve to feel like themselves? Nothing really makes me feel more me than pretending I'm in a will-they, won't-they situationship with my brother's best friend. It's sort of the trope of my childhood, and avoiding adulting right now is very tempting. And last night, just like every time Ashton and I played it out, I'm not even mad about it. It's like watching your favorite Christmas rom-com, knowing the ending and still feeling satisfied.

Only that six-five hunk of man could turn me down and make his rejection feel like a comfort blanket. I had fun last night. And I woke up wanting to do it all over again.

But am I still pretending? The fact that I didn't sleep a wink suggests I'm not. Also, in the delirium of the night, I thought about a million and one mischievous things from what it would actually be like to bang him, to what it would be like to turn him down if he acted on that glint in his eye.

I didn't get the obsession out of my system, and when I arrived at Moon Ridge Ranch the next afternoon, if five minutes went by without peeking behind me to see if Ashton was anywhere around, I was lucky. When Monica Dane comes to help me at three to set up for the children's barrel racing class, she calls me out.

"You got a problem with your neck, sweetheart?" she asks.

She must know. My childhood crush was no secret, and my identity as his admirer carries into adulthood. Every Scorpions game I've been to, when Ashton scored, Monica looked at me and hugged me like I'm proud of my man. But he's not my man. And the fact he didn't show up here today proves it.

"Yeah, I have a crick," I say as I shove a barrel on its side to wheel out into the arena for tonight's session. She'll either feel sorry for me or think I'm full of shit.

Because it's Monica we're talking about, it's the latter. "Ashton had to go to physical therapy today. Then he met with his agent and accountant." She heaves the barrel forward. "He was smart with his money on some level, but I still can't believe that little hussy got more than half of it."

I help Monica put another barrel on its side so we can roll them out together. "Hussy? That's a specific word."

"I've said too much and yet, not enough. Ashton tells me it's his business, but I hate that the media is portraying a situation that in reality is very much the opposite."

I get my barrel to its spot and pull it back upright. "Chloe cheated on Ashton?"

"Did I say that?" She grunts quietly, pushing her barrel upright a small distance away from me. She puts her hands on her hips and takes a breather from the manual labor. "Ashton doesn't want me talking about it. Hell, he wasn't even going to tell *me* what happened but I mom-guilted him."

I nod. I knew he wasn't a cheater. But why would he part with his fortunes when he didn't have to? And why doesn't he deny the rumors? It doesn't seem like the Ashton I know. Sure, he's never been the swinging dick in the room, that he left to Logan, but he sure as hell knows when to speak up and give a piece of his mind and then some if required. It doesn't make sense.

"I get that maybe Ashton doesn't care what the media thinks about him, I mean, he's always been his own man and not too concerned with reputation, but why didn't he even want to tell you about it?"

"I don't know. And anyway, the cheating is the only thing he told me about. When I asked him about the ridiculous settlement, he zipped those lips. He'll never tell me. There's something fishy going on. I always knew that woman was trouble, and not the good kind. But you can't control your kids forever."

That much is true. If I listened to my mom and Logan, I

wouldn't have stayed with Eric for more than a month either. Some of us just need to touch the stove to believe it's hot.

We head back over to the edge of the arena where the students will come any minute now.

Monica dusts off her hands. "Probably best you don't bring it up with Ashton. He told me to keep it private, but I couldn't bear the thought of you thinking less of him. I know we've teased you a bit over the years about him, but you've always had genuine care, and he deserves that friendship. I wasn't sure if your opinion was affected by the noise online or not, and somebody has to defend his honor."

I never doubted Ashton and now I'm glad I didn't. "You know nobody can say a bad word about that man to me."

Monica's smile and her arm around me are as warm as my own mother's. "I know, sweetheart. Thanks for your support. I'm glad he's getting a little time with you to find himself again. He needs that grounding. He was happier than I've seen him in years this morning. You two had a good night, I take it?"

"It wasn't a big one, but yeah... same for me. It was just nice to do something that felt familiar and normal."

Monica rubs my arm. I haven't explained to her why I'm here, but I'm sure Colt did, and she thinks maybe me and Ashton can lean on each other. But he decided not to even say as much as boo today so...

Voices reach us from outside in the corridor, and then one becomes distinct.

"I'll be here, too, so you're safe with me. I'm sure you'll be off to that competition in Florida in no time."

"Thanks, Ashton," a young lady I know answers back.

And then *he* turns the corner and enters the arena, all

tall, dark, and handsome with my sister-in-law and niece right behind him. He limps over to me and his mom. "Hey."

It's a casual entrance, but my heart flutters like he's the king of... well, I can't think of any famous kings, but the king of somewhere. And a goddamn handsome one at that.

I shake loose from my need to stare. Does he know I love him in a baseball cap? Is he taunting me? Torturing me by being so sexy I need to clench my teeth? But I got good at playing it cool then and I'm even more robust now.

I smirk. "You've come to bother me again today? Nothing better to do?"

"I'm not sure anyone has anything better to do right now." He places his hand on my niece's shoulder and gazes down at her. "Eve here was just telling me that she's come to prepare for a barrel racing competition with the Special Olympics."

Sam, my sister-in-law, comes over to give me a hug and whispers in my ear, "I'm trusting your judgment." Her comment is soaked with meaning. Sam is about my age, but she has a similar way to my own mother in that her most diplomatic words still sound like a threat.

My niece has Down syndrome and has been riding for years, but only in the past few months have any of us felt ready to have her try something more than trail rides and Western dressage. When she read about the equestrian competitions at the Special Olympics, the determined thirteen-year-old asked to join in on my mom's Pilates class and has been going three times per week for a while now.

Eve's core strength has improved, and much like the rest of the Hunters I know, she's a bit of a daredevil. It was always going to be hard to stop her from trying something quicker paced, but it is a lot of responsibility for me. It's a class for under twelves, but in this community, I could be getting a bunch of total yeehaws and struggle to keep an eye on her. And I did see that little redhead Gareth's name on the list. But Eve is experienced, and I'm sure she'll be sensible. Still, she'll be on a horse she's never ridden before, and I have to admit, that makes me nervous.

I glance over at the ponies Monica and I brought out. They are all tried and tested barrel ponies and seem calm now, but animals are unpredictable.

Monica says to her son, "So you two have it covered?"

Is she leaving? "I thought we were teaching together tonight?" I wiggle my finger between me and Monica.

"Oh, I just thought Ash could stand in for me. I invited Sam over for some cake during the lesson, and your mom is joining, too. That's okay, sweetie?"

That is one good cover, but I'm pretty sure I know this is a setup. The only question is, whose idea was it? My mom's? Or Monica's? They both want more grandchildren so badly they forget Ashton would never cross the line.

Though last night, he seemed to forget that, too.

"Course." I wave them off. "All good. Enjoy."

Monica heads out, and Sam watches over her shoulder for a few steps before throwing caution to Eve.

"Evie Bean, just remember it isn't Claude, so be more careful than usual with this pony."

"I know," she says. "It's going to be great. Promise."

Ashton reassures Sam, "I'll keep an eye on the situation."

As if I need his help. I don't. But when my eyes trace him from head to toe, I know I don't *need* his help but I sure as hell want it.

I tell Eve about her horse—all are tacked up and tied on along the wall. "Eve, yours is the painted one on the end. Her name is Grace."

"I'm so excited to try a new horse." She claps her hands together quickly, the way she always does when she's jumping out of her skin. She beams.

I bask in her sunlight. She has a way of making everyone smile.

"I'm stoked for you. I hope you're going to invite me when you go to the Special Olympics. We'll get you prepared in no time."

"Of course you're invited!"

"Me, too?" Ashton butts in.

Eve cocks her head. "Do you like barrel racing?"

"Who doesn't?" He wobbles his head like it's a silly question.

"Then come!"

Ashton glances at me. "We should get some of those foam fingers and we can write 'Eve' on them."

Eve giggles. "Those are for baseball games."

He points at her. "Not anymore."

She laughs again. "I'm going to say hi to Grace." She walks over to her pony, slips a tail comb out of her pocket, and has a go even though Grace is already groomed. Eve has always loved grooming.

I walk toward the door to the arena, and Ashton follows me.

"You're just butting into anything and everything now. Taking over my class. Wiggling your way into family trips..." I peek through the doorframe to see if anyone else is arriving and tease. "You're getting roped left and right these days. Yesterday, Gareth. Today, your mom."

A father and son arrive at the far end of the corridor.

Ashton leans into me, and I don't turn to face him but taste a tall drink of Cool Water cologne.

"I would have come even if she didn't make me"

I don't want him to see the satisfaction bursting my heart right now.

He adds, "I had fun yesterday."

I greet a student and his father. "Come on in, Brant. Sir, you can just come back in an hour."

The father tips his hat and doesn't waste a second to leave, sliding his cell out of his pocket.

I lean down. "Brant, at the end is Eve. You have the dark bay next to her, and his name is Slim."

Brant walks off, kicking through the sand as he goes.

I still stare into the corridor, gaze averted from Ashton. I can't face him or my body would burst into a sunbeam at the thought of him wanting to be here, at him having fun. I did, too, and I should admit it, but it's nice for the tables to be turned. "You had fun last night and so you came back willingly to annoy me again?"

He pokes his tongue in his cheek. "You didn't seem annoyed last night."

I shake my head, and the smile escapes.

Gareth and his mom walk up toward us, looking like she might have just had a moment with her son. "I told Gareth to behave..."

My voice is sugary sweet. "Gareth? He doesn't need to be told to behave. He's a model student." I glance down at the cheeky boy. "In fact, he's perfect."

Gareth darts his eyes back and forth, and his freckled cheeks round. "See, Mom?"

She doesn't believe me, of course, and shouldn't. I put my hand on her arm. "Seriously, he's been fine. Better than. Come back in an hour, Mrs. Mason, and enjoy yourself in the meantime."

She leaves, and Gareth sticks his head out the doorframe to watch her go. When she's gone, he turns to me and hooks his thumb in her direction.

"Thanks for covering for me, guys."

We both let out one syllable laughs; he's the worst cutest kid I've seen. I just have a thing for kids who are a little naughty. I see it as character.

He puts his hands out as if she's been exhausting. "I mean, she just doesn't understand that a cowboy needs an attitude."

Ashton nods like he totally gets it, hiding his amusement under his boyish lips. He's so good with the kids.

Gareth checks out the two remaining ponies and asks, "Can I have the palomino?"

"All yours," I say.

He pulls his arm down in celebration. "Yes!" He jogs off, his tiny chaps slapping his legs.

Ashton watches him with a faraway smile on his face. "I want one of those."

"Me, too."

Our gazes snap to each other, as though we just said something we didn't. But it isn't awkward.

Not for Ashton. "You want kids?"

I lean against the doorjamb, glance at my watch, not because I think my last student will be late but because gazing at Ashton right now is a bit much. He doesn't know it, but once upon a time I thought I'd have kids with *him*. I haven't thought that way since I was fifteen or so, and then my hormones started taking over and I thought more about what it would be like to *make* one than to *have* one.

"I do. Love kids. Spending time with Eve is a highlight in my life now. But I have learned it isn't easy. It's the worry I'm worried about."

He laughs lightly.

"Yeah, that sounds like I have serious issues. I'm happy you and Chloe never had kids, this all would have been worse, but you were married for a long time. Did you never talk about that?"

He lowers his gaze. "Nah. She didn't want to ruin her career."

"Pzzzt."

His expression is suddenly serious. "People are entitled to any opinion. And women don't have to be baby makers."

I don't like that he's defending her, but at the same time, he's right. Chloe didn't have to have children, and any reason is valid. Still, Ashton being so fair to someone I just found out did him wrong makes me shudder. Does he still love her?

"You're right," I concede, reaching deep for the maturity it takes to give Chloe any credence.

"I wish we talked about those fundamentals before we got married." His eyes are distant again as he ponders that thought. "Then again, we'd probably have kids now and that would be a disaster." His gaze connects with mine. "What will be, will be."

"Did you get that out of a fortune cookie?"

He offers me one of his famous half-smiles. "There's Chinese in the Canyon now?"

"Ha. I wish."

We're interrupted by the last student running up the hallway toward us who doesn't even say hello, just races between us and heads straight to the fourth pony. This one must be a regular.

Ashton adjusts his baseball cap, as though it wasn't in the perfect spot already. "I'll keep with Eve if you want. You take the others?"

"She's thirteen, I guess she'd prefer *you* watching her."

"I'm an old man to a thirteen-year-old."

It's hard for me to see it. Since reuniting with Ashton, all I see is the boy from Moon Ridge Ranch. The one who was always nice to me when my brothers weren't. The one who skipped the awkward teen stage and went straight to man. The one I wrote about in my diary. But we are grown up now with a shitload of nasty moments between past and present.

"Okay, you stick with Eve, but let her be independent. Strike the balance. Don't be a babysitter or worry too much. She's a cracking rider."

"Got it."

We get the lesson going, and two of the four have already done barrels. It's not a speedy sort of class but one more about learning how to shift weight and center and recenter. One to learn about not just using the reins but leg and heel, prompting a horse into or out of a turn. Watching the kids, even going slowly around the barrels, trying to use their legs instead of their hands to show the horses where to go, has me missing all of this. It's the thrill of getting it right. The thought of working toward something every time you practice—like how Eve has Special Olympics in mind or Gareth told me he wants to enter the Mini Masters in spring.

It's heartwarming to think about these kids achieving what they set out to do and I'm part of it.

My three students are pretty independent, and I let my eyes wander over to Ashton with Eve. He's bending down to show her which part of her leg is used to squeeze the horse's side. She must squeeze the horse then and there because all of a sudden, her horse starts turning away from Ashton who patiently guides the horse back to facing the barrel. I like the way he is with her. She's hanging on to his every word. He smiles wider than usual when she gets it.

It adds to the feelings building inside. Ashton senses me watching, and his gaze snags on mine. He shoots me a look that tells me Eve is doing great. I nod.

The lesson was a good one, though when we're done, Gareth has no end of wishing he was already God's gift to rodeo.

"Miss Hunter, we didn't even get out of a trot," he complains.

"When you can get the horse around a barrel using only your legs, you can go for it."

"I did."

"I must have missed that, but tell you what, next week, I'll let you try just once if your parents give me permission to let you."

His face twists with uncertainty. I get the impression his mom is pretty strict. But it's something else altogether.

"It's just Mom." He's a tough nut but he can't hide the sadness that tells me his dad is gone in one way or another.

I put my hand on his shoulder. "I'll see if I can soften your mom to the idea."

His smile is back.

Ashton and I say goodbye to the kids, and like last night, he stays to help me put things away.

"Your ankle will never get better if you keep putting weight on it."

"Maybe I don't care if it gets better."

Is he flirting with me? "Lies. You can't wait to get back on the ice."

"I want to play," he admits. "But I like being here, too. It's a crazy kind of peacefulness that doesn't exist anywhere else."

His comment hits me. It's the exact description for how I feel about my hometown. And being with Ashton. It's crazy peace. "I know what you mean."

When the barrels and horses are put away, we stand there together, and I rock on my heels.

"Thanks for your help. I probably could have taught on my own—"

"I know…"

I can't make out his thoughts in those deep-brown eyes, but he stares at me, and there's some sort of stop-start motion going on between us.

I slide my hands into my back pockets, considering if I should hug him goodbye, but I'd come away with diamond-hard nipples.

He interrupts that thought. "What are you doing now? Want to grab something to eat? I haven't quite gotten used to having dinner in the main house with my mom and dad. I'd rather be out, if you're up for joining me?"

My heart dances like a little girl with a golden ticket in her hand. But then responsibility hits. I'd love to take a drive with Ashton out of town for some food but I can't. "I have the chickens. I need to shut them away because I'm pretty sure the perimeter of my coop isn't totally secure. I haven't had time to fix it since I got them so I need to make sure they're in their hutch. I risked it last night. Can't do that twice."

He nods like he's not sure if it's an excuse or a reason. "I'm happy to head to yours if that's where you need to be."

An insistent man is so damn hot. "Okay. I could whip up an omelet."

"You're going to be one of those people always pawning off your eggs now, aren't you?"

"Pretty much."

"Okay. Sounds great."

This feels like a date. A date we probably shouldn't have. One with potential for hurt feelings and turndowns that will ache. But Ashton in my house tonight is not something I intend to pass up.

We walk slowly, Ashton's limp more obvious now that he spent the last hour and a half on his feet.

"I'll check out your hutch if you like," he offers.

It's been a long time since anyone offered to help me with the more mundane things in life. My brothers and mom would always come by and lend a hand, but I typically have to ask. To me, his offer is about so much more than the chicken run itself.

But if he doesn't respect his orders to rest, one of us should. "I don't want you on your feet anymore."

"Starlight Canyon breeds tough stock. I told you I'm fine. Plus there are no classes tomorrow, so I'll be bored with my foot up for hours."

We reach the cars and climb inside. He follows my SUV even though he knows where I live. I think about his last words as I drive. There are no classes tomorrow. In the rearview, I make out his chiseled jawline and intense hooded eyes and wonder how late he'll stay.

Chapter Eleven

Ashton

Why am I doing this? I question myself the entire way to Bird's Eye, Jolie and I catching glances in her rearview mirror. Maybe she's thinking the same thing. *Is this a good idea?*

I caught myself one too many times stuck in a spiral of thoughts about what a stunner she is now. If it was the same Jolie from years ago—the one who seemed a hell of a lot younger, the one who seemed like a little sister—I wouldn't be wondering why I'm catching a bite to eat at my friend's house, someone I've known since I ever remember knowing people. I wouldn't question my motives if I hadn't stared at her round, filled-out jeans and her full breasts. I'm a warm-blooded male just like any other.

But I do want to know more about what's happened in the past years and what's going through her mind as she questions abandoning a career she worked damn hard to qualify for. Is she okay? There's a haunting glint in her eyes now I don't recognize, even though I spent years getting to know every last shade of green in every sliver of her irises. I know Jolie. Or at least I've always thought I did. And now I can read a lot of her movements, but others are a mystery.

I get out of my car, and Jolie, who just parked, comes over to me.

"I'll just grab today's eggs to add to what I have inside."

I follow her to her hutch and chicken run that's about thirty yards from her house. Her *big* house. It's a lot of space for one person. She must be knocking around inside there like a pinball. Jolie isn't as bad as Logan, but I know she's never been big on being alone. Not like Dash who craves solitude. Even Colt is better at being alone than Joey, though now he has a wife and daughter, I bet he never is. It must be the best feeling in the world to know you'll always have someone to come home to.

When Jolie steps into the chicken run, her hens come running over to her. She reaches into her jacket pocket and tips out some feed. I always keep a few treats in my farm jacket pocket, too, and for some reason, even though a lot of ranch folk do it, my heart warms because Jolie and I are kindred. I just lived in a place for a very long time where most of the company I kept wouldn't have dreamed of keeping crumbly chicken feed in their pockets no matter how much joy it brought to their hens.

Joey throws the food down and crouches to scoop one of

the hens up, nuzzling it with her cheek. "This is Phoebe." She nods to the ones pecking at her feet. "And that's Rachel and Monica. I got them from Luis Mendez."

"Still into *Friends*?"

"Course. Who isn't?" She takes Phoebe over to the hutch and gently ushers her inside. Monica and Rachel notice and head for the steps leading up to the hutch.

Watching Joey with the animals has my heart twitching. It's just... cute.

Too cute. She closes the hens inside and reaches around back, taking out two eggs. "This will literally never get old." She lifts the white, ovular gifts to show me.

"Yeah..." Suddenly, the way I'm feeling right now makes me wonder why I'm here again. I told myself after Sly's it was mostly the alcohol that had me wanting to gather Joey up in my arms, but then, in the arena, here... it's...

I need to chase these thoughts away. "Why don't I inspect the chicken run barrier while there's still a bit of light?" I notice some supplies on the ground and point to them. "Is that what you have, if I find a problem?"

She nods.

"I'll meet you in the house."

"Are you sure? I didn't bring you here to work." She smirks, her gaze wild. "I brought you here because you invited yourself to dinner."

I rub my forehead, hiding a smile, then glance up from under my eyebrows.

"Thanks." She leaves the hutch and takes her eggs over to the house, her hips swaying under the hem of her jacket.

I let out a long, slow breath and crouch on the ground next to the chicken wire. I shouldn't be hanging out with her again, feeling the way I do when we lock eyes. The way

I want to take her flirt and turn it into something more. I found the strength to walk away after Sly's and rowed right back out into the storm. What the fuck is wrong with me?

Where the hell has my self-control and decency gone? I'm staring at my best friend's sister in ways I shouldn't and pushing my ankle to the goddamn limit just to be around her. I wish it was just her looks. Something shallow like that I could get past, but it's more...

I don't really see that little girl anymore, but in her place isn't just a woman very much my type. In her place is a woman who picked up some darkness, and no matter how bright Jolie still shines, I know it's in there. I've always seen it as my job to care for her, and the distance and time never changed that. Yeah. I'm doing the right thing being here. Getting to the bottom of what's up with Joey is the goal. I'm here to help her get talking.

I find a breach in the chicken run, almost big enough to let in a fox, so I grab the supplies Joey dumped outside the run. I cut some chicken wire to patch up the hole and get to using the twist ties she put there to make it an easy job. Easy, but not resulting in expert craftsmanship. I hope she doesn't tell anyone *I* fixed this fence.

Especially not Logan... *Logan.* I stand and dust my hands off on my pants. There is no way he won't find out I hung out with Jolie tonight, which means it's best if I'm the one who tells him. I slide my cell from my pocket.

ME: HEY, JUST HELPED YOUR SISTER FIX HER CHICKEN RUN. WHAT KIND OF BROTHER ARE YOU?

The time on my phone reads five-thirty. I might catch him just before the pregame briefing with Coach. My stomach churns with what he might write back, and I remind myself Logan can't see inside my head no matter how good we've gotten at guessing each other's thoughts. He doesn't know I wanted to peel off her pants last night at Sly's.

My phone buzzes.

PUCK BOY: I LEAVE THAT SHIT FOR YOU OR ELSE YOU COULDN'T FEEL LIKE A HERO. WHO WOULD YOU EVEN BE THEN? JUST CLARK KENT.

ME: SOME PEOPLE PREFER CLARK.

PUCK BOY: NO THEY DON'T. FIND OUT WHY SHE'S WORKING WITH YOUR MOM. COLT SAID SHE NEEDS A BREAK? FROM WHAT?

His text lowers my blood pressure. He thinks nothing of me being here. On the contrary, I know Logan. He's glad I'm helping her out, and moreover, he trusts me. *He. Trusts. Me.*

ME: I'M HAVING SOME GRUB WITH HER TONIGHT, SO MAYBE SHE'LL TALK ABOUT IT.

PUCK BOY: BE THAT HERO AND GET TO THE BOTTOM OF IT. MAKE SURE THAT FUCKWIT OF AN EX ISN'T BACK IN THE PICTURE.

Eric Larose? They must have broken up over a year ago at least because I've seen pictures of him with the latest snack on his arm. Why would he be around? And why is my heart beating like a caged gorilla right now? Logan has always hated that guy, but in an unusual display of privacy, he never said much when I asked why he had those feelings. He never opened up about what was happening between Eric and Jolie. I figured it was standard relationship mess and Logan was just being protective.

But right now, those explanations do nothing to satiate my curiosity.

I glance up at the house. Is Eric actually the problem?

ME: ON IT. PLAY STRONG.

I step through the front door and into the kitchen prepared to be the man Logan needs in his stead, but as I slip my shoes off one by one, the anger at Eric Larose possibly having an effect on my Jolie melts into a swirl of other emotions. I take in the sight of her... she's stripped off all her layers except for a spaghetti strap, low-cut, very thin camisole. And to top off the allure of her breasts spilling out of the virtual lingerie, she's vigorously whisking eggs and her chest bounces invitingly.

Her hair is pulled up, exposing a cape of perfect milky skin. She blows a rogue tendril off her forehead. "Hot in here."

The smile that follows is the same one I adored when we were younger, the one I couldn't really read but was full of the kind of irresistible mischief any young man would like.

She takes a quick sip of an amber liquid with ice in a highball glass and then hands me one of my own. "Bourbon." She wiggles her eyebrows. "Neat."

When I take my drink from her, our fingers touch, and it's enough for me to forget why I'm here at all. I sip, hoping some desire swallows down with the alcohol. This one isn't as strong as last night's, but it goes down with a warm familiar sting and when the burn fades, all there is in the world is us.

I take another drink, and the epiphany hits me. I've lived a life for a very long time where nobody really knew me. All those years playing without Logan, and especially the ones with Chloe, people concocted stories of me being some man I'm not. They'd write I was a party animal. They'd write I was addicted to spending money or that I had a bromance going with some actor I only met once.

That's the beautiful thing about roots. About having a home. You can't pretend but you aren't misinterpreted either. I used to think that was a hindrance when I was younger. A lot of teenagers want to reinvent themselves at some point in their lives, but now that I'm older, now that I got to try on a few costumes and play roles I never asked to be cast in, I know there's no happier feeling than being seen for who I am.

And that's exactly how Joey looks at me right now.

"What are you thinking about?" she asks. "A Mento for your thoughts?"

Her question draws me in even closer to our shared past. Whenever I could tell Joey was upset about something, I'd offer her peppermint Mentos, a treat I always had in my pocket for the horses. Sometimes she'd talk. Sometimes she wouldn't, but the treat would always get me a smile. I don't answer, but goddamn does her question tug at the loose string in my heart seams and threaten to unravel me.

I make my way closer and plant my hands on the other side of the breakfast bar to where she's whisking. I peer in the bowl. "Are you feeding an army?"

"You're pretty much two men. And I'm damn hungry after this day. Your mom is relentless. She must think I'm still sixteen the way she's working me."

I strip off my jacket, peel off my static-filled jumper, which only adds more electricity to the situation. I perch on a stool.

She considers me, laughs through her nose, and leans over the counter, exposing a view of her curves falling damn near out of that top of hers, and smooths my hair. "It's all standing up."

I swallow hard, working even harder to keep my eyes where they belong. "Static." I clear my throat. "Why is it so hot in here?"

"I think maybe the thermostat isn't working? I can't turn down the temperature." She takes the eggs over to a pan she clearly had already heated up because she pours the eggs straight in. "I don't know." She peeps over her shoulder seductively. "But I like it hot." She turns back to concentrate on the pan and adds, "I can sleep naked."

I try. I *try* not to picture Jolie naked, but my brain force-feeds me the image. I stare at her ass in her tight, filled-out jeans, and think about how those hips would feel in my hands. Round ass. She probably has smooth skin like the back of her neck...

She sprinkles some chopped vegetables and cheese into the frying pan. "I hope I'm able to flip this omelet without breaking it. I've never been good at these. Especially in a big pan like this."

"As long as there's cheese in it, doesn't matter what it looks like."

She points the flipper at me. "My kind of man."

And damn, if Jolie hasn't grown into my kind of woman.

She attempts to flip the omelet over, but it falls apart. "Shit." She doesn't face me but throws her hand on her hip and shakes her head.

Scratch that. Jolie hasn't grown into my kind of woman. She's *always been* my kind of woman. Bold. Playful. Puts her foot in it all the time but she's so well-meaning. She has a litany of qualities I've always admired and thought a few times, especially after prom when my mind first wandered to that *what-if* space in time, that I might end up with a woman like her one day.

I drink again, and the bourbon asks me what it would feel like to ease in behind her and put myself flush up against that ass of hers and inhale the back of her neck where the faded, earthy scent of patchouli and a hard-working woman would be the biggest turn-on I'd ever experience.

Being around Jolie is comforting. But also alluring. And worrying. And... Well, just like the girl, the woman makes me feel a lot of things. I rub my thighs to ground myself, bring me back to reality. It doesn't matter what I feel. I'm here to figure out what Joey feels. Like Logan said, there's something wrong, and I need to get her talking about it.

She puts the eggs—now more of a scramble than an omelet—on one plate and brings over two forks and takes the stool next to me. "I hope you don't mind sharing a plate. I hate doing dishes."

She sits with her legs wide open, and that same seam from Sly's tempts my mind away from reason.

I pick up a fork and wonder if she can read my thoughts. *God, I hope not.* "I don't mind sharing. But for the record, I would have done the dishes. You cook. I clean. Seems fair." I stab some eggs. "Believe it or not, I actually like doing dishes. It's relaxing. I hated having a cleaner back in LA."

"Oooh. A man who likes cleaning. You really are still so perfect, aren't you, Ashton?" She takes a bite, and her pouty lips move subtly as she chews. She has a damn pretty mouth.

We eat and talk about the kids in the class this afternoon. We laugh about a few of the things Gareth said, and Jolie tells me how his dad is gone and she looked it up in her car before driving here. Gary Mason died two years ago. I melt in the presence of this caring woman. She knows a lot about the history of the students, and her empathy has grown from what it was when we were kids—from concerned neighbor to a woman who has the intentional attentiveness of a matriarch.

We finish the omelet while still talking about Moon Ridge Ranch. I head to the sink, and Jolie enlightens me on all the things she's caught up on since returning to Starlight Canyon so many months before me. The town gossip. The fact that there's only one carrot cake per day being sold at CCs now that Shay Mendez is setting up her own business.

Talking about home together is the most comfortable I've felt in a long, long time. It's a shame I need to steer this conversation elsewhere.

I turn off the faucet, having finished washing the pan while Jolie chatters away, and I follow her over to the couches in her living room. She's refilled our bourbons. I tell myself not to have another one or I'll need a straight-jacket. Jolie laughs a lot, even when she's being serious, and every time she does, her full, round tits laugh along with her, calling to my fingertips.

Jolie plops down on a sofa. "I'm making up for lost time with Eve, but it's great she's a horsey girl. I can't wait to go to Florida with her for Special O."

I take the cushion next to her. "A lot happened while we were away. Like Eric..." I dare to meet her eyes, which have instantly changed at the sound of his name. "You two were together for a long time."

She finishes her drink in one go and puts her glass down on the coffee table. Her voice is raspier than when I came in an hour ago. Her eyes are lazy and hold nothing back.

"Yeah, he loves to come crawling back whenever he

needs someone who can string a sentence together at an event. I'm getting old for his taste now, though."

Loves. Present tense.

I put my glass down. Maybe I've had enough, because an inappropriate amount of jealousy makes tracks through my veins.

"Do you still wish you were his taste?" The minute the words come out of my mouth, I regret them. It's too much innuendo, and the thought of another man's hands or mouth on Jolie makes me want to grind my teeth.

She leans into the back of the sofa right next to me, and the cushion gives way slightly so my body collapses a few more inches toward her.

"I was a fool to ever get involved with him. And a fool a million times more taking him back and being on that seesaw from hell." She lets her hand fall to my thigh and pats me as she speaks. "But you know all about being foolish, so I don't feel so bad admitting that to you." Her words aren't full of anything but honesty.

Her feminine hand rubs my leg, and she talks at the same time, staring into the distance. Her mind might be elsewhere, but mine is firmly planted under her palm. She strokes back and forth, mindlessly, far too close to my dick, and I swell in my jeans.

"He cheated on me three times. And that's what I know of. And I still took him back. I bet you wouldn't have done that, though."

I can't tell if it's a question or a statement, and with half the blood in my body navigating away from my head and straight to my groin, it takes a minute for me to think about anything other than grabbing her wrist and guiding it to my cock for the friction it craves.

She's spent a bit of time with my mom now, though, so I

assume she might have told Jolie the story. In fact, sitting here now, feeling like Jolie might know it wasn't me who cheated… I realize how badly I want her to know. "I'm a no-second-chance type. I didn't take Chloe back after I found out. But I also suspected it for a long time and did nothing."

"So she cheated on you?" She's not surprised. Her question is a confirmation.

"Yeah."

Jolie's head settles on my shoulder, and that mango-and-sawdust smell I love so much overwhelms my senses.

"Sucks doesn't it? Even if you don't really love the person anymore." Her voice is laced with sadness that doesn't belong there.

I hate thinking anyone has ever made her feel the unique humiliation of being betrayed, because I don't care what anyone says out loud, or how many times other people tell you *fuck 'em*, it's impossible not to feel inadequate when it happens.

And my Joey is anything but inadequate. She's a once-in-a-lifetime catch, and Eric Larose is one blind bastard who I could fucking pummel right now knowing he treated this diamond like a disposable object.

I snake my hand around Jolie's waist and tug her into me. I've given Jolie many hugs before, but she feels different in my arms this time. She feels like… a perfect fit. I know I'm supposed to be comforting her, but her body snuggled into mine… it has me breathing deeper. "Eric doesn't know a good thing when he sees it."

She lets out a sad laugh. "Apparently, that's a theme in my life."

I know she's talking about prom night. "That was totally different."

But right now, prom night feels like my biggest mistake

because I could have saved both of us from a world of pain and been sitting here every night with Jolie's head on my shoulder, feeling at peace.

But I can't tell her that. I shouldn't anyway. But then again, I should. Why would I let anything stand between me and making her feel worthy? I brace her arms and spin her to have her look me in the eyes. For the first time, maybe ever, she struggles with eye contact. Her confession drained her confidence, and I'm determined to put that glint back in that green sparkle.

"Joey, I never said no on prom night because you weren't everything a man could dream for. I never said no because you weren't beautiful, smart, witty, hilarious, fun as hell... you are all those things and more."

"But—"

I shake her biceps in my palms. "No buts—" Her gaze connects with mine, and I dive into her emerald eyes. "You are perfect, Joey..."

She lowers her hands to the tops of my thighs, leaning closer.

I close the space between us. "As perfect as they come."

We're face to face. Inches away from my lips on hers. My mouth lowers in slow motion and her strawberry lips part. And I know... I know I need to kiss her now. I can feel her breath on my mouth, steaming hot and ready for the most romantic kiss of my life until I'm not sure if our lips touch or not, but she turns her head, giving me a cheek instead. I'm dead still, ready to devour her ear now, but she refused me?

She squeezes the tops of my thighs, and her cheeks round with a smile. "I've dreamed of turning you down for years, Ashton Dane."

A coy delight paints her features, and I can practically

see her pulse beating beneath the flesh of her neck. She might be turned away but she's still in my space. *Our* space.

A devilish laugh escapes me. "Is this you refusing me? Your fingers digging into my legs? Your neck craning so you can feel my breath?"

She wraps her hand around my waist, buries her face into my neck, hiding. "I told you—you had your chance." She continues the game.

She feels perfect in my arms right now, her lips on my neck, soft hair on my cheek. I smooth my hands along the humps of her ass and crush her body even closer into mine.

"Oh yeah?" I kiss the top of her head. "Are you saying no? You want me to leave?"

Jolie crawls onto me, straddles me, and eases her head back to gaze at me. "Ashton..." She combs her hands through my hair and tugs the tufts at the base of my neck. "I never wanted you to leave."

I swipe my thumb across her lips and stare deep into her until I see the game is gone and years of meaning, wanting, and desire are there instead. It's not a game to me either. There are real feelings here between us. History. "If I kiss you, Joey, I'm not sure there's any coming back from it."

Her warm palm cups my cheek. "See how silly you are? Where am I going back to? Just the place I've always been."

I kiss the corner of her mouth. I need to put my lips somewhere as I search for reason. I want to tell myself it's the bourbon. But it isn't. The only thought that comes to mind is how I've already wasted enough time, how I had this tailor-made woman right here all along... how wide she can open her legs to wrap them around my hips...

She kisses the corner of my lips in return and whispers, "You've never been *just* a friend to me." She lowers her core onto my now rock-hard dick and rubs herself on me. "And you never will be."

I can't wait another second to have her. I crash my lips into hers, and the minute her hot, sweet mouth connects with mine, the moment I snake my tongue inside and taste the delicious insides of Jolie Hunter... I've never wanted to possess something... *someone* more in my life.

I'm done. Here and now. There's nothing after this. The way she kisses me back with feverish mewls, she erases any memory of anything before.

It's as though it's always been her and always will be.

Chapter Twelve

Jolie

THE WAY MY CORE TINGLES, touched only by the firmness of fabric between us, doesn't seem possible. My clit weighs heavy, and I swear I can feel my pulse down there.

I've imagined this moment a few times before. Hell, way more than a few times. I imagined it a thousand times after prom. It went away for a while, but sometimes in my moments of rejection from Eric, Ashton would sneak back in, and I'd think about how one day, I'd say no to him. But I just tried.

"I've dreamed of turning you down for years, Ashton Dane."

I tried to reel Ashton in and then release him, but as I sit here with my face buried in the most muscular, sexiest neck in the universe, it still smells just like it did when I first fell in love with him as a girl. That classic scent he never changed brings back a world of wanting within me, and there's no way in hell, even for just this one night, I can pretend I don't want him. But I've always been on the sassy side despite my best interests.

He's thick between my legs and calls my bluff. "Are you saying no? You want me to leave?"

I can't even pretend for another minute. God, I just want him to kiss me. "Ashton... I never wanted you to leave."

His thumb grazes my bottom lip, and my core grows even heavier.

"If I kiss you, Joey, I'm not sure there's any coming back from it."

Going back? To the past where I always wanted him? "See how silly you are? Where am I going back to? Just the place I've always been."

He kisses the corner of my mouth, still seeming unsure. Will he? Will he relent this time to what *I* already know was always meant to be? Or will he delay the inevitable? Because if it's not Ashton, it's nobody for me... and I already wasted years with his placeholder.

I kiss the corner of his mouth in return, and there's not one ounce of play left in my words. I've never been more serious in my life.

"You've never been just a friend to me." I roll my hips back and forth, relieving my ache just a little on his tented zipper. "And you never will be."

Not another moment passes before his lips knead mine. It's the most tender but firm kiss I've ever had in my life. The moment his tongue slides into my mouth, I'm possessed. My body grinds on him without permission, pure passion and years of wanting take over. I press my tits into him as hard as I can, and rub myself back and forth like I've been waiting even longer than forever for this. My pebbled nipple snags on something under his t-shirt, and I slide my fingers under the fabric, feeling every lump of six-pack and taut muscle. My fingers find a necklace, and I anchor my grip on it to stop my hands wandering elsewhere.

This kiss is leading my need quickly toward home base. "You taste better than I dreamed you would..."

I draw my tongue along his, reveling in the bourbon- and tobacco-like taste of this man. I circle my hips to get more friction. It's hot and heavy between my legs, and I crave more so badly. He takes one hand and grips my ass, smashing me against him. He hangs on to my hips tightly, forcing me back and forth over him... he needs this, too. I'm breathless, panting for more when he tugs me down on top of him on the couch.

My breasts fall against his gigantic chest. He glides his fingers up my torso until his thumb grazes my nipple, and it sends a rush of hot desire between my legs.

I moan the words into his mouth, not wanting to detach myself. "You touch me like that and we'll do more than kiss."

He snatches his hand away from my breast, which is the opposite of what I intended with my saucy comment, and holds both sides of my head, as if securing his hands there so they don't wander elsewhere. Maybe he's thinking this is going too far...

I take one of his hands from my face and place it back

down on my breast. I stare deep into his chocolate eyes. "Pup, that wasn't a warning. It was an invitation."

I sit up, still straddling his giant hips—thank God I'm used to riding horses—and peel my shirt off, wasting no time taking off my bra. My tits tumble out, my nipples so pert they're stimulated by his gaze alone. He fondles one in his hand, stares at my chest like it's treasure, and sits up enough to take my nipple into his mouth.

I suck my teeth, and the pleasure runs straight to my core. I want to give this to him, too. I want to touch him everywhere and smooth my hands up his torso to push up his shirt, revealing that chest I used to drool over so long ago. It's better now. It's thicker and more manly with the perfect amount of hair to let me know he's just the kind of beast I want ravaging me tonight.

But suddenly, he lets his head drop back against a couch cushion and closes his eyes like he's not quite as savage and senseless as I am. He's slowing down while I'm speeding up. I tug his shirt upward, and he lets me, but I see it, something swirls around in his head. And that something doesn't seem like dirty thoughts of railing me.

I throw his shirt on the floor and lay my bare chest on his. I find his necklace chain again and run my index finger along the chain. The methodical movement slows my heartrate and I catch my breath. Under my cheek, he's balmy; his fingers run up and down along my spine in the most comforting way. We lie there half naked. I listen to his heart booming and wonder what's going through that head of his. His fingers feel so good on me, trailing up and down my back like someone who cares, and I know he does. But he's... well... he stopped.

"What are you thinking?" I need to know.

A kiss lands on top of my head. "I'm thinking we're not

stupid teenagers and this isn't some horny first date where the parents aren't home."

My cheek rises and falls along with his breath. "What's that supposed to mean?"

"I know you've had a crush on me since we were kids…"

"A crush hardly describes it…"

"Well, a crush hardly describes how I feel about you right now either."

The air is trapped in my lungs. It's words I've waited a lifetime to hear and yet…I can't look at him if he's about to turn me down again.

He cups his hand at the base of my skull. "If this is just sex to you, Joey… I can't."

My eyes flit around the room but focus on nothing, and finally I sit up, my boobs pooling on his chest. "You think I just want to have sex with you and that's it?"

"You said you're back to where you've always been. And prom night… It was about sex."

"Fuck… are you serious?" How can he even ask such a thing when every person in Starlight Canyon knows I've been in love with him since I was knee-high?

And then it hits me. The cheating. The deceit of his wife. The doubt that comes with that humiliation is something that needs a hell of a lot of reassurance.

"You know why you're in doubt and I'm not?" I stroke his cheek.

He stares at me, waiting.

"Because the reason I fell in love with you as a girl is that you've always reassured me. Even when you rejected me that night at prom, you came to my window to have a chat with all that tape in your hand to stick my heart back together. Whenever I was down, Pup, you were the one to be a little nicer to me. You were the one to come and ask if I was okay. If there was anything you could do to make it better, I know you would have done it. Who wouldn't love that? I fell for you then, and it's never gone away. You're the most comforting person in the world to me."

His gaze deepens. "I care about you..."

"I know you do. I never thought you'd fuck me but I always knew you cared about me. Always." I take his chin in my fingers. "And you need to know I care about you, too. If you let me... I'll show you." I kiss his lips. "I won't let you down. I'm big enough to take care of you now, too..." I kiss him again. "And this is a lot more than just sex to me." I gaze at him playfully. "If you say no again, though, there might be a crime of passion in this house tonight."

An amused laugh leaves his lips, and I kiss them again.

He laces his fingers through my hair and manhandles the base of my skull. "Don't think this means I'm going to be gentle just because I'm fucking smitten." His crooked grin is full of lust. "Nailing the most forbidden woman in this town... fuck, Joey, having you straddled over me is enough for me to come in my pants." He circles my nipple with his thumb and takes a big bite of my tit. "How did you get to be so perfect?"

My head falls back, and I close my eyes to enjoy the sensation of his hot, wet mouth on my nipple. Blinded by the feeling, I am somehow still able to find his button and zipper and get his jeans open to access his dick. I feel inside, and lined by a thin layer of cotton is what feels like the biggest cock in the world.

I'm in fucking trouble tonight and I can't wait.

He groans when I run my hand up and down his clothed sheath and undoes my pants, too, and I stand to wiggle them down. He watches every inch of them sliding off me with a captivated hunger that makes me feel like the most special woman in the world.

He reaches his hand out and trails a finger from my belly button down to the seam of my pussy and lightly glides along, easing it slightly into the wet space, but only enough to trace me. Such an enormous man. Such a gentle touch. He uses two fingers to ease open my folds and finds my clit, rubs circles over the sensitive nub. I bite my lower lip in absolute ecstasy. He's not in a hurry. He's not furiously rubbing to bring me to orgasm so he can have his turn... his stroking is calm, sensual... slow... and making my legs shake.

I drop to my knees next to the couch and start to pull his pants down, and I can't believe I'm about to see the dick I've drawn images of in my mind's eye nearly every time I masturbate. He lifts his hips to allow me to pull off his pants, and the most proportionate erection springs out. I'm a tall girl. I'm not small, but this thing surely can't fit.

"Jesus, Ashton," I say, staring at the crown of his dick, wondering if I'll even get the tip in.

He tosses me a sly smirk. "You like what you see?"

"I'm borderline nervous it won't fit." I grip his cock and stroke it root to tip. It's a fucking monster.

"I'll stretch you nice and slow..." He takes my hand off him and holds it. "If you have a condom?"

I tug at his hand, and he stands. I trail us up to my bedroom. I can't believe I'm buck-ass naked, walking through my house with Ashton Dane's cock like a sword fight in space, and it's... the most natural thing in the world. Like this was always supposed to happen. But when we get to my room, my intimate space where no man has been, and I turn to face him again... nerves kick in. I've never invited a man into this room. And now one of the most important ones in the world is here.

I've always been one to dive in head first. It's how trouble has always found me. I went bulldozing into vet school without thinking about my weaknesses. Blazed into a relationship with a man everyone warned me was an asshole. I've always whipped into the world without thinking through consequences until they are right there on my doorstep and they already know I'm home.

And now, Ashton's fingers are laced through my hair, and he stares at me like a man in need of my body, and my stomach drops. Will this hurt tomorrow? Was he right to be worried downstairs?

Ashton's gaze is intense, and he reads my thoughts. "No more questions. I made up my mind." He kisses me. "You're mine now."

Ashton puts his hands on either side of my waist and lifts me. I wrap my legs around his middle and hold on to his thick, strong neck. I'm overwhelmed with emotion when he lays me on the bed and stares at me again. His eyes scan every millimeter of my body, head to toe. He trails a finger down my breastbone.

"I want to memorize every piece of your skin. Every curve... Fuck, Joey..." He talks almost like I'm not here. "I fucking wondered what this body looked like under those clothes. You're a goddess."

He hovers over me and kisses me from my neck down my collarbone, peppering soft lips along every inch of my body until he hits my belly. "I can't wait to taste you... I'm going to worship this pussy..."

I widen my legs for him as an answer. If his mouth is anything like his finger was earlier, I can't imagine...

His warm, moist tongue lands on my clit, and I let out a

sigh. He laps down there slowly but eagerly, he moans into my core like he's enjoying it as much as I am.

"I could stay buried down here 'til I die. Fuck, woman, you smell and taste like heaven."

I weave my fingers through his wavy locks and hold on like his hair is the reins. If I don't, I might float away. His tongue drags over my clit with the perfect amount of pressure, a smooth gliding motion like he's reading my mind, knowing just where to touch, just where to circle... exactly where to suck. He pulls my clit into his mouth hard enough to make it stand tall, and when he takes his mouth off, he pinches my nub between his fingers. My legs open wider for him all on their own.

"Jesus, you're an expert at everything you do..." I groan, grinding my core shamelessly against his mouth. The five o'clock shadow on his chin scratches delightfully at my entrance. Pain and pleasure. He's always been the source of my most extreme emotions.

He sticks a finger inside me, and the slick sound of desire is impossible to escape. "You're soaking me." He pulls his finger out and licks it off then lines my lips with the sweet combination of his mouth and my deepest desire. "You wet and dirty little girl."

My words are breathy as he brings me close. "Only for you, Pup."

He adds two more fingers, and I'm so wet, the stretch is fucking everything, but it occurs to me will be nothing compared to his massive cock.

He twirls his tongue in a circle, firmer now but still in no hurry while my mind races and my core throbs, wanting him.

"More," I pant.

He sucks my clit between his lips again, and I nearly

shatter, the feeling is blinding. He pumps his fingers in and out, and though I love the fact this man would worship my pussy for days, he's a borderline tease. I take his hand and force him to drive his fingers deeper into me.

"Ashton, fuck... give it to me..."

I don't need to say it twice. He plunges his fingers in and out, circles my clit more viciously with his tongue, harder and just fucking right... My body surges, my toes curl, every muscle in my body tenses. I let out a tight groan, my pussy rippling and pulsing under his tongue. He paints it up and down, over my thumping clit, drawing out the orgasm for longer than womanly possible.

When he pulls his fingers out, I still have my eyes closed and am riding the wave, but I lay a floppy arm on my bed and point to the bedside table. He knows what I mean and crawls over. The drawer rumbles open, and when my eyes finally focus on him again, he's hovered over me, tight abs, perfect sinewed forearms, and veined hands rolling a condom over his thick cock.

He crawls between my legs and eases the crown to my entrance, and if I thought three fingers was a lot, taking a six-foot-five proportional man is playing in the big leagues now.

He dips in but only a little, drags himself out his eyebrows pinch together in concentration. In... out... "You okay?" he asks, he bites his lip like he's holding back.

I'm so stuffed, it's like he's fisting me. The stretch is dirty and indecent but at the same time sensual and loving.

"I'll take my time. I want it to feel good for you."

"It feels so good, Ashton."

"Almost in..."

God, he's not all the way in? I let out a deep exhale and feel him inch in farther; my pussy is burning now, but the fire Ashton brings is the kind that ignites my soul. He pumps in and out, and I adjust to his size.

"You're so tight, baby," he groans into my neck and nibbles on my skin.

I open up to him even more. "I want it harder. I can take it." I arch my back and press my tits up into his chest. The tingle on my nipples touching him loosens me yet again. "Give it to me."

He dips in, farther and farther, nudging into my slick core, filling me full like I didn't think possible.

He reaches the end of me and, sunk deep inside, he stops his methodical, deliberate thrusting, my core is stretched and full. His hot breath whispers against my earlobe. "You were made for me, Joey. It feels so good inside you."

His words wind me up, and I grind into him, splay my hands across his steely ass, and slam him into me, urging for more. I waited what feels like all my life to have this man inside me. He drives in and out again. Every vein and ridge of his cock massages my insides and I can't help myself rolling my hips. I rise and lower, move them in rhythm with his motion; his arms go impossibly tense on either side of me.

He growls, and I know he's gritting his teeth.

"I can't hold back much more... you're so fucking tight and so damn wet for me."

I want to give him the most blinding orgasm of his life. I murmur, "Just for you... always for you... Come for me, Ashton. And then I'll soak you just like you asked."

"Fuck, you've always been a naughty one, baby girl." He presses his hands under my ass and flips me up and over so now I'm on top of him. "I want to watch my naughty girl.

Watch your tits bounce and watch you spread open just for me."

He's even deeper now in this position, and his cock touches every part of my insides. I wonder what my face looks like working so hard to relax myself. He's filling me to the brim. He picks up my hips and slams them down. He said he wouldn't be gentle... it's fucking intense.

Seeing his insane pecs and gorgeous face and those eyes I've always drowned in under me, lazy, possessed... mine... the base of my spine tingles, and I throb deep inside, then my body releases all over him. I drop myself onto him, holding on to the back of his shoulders for dear life while the orgasm crashes through me.

His hands spread across my ass cheeks, and he grabs them, forcing me up and down, harder, faster, until his breath hitches and his dick pulses inside me, the hot lava of his euphoria inside... I ride him, trying to give him the biggest release of his life. *Me.* I want it to be me. *Always me.*

We pant, and I'm still on my knees but let my chest fall to his completely. He holds me with his long arms and big hands, and it's like he can take my entire body between just his two arms.

He kisses the top of my head. "You okay?"

"Okay? Is that... like, *fine?*" I ask.

He releases a laugh-like hum.

"Let's just say you were better than you let on on prom night. I thought you said you were shit at sex? I guess you learned a thing or two."

He slides out of me, and I take a place alongside him. His arm still tucked around me pulls me close. "There's nobody else in this conversation anymore. Let's just say me and you are all that ever existed."

"Are you the jealous type?"

"I am when it comes to you."

"Well, that'll work just fine." I kiss his pec. "Because like I said"—I press my lips into his—"it's only ever been you, Ashton."

He stares into my eyes, lazy satisfaction and ecstasy still warm inside them. And then he says words I wrote over and over in my diary as a little girl, right next to heart doodles dedicated to him.

"And it will only ever be you."

Chapter Thirteen

Ashton

Though I never let my mind wander too much to the forbidden thought of being with Jolie Hunter, I still somehow knew that if I ever went there, I'd be done for. Done. And that's exactly what's happened.

Jolie and I spent the hours to come letting ourselves fall asleep only to wake up and grind each other raw all night long. The woman has turned me into some sort of nymphomaniac.

But at eight in the morning, reality sets in. She needs to

get to work at Moon Ridge, the very place I didn't leave my car last night, and questions will be asked.

It's the beginning of the beginning.

"I better get up and shower," Joey says.

I laugh lightly. "That's the third time you've said that."

"You're not moving either, Mister." She snuggles into the crook of my arm more deeply, burrowing like yet again she has no intention of rising. Her voice is muffled, buzzing against my skin. "Guess it's time to face the truth?" She peeks up at me with her emeralds dancing. "What are you going to tell your parents when they ask where you were last night?"

I've been considering that for the last half an hour. Is it better to tell the truth now? Later? Don't Joey and I have the right to figure this out in private? Then again, what's there to figure out? It's not like I have any plans of letting her date anyone else ever again.

"You're spinning." She reads me perfectly. "Just tell me what you're thinking. It hurts less to know than not—"

"It's nothing bad. Not about you at all... I said what I said last night and I mean it."

She tosses me one of her honest smiles. The kind of smile that's so fucking genuine, it makes me want another one.

"I told you—you're mine now."

Her body relaxes, and I love seeing her that way. Comfortable. With her guard down... that's how I want her to feel every day but I'm not so sure I can promise that. And that's what's gnawing at me right now.

I caress her arm. "I just wonder if you and I deserve some time to enjoy this before the dramatics start."

"You mean Logan?"

"Mmm," I respond, even though he wasn't the person to

come to mind. Nor the next ones I mention. "Our parents, too. It's just—"

"Small-town meddling." She knows there are rarely only two people in any small-town relationship. Especially with families like ours.

"Mmm. And the press. I don't want you getting caught up in any stories. It's not fair to you. There's a lot on my mind. Hard to even articulate it all."

"As usual, I didn't think much about it." She wraps her arm around my chest and hugs me tight. Her words are sincere as always. "As long as I get you in the end, I don't care."

Goddamn, that's what I've always adored about my girl. She's so wholehearted. Always diving into life headfirst, Jolie is tough. And she isn't naive... but she doesn't know Chloe. Dread pools in my stomach at my ex hearing about this too soon, when there are still stories out there about my supposed cheating. How will a new relationship with an old friend so soon after the official story of our divorce breaking hit her? She'll be humiliated by the new narrative rather than concentrating on the truth.

Image is everything to her.

But I told Jolie not to bring up our past so I sure as hell won't. Maybe that was dumb of me. Avoidance. Maybe it's unhealthy, but thinking about Eric really has me losing my shit; my blood boils immediately upon mention. And Chloe is a drama Jolie doesn't deserve.

"We don't have to tell Logan right away. He'll be, I don't know, at minimum a sourpuss. I've *never* been with another man before," she says, playing into our charade of no other. "I was a total virgin when we got together last night, but Logan knows what jerks men can be. And he's very protective. All my brothers are."

Logan is the most emotional one, too. Colt is level-headed and has always liked me. Dash would probably give me a chance but watch me like a hawk for one slip up. Logan? He's the kind of guy who could fly off the handle. And I present two reasons for him to do it. One, I'm about to lie to him as he can't know that Jolie and I are together just yet. Two, well... two is bigger than one.

I shake my head because first, I need to explain things to my parents. "I'll tell Ron and Monica I went to see some places in Santa Fe and got a hotel to see more today."

"Will they believe that?"

"Yeah."

She pushes herself up, and the detachment makes my body ache. It's cold without her on me.

"I better wash your smell off me then."

I tug her back into me, and she didn't expect it so she flops on my chest.

"Do you have a lunch break today?" I ask.

"Yeah, but I might be busy," she teases.

"You'll definitely be busy. Can you meet me in the empty hay barn at noon?" I kiss her shoulder.

"My God. You made me wait for twenty years but now you can't wait thirty minutes?" She rolls her eyes dramatically but with a wide smile. "Okay. I'll be there." She boops my nose. "And I'll wear my crotchless panties."

Oh, this just got interesting. "You have crotchless panties?"

"No... you're going to buy me some at that adult toy store on your way back from Santa Fe."

I text my dad to say sorry I forgot to mention my trip, it was last minute, yada, yada, and he texts back with a no-fuss message like usual: *You're a grown man.*

A few minutes after that I get the usual one from my mom: *You're not moving to Santa Fe.*

Either way, when I get back to the ranch at quarter to twelve with a pair of crotchless panties stuffed in my pocket, I pass both my parents in the kitchen preparing lunch, and neither seem fazed by me not being here last night.

My dad glances up from a pan where he's making two grilled cheese sandwiches. "Ah... you want one, son?"

"Nah. I grabbed a burrito on my drive back."

"Any good property?" he asks.

My mom stares at me intently. She scans me from head to toe, inspecting me. Is she suspicious? *She's always suspicious.*

"No. It just confirmed that I really do want to settle in the Canyon. But it's not easy to find places here. Not much comes up, and people hold on to property like the gates of Heaven are on their land."

My dad chuckles.

Mom says. "Why don't you talk to Colton?"

"Colton Hunter?"

"Yeah. He knows everybody's business and charms the panties off a nun." She corrects herself. "But not any more, of course, because he has Sam."

"Sure. I can ask."

Dad plates up the sandwiches and puts one in front of my mom. "Maybe one of you boys wants to take over Moon Ridge?"

Shit. I have a date with Jolie in fifteen minutes, and my dad starts talking about succession planning?

It's rude, I know, but I cut him off. "I'm not in a big rush. Apart from getting to PT."

"You have PT today again?" Mom asks.

"Every day. Not that I need it. I'm feeling perfectly fine now but, you know, I want to get cleared."

Mom bites into her sandwich, but her eyes are firmly fixed on me. "See you later."

I rush out of the house, as best I can with my ankle still a little sore, but already feeling better which makes me realize, this time with Joey is more precious than I think. For the past twenty-four hours, I've been pretending I don't have a job and that I don't have to get back on the road soon with the Scorpions.

Arriving at the hay barn, I slip inside and wonder if she's already here. The barn is empty apart from the haunted house stuff that's still set up from a few weeks back. I wander past a tractor where I remember being hidden and Jolie inching by me in the dark. I loved her perfume. Her wild energy grabbed me by the lapels right through the darkness. And I wanted to touch her but didn't. I could have fucked her a thousand more times by now if I had.

"Pup?" Her voice calls to me from within the barn bathroom. "Is that you?"

"Yeah..."

"It's kind of cold with my ass out. Did you bring my present?"

I rub my eye sockets. This woman never ceases to make me smile. I bought them, but in the back of my mind, on my way over to the barn, thought maybe she wasn't serious. I reach into my pocket and feel the small, delicate lace. "I'm not sure what I brought will warm you up."

"As long as it warms you up, that's what matters." She sticks her arm out of the bathroom.

I hand her the panties.

She closes the door. "Ooooh. Cute. I'm glad you didn't get red ones. Red isn't my color."

"Joey, your pussy and ass would look good in anything. Now get out here as fast as you can before I lose my shit." My dick is already thick just thinking about her sliding those little panties over herself.

She saunters out wearing a long cardigan that goes down to her knees with nothing underneath but the panties. "Is this an outfit or what?"

I grab her. "Come here. You're like some sort of Swedish model ready to skinny-dip."

"A Swedish model? I'll take that. I just didn't think goosebumps were sexy so I brought my cardi..."

I slip my hands into her draping sweater. "Everything looks good on you... Damn, girl, I feel like I've been away from you for a century." I lower my lips to hers. They're cold. She's been out here waiting for me. *For me.*

I scoop Jolie into me and stumble backward to prop myself up on a ride-on lawnmower and take the weight off my ankle. She kisses me furiously, matching my need. Now that I've tasted Jolie, I don't know how I ever resisted her in the first place. Our tongues intertwine, and slowly her lips warm up. I open my jacket so she can cuddle into the heat of my chest.

We devour each other in the cold autumn air, gentle light making its way through cracks in the doorjambs and moss-covered roof windows. The cavernous space could only be romantic to two lust-filled country kids. It's so me. It's so *us.*

We kiss, and I knead her full breasts into my palms and

nibble her neck until we're both flush with lust and wanting. All I can think about is those panties and sinking my dick through those slits of lace...

She eases back from our embrace. Her chin is pink from my stubble. She dots tiny, feverish kisses on my lips in between her every word.

"Are you going to try out these panties or what? I only get an hour break."

"You look so fucking sexy in these." I snap the side elastic. "I'm only going to need two seconds inside."

She hitches her leg around my waist and nestles into me. "Just fuck me, Ashton. We can take them for another spin later. I need your dick inside me."

Her words make me an animal.

I bite her neck, and she sucks her teeth.

"Mmm..."

I unbuckle my belt and manage to play with her nipple, gnaw her milky neck and get my dick out from my pants at the same time. Her hand falls down to find my cock, and her palm is cool stroking up and down my shaft.

Tracing her earlobe with the tip of my nose, I growl in her ear. "I'm not fucking your hand, Joey. Spread those long legs nice and wide for me."

We flip positions, and she tosses the cardigan over her shoulders, baring them, her breasts, her soft womanly stomach, and... the white thong I'm about to get very, very dirty. I slide a condom from my back pocket, and with a saucy shimmer in her eye, she snatches it from my fingers.

She tears it with her teeth and takes possession of me with her gaze. I love how wild and unhinged and absolutely beautiful this earthy goddess is. She's as natural as the goddamn wind and can kill you just the same. She drops the wrapper to the floor and rolls the condom over my shaft then lifts one leg and props it on the hood of the mower. The gesture opens her pussy lips ever so slightly, and the lace falls open not at all wide enough for my dick, but it's a welcome sight.

When I slip my shaft through the pretty lingerie, I'm not as careful as I should be, and Joey grabs at the steering wheel of the mower to brace herself.

"Fuck..."

"Do you know how hard it's going to be to take it slow with you looking like this?" It's taking all my restraint to not totally rail her right now. I've never had anyone dress up for me, be this playful, this... *joyous* about sex.

She pinches her nipple and bites her lip like a sex kitten purring her plea. "I want it hard. I can take it."

Her eagerness does nothing to hold me back. "Such a naughty little thing." My lips follow the curve of her neck, peppering kisses as a way to distract myself from her tight walls, squeezing my dick but the scent of her only makes me unhinged. I bite her shoulder. She gasps and it's a sound I'd love to hear again and again.

I thrust in and out, each time needing to restrain myself but finding it almost impossible. My muscles are taut holding her up, tensing my abs to not blow inside her this instant. Her pussy is so tight, wet, and my dick is glazed with her arousal. I sink in deeply, dragging in and out as slowly as I can. But every time I drive into her, her breasts bounce and dance for me, just another temptation to release, so I still them by sucking her nipple into my mouth.

"Mmm," she mewls. She positions herself so I don't have to hold her steady and puts her foot up on the machine, her legs wide. She drops her fingers to spread the fabric wider, giving me a glimpse of her clit before she fingers her nub. "You like what you see, Pup?"

"No better view than your pussy, Joey..." I pinch her nipple and the sight of her pleasing herself has my mouth watering.

"I'm so damn close," she's breathless. "If you don't fuck me hard, I'm going to have to finish myself off."

"So greedy," I growl and sink back inside, filling her to the hilt, and this time, hold nothing back, just like she asked. I keep myself steady as I can at first, but she's like a vise, every ripple of her insides makes me ready to explode. Seeing her like this, my cowgirl sprawled out for me, pleasuring herself while I ride her pussy through dirty little panties... She's a dream I never dared to have. And she's mine.

Mine.

She bites her bottom lip, and her brows furrow. I know she's close.

"Come with me, Pup." Her head falls back, and her pussy ripples around me.

Her release pulses around my shaft, and I fall apart.

My dick surges and spills the most powerful fucking orgasm since the last one I had with this siren. Every new time with her is more perfect than before. I drive into her, nearly losing control of my legs. They're weak, fucking fuzzy, my vision goes blurry, and I come so damn hard I almost lose myself to the other side.

But just when I think I'll crumble into oblivion, my woman takes my mouth with hers. And when we kiss, her lips still slightly cool from an entire morning in the November mountain air, I thank the Lord this is actually real. That after all these years, I'm here, back in my hometown, with the most genuine woman in the world. It's moments like these I believe I'm not such a bad guy after all because karma is on my side.

I help Joey back on her feet which must be absolutely frozen on the cold, concrete barn floor. "You didn't have to do all this for me."

"For you? Boy, I'll be fulfilling my crazy fantasies for years to come. This one wasn't yours." She heads toward the bathroom but tosses me a sassy smirk over her shoulder. "It was mine."

When she's dressed again, I insist I get her something to eat because even though my mom would have given Joey a schedule, she isn't keeping tabs on her. My cowgirl surely has an appetite now, and I can't stand the thought of her working the rest of the day without food in her belly.

I drive her over to CCs. The rest of the Canyon—as far as Jolie and I are concerned—will see our lunch as a meet-up not a date. Because we're friends, right?

All the way over, I think again about how she's here on my ranch. About her job. About how even though we disappear into perfection when we're together, our imperfect lives are always there waiting for us when we open our eyes.

And I want to fix that for her.

At the counter, I order her a tuna melt without even asking, recalling it as her favorite. When I glance back at her to confirm, her wide approving smile is everything. It's what she always had when we were younger. Unless there's tomato soup. I love the predictability. The stability... home.

We sit and eat, and I have to admit, I'm famished, since I never actually went to Santa Fe and I could have gone for that imaginary burrito. CCs is comfort food for us both. Or I hope it is because I'm about to dive into some uncomfortable conversation. I want to get to the bottom of what's eating Jolie up and why she's at Moon Ridge.

I take a drink. "As much as I'm sure my mom loves

having you around, and I'd love to have you at Moon Ridge anytime I come home, I'm still curious..."

Her gaze is fixed on the ceiling. I know she doesn't want to talk, but she has to.

"... maybe you need to talk about things, Joey?"

She sips through her straw and keeps it in her mouth, mumbling. "Maybe."

"You know you can talk to me. No judgment."

"I know." She lowers her eyes, and immediately her aura shrinks.

Jolie has always radiated, and every time I bring this up, it's like watching a sunset fade into black.

How could I have let myself lose touch with her all these years? I could have been supporting her all this time instead of having to face the now-hollow expression in her eyes while she considers telling me what's going on.

"Tell me why being a vet is just fine. And why are you really working at Moon Ridge?"

"Geez. Going for the jugular. Where's the segue, Dane?" She sits back and crosses her arms.

"A Mento for your thoughts? I'd buy the whole damn company to know what's up with you."

Somehow, my comment makes her smile, but it quickly flattens when she decides to open up. "I thought it was the euthanasia. That's what I thought it was mainly, but these past few days, I realize it's not even that so much. It's not like I put healthy animals to sleep. It's the up-and-down constant rollercoaster of fake or real emotion... I don't know which way is up anymore. One minute I'm happy for a birth, the next I'm giving someone a sympathy hug. It's fucked. And I might be able to manage the emotions if I had a minute to myself, but it's like I'm on call twenty-four seven."

In all my years and all the people I've met through teams and otherwise, I've never come across someone as sincere and direct as Jolie Hunter. She was born without a filter, and even though her candid nature could land her in the doghouse sometimes, it is what I love most about her. There's something wonderful about being with a person who wouldn't—hell, couldn't—lie to you.

"I can see how that would be especially hard for you. For an authentic person like you..." I take off my cap and scratch my head. "It would be hard for anyone... but especially you."

She reaches out to touch my hand. "Thank yo—" She rips her hand away and glances around to see if anyone has seen her do it. "Thank you. Colt said he'd support me no matter what, but I don't think he gets it. He's able to do what has to be done in any situation. He has morals and everything but he can change his colors and still feel like the mere fact of being a chameleon means he's grounded. Me? I'm just... me. I'm not good at being composed; it actually takes a lot out of me. But he was right about one thing. I'm so glad I don't have to deal with small animals very often. Thank God Colt put me off opening an actual practice here. Guess he read me pretty well in the end."

"You can handle anything—"

"No I can't." She dips her straw up and down, staring at it like she wants to dive into the pint glass of Coke. "I'm not classy and professional like Colt is."

Putting herself down is not an option in front of me. "I've always admired how frank you are. I think it's a superpower. You take it for granted how easy it is to be honest. Just like Colt thinks his strengths are normal, but they're not. Maybe you should lean into it instead of shying away."

"Unfortunately, having a mask on is just part of the

profession, Ashton. Hockey players wouldn't understand. You get to fly off the handle and express yourselves however you damn well want. You have no idea how many clients I've wanted to slug and couldn't. The people are the real assholes most of the time."

"Trust me, I can't do whatever the hell I want all the time." I smile, hoping it infuses her with more positive energy. "But it does feel good when I get to let off steam. Not gonna lie. But let me ask you a question. Do you really not want to be a vet anymore? Like, is that what your heart is saying?"

"Well"—she swirls her straw in her drink—"no. It hurts to put animals down, but more often than not, it's merciful and at the end of a full, long life. And even though I'm not Dr Doolittle like Dash, I do think I have a gift for hearing creatures out. You know?"

"Then..." I hope what I say next doesn't sound flippant. "Be yourself and see what happens."

She stops stirring her drink. Her paper straw has practically disintegrated, her nerves have kicked in as we speak. But she's thinking hard, she runs through scenarios behind her jade eyes, considering what I said. And that's the other thing about Joey I adore. Though anyone who didn't know her might not think so, she's not stubborn. She takes what you have to say on board.

It's refreshing. Especially when in hockey, every player I know thinks they're never in the wrong, and my years in Los Angeles, hell, that place was full of pretentious mother-fuckers.

People don't value humility anymore, though it's the one quality my dad told me and my brother to never forget. *Stay humble. It's grounding.* I can't give her a silver bullet but two people asking questions instead of giving answers is as honest as it gets. I hope it eases her anxiety.

"Do you think that would actually work? Isn't it my job to shore up the client? To take the emotional load?"

"No. That's definitely not your job. Sure having a good bedside manner is something anybody in the medical profession should work on but maybe it's time people stop expecting vets to be therapists. You could start a whole movement of redefining the job."

"I can already see the shitty reviews popping up on Facebook."

"So the fuck what? Counter it with a blog. You have a voice, too. And at this point, you have nothing to lose and everything to gain. And if it doesn't work out, there's always a job at Moon Ridge."

"Yeah, it pays like shit, though."

I laugh. "What do you need the money for?"

"I want to go on safari."

Her answer surprises me. "Safari? What, like in Africa?"

"Yeah. But. I've been saving up, but the place I want to go is mega expensive, and Ted has been a bit of a money suck. He's getting older and needs medication and organic hay that cost a fortune."

Her horse, Ted, has always been a money suck. All horses are, but especially when you pamper them the way Jolie does. But as an animal person myself, I get it. They always come first. Before new clothes. Before new cars. And before trips to Africa.

"Well, if you end up not making the vet thing work, I'll talk to Monica about a raise. She holds the purse strings."

"Gee, thanks. Might get fifty cents an hour more." She takes the last bite of her sandwich and talks to me from behind her hand. "Honestly, though, I'm just so grateful I don't have debt. I focus on that all the time. I am lucky so I don't want to come across as a whiner. Just... figuring things out."

"You don't whine. I know that about you."

"Well..."

She stares at her plate, and something pangs inside me, and I just know. I know someone made her think her feelings weren't valid.

"You don't have to justify yourself to me, Joey. Or anybody for that matter. If anyone ever told you otherwise..." I grit my teeth.

I'm guessing I'll meet this person on the ice.

She leans down and reaches under the table to rub my leg. "You always know how to make me feel better. That's why I L you."

Her private but public declaration fills my chest like a sunrise. My cowgirl and I are a new chapter of the best story of my life.

"I'll always take care of you." I put my hand under the table, envelop hers, and squeeze it. "Because I L you, too."

Chapter Fourteen

Jolie

ASHTON SPENT the rest of the afternoon in the yard with me. It was luxurious. With hardly a soul around, we could kiss when we wanted to, feel each other up, laugh and touch as much as we goddamn wanted. I understand why Ashton wants to keep the gossip at bay for a while longer, but I also cannot wait to come out of the shadows. And for everyone to know he's mine.

I glance over at my long, gorgeous man sitting at a picnic table outside one of the outbuildings where I'm sweeping up. I told him to sit. I know he said he's feeling better, but he has another checkup tomorrow, and as much as I want to have him here forever, he has a job to do. He needs to heal and get back on the ice. In fact, Logan has told me Ashton wants to retire soon. He deserves to go out with a bang not a life-changing injury because I want him to fuck me standing up again.

I sweep mindlessly because I can't take my eyes off him. He's scrolling on his phone with his backward baseball cap and gorgeous cheekbones and jawline. Even his nose is cute. But Eric was a handsome guy, too, and never made me obsess the way I always have over Ashton. I can't even get on with my work. I keep having to pause to make sure he's still there, to make sure this isn't all just some super-long, lucid dream.

I try to get back to my work, and while I stare at a pile of hay dust and leaves, our conversation from CCs plays on my mind. Ashton has always known how to make me feel better. Stronger. Happier to be, well, me.

When I told Eric about my feelings a couple of times after becoming a vet, he thought I was being dramatic. He said I made my bed and I needed to lie in it and I needed to check my privilege. I was a doctor coming out of school with no debt, thanks to my family's position. And he'd tell me I already knew what the job entailed so why complain about it now.

As a woman growing up with a lot of men in my life, I knew they weren't always the most sympathetic. But Eric was downright cruel sometimes. And now, talking to Ashton, I can't believe I wasted so many years not seeing how Eric pushing me down was also him keeping me right where he wanted me. Under his skate. Ready to pick up whenever he wanted. I told myself he wasn't important to me and he was as throwaway in my life as I was in his. I never loved him. But allowing him in my life was more damaging than I realized because it doesn't matter if you're made of steel. When someone shoots at you, if it doesn't leave a hole, it still leaves a dent. I let his words wear me down into silence.

And it's so clear, now that I have Ashton who won't let me hide within myself. Never before and not now. He just has a way of getting me to talk and open up.

I stare at the country hockey boy in his element, hunched over, his thumb flicking upward, and God, I remember how well he flicked me... He senses me staring and glances up from his phone. I snatch his gaze into the palm of my hand and send a smile on the breeze across the yard. The corner of his mouth lifts, and our eyes lock long enough for me to want to run across the pavement and jump onto his lap.

"There you are!"

A woman's voice startles me. Startles us. Ashton quickly lowers his eyes to his phone again.

There, coming into the space, are our mothers.

Monica heads to Ashton's side and puts a hand on his shoulder. "Good to see you're resting. You've been out all day."

I get back to sweeping as if it's the most important task in the world, but I feel her eyes dart to me anyway.

My mom approaches, pulling her coat tighter around her slim middle. "Are you okay?" she asks in that very particular way moms who know you're not quite right, ask.

I know my mom knows everything, even though I haven't told her. Colt would have told everyone in our family. I'm sure my mom is terrified of how fragile I could be. I should talk to her.

I've avoided just about everyone in my family like the

plague since talking to Colt. Logan's been blowing up my phone. Dash has asked me for coffee more than once this year which is a new record for him, since it's me who always dishes out the invites. Colton sent me a few therapy appointments that might "fit my schedule."

They're all worried I'm severely depressed. They know my profession claims lives. I'm lucky. Some of the vets who haven't made it didn't have anyone. I toss Mom a true smile, because since talking to Ashton, I'm feeling optimistic for the first time in years. I don't know if I can just be myself like he says, hell, I probably won't be able to retain clients if I don't keep some filter on, but his validation meant everything. Sometimes, all we need is to be seen for who we are to gather up our weapons and fight another day.

"I'm good." And I mean it. I am good about what she's asking, and if I included finally getting with the man of my dreams in this equation, I'd be a lot better than good. But she's not asking about that, and I can't tell. Not yet.

Mom smiles back, and visible relief washes through her because she knows if I'm not okay, I usually stop talking to everyone altogether. "Yeah? That's... great."

Monica asks, "You two want to come in now? We have the caterer inside and we're picking buffet items for your dad's surprise sixtieth."

Ashton taps his phone and slides it off. "Sure. Man, the party is sneaking up on us."

"Mmm. Not long now. You have a game on Thanksgiving, so we made it the Friday after because your brother might be able to come home, too. You both have it off."

"Might?" Ashton barks. "What the hell would he have going on that's more important than Dad's sixtieth?"

"You know how Fletcher is."

Ashton's younger brother and I went to school together.

"He's just like Logan. How can he make an entrance if it's not a surprise?" I say.

"Exactly," Monica agrees. "You look done here, sweetheart. Want to come in the house for some hors d'oeuvres?"

"You don't have to ask twice." I pop the broom back in the outbuilding. "I'm starving."

Monica says, "You two will be helpful. Joy and I don't exactly agree on spice levels."

My mom shrugs. "What can I say? I like it hot."

Ashton and I stand next to each other on one side of the table. I planned on not standing next to him because if I thought I craved him before, now that I know what he has under those clothes and in that heart of his, all that L for me? I want to touch him, squeeze him, hold him, and talk to him all night long.

Ashton being so tall, he's always had an imposing energy, but now, he's a wall of red-hot desire next to me, and it's pretty damn hard to focus on the food.

Monica coughs into her hand. "What the hell, Hux," she says to the caterer, who is also head chef at our family's ranch hotel. "You said these were mild satay skewers. How much chili is in these? I think I'd rather poke my eye out with the bamboo stick." She coughs again and tries to wash down the spice with some water.

Hux hides a smirk behind his handsome full lips.

My mom stands close to him and bumps into his side. "I think it's perfect. Mmm..." She glances at Monica. "Trust me, these are a go for anyone who's not a wimp. Hux, what's in this?"

Huxley talks to my mom but passes a plate with a skewer over to me for Ashton and I to share.

"That's cayenne." He glances at Monica. "I swapped out the usual Bird's Eye chili to take down the heat like you requested."

My mom teases her friend. "I thought these weren't as spicy as the ones I had at the hotel. Monica, you need to get out more, woman."

Monica downs the rest of her water. "Beelzebub is what you are, Joy Hunter."

My mom laughs. "You need these on the menu."

I turn my attention to the plate on the table between me and Ashton. When I reach out to pick up the skewer, he does it at the same time, and our fingers collide, both of us accidentally grazing the saucy kebab with our fingers.

"Oh, sorry," I say and put my finger in my mouth to lick it off.

Ashton stares at me, transfixed on my finger and mouth. I take my time sucking off the sauce, because I know what he's thinking when his brown eyes stare at my lips. The sauce is more than gone, but I pretend it isn't just to let him watch me dip my finger in and out a few more times and make him want it as much as I do right now.

Eating makes me horny. Food and sex are the ultimate combination.

But our moms are here, so I quit before either of us becomes too obvious. "Mmm..." I say, edging toward being sensual but not so much I garner a side-eye from the others. "This sauce even tastes good off my finger."

"Ha..." My mom lets out a little laugh and shakes her head as if I've said the darnedest thing.

I pick up the skewer and tip it toward Ashton. "You first?"

His long finger and thumb pull off a nugget of chicken, and I watch him open wide and put the piece in his mouth whole, wishing I was that chicken. God, I want to dive onto his lips, legs wide open and sit on this man's face.

I slide a morsel off the bamboo, and the delectable canapé makes my mouth water more. It has a sweetness with the perfect amount of kick. I stare up at Ashton again whose neck is creeping with red as he chews.

I finish quickly and hide a laugh behind my hand. "You all right, Ash?"

His eyes have begun to water.

He swallows and clears his throat. "Fine. Why?"

Monica rubs her son's arm. "Don't worry, bland palate runs in the family."

"Except Fletcher." I recall an incident years ago. "I saw him once take a dare in middle school to eat a habanero from Victor Mendez without even blinking."

"Yes. Fletch is the exception—" Ash starts coughing.

His mom picks up his water and passes it to him.

"Sorry, Huxley, but I need to veto these. Mr. Dane isn't any better than the pair of us with spice, I'm afraid. And it's his party."

Huxley leans over and feigns a whisper to my mom. "I'll sneak in a couple for you, Joy."

"Make me a special spicy plate, honey."

"You got it." He winks. Then he rubs his hands together. "Last is just the birthday cake. I have chocolate, white and lemon... but I'm guessing this is mostly for show, or if Shay isn't available to make you one?"

"Actually, Hux, sadly for my husband, he's allergic to nuts. And I wouldn't dare ask her to alter the recipe. I'll have her carrot cake there, but we need a second."

Huxley passes over plates, one at a time, each with a

different flavor and fluffy frosting. And it's impossible not to think of it. I wonder what it would be like... to sample wedding cake with Ashton Dane. I think of the thousands of times I wrote Jolie Dane in the margins of my diaries, and my heart glows. I'm a million miles ahead of myself, but I'm not the only one with fairy tale dreams.

"Look at you two." My mom's eyes are all gooey, and her head tilts to the side.

I know exactly what she's thinking, because when it comes to Ashton Dane, I have never evaded the teasing, I just hope she doesn't say it.

She doesn't. "It's so good to have the two of you back here in the Canyon."

Ashton lifts a plate of chocolate cake to offer it to me. "It's good to be back. So good I don't think I could ever leave again."

Monica swipes a tiny bit of frosting off the top of one cake and licks it. "Please don't. Neither of you. I just love having the two of you back in my kitchen again." Her eyes shimmer with something I can't read. "And having you back enjoying the ranch."

Enjoying the ranch? I can't help it. My face flushes immediately dreaming of my baptism on their ride-on lawnmower.

I shove the cake into my mouth quickly. Ashton follows suit, but I don't know about him, I don't even taste it. Could Monica somehow know about the crotchless panties? Both our moms are switched on, and I don't think I've ever pulled a fast one on my own. Monica is an eagle mama just like Joy.

We all finish tasting the cake and decide on chocolate, and by this point, it's seven o'clock. Huxley has made all the notes he needs and clears up his supplies. Ashton and I are stuck. Is he asking the same question I am? How on earth am I going to get from the watchful eye of my mom up the stairs and into Ashton's bedroom?

"Jojo." My mom puts on her coat. "You wouldn't mind dropping me home on the way to yours, would you? Monica brought me here. Seems silly for her to drive me back when you're passing."

"Course." I dart my eyes to Ashton, guessing tonight isn't meant to be. "Good luck with your physical therapist tomorrow. Let me know how it goes?"

"Will do."

His eyes are apologetic, but I have to accept we won't be knocking boots tonight.

I'll have to settle for my fingers because Ashton is up at the crack of dawn for PT in Santa Fe.

When I get home, I shower and tell myself it's a good time to catch up on my book. But I'm less than ten pages deep when my phone beeps.

PUP

YOU KNOW WHAT I'M THINKING ABOUT?

I place my book down on the bed beside me, smiling at my cell.

ME

SPREADING FROSTING ON MY PUSSY
AND LICKING IT OFF?

I moisten my fingers and glide them across my seam but I'm already wet, so I guess my pussy read his text before I did.

PUP

THAT'S BETTER THAN WHAT I WAS
THINKING…

My fingers work more swiftly knowing I pleased him and I wait for another text but my cell rings instead.

"Are you touching yourself?" His deep voice rumbles like low, distant thunder from a storm I wish would come here quick and soak me.

"Yes. Are you?" I rub in rough circles now, knowing he has his cock in his hand makes me hot.

"I'm thick as fuck right now thinking about that frosting spread on you. No way anything could make you taste better than you already do. Dip your fingers inside and have a taste for yourself."

I've never tasted myself before. I do as he says and sink a finger inside me then lift it to my lips. "Mmm. Not bad…" I giggle at myself.

A dark laugh joins me from the other side. "You make me laugh, naughty girl… and that makes me even harder. I wish you could see how swollen my cock is for you right now."

"I love your dick…" My clit is absolutely swollen at the thought of his manly hand wrapped around his enormous cock. I run longer, more even strokes over my nub because I'm already close.

"Everything about you makes me wild, Joey. I want you all the time…" His voice is becoming grainy.

"Mmm…. Me, too…"

"Touch that pussy for me, Joey. Put your fingers inside…"

I dip one inside again, even though he can't see me I want to do as he says.

"Put more in," he commands. "Stretch yourself with your fingers... fuck them in and out and imagine my cock when you do it."

I'm wet as hell, and three fingers glide in easily. I fill myself, imagining it's him even though the girth isn't even close. "I wish it was you. Fuck, I want your dick right now."

"How many fingers do you have inside?" He's more breathless than before.

"Three." I pump them in and out.

"Oh, good girl," he grunts. "My naughty girl."

Hearing his panting ramps me up to the next level, and I have to pull my fingers out to give my clit some relief. "Even over the phone you're the best lay in the world, Pup."

"I'm going to stretch you wide open. I can't wait to sink into your pretty pussy again."

Jesus... my clit is on the verge. "I hope you're close... I'm fucking close and I want you to come with me." I swear I hear slapping noises on the other end. "Did you lube yourself up for me?"

"Just like your creamy, messy pussy..." He moans again. "I'm going to come..."

I close my eyes and play out our porn on the back of my eyelids. His pecs and his flexed biceps glisten with sweat and his giant cock and manly veins pump in and out of me. "Shit," I murmur the word, something between a word and a groan. My release surges through me, a hot, heavy wave. I ride it out as long as I can, whimpering as it comes. "Ashton, I want you inside me..."

"Ahhh... I'm going to fuck you so hard, Joey..."

A sound like him gritting his teeth and biting down a groan sounds in my ear, and we come together hard.

When I open my eyes, I literally see stars.

His moan of satisfaction slows by breath in the way only

he can calm me. "Mmm." I can practically feel his deep voice vibrate my earlobe.

"Mmm," I moan back, because my brain won't form words yet.

"I wish we could sleep together tonight."

"Me, too." My eyelids are heavy.

"Every night." His voice is sleepy.

But my heart awakens at the thought. *Every night.*

I squeeze my eyes shut more tightly as if to capture this feeling of being wanted by him. "Night, Ashton Dane. I L you."

"I L you, too."

Chapter Fifteen

Ashton

My cell beeps, and a smile crawls across my lips, slowly and sensually, just like Jolie has been crawling up and down my body in my dreams.

But when I flip over my phone, I'm awoken straight away from my fantasy because it's not Joey... but her brother.

Fuck. I never texted him back after he asked about Joey or even yesterday. Normally, we text multiple times a day.

PUCK BOY

DUDE, YOU NEVER GOT BACK TO ME. I
HAD AN EXCUSE… TWO EXCUSES,
ACTUALLY, IF YOU MUST KNOW, BUT
WHAT'S YOURS? UNLESS YOU'RE
TELLING ME THAT SOUTH-AFRICAN
EXCHANGE STUDENT CAME BACK TO
SC, I WAS HOPING YOU'D HAVE A
REPORT ON JO. I THOUGHT YOU HAD
DINNER WITH HER?

My eyebrows go tight, me thinking how many times between then and now Joey has been the main course. I sit up and stare at my cell for a minute. What the hell am I going to say? Lie? To my best friend? I just need a little more time. More time. Like more time will solve the real problem… I press my fingers into my eye sockets and wonder how Lo will take this when he finds out.

On the one hand, he knows I'd never do Joey wrong. On the other hand, he's been more protective in the last year than I've ever seen him. And that's saying a lot because he didn't even want her to have a real prom date. He spits venom when it comes to Eric Larose. But Joey is thirty fucking years old now. She's an adult. And she chose me.

Maybe I should just tell him now.

I don't answer for too long, and the next thing I know, my cell is ringing.

"Yo," I answer.

"I got practice in thirty," he says. "Did you get my text?"

"Yeah. Course I did."

"So did you talk to Jo about everything? I'm worried she's not all right. It sucks not to be there and see for myself. What's the verdict?"

"We talked about her job and the struggles with that… She's feeling unsure, but I think talking made her feel better. We'll keep an eye on her; she doesn't want to quit but she knows we all have her back if she needs to."

"Do you think she's depressed?"

If she is, I don't see that side of her very often.

My answer is diplomatic. "You should still reach out. The more people who care the better. I think she'll be all right."

He pauses. "So she didn't say anything about Eric? Did you ask?"

"Why would I ask about Eric?" I try to keep the venom off my tongue. I can't sound like I feel. Like I have no fucking interest in ever hearing the guy's name again.

"Man, between me and you—the fuckbag is a manipulative user. I think Jo has been off him completely for a few months before she moved back, but the maggot has a way of wiggling in every once in a while. I was worried maybe she had that going on, too. I fucking hate that guy. He's brought her to tears more than once, and you know Jolie doesn't really cry. That's how bad he is. I've only come across him on the ice a few times, and it took everything not to slam him into the boards... or worse."

I want to ask exactly what he's done but don't. Was it the cheating? Or more? My blood boils, and I'm hot now, so I throw off the covers. "I'll hang with her again tonight and see if he's on the radar."

"You don't have to spend all your downtime with my sister. Just wondered if she mentioned it."

"It's cool. We're catching up on old times."

"Well... you're a good brother."

Brother. I don't know if he means I'm his brother or hers. Guilt tangles my intestines. "I have PT in an hour so I'm going to get going. I think I'll be cleared early."

"That's a relief. Last two away games we just squeezed

by. We've got that winning streak so far, but I think we need some more muscle to keep it."

I circle my ankle; it's feeling perfectly fine. "Well, especially since we have the weekend off, I'm sure I'll be back next week. Are you coming home this weekend or are you off galivanting?"

"I have an appearance in Vegas opening a new club."

Logan is a high-profile hockey player who often dates—if you could call it that—actresses and models. The pair of us were two of the most photographed athletes at one point when he actually managed a two-month monogamous stint with one of Chloe's A-list friends. Now, Logan has become a celebrity in his own right, endorsing sneakers, soda, and his agent is in the middle of a deal with a fragrance house now. That guy has only gotten better-looking with age. He's the Canyon's own David Beckham.

I remember Chloe being pissed at me for turning down a lot of those offers. After winning the Hart trophy my third year, I had endorsement deals, too, but I hated it. I play hockey because I love hockey. And without hockey, I'm just a country boy who likes the simple things in life and is always eager for time with the horses. Giving them up to go pro was a devil's dilemma for sure. Any way I slice it, I don't want to be a supermodel and I definitely don't want to see my mug plastered on a billboard. How I didn't think about the invasion of privacy when I plunged headfirst into a relationship with a media-hungry person like Chloe is beyond me.

We all make mistakes.

And I hope Logan isn't about to make one soon. "So you're in Vegas... not drinking? That's impressive. And I'm sure Coach will believe that." Sarcasm dominates my words.

"It's work. I'm under contract. I have to be there, so he'll have no choice but to deal with it."

"You only do those stupid appearances to pay for what you spend there. It's breakeven."

He puts on an accent. I think he intends to sound British. "Aren't I clever?"

"Yeah. Spending everything you earn doesn't sound stupid at all." I snort. "Well, I guess I'll see you next week then."

"All right. Don't get fat. I know your mom's a feeder."

I end the call and think about how this time next week I'll be back to practices and commuting to and from Santa Fe and not seeing my Joey in her tight, dusty jeans. Better make the most of it.

I got the all clear with the PT, a week earlier than Coach expected, and when I get off the call with him, the countdown begins. I only have about five more days with Jolie before it's going to be tougher to see each other. So since I have the green light to be on ice, that's where I want to be with her.

Thirty minutes outside Starlight Canyon, in the middle of nowhere, is the rink where Logan and I first learned to skate. It's an outdoor rink that is wonderfully quiet because it's too far from any major towns to get busy. Nonetheless, I phoned ahead to purchase every ticket for the evening so Joey and I can have a romantic public date in private. By the time of night we arrive, darkness swallows the unlit, deserted, single-track highway until the welcoming orb of floodlights illuminates a dome in the sky above a simple marquee tent, and next to it, the sparkle of the ice rink. It's almost surreal, and to me, it's heaven.

As was my plan, the place is empty apart from a few workers, likely from the next nearest town of Blackhawk. Neither myself nor Joey recognize the teenager checking us in.

Joey's sweet nose is a little pink in the cold November air. "Are you sure you're alright to skate? I don't want to break you."

Feeling confident being outside of the Canyon, I scoop her into my arms. "You've already broken me, baby girl. I'm yours to ride now."

She slaps my chest, clearly loving the wild stallion reference, and pours herself deeper into my chest. Having her here in my arms is the best feeling in the world. I thought I would die of starvation yesterday in my mom's kitchen, not being able to touch her, feel her, and eat her. I didn't give a shit about canapés.

I kiss her often, between my words. "Do you remember coming here when we were younger?" I glance around. "It hasn't changed. Just what I hoped for tonight."

Joey and I walk over to the benches rink side. She shoves her foot into her white hockey skate.

"Are those the same skates Logan got you for graduation?" I ask.

"Yeah." She laces up the other one. "Shamefully, they haven't had much use."

"We need to change that." I put on one of the spare pairs my mom kept all these years because my usual ones are still with the sharpener. I'm fast and adept after years of doing it and manage to stand before she does.

"Holy shit, Ashton. You're a giant with those few extra inches."

"Say that later... I like the sound of it." I bite my lower lip and offer her a hand, hoisting her up to standing.

She is gorgeous in her skates, and her already long legs now stretch for miles. I don't think I could love it more if she was wearing those crotchless panties again. Naked in skates... now that is something we need to try.

I take her hand, and she wobbles along with me. We head to the ice, and I glide out first and offer her my hands. She must have told me a thousand times in the car ride over that she hasn't been skating for a long, long time.

"I got you, Joey. I always have you."

"It's not like I'm afraid of falling or anything. I ride horses, for God's sake, but I can say, the last couple years my ass doesn't take it like it used to."

"I need you to tell me more about that..."

She smiles slyly. "I'm lucky to have a man as dirty as I am." She holds my hand firmly and steps out with me.

I skate backward for a while and hold her hands as she gets the hang of it again. "It'll come back fast. You skated loads when we were younger."

She stares at the ice like it might jump up and bite her. "Do you call that skating? Most of the time I just had to make it out to the net and stand there getting pummeled. I didn't skate much."

"You were damn brave to do that with us."

"Yes, I fucking was. Especially once you both were over six feet and eating two steaks a day for dinner. And I was just a weed back then."

She was. But still the prettiest girl I've ever seen. "Your skates are too straight. Try to angle them. Push and glide."

She laughs. "Every goddamn thing you say right now sounds dirty..."

We're near the edge, and I slam my back into it, pulling

her hands so she falls into me and I catch her. I hold her tightly into me, my dick immediately thick with her flush against me.

"If you keep saying naughty things, I'm going to throw you down and melt this ice with your bare ass."

I take her mouth in mine, snake my tongue into the warm space between her lips, and swallow her laughter because I want so badly to take it on the road with me.

"You're the one with the innuendo, Pup." She skates backward, not without effort and a wobble, but there's that sassy glint in her eye she always had when she had something to prove. "Waiting makes the heart grow fonder." She turns forward but tosses me a glance over her shoulder. "Trust me. I would know."

I skate over to her, and she's doing just fine, but I still keep my hand over her back just in case. Jolie has always been athletic, but her technique needs some work, and I'm glad for it because teaching people things is something I love.

"Do you remember how to stop?"

"I used to just throw myself into the side of the rink."

"You never learned?"

"No. Where would I have learned? I only skated with you two, and we just talked about what that was like for me."

I can't believe I think of him at a time like this. But the fact that my next game happens to be against Larose's team has her ex on my mind more than I'd like. I don't want to think about it but I can't help but wonder how she was on and off with a pro-hockey player for the better part of her twenties and he never took her skating. It was the classic first date for a lot of us. Get to show off some skills, have a reason to touch the woman...

"What are you thinking about?" she asks. "You have that grimace of yours going on."

I nearly keep it to myself. After all, I was the one who said we shouldn't talk about our exes. But it's not realistic to think we can grow close without getting to know it all, so I'll have to grow up and get over that at some point. If we want to be close, she needs to be open with me. I need to get a strong, steel leash for my jealousy.

"What is it?" she repeats.

"I just find it weird that Eric didn't take you skating enough to get good. That's all."

"Did you take Chloe skating?" She asks the question quickly as if trying to get it out before she stops herself.

I consider not responding. I don't want to talk about Chloe, even though I know we have to. Maybe her segue is gracious. "Yes, I took her skating. Three times. Until she didn't want to go anymore."

"Three times? That's not much; you were married a long time."

"She didn't like it."

A scoff leaves her cherry lips. "Red flag."

"Yes, it was. But we're not talking about Chloe." I try again. "Did Eric not take you skating?"

"He only took me twice—very early in our relationship."

"That's not much either."

She shrugs. "I would have gone more. I'm a novice but I like it. It always made me think of good times..."

I love working our way around the ice, floating effortlessly, the sparkle of eternal winter all around us. I should leave it and lean into the romance. But... I can't help the jealous need inside to know everything, and to rectify it. I don't want to hear about her asshole ex and at the same time

I do. That's the irony of being a protective man. I usher her over to the edge again, this time, cornering her to the side. I cage her in with two arms and press my hips into her to hold her up with them when she slips.

"Ooh. Nice move, *Great* Dane," she teases.

I ask more forcefully than I mean to, but my words come out as a combination of jealousy and sensing something was wrong. "Why did Eric only take you twice?"

She gyrates her hips, as if she can dance out of this. "I like this..."

"You can't get out of the question like that, Joey."

She smirks. "The second time we went, I told him about how I used to play with you and Logan when we were younger..." She sighs, and her eyes lower. "He would do that. If he felt jealous or thought I got pleasure out of something, he'd take it away somehow. So after he knew I loved skating with you, he took it away as a means of control, I suppose." She gazes at me again. "He was jealous of you for sure, and he probably assumed skating only made me think of you." She quirks an eyebrow. "Even though it was a dick move, he was right. I've always talked about you with love."

I think about how Chloe would respond when I spoke about Jolie. It wasn't as extreme but similar. "I've always talked about you with love, too, Joey." I lower my lips to hers and whisper a frosty puff of adoration across her mouth. "Because I love you."

All bravado drains from her features and nothing is left but the beautiful, honest goddess I know her to be.

"You do?" She says, quietly.

"I love you." I press my forehead to hers. "I always have."

"But now you love me as more than a friend, right?"

The corner of her mouth dances with delight though she doesn't let herself smile.

I bear down weight onto her frame, still stabilizing us both with my arms against the sides. "I love you as my friend. As my lover... I love you as everything. And I shouldn't have said we can't talk about our exes. I want you to be able to talk about anything with me. But it is hard to hear about other men."

"There was only one. It was enough for me to know none of them would ever compare to you."

My heart thumps against my ribcage. But if she knew that... "Why did you stay with him for so long? And take him back when he wasn't good to you? It doesn't line up with the woman I know. If anyone can tell a guy to fuck off, it's you."

She laughs lightly. "Yeah, well, Eric had a way of... it's hard to explain." Shame chokes her up, and she drops her gaze to the ice again.

I tilt up her chin. "Hey. You can talk to me."

"This one is hard to admit. It's... it still hurts. His words still make me wonder... I still ask myself if he's right..."

"Tell me." The haunted look in her eye is back, and I need to exorcize this demon Eric put inside her. It doesn't belong there.

"When Eric did his childish man-boy stuff, I saw it for what it was. Like he doesn't want to skate anymore with me because he's jealous? Whatever. I just didn't really give a shit. I wasn't that invested in him anyway. But I think he might have felt that energy from me, and when I stopped caring so much, his methods of controlling the situation got... meaner. And sometimes, he said things that I actually wondered if they were true and maybe they weren't mean at all."

She reflects, her eyebrows furrowing with her remembering conversations I wish I could erase from her memory because they clearly still hurt her.

"Like what? What kinds of things would he say?"

"I don't want to go there. We're having fun."

I grab her hand and circle the delicate bone of her wrist. "And it's even more fun to connect with someone."

She reaches her thumb onto my wrist and strokes me back. Her gaze is low. "He told me I was hard to love."

Her special spark falls down and out of her, extinguishing on the ice below. Her ember may have gone out, but mine has only just now burst into flames. How *dare* he talk to her like that?

"That's not an easy thing to hear," she says, "especially when he seemed to have valid points."

I want to cut her off and say how wrong he was. But I let her talk, even though I'm now raging. Right now, this isn't about him. It's about Jolie getting a chance to get it off her chest and have a moment to process her feelings with someone who makes her feel safe and valid. It's not about showing him how much I disagree.

Later.

Next week.

On the ice... that's when I'll make this about him.

I tuck hair behind her ear, and it brings me back to the one who's important. Her. My Joey.

"He used to say I would just blurt things out with no consideration for people's feelings. That it takes a strong person to love someone so insensitive and tactless."

How dare he make my favorite part about this beautiful human a blemish? I swallow down my need to rage. My feelings don't matter right now. And she's talking... and I get the sense she needs it.

"And he's kind of right. So because he was right about me being tactless, it begged to reason that he might be right about me being... hard to love."

I take her head against my chest. She can probably hear my heartbeat right through my jacket. It's pounding so hard. "You are not hard to love." I ease her back and gaze into her eyes. "Your unbridled honesty is my favorite thing about you. It takes a strong man to be with a strong woman, and he clearly isn't that."

She offers a crooked smile, but his words so obviously cling to her memory.

"Joey, you can say anything you want around me and I'll love it. I'll never shame you for the things you feel, think, or want. Your honesty is everything to me, and I'll take it as it comes." I cock a smile. "Diplomatic or not. I don't care. Truth is intimacy. I've never had that with anyone and I know I'll always have it with you because it's woven through the very fabric that is you. And that? That's the easiest thing in the world to love."

Her eyes glass over, and her nose goes red.

I kiss it. "You're mine now. And you'll never deal with that prick, Eric Larose, again, because I'll do it for you."

She laughs.

But I don't.

Her gaze steadies, and her words are like a warning to a child. "Ashton... you play the Huskies next, don't you?"

I don't need to say a word.

She knows.

"You can't..."

"I can, Joey. And I will."

Chapter Sixteen

Jolie

I HAVE NEVER FELT LIGHTER than I have since Ashton and I have been together. Even in the middle of big problems and small ones—I still haven't gone back to work, and there's still telling Logan—I'm breathing more deeply than ever.

The epiphany hits me. Being in love isn't taking your breath away. Being in love is breathing more deeply, filling your lungs with so much life it feels like it will go on forever. Ashton makes me feel invincible. It's as if no matter what happens, I can handle it. So when he goes back to Santa Fe to resume practice on Monday, and stays the night because he has physical therapy after, I decide to take my issues public. Well, Hunter-style public, and I invite everyone but Logan—who's staying in the city with Ashton—over to my place to clear the air.

Bird's Eye is a proper family home that my dad built with the intention of putting a roof over his four children in mind. I live here alone now, and even though I don't exactly mind being alone, it's not my preference. I want a house bursting at the seams with Hunters. They pour in on time, with Dash the last to arrive, very disheveled, I might add. All I can think is he must be nailing Molly. I have a gut feeling we'll all find out about it soon, and if he is, he'd better not fuck it up.

Sam, Colt, Eve, my mom, and Dash are all reading my napkins to each other at the dining room table. The napkins have Christmas jokes on them, and I figured if for some reason I seized up tonight, they'd be good icebreakers. I don't usually struggle to talk, I just find it hard to do it coherently. Especially when I'm emotional. But as I take my quiche out of the oven, I don't feel in the least bit worried about it all coming out right. Ashton builds me up. His support is like the best foundation. And talking to him helps me process and have clarity I just don't find on my own.

Everyone needs an Ashton.

I walk toward the dining table, and for some reason, being here now, thinking about Ashton and how he fits within all of this... My heart swells with gratitude for his support. As with these people sitting around my table, I can be my true self with him. His favorite thing about me is the one thing another man hated. He encourages me to find my authentic place within my profession, or not, and that either outcome is okay and I'll still find happiness in this world.

I've never felt more validated and seen than when I'm basking in his melted-chocolate gaze.

I place the quiche down on a trivet in front of one of the empty chairs at the ten-person table, and it's the first time in a while I think about how my dad should be in one of these. I miss him but don't think about it every day. But with all that's been happening, returning to Starlight Canyon, finally getting with my forever crush, life seems to be coming full circle, and the only thing missing is Dad.

He used to say that families were branches growing on a tree all in different directions but that share the same roots. Dad would have loved me and Ashton together. Suddenly, I'm overwhelmed thinking about it—how lucky it is I'm ending up with a man who knew my father. It's the best I could ever do.

"Honey, are you okay?" My mom stares at me, a deep line of concern between her eyebrows.

I shake my head before my eyes grow glassy with sentimental thoughts. "I'm great, actually."

"Yeah?" she asks again.

This time, Colt glances at me, examining my face, deciphering it like it's code.

Sam finishes laughing at the joke Eve just read to her and gives me a sideways glance, too. Dash has his hands folded in front of him on the table, staring at me like he lost his eyelids. Everyone knows there's some kind of announcement about to happen. It's not like we don't get together for dinners and drinks. We do it a lot. But not usually on a Monday.

I cut into the quiche and admire how well I did getting a nice brown top. "So..." It's better not to make eye contact just yet. "I did bring you all here to have a little talk about me and to put to bed any worries you might have."

"Dad said you have a lot of eggs to get rid of," Eve adds.

I gaze at her and laugh. "Well, that, too. I hope you still like baking because I don't."

She nods. "Can I collect them myself out of the hutch sometimes?"

"Of course. If you come in the morning around nine, they might even be warm still. They're mid-morning layers. Come on Saturday, okay?"

Colt and Sam simultaneously wrap their arms around Eve, one draped across the back of the chair, one over Eve's shoulders. Like King and Queen Hunter, they stare at me, waiting—patiently but somehow not. They're both so damn put together compared to me.

"Well, anyway." I dish a piece of quiche onto a plate. "I know you've all been worried since I've needed a break from the whole vet thing."

"Why did you need a break, Auntie Jojo?" My niece's face is bright with her innocent question.

When I invited Colt and Sam, Colt knew I might want to talk. He offered to ask Eve's friend, Macy, to have her over after school, but I said no. It's important Eve hears these kinds of conversations. She's growing up, and feeling like shit and working through that is part of becoming an adult. And knowing that it's okay to falter is part of life. Everything doesn't have to go perfectly for life to be happy.

I know Eve looks up to me. It's important for her to know I find life tough sometimes, too. I'd rather be human for her than a hero. It's the best thing I have to offer.

Equally, I temper my words knowing a kid is here, and try to explain without upsetting her. "Sometimes, Eve— well, all the time actually—there are parts of jobs that can be hard and stressful. Sometimes the stress can get over- whelming, and we need to take a step back to see what's really important. And it's okay to do that. It's okay to take a quiet moment to yourself, to figure things out. And that's what I needed to do. I needed to think about whether or not I wanted to accept the stressful things about being a vet or not. And I needed a little break to think about it because that stress was really hurting me and almost making me sick."

"You're going to quit being a vet?" She can't help herself. She's disappointed.

To her, just like it was for me at thirteen, being a vet sounded like the coolest thing a girl who loves animals could do. Eve herself has told me lots of times she'd like to be one. And once in a while, I fantasized about how nice it would be to have a practice here in town where she could come work with me on whatever level she's capable.

That was until I questioned my own ability. But I don't anymore. "I decided I'll still be a vet and I was really lucky your dad helped me take a step back so I had time to think about it."

I glance up at my brother. "Thank you for helping me, Colt."

He simply nods. I plate up more quiche, and my mom passes plates in a circle until everyone has one.

She serves herself some salad I put in a bowl on the table. She's thinking a lot harder than a person needs to to spoon salad. "You worked it all out in just a week? It's okay to take more time if you need it. Monica loves having you around, and there's no hurry."

I reach out and put my hand on hers. "Seriously, Mom. I gotta give it a go now."

Dash hasn't moved a muscle. He stares at me with such concentration, taking in every word I say as if each one has a thousand syllables. He's always been a good listener. And he learns through questions. "What's changed that makes you ready to go back so soon?"

Ashton. Having a rock and someone steady in my corner. But I can't say that, of course. "I have no idea if I'll be able to cope with the pressures but I realize I was trying to do it all alone, be strong, grit my teeth... that's not going to work. I know you're all here to support me whenever I need it, but like most people, I don't like asking..."

Sam nods, knowingly. I know she gets it. She's a tough cookie, too. But she taught me a lot over this time of knowing her; watching her be honest about her struggles has only made her better.

I continue, "So first I hope you don't mind, but once in a while I might need to vent. Maybe even..." I say it dramatically, "...cry from time to time. But mostly I hope it's okay for me to come to all of you for support. The job can be so draining, and I know now I can't shoulder the burden alone."

"A problem shared is a problem halved, right?" Eve says.

It makes my heart smile because I've said that to her so many times but never actually did it much myself.

"And also, I need to draw boundaries. I've read a lot about it online." I dart my eyes to Colt. "Thank you for the links. I did actually read them..."

Colt salutes me.

"And I need to set boundaries and take care of myself more. I'm getting a new cell for personal life and won't tell clients they can call me twenty-four seven when there is a vet on call at the emergency clinic."

Dash adjusts in his chair. "Much as I enjoyed hanging out with you and Romeo, I approve. You wore yourself out and went straight to other appointments. I told you to go home."

"And I should have," I agree. "In part, I think my burnout and inability to deal with compassion fatigue is from overworking and lack of sleep. So I'm also going to try and get better sleep. I just need to take care of myself."

Colt and Sam share a conversation in their connected gaze and I can't quite translate. These two speak to each other without language.

Colton takes a bite of quiche and points to it with his fork. "This is really delicious."

"Yeah. It's the fresh eggs that make the difference," I say, having not had a single bite of my own.

He finishes chewing. "Not that it matters what I think next to what you think, but I believe you were born for this job. But none of us can take care of others if we don't put our own oxygen mask on first. And don't be so afraid to talk to a therapist either."

"I won't."

He points his fork at me. "We all need rebalancing sometimes. I think this family has a lot to offer in terms of support, but there's no shame in seeking help elsewhere either."

"I know. It's just hard for me to admit my weakness. Shit, I would have never made it with three brothers if I didn't get good at that."

Dash mumbles. "It's our job to take care of you."

My mom brightens. "It's our job to look after each other." She sighs. "Thank you for bringing us over and talking to us. I've been scared shitless with you pulling back into yourself. Only person you seem to talk to these days is Ashton."

Dash's eyes flick up. Colt stops chewing for a moment, and one of Sam's eyebrows seems to be having a gossip with the ceiling.

"Anyway." Mom's comment wasn't a segue, so I get back to the topic at hand. "I don't know where the chips will fall but I'll control the things I can right now and get back to work. I'm ready and I want you all to know I'm going to be okay no matter what happens."

My mom nods. "Boundaries are important, Jolie. That will help you in a marriage."

I can't tell, but when she chews her next bite, she might just be smiling.

Sam leans on her elbows. "Teaching can come with some of the same problems. It's one of the reasons I was glad to settle into a much smaller school. Nobody in any profession should be on tap."

Colt clears his throat. "What about"—he clears it again to indicate exactly what he wants to say without saying the word euthanasia while his daughter is next to him—"what about the other thing we talked about? The ups and downs? The roller coaster?"

"I'm a ranch girl. I've seen it. I don't like it. None of us do. But I've had time to think now and I hope setting boundaries will go a long way to making this better."

"And if it doesn't?" my mom asks.

"Then hey... we all have to pivot in life sometimes, don't we?"

She reaches out, her soft, warm hand on my forearm. "We're here for you, Jojo. I've said this many, many times and I'll say it again. In this family, we catch you when you fall." She glances over at Sam, and they share an affectionate smile.

"I know, Mom."

"I don't want you disappearing again. It feels like I haven't seen you at all lately."

"Yeah..." My voice trails off as I consider how if Ashton

and I don't tell everyone about us soon, she won't see much more of me as I live out my secret relationship.

And even though everything isn't ironed out and I'm still not entirely sure if my shiny new mindset will help me at work, a sense of wholeness fills my chest.

I go to bed super early that night in an attempt to get extra sleep while Ashton is gone, and I'm so full of calm, I hardly even notice my eyes close.

* * *

Tink.

Tink.

Tink.

I wake up only a couple of hours later to the sound of a branch or something at my window.

Tink.

What the hell? My window echoes out the sound and I squint. It's not a branch. Stones hit the glass. I race to the window and there he is. A rush of prom night memories swirl around me in the winter breeze as I gaze down at Ashton with a handful of stones. I throw open the window, and my bare nipples tighten both at the cold air and the prospect of his tongue flicking them... sucking them. *He's here...*

"Oh my God, I couldn't have asked for more..." he says, clearly referring to my boobs.

I glance down at my breasts and give him a sideways glance. "Told you I like sleeping naked."

"When are you going to cut me a key?"

"What are you doing here? I thought you were staying in the city?" And why am I having a discussion out the window when I could... "Just a minute."

I run down the stairs, my tits bouncing up and down because why would I dress to open the door? Moments later, I open it in nothing but panties. He's tall, gorgeous, and throws a large duffel and a hockey bag down.

He glides his hands down my waist and slips fingers through the sides of my panties. "What are these?" He pulls them up high so they press firmly against my core, igniting that fire between my legs. He then lets them slap against me with a subtle sting. "I thought you slept naked."

He gathers me into his giant, cool embrace. We kiss like we didn't just do it yesterday, and my heart flutters at the thought of him driving just to see me.

When we finally come up for air, I ask, "What happened?"

"Practice. PT. Then Logan asked me for dinner because he was staying overnight, too, and as soon as we finished, I said I was hitting the hay and drove back. Sorry, you're in bed a lot earlier than I thought you'd be."

"I thought I'd catch up on sleep while you're away. What about tomorrow, you'll have to leave so early? You need sleep, too."

"You're worth it." He cups my breast and rolls my nipple between his fingers, sending shivers down my torso.

I shove my hand up his shirt and enjoy the rock-hard muscles underneath. "I just told my family I was drawing boundaries."

He bends over and takes a soft bite of my neck. My head sighs back, and he traces the shell of my ear with his lips. His murmur rumbles through me.

"If you want me to leave, I'll go."

He kisses me harder, my nub tingling so strong I'm weak in the knees already.

"God no, Pup, you're the best self-care I can think of… but we need to sleep."

He gnaws my neck just short of actually biting me. "What's your bedtime?"

"Before midnight." I'm already breathless.

He starts toward the couch. "We have an hour then. Enough time to taste you, ride you… make you scream."

We reach the couch, and he lets me fall, unbuttoning his pants as he backs away toward the door.

"I'll give you something to dream about."

He unzips a bag and takes out a hockey stick, and for a minute, I'm almost scared. *What the hell does he think we're going to do with that?*

"I got you a present."

His gaze is dark, or at least I think it is. He runs the handle of the stick along my jawline and traces my collarbone.

"What am I going to do with that?" I swallow hard.

He passes the handle over my nipple, flicking it with the solid carbon fiber that's still cold from being in his car. "We're going to play together."

He slides the stick down along my body until it's flush through my middle, stiff firm pressure from under my chin over my breastbone, along my tummy, the stick forming a sensual line from my chin through my seam, the blade curving down along my backside. He presses the stick between my legs, and the rock-hard friction floods my core with blood supply. I spread my legs wider, opening myself farther so the rigid surface can access my sensitive nub.

A shady laugh leaves his lips. "You like that, don't you?"

I bite my lip. "I like anything you do." I grind myself on the stick where he leaves his hand so it stays against me. "But this? It's nothing compared to you."

"But I like seeing you ride it, Joey. I like watching you grind your pussy. Play with it for me."

I love that he likes watching me. And the rigid surface is like nothing I've ever felt. It's as relentless as Ashton's gaze. I ride my man's favorite toy, the surface doing inexplicable damage to my willpower, and within a second, it isn't a dry hump anymore. My panties are soaked. "If I hump on this stick any longer, I won't be able to come on yours."

He shoves his hands in his pants and frees his cock, pumping it in his hand a few times. "You are so fucking hot like this. Two of my favorite things are under me."

He slides his hand from the top of the stick downward until his enormous hand cups both the blade and my panties. He gently rubs it over the fabric, like the hardest fucking dildo in the world. My hips roll uncontrollably. God, he's a tease. Then, he takes the stick off my body until the handle is in his grip. He positions the blunt end right at my entrance and presses it in gently, easing into my slit. The satin fabric of my panties pushes into me along with his creative sex toy.

My legs have a mind of their own and fall open more, giving him better access. I know he can't put it in much farther, but at this moment, I want him to. He teases it as far as my panties allow, and spins it in a circle slowly. The feeling is like none I've ever had before.

He takes my hand and places it on the stick, so now I'm holding it instead of him.

"Keep that right there, baby girl. Keep it right where it feels good..." Ashton stands and pulls his jeans and boxers down then jerks off his steely dick. "Open wide, Joey. I'm going to fuck your mouth the way I wish I could fuck you with that stick."

"Jesus, you're dirty."

He pumps himself. "You like my imagination, though. Look at you wanting to just shove that stick inside. I bet you want to..."

It's impossible but... "I do." I keep the stick on my core. It will have to do until I have him inside me, but to be fair, I need friction badly. My clit throbs begging for his touch. My pussy drips and my desire is now a wet spot on the couch.

"Naughty... naughty girl." He rolls my nipple between his fingers and brings his dick to my lips. He traces precum over them like musky, salty gloss. "You want me to fuck your face?"

I nod and open my mouth, hopefully wide enough for him to get in. And when he puts it in, his girth is so thick he scrapes my teeth. I try to hollow out my cheeks and suck, but there's hardly room for his cock, let alone my tongue to give him more pleasure by dancing underneath him. The taste of him sends me wild, and I throw down the hockey stick. I just want to devour him now. I want to make him so hard he feels just like that stick when he forces himself inside me.

I shove his pants down farther, my nails scraping his ass and he plunges his dick in and out of my mouth, slowly, going deeper down my throat each time. I play with his balls and suck the best I can.

"You take me so good," he moans.

I hum on his dick and let a finger slide to the sensitive place just behind his balls and his backside and press down harder, circling, sucking at the same time until his thighs quiver in praise for doing this right. My eyes are fucking watering, he's so big, so deep. And he laces his fingers through my hair, driving in.

"You keep doing that... and I could fuck your face 'til you choke."

He thrusts a couple more times. With each one going deeper, the water in my eyes trickles down, and I have to concentrate hard to relax my jaw enough to allow him in, and just when I think he's going to release in my mouth, he pulls out.

"Not in here. I need that pussy now."

When he reaches down into the back pocket of his pants, I take the time to yank my panties off and widen my legs as far as they go to let my beast of a man between them. He rolls on the condom, quickly with a wild look in his eye, while I finger my nub, knowing the minute he's inside me, I'll let go all over him.

He lowers himself over me, positions his cock at my entrance. "Such a tight girl. So fucking tight."

I don't know if I'm tight or he's a fucking mutant as he sinks his thick cock into me, filling me to a level of full I didn't think I could take. He yanks my ass to the edge of the couch and rails into me on his knees.

"You are everything, Joey. You ruin me."

He uses his thumb to give me pleasure, circling my swollen clit, while driving into me in a way I know neither of us will last. His hips meet the cradle of mine, and wet slapping sounds fill my home.

"You're so messy for me. So wet, I want you dripping down my balls." His jaw clenches, and then he gives me his best move yet and gently pinches my clit.

"Holy shit." I arch my back. My spine tingles. "I'm going to explode all over you, Ash... right now." My pussy flutters and pulses around him, and I can't even help myself, I let out a loud moan while squeezing the couch cushion underneath me as he pounds into me to get his.

He uses my hips to brace himself, and the force of his muscular glutes driving into me is almost painful. He thrusts one last time, and his dick swells, the heat of his release fills me. The thrusting motion slows in the same rhythm of my breath until he pumps a few more times before sliding out and collapsing half on top of me on the sofa.

He kisses my cheek. "Time to get you to bed, cowgirl."

Ashton takes off the condom and politely throws it in a trashcan across the room, and I get the best view of his powerful buns. Goddamn, I'm a lucky woman. He hoists up his jeans and then scoops me off the couch, cradles me into his arms like I weigh nothing at all, and somehow shimmies both our tall asses up the stairs without bumping me once.

We spoon in bed, and he holds me. After fifteen minutes in his arms, I'm horny and having the feels all over again. I reach behind me to have another go at his dick.

He swats my hand away. "Sleepy time, Joey."

I giggle and take my hand back. He holds me tighter.

I concentrate on his warm breath on my neck, and my mind wanders to a million different places as if the past weeks have years' worth of memories. But as fatigue sets in, so do a few intrusive thoughts.

"Ashton?"

"Mmm?" His voice is tired.

"How did you end up with a person like Chloe?"

He heaves in a large, long breath of air and lets it out deliberately, like a yoga breath. He pauses for what feels like a long time, I wonder if he drifted off. But then he kisses my back.

"I only knew for sure what love was when I found out what it wasn't." His lips land warm and soft on my shoulder blade again.

My words are hopeful. "And you know for sure what it is now?"

"Yes. And now *I'm* right back where I've always been."

His reminiscent words glow inside me like a hot ember, and a smile tugs at my cheeks.

"I love you, Joey. I love you with everything I've got and I always will."

"I love you, too, Ashton."

He kisses me again, and his body aligns to mine in a perfect embrace. "Now go to sleep."

Chapter Seventeen

Ashton

I snuck back to Starlight Canyon the next two days after practice, but rather than draining me, being with Joey energizes me. Her wild laugh echoes in my mind along with the clink of our forks touching on a shared plate of food because now it's not just practical, it's romantic. We made love and talked until midnight both days about everything in the world, and I find the same peace she does when she talks about her first day back treating animals and how quiet her personal phone is now that she has a dedicated work one.

Nothing earth-shifting happened those two days, and yet it's the dawn of a new normal I hope to revolve around forever.

But today, a lot of the calm of the past couple of game-free days passes when I lace up my skates, ready to play the Huskies. And Eric Larose. Coach gives the pregame talks.

"The Huskies are our hardest game yet. They were last season's number one, and you all know the focus this team has. I know you're thinking they're potentially the ones to break this streak we're on. I don't believe that. I believe that this is the team that will be holding the Stanley Cup this year. I believe you boys know how to make mistakes, pivot and stay loose. We're home for this one, and it's a big advantage as there are no better home fans than the Scorpions who are up in the stands willing this win. With the team we have, the crowd believes this is the year. We have every reason to believe in ourselves. We have Dane back, a full roster, and they're down Polakowski and Kurtz. This night is yours, gentlemen. Make the most of it. Skates on."

We all file toward our lockers, but Coach taps Logan on the arm.

"As usual, you won't be on with Larose."

Logan flashes one of his charming Hollywood smiles. "I expected that much but I don't see why you won't let an old boy like me have one last hurrah."

"Case in point."

Coach walks off, and I'm thinking of Eric Larose all over again. Logan never told me just how bad that motherfucker was. I thought he was just being overprotective. But now I know why he rages at the mere sound of his name. Coach is careful. Fights are standard, but us players know our limits typically, and he knows bad blood in real life between players can get ugly. I wonder if I'll know my limits today. I hope I get a chance to find out, because I can't ask when to be on the ice, but one thing I do know is I'm first line and Eric is, too.

I can't believe I've shared the ice so many times before with Larose and did nothing. It's illogical, but shame courses through me, knowing I did nothing for years when I should have been defending Jolie's honor.

Hard to love.

His face will be hard to fucking love when I'm through with him tonight.

I step onto the ice, and we all warm up on our own halves. It's dangerous not to focus on my teammates, but I'm pre-occupied. My mind is glued to the other side of the rink. Trying to focus on the drill we're doing, I'm distracted by something else. In the corner of my eye, rink side, bouncy long blonde hair grabs my attention, and I glance over.

Jolie stands in a loose Scorpions jersey, and her matching sparkling jade eyes collide with mine. Her cheeks are rosy from the chill in the air. She's with her niece and sister-in-law who have woven their way down to watch warmup before cheering from the box our families share. Eve has a foam finger on, reminding me of how I said I'd bring one to her event. Joey splats a big white card sign onto the plexiglass that has a phone on it reading *Your Mom Called—You Left Your Game At Home.*

Eve catches my gaze and screams. "Go Scorpions! Kick butt!"

Logan glides past them when his position heads that way.

"Go, Uncle Lo!!" Eve shouts.

I'm still looking at the Hunter girls when someone shouts.

"Dane!"

A puck whizzes by me, and I miss the pass from a drill I've done a thousand times.

One of my teammates, a rookie named Mahmoud, skates over. "You okay, man?"

He's a talented guy who knows I should have had that pass. He doesn't say more, but his expression tells me he's not asking if I'm okay, but telling me he's not impressed.

We all want to win this game. Beating the number one seed in the league would cement our prowess. But number sixty-six on the Huskies, the douchebag who thinks he can wear a variation of the mighty Gretzgy's number, distracts me. I'm being unprofessional. I'm being... self-destructive.

But nothing dampens the rage building inside as I watch Eric Larose.

Logan skates dangerously close to the red halfway line where I'm sure a ref is watching carefully. He toes it but won't be stupid enough to get a suspension by going over.

"Larose!" he shouts loudly enough for me to hear yards away. Eric doesn't pay Logan any mind but it still doesn't stop Logan from spouting, "Eat shit."

Lots of players trash talk across the red line before games. And I've seen my friend do this several times since we've been on the same team. The same wave of guilt I felt over not defending Jolie all these years rises like bile in my throat over not supporting Logan, too. Not that either have said anything until my recent conversation with Jolie, but loyalty is one of those things friends don't have to ask me for. It's in my bones.

Warmups end, and just before the puck drops, Eric skates into position opposite me. In all the combinations of players who could be on the ice to start this game, I can't help but think that me being right defense and Eric left is clandestine destiny.

Be smart, Dane. I tell myself to keep it cool. A fight for no reason this early in the game, risking injury... I'm not a rookie anymore. I should know better. Nothing is more important than winning. I have a team. I have a contract. I'm not Jolie's boyfriend while I'm on the ice... I'm a Scorpion. But one last peek up toward the box, and I capture a heart-wrenching glance of that woman who deserves so much more than he gave her...

The puck drops, and adrenaline releases in my body like it always does, but this time it's joined by the intense urge to beat Eric Larose to a pulp. My eyes track him feverishly when he heads up the left side. He passes it off before I can check him.

I just need a chance.

I'm called off before I get one. Maybe it's just as well, because me being focused on Eric means I'm not focused on the basket. My teammates sink in a goal before the first period. Everyone is pumped up during intermission. I watch my best friend fist bump a teammate with a satisfied smile. Is my personal vendetta a bad idea? I know Logan wants a Stanley Cup win so badly. I know we're nearing the end of our ability to play at such a high standard. I'm not a kid anymore. This isn't the playground... I *know* this.

But I'm still blinded by some chivalrous need to teach Larose a lesson. I don't get another chance to face him until the third period... I'm too seasoned not to be smart about it. To make it look like a legit fight. But pucks fly and goals are made and skates make snow on the surface. The game goes by like a haze until total clarity overcomes me. Finally, Eric Larose has the puck, and he's coming straight toward me.

My skates are turbocharged, I hardly feel the ice beneath them, blitzing toward my enemy, my woman's enemy, and I body check him so forcefully, we connect with a bone-jarring clash. He blasts off his feet and straight to the ice. I'm not even thinking when I throw my body down on top of him. Rage fills my every nerve. The thought of him hurting my woman for so many years fuels my fists like they have a mind of their own. My heart pumps painfully, rushing blood to my arms so I can pummel down.

Our teammates flood the ice, surrounding us, ready to jump in with support at any time. A blur of green has my back, purple behind him. The crowd barks around us, encouraging me to keep fighting. "Woof! Woof! Woof!"

Eric is no small boy. He pushes back up on his skates and smashes into me. But he thinks this is some ordinary fight. It fucking isn't to me. Jolie's pride and self-esteem are everything. Fury rushes to my limbs, and a fist makes contact with his jaw while fierce, enraged thoughts flood my veins. *You stole her confidence. You tore her down.* My height advantage gets the better of him, and I have him against the boards, uppercut after uppercut, trying to get him where it hurts, under the helmet...

Finally, a ref dares to get between us, and I know I'd better stop because I'm already going to the sin bin for this one. I can't afford to be ejected. I skate away, ready to sit and stew in the penalty box. I'm not satisfied leaving Larose with just a bloody eye and a swollen lip. I leave him with some carefully selected words, hoping not to give myself away and at the same time tap into the real reason he deserved what he got.

"That's from Hunter."

The locker room post-game is celebratory, and spirits are high after our four-three win against the Huskies. It was an intense game, both sides fought with grit, and our center, Rosario, blasts a high-energy playlist after our showers.

Logan is uncharacteristically quiet when we gather around for Coach's brief. Rosario cuts the music, and the room goes silent.

"Gentleman, that's the intensity I'm looking for! I'm blown away by the teamwork. I haven't had a team gel like this one in years, and you executed the prettiest on-ice choreography I've witnessed since Gretzky and Messier." He laughs to himself. "Kidding. That's sacrilege."

Coach would never blow that much smoke up our asses.

"But seriously, if this team keeps playing hockey like that, we are making some memorable moments for our fans, this organization, and ourselves. You should be proud. I don't want to dampen anything but I just want to add that we need to keep our noses clean." He glances at me. "Dane, that's two for two now... and the last fight led to injury."

The first one wasn't my fault, but I know better than to speak up.

"Let's not do anything stupid, boys..." He speaks to everyone now. "One of the reasons we won tonight was we have a full, healthy roster. Let's keep it that way. Rosario?" He glances at Rosario and fans his hand upward, telling him to blast those beats again.

Dance music floods the locker room again, and Logan and I sit, shoulder to shoulder, both tying our shoelaces, almost ready to get out of here. He hasn't spoken much. We pretty much always leave together, but he seems to be dragging, and I want to get back to the Canyon tonight so I decide to grab my things and go.

"See you, man." I make it two steps down the hallway when I hear his voice behind me.

"Dane!"

I turn, and he strides toward me, brows furrowed. "Which Hunter was that brawl for?"

I didn't notice Logan come out on the ice when I fought Eric. But he must have been there with the others who came out to back me up.

"What do you mean?" *I know exactly what he means.*

"You heard me. You told Larose he got it for Hunter."

I don't want to lie. "Why are you asking?"

He runs his fingers through damp hair. "Why aren't you answering?"

But before I say another word, he shakes his head, a disbelieving, flabbergasted smile on his face.

"I can't fucking believe this." He combs his fingers through his hair again. "You. It's you."

"Who's me?"

"Are you and Jolie together?" He's dead serious now. "Don't fucking evade the question, Dane. Are you and my sister hooking up?"

I don't want to lie. I don't want to answer. But he reads me like a book after all these years of friendship.

"The fuck, Ashton!"

"I would have told you..."

"When? Clearly not before I was able to put two and two together. Way after you *should* have told me... I'm such a dumbass. I never even suspected it until tonight. But... the fight?" He shakes his head then offers more. "I haven't really heard from Jolie in weeks, which is unusual, so I called my mom. She said Jo seems pretty happy. Happier than ever. That Jo has really healed from her time with you... and I actually thought you were just being a good friend, but you were being so much more than that. Weren't you?"

"I'm still figuring it out..." I glance around, hoping no one is listening. "Lower your voice, man. Just..."

"Oh, you need to keep my sister a secret?" He's pissed now. "She deserves better, and you of all people should know that."

"Logan. Just..." I need him to calm down. "Look at me."

He's fuming, but clenches his jaw and braces within to listen to what I have to say.

"I should have told you. I should have told you the minute I saw her again and feelings came flooding in."

His eyes widen. "How long have you been keeping this?"

"Not that long... too long, though."

"Yeah. Lying by omission is fucked, Ash."

"But—" My eyes dart up to a rookie who's leaving and passes us, but thankfully he has earbuds in. "I didn't tell you for a reason. I'm... the divorce news, and how Chloe is. You know it's a problem, Lo." I glance around again. This is far too public for a conversation like this. "I'm worried I'll draw Jolie into unfair bad press and Chloe will... I thought if we lie low for a while longer..."

More teammates pour out, but they're engrossed in conversation and don't pay us more than a chin wag.

Logan speaks through his teeth. "Does Jolie know everything? Like, she knows what *I* know?"

"No... but..."

A sordid laugh escapes him, and his words are unhinged. "You're such a dick..." He gazes at me with wild eyes. "You better fucking love her... I mean, like as in I better be your best fucking man in a year's time, because this shit?" He pokes me in the chest. "Tell me you have a plan. I need to know how you're going to deal with this mess."

"I'm thinking about it."

He throws his head back and stares at the ceiling like it understands him better than I do. When his gaze returns, he's more centered but still full of warning. "I want to be happy for you two. Jolie has always cared about you, and you're my best friend. I'm not one of these dumbasses who can't see how cool that would be to be your brother. For my sister to be with a man I actually think the world of. But... I don't trust Chloe if she hears about this. And my sister just came off a lot of years of, well, judging by what happened on the ice tonight, you know all about Larose."

I clench my jaw.

Logan's eyes chastise me. "You should have never caved to Chloe."

"Yeah?" His words rile me up. "And what was the alternative? Tell her to go to hell and let my family unravel?"

He reaches a hand up the wall and drops his head, defeated.

"I'll handle it," I reassure him, even though I have no idea what to do... apart from waiting for Hurricane Chloe to blow over.

Logan's jaw tics. "I'm sorry, man. This time I... for once in my fucking life I'm speechless."

"Will you keep it to yourself?" My stomach is sour now with me knowing I'm getting closer to some sort of inevitability I didn't plan enough for. I need more time to find a way out, to figure out the right thing to do.

His expression says I'm an idiot. "I'm not going to tell anyone." He turns to leave and throws an exasperated hand in the air. "Figure it out."

I watch my best friend walk away with a sinking feeling in my belly even worse than the sour taste on my tongue.

That night, I don't tell Jolie that Logan knows. I let her fall asleep hugging me like a hero for pummeling Eric Larose.

I might be her hero. But when I finally drift off, I feel more like a traitor.

Chapter Eighteen

Jolie

ASHTON'S ARM is a crescent around me, and I stroke his skin lightly, having woken up long before him. Replaying the events of the past twenty-four hours, the cavewoman in me is elated. Watching Ashton beat Eric was cathartic. I've never told Eric just how much he hurt me. I didn't want him to see my weakness, because the one time I did, he proved to me what a bad idea it was. So all I did was walk away and tell him never to come back again.

It was a loose end. And Ashton tied that shit up in a knot so compact it will never unfurl again. Finally, it's the end of the Eric saga. So yes, the feral, illogical, and let's face it, slightly immature young woman inside me is celebrating the payback. Eric's face looked like my heart did so many times in our relationship.

But... Ashton... something is different. He was quiet last night. He's never been a man who needs to assert his words, not like Logan, not like me, but the quiet moments weren't comfortable yesterday like they usually are.

My big spoon stirs behind me, and his morning wood pokes me in the butt. A kiss lands on my back before his groggy, croaky low voice wafts in my ear. "You're up before me."

"Yeah."

"What time is it?"

"Seven-thirty."

"Shit," he groans.

"I was just about to wake you. But you were so peaceful."

Beep. Beep. Beep. Ashton's phone alarm goes off. He reaches over to the side table behind him, and cold air rushes between us. He turns off the alarm, rolls back into our groove in the mattress, and warms me back up again.

"I don't want to leave." He inhales my hair and holds me affectionately but doesn't make another move.

I'm pretty sure one of two things is supposed to happen now. Either he's supposed to stick that wood in for a quickie or we should have a little talk before he heads off, because the man has to be back on the road in thirty minutes. I definitely want to bang him, but Ashton is... still different. Just like he was last night.

Because normally by now, I'd be stuffed with nine inches, so he must have something on his mind, too.

Something is wrong. Is it me? Is he hurting from the

fight? Sometimes, when my brothers were sick or had an injury from sports, they'd go quiet.

"How is your body feeling after that fight?"

"I'm fine. He only got me once on the side, so I hardly felt it."

"That's good."

"Yeah. It was stupid." He wrestles me in his arms. "But worth it."

I smile, but it's half-hearted. A woman's gut is her greatest gift and her worst torture.

Ashton gets out of bed, and his perfect glutes head toward my en suite bathroom. "I wish I didn't have to go."

I sit up and pull the duvet up over me. "Me, too…"

He almost gets the door closed before I blurt. "Ashton, get your ass back here."

He peeks out of a crack in the door, his eyebrows furrowed, but for the first time since the incident on the ice, he has a little smile on his face. "Excuse me? Are you bossing me around?"

I pat the bed beside me, and he comes over, propping himself up on his elbow beside me. I try to stay focused, but his big dick, softer, is sprawled out like a very tempting snake. Still, I don't want him inside me nearly as much as I want to be inside that head of his right now. I slide my hand down his long, strong body from his shoulder down his arm and rest it on his hip.

"I feel like you have something to say but you aren't saying it."

He swipes his fingers over his mouth, staring at the ceiling, thinking, so obvious that I hit the nail on the head. He doesn't answer, just keeps stroking his boyish lip in thought.

"It's going to kill me thinking about this all day. Did I do something wrong?"

"No, Joey... never. You're perfect as always."

"So why no morning nookie or even snuggle convo? Please don't say you're just tired because I won't believe you."

He takes some of my hair between his fingers and twirls it. "There isn't time to unpack it all right now."

"Well, let me have a peek in the box at least. Are you coming here after tonight's game?"

I'm trying not to be needy. Ashton is coming off an injury and has back-to-back home games. Plus, instead of staying in his bolt-hole apartment in Santa Fe like my brother does, he's getting less sleep coming back to me.

"You don't have to come back if it's exhausting."

He doesn't stop me from talking, so in my typical fashion, I just keep going. "Sleep will probably do us both good."

It's the sleep he needs, right? That's all this is. He's tired, and running this schedule with me is hard on him.

I blurt. "And you only have one more game then off days before leaving. Maybe I could come to the city... instead of you driving here?"

He drops my hair along with his gaze. "It's Chloe."

My heart bursts, and my throat swells. "Chloe?" I never expected to hear her name this morning.

"It's not you at all. You've done nothing. I love you as much today as yesterday." He hesitates.

Dread pools in my gut. Why would we need to talk about his ex? What the hell could there be to unpack? "Ashton, just tell me."

"I..." he starts but shakes his head. "I'm worried about the whole world knowing our business just now."

Chloe is the reason we're keeping this quiet? Not

Logan? "Is this about why you took the blame for the divorce?"

He nods and struggles to find words. I see a battle play out behind his deep-brown eyes.

"You can tell me," I reassure him.

"I know I can tell you. I know. I trust you. But it's a long story, and I want to give us time to talk. You said how important sleep is. Tomorrow night is better when you don't have clinic the next day. It's not you, I promise."

A knife twists in my gut. I can't wait. How bad can this be? "Most long stories aren't long at all, you know. People say that all the time. It's a long story, but then really it can be told in one or two sentences."

He sighs. "This one is actually long. We need time to sit down about this. You don't deserve me dropping a bomb and running."

I scoff. "That's already what you're doing."

He laces his fingers through my hair. "You have to trust me. I love you. Nothing has changed that and nothing ever will. But there are some things we need to talk about, decide together how to move forward and what that looks like. I'll tell you everything. You and I are completely inseparable." He drops his forehead to mine. "Do you believe me?"

I don't answer. My belly wobbles like I'm going to be sick.

He tips my chin up with his finger and gazes at me deeply. "Hey. You and I will make it. Promise. It's not the kind of stuff we can make off-the-cuff decisions on, and I don't want you thinking about it all day at the clinic."

"So it's about Chloe?" I confirm again it's her, not me who's the problem. *Why would she be a problem?*

"Mostly."

I don't feel right, and he knows it. His gaze is soulful and affectionate.

"I love you," he says, considering me.

I give him as much smile as there is in me right now. He said we need to make decisions. What decisions do we need to make that would ever concern his ex? The worst thought crosses my mind. "You and Chloe *are* officially divorced, right?"

"Yes, baby girl. Definitely a hundred percent."

So why does she matter at all anymore? I want to squeeze more out of this conversation, but Ashton can't be late. He'll have no excuse for his coach, and worse, Logan. He's supposed to be staying overnight at his apartment in the city right now, and that apartment is in the same building as my brother's. Being late requires way too many lies, so he needs to get out of here.

Ashton kisses the back of my hand. "I want to hear you say it." He moves my lips with his finger and makes his voice a little higher as if it's mine. "Ashton loves me."

His silly gesture has me rolling my eyes and grinning involuntarily. He's trying to lighten the mood, and I have to admit, I appreciate it, because dark thoughts are creeping in.

He traces my lips. "Go on, Joey. Say it."

I heave out a frustrated sigh at how easily he can transform me from worried to lighthearted. He's always been a master at the controls.

He kisses me gently. "I need to hear you say it. I can't leave here unless you say it." He cocks one of his famous half-smiles.

"Ashton loves me," I concede.

"That's my girl." He cups the back of my head and pulls my lips against his. "Don't you worry today. I'll be back after the game tonight, and we'll get up early tomorrow morning."

He heads to the bathroom again but turns, giving me a full frontal of the most manly beast with the kindest heart. He points at me. "Ashton loves me."

"Ashton loves me."

I'm back at my consultant work with Starlight Vets, treating all animals large and tiny, and today is as crazy as all my in-clinic days have been before. The Canyon being a small place affords me the opportunity to be a mixed-practice vet. Starlight Vets has been the only clinic in town for as long as I remember, and I still can't believe when I returned to the Canyon, I actually wanted to open a rival clinic. That was me falling into life as usual.

I inwardly thank Colt again for stepping into the mentor role. He does it for all of us. No wonder he chose someone like Sam, who bosses him around from time to time. He probably likes not making all the decisions every second of the day.

Over the past week, I've thought more about how to make sure I protect my mental health in this job. I considered concentrating on farm animals only. I love being out in the fresh air. And even though horsey people often think they know what's going on with their horse better than I do, the farmers and ranchers are more down to earth. I still come across the same sad days there, but often, they're more practical about things which brings a lot less stress into the situation. But I know that line of work, when doing it full time leads to physical problems, as getting pushed around by cattle or manhandling a goat isn't easy on the bones.

It replaces one problem with another.

So boundaries is my answer.

I'm in the clinic with the little furballs and I'm glad to be here. There's nothing like a brand-new kitten or puppy or fluffy baby rabbit to brighten a day. And right now it's time for vaccines for the cutest fluff of a collie I've ever seen. The black-and-white furbaby sits in the arms of another youngster I like—Gareth from Western skills school.

I bend down to pat his new pup on the head. "And what's this little guy's name?" I already know it's Rocky, because I read the paperwork, but every kid likes talking about their new dog.

"Rocky." Gareth wraps his arms around his pup, hugging him.

His mom gives me a thin-lipped smile, and I think about the hole Rocky is filling and how well animals do it. There were days after my dad died where our shepherds were the only thing that made me get out of bed in the morning. And they were the best listeners. Them. And Ashton.

Back then, Ashton could even hear the words I didn't speak. And that's why I've never been able to give up loving that man.

I prepare the needles and double-check the doses on a side counter because I only have ten minutes for the appointment. I wish I had more. I'm sure Gareth would love to talk about his puppy all day long. "You're not afraid of needles, are you, Gareth?"

"Nah. I'm not afraid of anything."

"Oh yeah? That's a shame." I pat the exam table, indicating for him to bring Rocky over.

He places the collie on the table. "Why is that a shame?" He smooths Rocky's fur.

I pat the pup, too, trying to impart a lesson my dad

taught me. A lesson that, just maybe, a kid like Gareth could do with. "Because fear usually tells us what's important. It can be kind of helpful in life if you don't let it beat you. There's no shame in being afraid."

I listen to Rocky's healthy heartbeat. Gareth is quiet next to me, likely thinking about what I just said.

I go to get the first needle off my stainless-steel prep tray and lift it in the air to give it a tap.

Gareth's eyes go wide. "Maybe I'm a little nervous for Rocky."

I smile. "He'll hardly notice it. But your fear is telling you that you care about him." I administer the shot, and Rocky takes it like the champ he's named after.

Gareth puts his face in front of the dog's and gets some anxious, slobbery kisses. I finish the rest of the shots, and Gareth scoops Rocky up in his arms.

"Good boy."

"Now keep an eye on him over the next twenty-four hours." I hand Gareth's mom a paper with Vaccination FAQs including side effects.

She, like many clients, didn't listen closely to the vet nurse talking through possible side effects, but now, reading them, and they all sound life-threatening, because they are, her steps slow as she approaches the exam room door. "Wait... so do I call you if any of these things happen?"

"First, these are very, very uncommon, so don't be too alarmed. But second..." I want to give her my number. Clients always have a sense of calm when they have a name and a face to call in the middle of the night. But I can't. *Boundaries.* "There is an emergency number on there, and there's someone answering that number twenty-four seven. It might be me or someone else."

"I'd feel better if it was you," she pushes.

A lot of clients push. And in a small town, it happens more than elsewhere because helping neighbors is what we do.

I put a hand on her arm. "I'd feel better if it was me, too, but the important thing is that you get an answer and someone who is fresh and prepared if Rocky gets sick. If I were to be on call all the time, I'm sure I'd be useless at some point."

She gazes at me knowingly. "I get it. I'm a mom."

I'm pretty sure that job is harder than being a vet. At least in my house it was.

I walk them to the door.

Gareth asks, "So are you going to be at my next roping lesson? I've been practicing on a stump in the backyard and I'm going to get Ashton next time, I swear."

I laugh. "It will be back to Mrs. Dane next time. I'll miss you but I had to get back to helping all the new Rockys."

"Dang. You two are funnier than Mrs. Dane. You work good together."

"Gareth..." His mom palms her face.

"We are a good pair." I think about Ashton all over. But instead of a warm feeling, it's one of melancholy and questions. I wish we could have just talked this morning. Patience is not my strong suit.

They begin to leave to go back to their new paradigm, a very different trio from what they once were, and I can't help myself.

"Mrs. Mason?"

She turns.

"If you ever need a babysitter for Gareth, or a dog sitter for Rocky, drop a note to Monica with your number, and I'll help you out."

She lifts her eyebrows. "I don't think many people can handle Gareth for a night."

"I'll wrangle my teammate he likes and I'm sure we can manage together."

She offers a soft smile. "That's really kind."

I watch her leave and wonder if that was crossing the boundaries I'm trying to draw or not. But Ashton's best advice was to be myself, and in that moment, that's what felt right, helping a tired single mom and offering a little boy a village to care about him.

I guess you can take the girl out of the small town, but not the small town out of the girl.

Chapter Nineteen

Ashton

I HATED LEAVING Jolie behind this morning, not being able to tell her everything. I've already kept it to myself far too long. Logan is right. She deserves to know. I should have just shared it with her. But doing that also puts a burden on her, and I guess for a while I hoped some uncomplicated solution would fall from the sky and I wouldn't have to drag her into this mess.

But there isn't one. The only thing I can do is trust that we'll be in this together and that time will give Chloe a different man to blackmail. That her narcissistic need to be the one and only woman to me, even though I wasn't her only man, will fade. She doesn't need the money after all. That woman is mentally ill and has a severe lack of morality.

The only thing I can see working right now is Jolie and I lying low for at least six months, maybe a year. By then, Chloe will be thinking about someone else, or many someone elses. By then she'll be another film deep... I'll maybe even be retired this season or the next, and nobody will give a shit about telling the world I have a girlfriend.

But that thought is quickly obliterated by reality.

When I walk from the parking lot to enter the stadium for today's pregame action, Logan, who has clearly been waiting for me, bullrushes me with his cell in his hand. He's angry in a way I haven't ever seen him before. I've seen him fight on ice, but somehow, it's always been fun and games. Now? He is livid.

"The fuuuuuuck, Dane?"

I stop in my tracks because I'm not taking his volume inside.

"You stupid motherfucker." He swipes his cell a few times and shoves it in my face. "I thought you said you were lying low? Keeping it quiet?"

I try to focus on the screen he handed me, but he keeps growling at me.

"You ask your best friend to keep a secret but are stupid enough to go out in public on a date?"

I tilt the screen so I can see better, and there we are, me and Jolie at the ice rink in Blackhawk, and we're all over each other. My heart sinks into my gut. I never thought... that place is in the middle of nowhere? I bought it out for privacy. I stiffen at the thought of it. I try to see what site the photo is on, but Logan yanks his phone back.

"And before you even dream of thinking that nobody but me has seen this, let me show you something else, you dumbass." He swipes a few more times then shoves it back in my face. "Read it."

ROSALIND

MY GOD, LOGAN, I'M STILL THINKING OF YOUR COCK THREE DAYS LATER, YOU'VE TOTALLY RUINED ME. I'M STILL SORE. ONE MORE TIME?

I shove the phone into his chest and bite my lip, waiting for him to pull up what he actually wanted me to see.

He reads his phone, shakes his head, and swipes furiously again. "Here." He wiggles the phone in front of me to take it again.

ROSARIO

BRO, IS THIS YOUR SISTER WITH DANE?

My jaw goes slack. Shit. I gaze at Logan who is shaking his head. He found out from our teammate?

"I found out from Rosario," he confirms. "You know, because rookies love looking for their names on puck bunny blogs."

I glance back at the incriminating text before he snatches the cell out of my hands yet again and swipes his finger all over it like a mad scientist or something. "It's plastered all over these puck bunny fan sites. If Rosario has seen it…"

Chloe has seen it. My ex-wife had real obsessive tendencies, trust issues, and a jealous streak to rival Haley's comet. During our marriage, she never missed an article about me, even if it was a silly blog on a website designed for hockey-mad young girls. I can't expect she'll have outgrown that by now.

"Tell me you told Jolie about everything last night?" Logan pleads, knowing how insane Chloe can be.

"I told her we'd talk tomorrow morning..."

He clenches his fists tightly, like he's trying not to let them take a swing at me. "How could such a smart guy be so damn stupid? Now we're here... all damn day and all damn night at the arena, and Chloe is not known for being reasonable. I'm thinking of that time she flew all the way to Boston to confront Zara Thomas."

Chloe has never been level-headed. Logan is right. He's referring to when Chloe confronted another woman I dated after she texted that she missed me. Mania shudders through my body, and I'm caught between the push and pull of needing to be in that arena and wanting to hightail it back to Starlight Canyon.

Logan finally calms down, and thank God, has nothing more to show me on his phone as he slips it in his back pocket. "Good thing my sister knows how to handle herself. I don't even want to think about a showdown between those two."

"She'll be after me, not Joey."

"Oh really?"

He draws out his words, giving me time to realize how naive the assumption is.

His features are unconvinced. "Yeah, I've seen what that woman does when she's feeling jealous. Ice-bucket tantrum in Vegas? That poor server..."

Chloe's jealousy rivaled any woman I knew. I

remember that night. A pretty server recognized me and Logan at a club many years ago, and she was a huge hockey fan. She bantered with us more like a guy than a puck bunny, but that's what Chloe hated most about it. The server connected with me and Lo on a level Chloe never cared to. She didn't give a shit about hockey. We spoke to the server for no more than three minutes when she said she needed to get back to her job but asked first for an autograph. Though it looked like she was going to ask for one on her boobs, she was actually pulling out a miniature notepad she had tucked in there for orders. Chloe didn't wait long enough for it to come out and whipped our champagne from the ice bucket, then threw the frozen contents over the waitress.

That's the kind of woman Chloe was.

Is.

And if that was all there was to be going on, Jolie dealing with a high-octane, jealous woman, I'd back my little Hunter every day of the week. But that's not all there is to this...

"Go inside," I tell Logan. "I'm going to try to call Jolie."

He glances at his Rolex. "You got like ten minutes before you need to get kitted up."

"I'll do what I can."

But Jolie's cell rings out. Three times I reach her voicemail because she's in the clinic today, and we talked about how those days she rarely even comes up for air. And if I don't touch base with her now, it's pretty much never today. I can't leave a voicemail about this. What the hell am I going to say? Even if I leave a message, she probably won't listen to it anytime soon.

I need to text her. Something short. Digestible. I open

up my messages and think of how I can summarize the drama that might be sitting on a plane right now headed to Starlight Canyon. Then again, I don't know for sure, but I can't do nothing.

ME

JOEY—I WILL ALWAYS PUT YOU FIRST.

Chapter Twenty

Jolie

Ashton's sweet but dramatic text landed funny today of all days. On a day when I know a serious conversation is coming, something that would normally make me swoon came across cryptic. Adding to that message he also called multiple times, leaving no message? My stomach gurgles on my drive back home, despite me having zero appetite.

I can't wait for tonight's game to be over. He'll get back, and we'll talk it out. I pull up the long winding drive to my house, bummed that I can't go to games on clinic days, but trying to be grateful that it was a good day. It wasn't without struggle, but I did feel a little better about the challenges today and am proud of myself for setting limits. It's a positive start toward feeling better about my job.

I squint up the road... Is that a car in front of my house? Apart from me, everyone is away for the Scorpions game. Delivery? Have I ordered something? No...

I get closer, and the view sharpens. A white Jeep I don't recognize at all, with Mavis rental plates, is parked in front of my house. I can't make out the face of the female driver, but intuition creeps up my spine and tells me to be on guard. What worries me even more is that I get out of my car, walk to my door, and unlock it before the person in the vehicle gets out of hers. If it's a delivery, surely she's been waiting for me and wants to get on her way?

I take one last look at my cell to see if I have another message from Ashton. I don't. By the time I throw my keys on the console table by my door and turn around to see what she wants, she's gotten out. The woman doesn't have a package in her hand. And, it's not just any woman.

It's Chloe.

I recognize her from all the pictures of her and Ashton over the years and all the B-rated movies I sat through in masochistic agony, wondering what kind of woman got to marry my Ashton Dane.

"What are you doing here?" I ask, because this traitor doesn't deserve a hello.

She smiles, and boy does it send a spike of adrenaline coursing through my veins.

"I was hoping to see my husband." Her perfect lips and straight white teeth beam at me with the most patronizing grin in the world.

"*Ex*-husband." I correct her.

"Oh, sorry. We were together for so long. But you know,

ex. Husband. Ex-husband. In my mind he was mine all the same." There's a menacing twinkle in her voice.

"I highly doubt his memory reflects the same fondness. And I'm going to need you to leave. If you adored him the way you say you do, you'd know he has a hockey game and his parents' ranch is four miles down the road. You won't find him here." *I hope you never find him.*

I'm proud of myself for keeping my composure. For not allowing the secret Ashton asked me to keep from slipping and tell this woman he's mine now.

Unfortunately, holding back is taking every bit of my self-control, and expletives are at the tip of my tongue. As she sways forward, clearly not leaving and appearing completely unthreatened by me, she somehow looks down at me even though I have four inches on her. My jaw clenches. I'm already starting to lose it. I've never been a calm person, and her steady steps and condescending features have my heart beating relentlessly. I swallow a hard, dry lump.

Her tone and everything else is haughty. "You see, Jolie... you *are* Jolie? Aren't you?"

I don't answer, because this woman already knows who I am.

She continues. "You see, I think I will find him here, because after me, Ashton went for the low-hanging fruit."

My temperature spikes. My cheeks flush. "Low-hanging fruit? It doesn't get any lower than you. I know what you did to Ashton. It's his prerogative if he wants to let you get away with painting him as the villain, but if you think I value the opinion of someone with zero integrity, you're wrong."

"Oh, he told you everything, did he?" she sneers.

"Yes, Chloe. I know you were the cheater. You let him

take the fall in the media. You took more than your fair share and you don't even need the money. What's wrong with you? Have some decency."

"Decent?" She laughs. "That's cute. You think your little boyfriend is decent?"

I should correct her but don't.

"Was it decent of Ashton to make me out to be a goddamn fool running home to get with his childhood sweetheart?" Her smile twists into something sinister. Her nostrils flare slightly, and her mask falls. Her fake sweet tone has melted into something more like the voice of a bitter witch. "Rumors of his indiscretion flood the gossip pages one minute, and the next second, the world sees Ashton tongue-fucking his lifelong crush back home in sweet little Starlight Canyon. Once an adulterer, now the beloved hockey boy has flipped the narrative in an instant, and the whole country is rooting for the friends-to-lover's story."

"What the hell are you talking about?"

"You know what I'm talking about."

My heart drops. What is this woman going on about? Ashton and I haven't told a soul about our relationship.

"Oh? You think you're smart, do you? No... no... no..." She laughs maniacally. "Ashton really is some clever boy, isn't he? Even I couldn't have come up with a plan like that. Of course, he let me look good, because he knew all along he could use you to come out on top like the golden boy. A sweet, innocent man coming back home to his cookie-cutter small town and the love story that never ended? I know better. He's just a scheming prick."

Her suggesting Ashton is using me to raise his profile in the media is a knife digging into my sternum. It's agony. But there is no way in hell I'm going to let this horror story of an ex talk about him like that. She can say what she wants about me. I don't give a shit what someone with rock-bottom morals thinks about me. But I won't let her talk about Ashton that way.

My blood works up from a simmer, so even though I want to make my way down my front porch steps, I stay put. "He let you have everything you wanted... Ashton has more class in his pinky finger than you'll ever have." I want to say more, but my heart thrums hard, and it's better we end this here. "Get the hell out of here, Chloe." I show her my back, but rage continues to build. "Ashton isn't here. Go back to LA."

Her venomous words waft over my shoulder. "You two will *not* humiliate me."

I turn. I shouldn't have. I should have walked in my home and left it. I should have gone inside, made a cup of tea, or had a shot of bourbon or something to calm down, because I am too hot-headed to deal with a conversation like this. I need to keep Ashton's confidence and I already feel my shield slipping. Chloe knows how to get under a person's skin. Ashton using me? It can't be true... but it hurts like it is.

And it hurts that a small part of me questions whether in her many years as Ashton's wife, she knows something I don't know about him. That she got parts of him I have yet to have. Did she come all this way just to insult me? Just to exchange verbal blows with me? This woman doesn't know I grew up with three brothers. And almost nothing was resolved with *verbal* blows in my house. My body tells me to settle this score with an uppercut.

But I can't do that to Ashton. I can't do that to myself... I have to hold it together, but facing her again was a mistake.

Her snide features, her beautiful skin, and her superiority complex all dissolve my restraint.

Just when I think she can't say anything to make this worse... she does.

"You know why you're going to follow my instructions to leave Ashton alone, *Jolie Hunter?*" She says my name with utter disdain. "I know the Danes' dirty secret. And if you two continue this farce, I'll make sure everyone else knows it."

My mind races for an answer. For a secret about the Danes. For anything at all that will tell me what she's threatening me, us, with right now. I've known the Danes my whole life. This must be an empty ultimatum.

Her expression is smug and cruel and makes me want to scream.

"Oh? Don't tell me Ashton doesn't share everything with his perfect *Joey?* He didn't trust you with his deepest, darkest secret, did he? Well, he trusted me. Turns out the Danes aren't picture-perfect after all. Because Monica Dane was a little whore, and the NFLs favorite quarterback is a bastard child."

Bile fills my throat when she insults Monica like that and... "Fletcher?"

"Oh, there is a brain in there, Scarecrow. Yes, Fletcher Dane is Fletcher... well, something, but he isn't a Dane. He's some immigrant worker's child because it turns out Monica liked spending more time riding than Mr. Dane did."

I feel like my world just tipped upside down and the contents of my life lie at my feet in a jumble. Fletcher and Ashton don't share the same father? Monica cheated? How dare Chloe spout lies like this. How dare she... My eyes sting with anger, my body bubbles with pent-up violence, and the heat that pooled in my guts just seeing Chloe's face on my property has grown into an all-out volcano inside.

She remains seemingly unbothered. "So Ashton didn't trust you with his truth, hmm? Well, he trusted me. His wife. Something you'll never be because you two are ending it today."

I shake my head. "I don't believe you."

"It doesn't matter what you believe, you hillbilly man stealer. It matters what the media thinks, and I have every junket on speed dial."

I speak through gritted teeth where I bite down on the big red button. "You can't do that." I step toward her. I want to swing. I want to lay into her gleaming veneers with the kind of punch that taught me lessons growing up.

"Stay away from Ashton," she commands.

My chest heaves with deep breaths, trying to keep up with the blood supply heavy and aching in my limbs. How dare this woman threaten me? Threaten the Danes? How dare she think she can come into this town and tear it apart? Tear everything I care about in the world away from me with her venom and threats...

I'm spiraling out of control. The pain of this being real, of me in a world without Ashton, takes over all my senses. Something between vengeance and self-defense seizes the last thread of self-control I have within, and before I can think again, I head just inside my house to grab one of the hockey sticks Ashton left. My strides hit the ground hard enough to make craters all the way to where Chloe's white Jeep sits. With the strongest swing I can muster, I whack the stick down hard, smashing one of her headlights.

"What the hell are you doing?" She takes a few steps back.

I go straight to the other one. It explodes under the crack of thunder. I lay into it with the stick.

"You stupid country bumpkin bitch!"

She's grabbing both sides of her face, and she should, because the way I'm feeling, those contoured cheekbones are next.

I raise the stick toward her. "Get the fuck out of here. You hurt Ashton. You threaten to hurt his family. We're done talking. Right now."

Her jaw is wide and slack.

I raise my voice and shout, "Get out of here!" I'm heated. And though I've never hit a woman, I have punched Logan before, and this is exactly how I felt before I did it. "Never come back here. You hear me?"

"Oh, I'll leave, just after I call the cops, you stupid bitch. I'm not scared of you..." But she keeps her eyes on me while she opens the passenger door to grab her cell off the seat.

I step closer, and she cowers against the car.

"You're a blackmailing, slanderous, greedy woman. Get in your car and leave. You're in the wrong place to make threats, Chloe. Nobody is on your side here. Least of all the sheriff."

"Let me guess? You're related. You're all fucking inbred."

I stride one step closer to where she stands, and she tries not to, but she flinches.

My voice is low. "Maybe I should tell the press what *you* really did? Hmm?" I pull my cell from my back pocket. "I recorded this whole conversation."

She tilts her head and narrows her eyes. "You didn't."

I wish I had.

"You wouldn't. You know I still have your boyfriend's little secret in my pocket. And that truth doesn't change no matter what happened here today. Don't treat me like I'm stupid." She heads over to her driver's-side door. "But I'll leave. I'll leave because you're not worth talking to anymore. I didn't come here to see you anyway."

"You *did* come to see me. But don't even think about waiting around town for Ashton. You're leaving now. And I mean now. I will make sure no hotel takes you in, no restaurant serves you food. Your next stop is the airport... or you're sleeping in your car tonight at the town border, and I'll be around to wake you up in the morning with this stick."

She mumbles something that sounds like *cunt* and drives off, tires skidding, broken shards of headlight plastic crunching against the gravel. Catching my breath, I watch the dust settle then, one heavy foot in front of the other, make my way to my house. Once the door is closed and I'm safe inside, the hockey stick falls from my hand and onto the floor with a deafening smack. I breathe sharply through my nose and drag my feet like I'm having an out-of-body experience. At the couch, I allow my body to crumble into the cushions. Diving face-first into a pillow, I can't help it. I scream.

I scream because that woman still has control over Ashton.

I scream because I let myself believe he was mine.

I scream because I'm fucking helpless to get what I want.

And then the tears flow. I hate the warm, wet heat sliding down my cheeks. I hate it because she doesn't deserve my tears but I can't help it. A painful stab of despair thrashes through my chest like nothing matters anymore. I cry out my frustration, wailing loud into the empty space.

Eventually, my sobs become sniffles, and sniffles become a clog in my throat and a tension headache of heartache. I sit up and try to pull myself together. What the hell just happened? Was what Chloe said true? Why wouldn't Ashton have told me? He told this woman, someone he supposedly didn't even love and didn't even know his family well about his secret, and he never told me? Doesn't he trust me?

My phone beeps in my back pocket.

MOM: WE MISS YOU TONIGHT AT THE GAME! BUZZER JUST WENT. I'LL KEEP YOU POSTED WITH THE SCORE.

Staring at her message, I wish I never had to come home tonight. I think about Ashton on the ice. How just last night he put himself on the line to defend my honor all over Eric Larose's face. While he's off there, Chloe was here, waiting for me. Waiting to rip my world to shreds. I swipe through my phone to my missed calls to check again if Ashton left me a voicemail.

None.

I read his text again.

PUP

JOEY — I WILL ALWAYS PUT YOU FIRST.

Instantly, my eyes brim with tears. He didn't put me first. He lied. I never thought he'd lie to me. He had to have known this was coming. He wasn't honest with me, and being caught off guard, letting Chloe rip into me totally unprepared was humiliating. He's never let me down before, and I can hardly even swallow or breathe thinking of how finally, after all these years, Ashton proved he is, in fact, only human. Only a man who makes stupid man mistakes.

I can't talk to him because he's at the game. I can't eat. I can't watch TV. All I can do is cry until my eyes are swollen and I can't even breathe through my nose anymore. He'll be back tonight. I try to stay up until he gets here, but the sheer exhaustion of hopelessness gets the better of me, and I drift off on the couch with reruns of *Gilmore Girls* flashing in the darkness.

249

Chapter Twenty-One

Ashton

I'D NORMALLY BE tired after a long day of hockey, but the insane worry over the conversation I need to have with Joey wins the round. That night, I pull up in front of her house that night, and the white stream from my headlights glint on something on the gravel. I turn off my car, step outside, and use my cell to illuminate the debris.

Broken shards of plastic? I scan my cell in the darkness, looking for something broken in the area, but don't see anything. Walking up the front door, I see all the lights in

Jolie's house are off, but through the living room window, I notice a flicker from her TV. Is she still awake?

Regret at not having talked to Joey before leaving snakes through me. I didn't want to make her worry all night. When I open the door, she's curled up in the fetal position, her Starlight Vets scrubs still on and her tied-back hair falling out around her face in tendrils. I smooth one off her forehead and kiss it.

She startles awake but quickly sees it's me. Her eyes aren't welcoming like they usually are. Her gaze is deep, and that haunted expression I worked so hard to get rid of is back. She's been worrying all day.

"Are you okay?" I ask.

She doesn't answer.

"What's on the driveway? Did you run over something?"

She pushes herself up to sit and draws her knees to her chest. "Chloe was here."

My heart all but leaps to my throat. "Here?" *Fuck.*

She nods.

I ease myself alongside her and wrap my arm around her, but she wriggles like she doesn't want it there, so I pull it back.

"You know I was going to talk to you tomorrow."

"Oh, were you?" She says it like she's not so sure, and it's a sucker punch.

Jolie, as long as I have known her, has never questioned what I tell her.

I inch closer, my thigh connecting with hers. "I was. You know that."

"Is that all we were going to discuss, Ashton?" She's cold, and her walls are up.

And it's no wonder. I know the kind of fork-tongued

creature Chloe is. She has a way with words. A way of sneaking into the one crack of vulnerability in your armor. Of finding your Achilles heel.

"Joey... we have a lot to talk about."

"Pzzt..." She stands, shouldering me, forcing me to get out of her way.

She heads to the kitchen, and I follow her. She fills a cup that was left by the sink with water and takes a long, deep drink. "A lot to talk about is putting it lightly."

I don't really know where to begin. But I hate where this is starting. "I should have warned you Chloe might come."

"Yeah, you think?" She raises her voice. "That was... literally the worst ambush in the world, and you could have prevented it. I'm fucking pissed at you, Ashton! How could you let that happen? Don't you give a shit about me?"

"I didn't know about our picture being on fan sites until I arrived at the arena today. I had no clue she'd know about us until hours ago and I'd already left here."

"Did you ever think of actually leaving me a voice message?" She's escalating.

"I did. I thought about it but I didn't think she'd come here right away."

"Well, you vastly underestimated that woman." Anger glimmers in her eyes, and her words cut deep. "Just like you did when you told her about Fletcher."

Those words shatter over a decade of secrecy. Something untamed releases into the dark between us, because now, she's not the only one who's feeling out of control. Chloe didn't come here just to pull one of her ice-bucket tantrums. She stormed in with wicked fury.

She told Jolie about my brother.

"Is it true?" She softens for a moment. "Is it true about your mom? And... Fletch?"

My nose stings when I recall the day. It was a day that Jolie herself was with me. "Do you remember prom night?"

She shakes her head, clearly wondering where I'm going with this.

"You kept calling me a space cadet. My head was gone. That was the night I found out. I was..." I swallow hard. "I was looking for a bow tie in my dad's drawer, without asking because at that point, I had my own ties and I didn't want him telling me off for forgetting mine at college. I rummaged around, and while I did, a false bottom popped out of place a little." Thinking of that night still makes me sick to my stomach. "As any young guy would, I was curious about the things my dad might hide and, well, it was a bunch of shit I took more than a moment to understand. Patronage affidavits. Paternity tests... contact information for some guy in Mexico, and my brother's name and year of birth on every single, confusing document."

Jolie softens with sympathy but doesn't touch me. "Ashton..."

I continue my story. "And I have no idea how long I stood there in total shock, but my mom came in the room to turn off the light—not knowing I was there. I'll never forget her face when she saw me, with evidence of her darkest moment in my hands. She darted to me, we shared hushed, heated words, and she begged me not to tell my brother, or anyone. She told me they'd managed to keep the secret all these years and urged me not to upend my brother's reality. She begged me. Can you imagine what it would look like to see Monica Dane beg?"

My mom was Starlight Canyon's co-matriarch along with Joy Hunter. These women ran political campaigns, donation drives, volunteered whenever it was needed. They were strong women. My mom was anything but weak. I hated seeing her that day, crumbling, practically hanging off the end of my dress shirt, pleading, praying I would keep it all hidden.

"I was in a hurry to get out the door to prom, to see you, and my mom was desperate with tears of fear and dread... and what else was I to do but promise her? I didn't want to hurt my brother or my mom, even though what she did was wrong. I didn't want to dredge up the past for my dad... so I kept the secret. I only ever told Logan."

"Logan knows?"

I nod. "I told him when I got back to Golden Sierra after prom. It wasn't like I just told him yesterday. I need you to know that."

A mix of emotions, none of them good, swirl between us.

The pain radiating off her shoulders is palpable. "But you told Chloe, too."

"I didn't tell her. I don't know how she knows."

Jolie's anger is back. "You really know how to pick a walking, talking red flag, don't you? Thinking with your dick on that one. That woman is vicious."

I try to take Jolie's hand and bring her into me. I need that closeness now. She needs it, too, but she snatches it away.

"And then you pick me, the low-lying fruit who will blindly follow you anywhere... blindly, like some puppy dog who will never question you, right?"

"Low-lying fruit?" *What is she even saying?* "You're not a low-lying fruit, Jolie. You're my everything. Now and always."

But she's not listening. The thoughts in her head are louder than the ones coming from my mouth.

"You told Logan and you didn't tell me? Don't you trust me? You don't think I can keep a secret? I actually care about you and your family. I've known Fletch as long as I've known you. And you couldn't trust me?"

"I told Logan right after it happened, Joey. I wasn't about to ruin your prom night and offload. Then I never even saw you again until about a month ago." I plead with her to look at the logic here, but that shame is back in her eyes.

The one thing Jolie doesn't like about herself is that people think she's too direct. I don't. I appreciate a woman who can express herself. But me not telling her makes her feel untrusted, and I'm not sure I could have done anything worse to her.

"I was going to tell you, tonight."

"No you weren't." Her eyes are glassy.

"I was! I swear to you. I know I can trust you, it's just... I wanted to figure a way out of this mess before we talked. But—"

"You didn't figure one out?" Her voice is hard.

"No. We'll have to do that together—"

"Together? You know why you couldn't find an answer alone? You didn't figure it out, Ashton, because there is no solution. There is no way out. There is no happy ending here."

"What are you saying? There is... I'll do anything to be with you."

I gather her into my chest, and she makes a move to create distance again. I hold her tightly this time.

"Stop, Joey. Stop fighting me. I'm sorry you're in this. I can't apologize enough times to let you know how much I regret Chloe coming into your world and knowing all this about Fletch. But we're in this together and"—I let out a stale breath, one I didn't realize I've been holding in for over a decade—"we're going to make it no matter what happens around us."

I hold her against my chest, and the weight of her head finally relaxes and falls into me. She's silent, and yet I imagine millions of words, a hurricane in her head, it's tangible beneath my palm. I've always had high self-esteem. Always considered myself to be a person who mostly did the right thing. But in this moment, I hate myself and feel like I made the biggest mistake of my life at the one time it mattered most.

I should have told Joey. Leaving here last night without being transparent was a tragic error. "I should have told you yesterday. Or this morning. I really had the best intentions. You have to believe me. I want to share everything with you. My whole damn world. All my secrets. Not that I have any more... I trust you, Joey. I do." I smooth the top of her head and kiss her sweet, soft hair. "And I need for you to trust me, too."

A warm, wet stain forms on my t-shirt, balmy on my chest. She's crying. Please, no... I made her cry. I stroke her hair and hold her more secure. "I'll do whatever needs to be done. I told you and I mean it. I'll always put you first."

"You lied." She snuffles into my chest.

Her words ache right down to my bones. "I fucked up. But I thought I was putting you first. Don't you think I wanted to talk last night? Of course I did. This has been eating me alive for thirteen years and has been like some sort of acidic torture since I got with you. I wanted to unload last night. I did. But I knew how important it was for you to be clear-headed in the clinic, to feel positive for your first days back. I made the wrong call, but don't say I didn't put you first. It would have been easier to unpack it for me and unload on you then run off to my game."

She snakes her hands around me and finally embraces me, but it doesn't feel like the love from before. Her arms are heavy with sadness and the worst thing in the world. Hopelessness.

I try to unlock myself from her to look her in the eyes, but she holds on tighter when I do it, and I know she doesn't want to let go. She doesn't want to show me her face. A lot like Joey is with trust, I am with promises. She can't handle feeling untrusted. I can't handle breaking a promise. And right now, I'm breaking two. Joey clings to me like I shattered her heart, something I vowed to treasure and protect. And the only way out of this is to break the one I made to my mom.

I have to tell my mom to tell my brother or let her know I will. And just as importantly I need to do all this before Chloe plays any cards. My body aches with selfishness, but it's the only thing to do. "I'm not letting you walk away from me, Joey, so don't even think about it."

My words make her tears flow stronger. Her body shudders in my arms, and I swallow hard, but nothing goes down apart from the rough dry feeling of hurting Joey.

"You know what?" Her words are muffled in my chest. "You'll have to—"

I stiffen. "Have to what?"

"You'll have to walk away from me."

I grab the sides of her arms, I need her honest gaze. I need to see if she means this? She resists me again.

"You need to look at me now, baby girl, because you are talking crazy, and I can only sort this out if we stare each other in the eyes."

She doesn't leave my embrace but peeks up. Her green eyes brim with tears like dewy grass, and I've never seen something more heart-wrenching than the meaning behind them in my whole life.

"We can't be together, Pup."

"How can you say that so easily? You're going to give up?"

My accusation fires her up, and she peels away. Instantly, I regret pushing her buttons with my comment because the sick feeling in my throat tells me that might have been the last time I hold her and I was a fool not to enjoy it for longer.

"Give up?" she asks, defiance in her eyes. "I have loved you for the better part of thirty years. I'm not giving up. I'm finally seeing that what you said on prom night is true. It's some pipe dream between us. We're just a fantasy. A cliché."

"You don't mean that." Her words twist my gut.

She shakes her head, and a tear escapes down her cheek. "No. I don't mean that, but I'm so"—her sobs strangle her words—"so angry. And I'll say anything now to delay what really needs to be said."

My heart fucking stops. This can't be happening.

"I've had hours since Chloe was here to run through the playbook. What could we do to get through this and not hurt anybody? There's no answer, Ashton. None. And I'm angry now. So goddamn angry."

She throws her hands behind her on the counter, and her breasts spill out toward me. They are round and beautiful, and underneath them is the heart I want to reach in and grab and protect. But she's guarded. She's building a wall between us.

She clenches her fist and brings it down with restraint

on the worktop. "I'm angry with your mom for cheating. I'm angry at your parents for keeping your brother's life a lie. I'm furious with Monica for asking her twenty-two-year-old son to let her indiscretion be his biggest secret. I'm angry at you, Ashton. I'm angry at you for choosing someone like Chloe."

My brows pinch so tightly listening to my girl, taking in all her validity. Every ounce of her vulnerability. But it hurts. It kills me.

"But most of all"—her gaze lands on me now, and our eyes connect—"most of all, I'm angry with myself." Tears trickle down, but apart from them tracing rivers on her pink, round cheeks, her face is unmoving and as serious as I've ever seen her. "For not choosing me."

I shake my head. "No. Fuck no. Not happening, Jolie."

"I can't do it. I can't make that decision. I can't be the person who tears Fletcher's world down to build mine up."

"No." I bring her back into me, but her body feels lifeless. "No, Joey. This is not the way this story goes. We make it."

"No we don't, Ashton."

"We do," my words are a plea.

She shakes her head slowly, deliberately, not saying another word but her gaze is filled with terrifying clarity. And then, she says goodbye.

"Can I have one last kiss?"

Time stands still between us. I search every inch of her face for doubt. There is none. And this time I have no answers. I can't save her. I can't save us. She won't let me. So all I can do is... kiss her.

I lower my lips to hers, and they're every bit as warm and soft and loving as the first time my mouth connected with hers. I stay pressed against her, my soul pleading with hers, begging her with my embrace to take my life back into her hands, the only place I ever wanted it to be. But before the spark ignites again, she smothers the oxygen, the fuel and the fire that made life worth living. She leans away from me, leaving a space in between, she draws her lips into a thin line.

Her gaze is lowered and in the distance. Mine is firmly attached to the woman I love. Neither of us speak. The room is so silent and still it's as if death has finally found me.

When the tick of her wall clock becomes audible again, reality resumes, and standing here forever in the dim light of her kitchen isn't going to change anything.

"What do we do now?"

Her voice is weak, but each word lands on me with a mighty crack. "You leave."

"Leave?"

She nods, tears rolling down her cheeks.

"I can't... just leave. And I can't leave you like this."

"I want you to."

"Nothing about the way you look right now tells me you want me to leave, Joey. Don't do this..."

"And don't make this harder than it has to be."

I flare my nostrils. "*Nothing* could make this harder than it already is. I don't want any of it without you, Joey. I don't want Starlight Canyon. I don't want to be in my family, dysfunctional or not. I don't want any of it without you. What's this town without us? It's always been me and you. Right from the start."

My words only make her cry more, and I'm torn between knowing I have to fight and hating that I resurrected her tears.

"I won't. I won't make that decision. I can't pull the trigger, Ashton. I'm sorry."

What can I say? What can I do when I can't give her what she needs? Or what she wants? The pain of turning the page before our chapter is over slices thousands of paper cuts inside me, and I think I might bleed to death from the inside out.

I go to the door, grab my jacket. My bag. And with my head slumped and palm on the handle, I leave her with the only words she needs to know. "Whenever you're alone and you think there's no one burning for you, I'll be burning for you somewhere quietly. Just like I always have. And you always have." I turn to see her one last time before I step out into the empty and unknown world that doesn't include her. "I refuse to move on from this. In this world or the next. Joey. You'd better come and find me. Because I'll be waiting."

Chapter Twenty-Two

Jolie

THE DOOR CLOSES behind the love of my life, and his words swim around inside me, drowning me, making it impossible to breathe. My lungs are heavy with an ocean of sadness. Outside, Ashton's car starts, and his tires grind against the gravel. The sound of his departure claws at me painfully and breaks any strength that holds me together. Tears pour out of my eyes, and I sob loudly, right through the stinging pain of my already raw throat, and the wailing is a desperate voice I don't recognize.

My house feels emptier than it ever has before. My

giant six-five beast will never fill the space with his crooked smile and deep-brown eyes. We'll never play around with either of his sticks, and I won't know where to go when the chips are down. I've never once felt so good in my adult life as when Ashton walked back into it, making me feel something between a carefree kid and the woman I was always meant to be. He made me whole.

I collapse on my couch and throw my face into the cushion that's still a little damp from where I cried myself to sleep watching TV. Now the moment I dreaded has come and gone, and all I can think about is my empty future. I dreamed of being with Ashton all my life. He was the only one to consume my heart and make it beat with the most special purpose in the world- true love. I thought about kissing him from the time I was small and medium and grown and I truly believe I'll ache in my bones when I'm old, the need for him still inside me.

Did I do the wrong thing? I want him back now. All I can think about is that last kiss and how I peeled away way too fast. I want his body back here. I want it back on my couch, in my bed, in my car, at Sly's, eating carrot cake at CCs, skating on pristine winter glass and everywhere. That's where I'll think of him. Everywhere.

The thought of it scares me. The fear of never being happy for the rest of my life is so overwhelming I cry so hard I choke on my tears. And I know... I know we're supposed to be a secret, but darkness is closing in on me, and I think about my mom, and her hand on my forearm, making me promise I wouldn't suffer alone.

I'm falling now. I want to let her catch me and smooth my hair and tell me everything's going to be all right. I won't believe her, just like always, but she'll make me feel better all the same.

Mom went to the game with Colt, Sam, and Eve tonight, and if Ashton is back, they'll be back. It's the night before Thanksgiving... they might still be up.

I look like shit but I'm pretty sure there aren't even smears or mascara crumbs anymore after how hard I've cried. Heading to the kitchen, I take two more long drinks of water. I'm cracked and dehydrated. Moments later, I'm in my car, meandering down the Hunter private road, thankful to my parents for making our ranch a sanctuary.

***

I take one last look in my rearview mirror to make sure I tidied up my eyes as much as possible. They're still a little puffy but the ice cubes I popped on them before leaving the house worked wonders. I almost look normal.

The lights are on in Sam and Colt's house. No doubt I'll be interrupting pre-turkey day meal prep. If I clean myself up good enough, I can pretend my intermittent tears are from the unimaginable amount of onion my mom likes to put in every side dish.

I sit in my car outside for a while. Is being here the right thing? The granny flat my mom lives in to the side of Big Sky is pitch-black. I know the routine on the night before any holiday. My mom always stays up later. Even more so in the years after Dad died. In the window, Colt emerges and peers down at my car. He must have heard me pull up and waves, gesturing for me to come in.

Colt is still up, too? I can't help an audible whine from escaping. I draw in a few deep breaths and prepare myself to be normal and go inside. I can't really talk to them. But I can't be alone either. And now that my brother has seen me, it would be really weird to head home again. So I climb the stairs, draw in a cleansing breath, and open the door.

Warm, succulent smells fill me with an instant comfort upon entering.

"Hey!" Sam glances up briefly from one of many pots on the stove, but doesn't really make eye contact, then finishes stirring. "Wow, you're here late. Why are you up? I thought you were going to try and get more sleep these days?"

"Yeah..." I forgot to think of a reason to be here. I hate lying and don't really do it much, which is probably why it didn't occur to me I might need one, or two, or many right now. I divert. "Can I help with anything? You guys all being out tonight probably ate into your prep time. I don't need to get to bed early since the clinic is for emergency only and I'm not on call. Day off tomorrow."

My mom sits on the sofa in the open-plan living room with Eve and spins to lift her mug of hot cocoa. "Pumpkin spice hot cocoa recipe."

"Is it good?" I ask.

"Not worthy of tomorrow, but decent." Mom keeps her eyes fixed on my face.

She searches me carefully, and I wonder if the ice cubes and touch up in my rearview mirror weren't enough to wipe away the past six hours of heartache.

She pushes herself up from the couch and joins us in the kitchen where Sam and Colt haven't paid me too much attention because they're working on putting things together for the meal. I sit on one of the breakfast bar stools.

Sam puts a plastic sack of peas in front of me and a bowl. "You want to help? Get shelling."

I reach into the bag and take a pod. "Is this necessary? In this day and age?"

Mom arrives by my side and puts her arm around me, kisses my cheek greeting me, and I try not to lean into her motherly embrace, the very comfort I came here seeking. I need to *act* normal to get to normal. Fake it 'til you make it.

Mom grabs a pod and opens it with her nail. "Frozen peas are for weekdays. Nothing but the best for holidays."

Sam blows hair off her forehead after checking the food in the oven. "Right. A couple more minutes for the breadcrumbs."

Colt wraps his arms around Sam. "Mind if I take Eve up to bed? It's late."

"Yeah, the girls are here now. Anyway, we're just about done."

"Don't take your eyes off the onions," he instructs.

"Burnt onion makes everything bitter," Mom adds.

Bitter, like my life.

"I got it," Sam says, not sounding like she has it at all.

It's creeping up on eleven, she's been at work, to and from Santa Fe for a hockey game, and still manages to prep for tomorrow. She is a superwoman. I wish I had her strength. But it's her first big holiday with us, and she must find horse folk crazy. It's tradition to stay up late in our family and get as much done as possible, because when you have a ranch and animals, the morning doesn't afford much free time.

When we were younger, our dad made us help with the horses every single day, and on no condition were we allowed to outsource our horse to the ranch hands. He wanted to instill work ethic. As such, if it was Christmas, Thanksgiving, or any other special occasion, we had to pull long nights to get everything ready because where my dad was immovable about us helping at the ranch, Mom was just as stern about us participating in the kitchen. I guess that's why none of us blink when we have to roll up our sleeves. All us Hunters are industrious. But also maybe why I was unable to see when I'd reached my limits. Grinding is in the Hunter blood.

Mom and I peel open green pods, not complaining about all the work with no reward. Like my lifetime of pining after Ashton Dane, these pods will take an eternity to shell and will be eaten in a millisecond, disappear within an instant, like they never even existed... like they never even mattered...

"Sweetie? You okay?" My mom's soulful, dark eyes reach into me.

But even though at my house I yearned to be held by her and comforted, this isn't the time or place.

One of the hardest things about all of this is that nobody will ever know. I just had the most euphoric, heavenly weeks of my life, and I'll never be able to tell anyone. I'll never be able to relive the memory. All these thoughts of unappreciated peas and having to repress the best thing that ever happened to me make my eyes well up.

"My eyes are dry and tired. Long day. Lots of onions in here."

"You sure?" She's not convinced.

I nod quickly. Too quickly. She narrows her eyes at me. My mom can have a storm of meal prep around her and still see where her calm touch is needed.

She drops her gaze to the peas again. "The boys did well tonight."

The boys. Logan. Ashton... the Scorpions. A lump forms in my throat. I knew they won because before I fell asleep and Ashton got back, my mom texted me the final score. And also, I have NHL and NFL score alerts on my phone.

I'll need to delete that app. Constant reminders of hockey will be excruciating.

"But Ashton seemed very off his game," she adds. "There wasn't one roar for the Great Dane tonight, I tell you. Missed after missed opportunity."

Makes sense.

"And you know, I haven't seen him play so horribly since his senior year in college."

Senior year in college. When he came to prom with me. When he learned about everything.

Guilt starts chipping away at my resolve. It makes me question if me running away, not wanting to be the one calling the shots in Fletcher's life, actually only made Ashton feel, well... all alone. It bubbles inside me like a putrid, squelching swamp, but I can't turn back because I'm stuck in it.

Maybe we should have talked about it for longer. Maybe I shouldn't have been so explosive and extreme about it. But really? What *can* we do? Chloe has a hold on both of us, and in order to break free, we need to hurt someone we both care about.

Mom and I finish shelling, and the bowl has about three tablespoons in it. Mom and I glance at each other, wondering what Sam will say when she realizes that she didn't buy nearly enough. Mom pushes the bowl toward Sam and conceals her amusement.

Sam peeks in the bowl. "Is that it?" Her gaze is full of shock. "I bought two pounds of peas!"

Mom shakes her head, laughing. "That's okay, city girl."

My mom using Colt's nickname for Sam nearly gets a smile out of me.

"We can mix them with frozen just this once," she adds. "But don't tell anyone."

Sam has her hands on her hips. "I feel like I've been cheated."

She puts a bunch of plastic containers on the counter. "Right, let's put these things away, because I think I have about ten more minutes in me before I collapse." She does look exhausted.

Mom stands and walks around to her side of the counter and takes the Tupperware out of her hand. "Go on upstairs, Sammy. Be with your family. Jolie and I will finish and lock up."

"You sure?" She sounds relieved.

I nod. Mom does, too, and Sam pads up the stairs in her fuzzy socks. Mom and I put the food away in silence and find nooks and crannies in the fridge to shove the sides into. I'm working slowly, not wanting to go home at all. I really can't imagine how empty I'll feel walking into my house with Ashton's stick still sitting near the front door and my bed surely smelling like Cool Water, because I made him spray some on my pillow before leaving for the arena this morning.

We finish, and my Mom considers me.

"It's late. Why don't you slumber at mine tonight if you don't have work tomorrow? Saves you driving back here in the morning to muck out Ted."

I don't have any pajamas and I'd need to change out of my scrubs before doing Ted anyway, but the look in my mother's eye tells me she knows that already and she's making excuses for me, so I don't have to.

I'm so grateful for her. The relief at not having to be alone tonight is overwhelming.

Half an hour later, I curl up on my side of my mom's queen bed wearing the biggest PJs she could find, but my ankles and calves stick out the bottom. She puts on *Sex and the City* which was her go-to show in the years after my dad died. I see why. Those women are real and flawed but badass and always get back up when they're knocked down.

About midnight, my mom leaves the room, and when she returns she has a hot water bottle for me. "It's bedtime. I got this for you."

The fuzzy warmth adds solace to this space. It's the best thing I'd ever be able to ask for right now.

She turns off the light, and I stare into the darkness, eyes adjusting slowly. I hug my hot water bottle. When my eyes can see clearly again, they focus on a little picture next to the bed on the side table. It's of my mom and dad with one of our old horses. They're young and happy in that picture.

Guess nothing lasts forever.

And some things don't last nearly long enough.

Chapter Twenty-Three

Ashton

Opening my eyes the following morning, I'm still breathing shallowly in my childhood bed surrounded by everything that reminds me of good times. Years when everything was simple and all I would have had to do for a lifetime of happiness was say yes to Jolie at prom. Last night, regret poured into me, and now my body is heavy and as thick as concrete. I have no idea how I'm going to make it through Thanksgiving today. How did I get myself into this position?

Jolie is right on so many levels. My mom fucked up and

asked her son to shoulder a burden far too big. I have no idea how I'm going to look her in the eye and not experience some kind of tension. But I really blame myself more. If I didn't pick Chloe, if I wasn't fooled by the excitement of Hollywood and her promises of paradise, none of this would have happened.

In my life, whenever I'd do something wrong or a bad thing happened, I'd always have a future moment when I'd think that mistake or challenge shaped me for the better. That will never happen in this circumstance.

By ten, when I know I should rise because the clatter of Thanksgiving preparation dances up the stairs and under my doorframe, I'm still facedown on my bed in my boxers, thirsty but too depressed to even get myself a goddamn drink of water.

My phone beeps. It takes me until it goes off a second time to peel my creased face off my pillow and have a look.

PUCK BOY

SO WHAT HAPPENED WITH JOJO LAST NIGHT? HOPE IT WENT WELL.

Shit. The Hunters always have Thanksgiving lunch, and soon, he'll be back in the Canyon after staying in the city. He'll see what I did to his sister. Flashes of Joey's face flicker in my mind—her red-rimmed eyes. Her pink nose and puffy lips swollen from crying. Over *me*. Over *my* stupid decisions.

Logan will be livid. But part of me is grateful Joey will have someone to talk to about it all. As much as I'd like to pretend this is all a terrible dream, I can't play dead forever, so I tell Logan what happened.

ME

> CHLOE CAME YESTERDAY. JOLIE ENDED
> IT WITH ME.

The ellipsis coming from Logan's typing and presumably erasing and typing again lasts forever. But I don't care. There is no reason to get out of bed today anyway. It's not like I'm in a hurry to get up and live life. Not even for my dad's insane gravy that I could drink straight.

Finally, my phone beeps.

> PUCK BOY
>
> WHAT'S YOUR PLAN?

For the first time in hours of being comatose, I sit up. My plan? What the hell does he think I'm going to do? Jolie doesn't want to hurt Fletcher. And understandably, she doesn't want to be dragged through the mud. *I* don't want her dragged through it. Chloe has a good relationship with the press, and I know what kind of damage she could do.

> PUCK BOY
>
> IF YOU GIVE UP NOW, I'M NOT GOING
> TO BE YOUR BEST MAN. AND MY
> SPEECHES ARE THE BEST.

Logan's positivity almost makes me feel better, until I realize that any sweeping, grand gesture to get Jolie back involves dealing with Chloe, or hurting my family, more likely both. I've already run through every possible reverse blackmail situation I could muster. There are a few. Chloe isn't such an innocent little sweetheart. She's done drugs in the bathrooms at parties. She got caught shoplifting when she was nineteen so, it's on her record. And, of course, she cheated on me, not the other way around.

But none of that changes the information she has about Fletcher.

PUCK BOY

MEET ME AT THE POND BEFORE FOOD STARTS.

The pond is more like a gigantic puddle than anything, but the thing about it is, being so shallow, it usually freezes over early, and Logan and I would get to mess around on its uneven surface and tight space even when our parents wouldn't take us to the most local ice rink.

ME

BE THERE IN TWENTY.

After sneaking past my mom while she had her head in the pantry and Dad was outside fetching logs, I arrive at the pond. Logan is already parked up and skating on its brown surface where he set up a few sticks and jumps over them.

I sit at the edge of my car and lace up my skates, then head over with my stick. Logan and I have been here a million times before. I know the drill. He'll have a puck out there, and we'll pass it back and forth. Talk. Sure enough, he skates to the side, grabs his stick and a puck, and by the time I step onto the rippled and unevenly frozen surface, he sends a pass my way.

The black biscuit slips across the ice in hypnotic motion, back and forth. Our focus is on the puck, and yet our muscle memory allows us to do this with ease and relax into the action as a meditation. Some have walking therapy. Logan and I have the pond. We've had some of our best chats here. But it's been a long, long time. The last one we had was the day we realized we were being signed by different teams and wouldn't play together anymore.

That was a day full of joy and melancholy. Today, I just have melancholy.

Logan pushes the puck over. "One thing I know about you, bro…" He receives my return pass because we're only several feet apart. "Is that you always know the right thing to do."

"I'm stuck this time."

"Talk me through the options."

I receive the puck and we begin the methodical movement back and forth between us, a hockey player's hypnotherapy. "I can put the shits up Chloe and threaten her back."

"Not your style." He flicks the puck back to me.

I hold the biscuit on my blade for a moment, along with my thoughts, then pass again. "Or I could take away her leverage."

Logan steadies the puck and gazes at me. "That's a bold move. You'll tell Fletcher yourself?"

"It's the only solution I thought possible before Jolie told me she doesn't want in this mess."

He tilts his head. "Is that what she said? She doesn't want part of this? That doesn't sound like my sister to me."

I shrug. "She didn't want to make the decision. She said she couldn't choose to tear down Fletcher just to build us up. Pretty much her words verbatim."

He nods. "That's fair enough, though. She doesn't want to be the one to decide or be the reason for the mess. Most women wouldn't be strong enough to walk away for someone else's good. I know. I've met more than my fair share of selfish people." He cocks his eyebrow. "Myself included."

He hits the puck back again. It catches on a ripple and glides to the edge. I skate to fetch it and turn sharply back, facing Logan.

"I wanted her to fight, though."

Admitting this out loud to another man makes me feel weak, but right now, I'm so rock-bottom I'm not sure there's anywhere lower to go.

He flaps his lips. "You think Jojo won't fight once you make the decision? It sounds more like you're having a pity party and dodging the hard stuff. Look, it's your decision to make. It sucks when we come to those crossroads, where nobody else can decide for us. I know you can be decisive. Hell, you already said you pretty much decided you have to tell Fletch. But you've always had another problem altogether."

"What's that?"

Logan always comes across playful and happy-go-lucky, but he gives me that other part of him right now that has always made him my best friend. Somewhere under his layers of party animal is a man with true maturity and wisdom and the guts to say what needs to be said. "You think every decision is either right or wrong, Ashton. You think there's some reward for one thing and damnation for the other. That's not how life works. You make a decision then you work around that decision. There's no right or wrong, bro, just a series of possibilities."

"And consequences."

"Fine, Negative Nancy. And consequences. My point is, you'll work it out either way. First you need to decide if you want freedom. And Jolie."

My words tumble out. "There's no life worth living if I'm not with Jolie."

Logan stops dead. "Wow."

"Yeah."

We stare at the brown ice for a moment while it sinks in that I'm in love with his sister.

I let out a long, slow breath. "I need to figure out the right time to drop the bomb."

Logan scoffs and shakes his head. "You're a slow learner."

I laugh lightly. "You're telling me there is no right time, Jedi Master?"

"Wrong." He picks the puck off the ice and points it at me. "The right time is always now."

"Says the most self-indulgent person I know."

"Hey. I got a smile on *my* face." He skates backward, his cocky, charming grin on full display. He's so damn carefree. But when he gets to the end of the glorified puddle, he skates back toward me and snows me when he stops. "I'm not making light of this, bro. I know it's going to fuck things up for your family. But in the infinite possibilities of decisions, I typically choose the truth."

He puts a hand on my shoulder, and that's what I've always liked about Logan. He brings light to everything he touches. He acts aloof and devil-may-care but he is one solid man. I've known what I needed to do since the minute Jolie and I kissed. I have known that hiding and waiting for Chloe to forget about me and her pride was not only stupid but cowardly. And I'm anything but a coward.

I know I can support Fletcher if this all goes public. Hell, my own media disaster is still recent news, so I have experience with it. But there's still a doubt in my mind now, now that Joey dumped my ass. "What if Joey doesn't want to be part of it? What if I do all this and she doesn't come back?"

"Well then, dude, you at least have freedom. And so does your brother, even though he might not at first believe it." He steps off the edge of the pond. "And once you clear this up, I am *so* telling the press that Chloe nailed that nasty old fucker."

A grateful laugh leaves my lips.

Logan and I wrap up the bromance and head back to our families for turkey. Even though Logan propped me up, I still have to drink a lot to numb both my urge to pull my parents aside and the pain of not seeing Jolie at all today. I text her to say Happy Thanksgiving, and she texted me back a pumpkin pie meme. It felt flat.

After my cousins and aunts and uncles and I wash up all the dishes, we sit down to watch the Thanksgiving football game my brother happens to be playing in. My eyes sting considering how much his life is going to change. How the man on the screen is about to turn inside out. Not even my straight bourbon dulls the sick feeling I have or quiets the demons in my head telling me I'm being selfish.

But by the time I crawl in bed, alone, my arms aching with the absence of the woman I love, I'm determined as ever to start a new chapter. For me. My family.

And with Jolie.

Chapter Twenty-Four

Jolie

I NEARLY CRY when Colt offers me a bourbon after dinner. It makes me think of Sly's, a moment that now feels so long ago. It's a lifetime away with a lifetime of problems in between. I can't face going home to my empty house and decide to crash at my mom's again, an easy excuse to make because I've had too much to drink to drive. Sadly, not enough to forget Ashton.

When I wake up in the morning, fresh coffee is brewing, and the cozy scent of toast encircles me. I crawl out of bed, keeping the warm duvet wrapped around my middle.

The weight of one too many drinks and helping myself to thirds adds to my impossible sadness. I drag my socked feet to the kitchen.

"Jolie Aiyana Hunter. Don't dirty my blanket on the floor." My mom gestures to the bottom of it.

I gather it up and bunch it around me when I sit on one of her kitchen chairs. It's a modest place compared to Big Sky, the house I grew up in and what Colton now lives in. Hell, it's a small place compared to where I live, too. "Do you like living here?"

She places toast on two plates, butters it with her back to me. "Love it. Not much cleaning. Warm in the winter. I don't want a lot of extra space."

"I get that." Neither do I. Especially when that space is empty.

She places a cup of joe and the plate with toast down in front of me, then hers opposite, and takes a seat. "Sorry it's nothing fancy, but I'm done cooking for a day or two. And we're going to be having all that party food later today for Ron's birthday."

I crunch down on my toast, grateful for something plain and simple after all the rich food last night. I consider not talking about it now but I can't go to Ron Dane's party. "I'm not going."

My mom stares at me over her steaming cup of coffee, occasionally blowing the warm wisps of air to cool it. She considers me, and I sit in silent wonder, waiting for her reply.

"Interesting."

Interesting, it is. Because me not going is loaded with backstory, and she knows it. For as long as the Danes and Hunters have been friends, we have shared a lot of big moments together. It's Ron's sixtieth and a big deal, too, because the guy had a heart attack a couple of years ago.

I chew slowly. It's cowardly. But I can't face Ashton.

"It would make sense to skip out if you were still in New York not just down the dirt road. Are you going to tell me why you aren't going?" Mom asks. "I'll venture a guess it has something to do with these sweet sleepovers we're having. Which I love, by the way. Just... curious."

I sigh. "I've been down in the dumps the past few days. I didn't tell you but I was seeing someone. Just testing the waters with him. And..."—a lump forms in my throat as I try to downplay my feelings—"and it's not going to work out, so I'm bummed. I started to have serious feelings for him. You know how it goes, seeing as you watch more reality TV than anyone I know."

Her gaze tells me I've just been sassy. "I don't need to watch reality TV to know how that feels. I wasn't born yesterday..." She waits for a beat, staring at me intensely. "Ashton?"

His name falls from her lips like a bomb. It blasts through my thin veneer of protection, the veil of strength I've been hiding under, and my eyes instantly brim with tears. My voice is high and squeaky. "Why would it be Ashton?" I laugh meekly, but it's the type that gives everything away.

"I know, honey." She takes my hand in hers.

She knows?

"How?" I thought we were careful.

"Monica found a condom wrapper on the ground in one of her outbuildings. Nobody but you and the Danes have a key to that barn."

I pull in a sharp breath. I'm both mortified and wish I

could melt back in time to live that moment all over again. I wince. "Embarrassing."

"Oh please, Jojo... Mon and I have seen it all. She used to find dozens of foils around when Nick and Randy worked at Moon Ridge. It was like *Brokeback Mountain*."

I bury my face in my hands. My words come out as a plea. "Mom..."

Her hand falls to my head and strokes my hair. "You want to tell me what happened?"

"I can't."

She tips my chin up. "Are you sure about that? A problem shared is a problem halved."

"I really can't. But all that matters anyway, is after wanting Ashton my entire goddamn life, I finally had him. And now I don't."

"Did he do it? I mean..."

"Break it off?" It's the first time I really think about it. It's been a whirlwind of emotion since I was blindsided by Chloe. And even though I told myself he didn't want me and that's why he was keeping secrets, the truth is, I ran away. I lift my head again and face her. "It was me."

She takes my hand. "Well, give me the gist so you can get it off your chest."

"It's pretty much a problem with..." I search for a way to explain that's both the truth and not exposing too much. "It's his ex."

Mom stiffens in her chair. I'm sure Monica told her about Chloe being the actual cheater in the situation. "No daughter of mine is going to allow a scandalous woman like that to stand in the way of her and her happily ever after. Is she?"

"It's complicated, Mom."

"I don't give a rat's ass how complicated it is, Jolie. You

can walk away of your own free will, but don't let yourself be pushed away by... *her*." She says it as though she witnessed firsthand what I did two nights ago.

"There's more. More that I can't tell you. The whole thing is bigger than me and Ashton."

She shakes her head like I just said something stupid. "Is he the one?"

"What?"

She repeats. "Is Ashton the one?"

Never in my life have I ever had eyes for another. "He's always been the one, Mom. You, of all people, know that."

She scoots her chair closer, wraps her arm around me, and gazes at me deeply. "If he's the one, it's time you heard this—a universal truth that exists in every single union of soulmates, every marriage, every forever love. If he's the one, then there is *nothing* bigger than you and Ashton. Not now. Not ever. Couples that are so-called meant to be are the ones who went through things that should tear them down, but they come out stronger than before. You gotta fight for it, my girl. And judging by the look of that jezebel, I reckon you can take her."

Her words make me laugh, but it very quickly transforms back into a gentle cry. "It's going to be hard, Mom. Really hard."

"It always is." She shakes her head, her eyes distant with memories. "It always is..."

Her voice trails off, and I'm sure she's thinking about dad.

"But every couple comes up against those us-against-the-world decisions. You have to be united. Stand together."

My mom is right. And I let Ashton down. I dropped the gloves when he needed me to fight in his corner.

Mom rubs my back. "When was the last time you talked to him?"

"He texted me 'Happy Thanksgiving. I love you.'" I shake my head, chastising myself for not saying something significant. "I texted him a pumpkin pie meme back. I didn't know what to say."

"Well, he probably took that as good news." She tightens her arm around me. "Pies are fun and games, right?"

My mom earns a soft laugh. "Seriously, do you read the urban dictionary or something?"

She shimmies her shoulders. "My book club. I know more than what pie is."

I let out a stale sigh and experience a million different feelings at once. Most of all, I wonder if after my dramatic departure from his life, asking for one last kiss... will he ever give me another?

Just then, my mom's doorbell rings. She rushes over and opens the door to Shay, Starlight Canyon's favorite baker and all-around wonderful human. If I didn't already admire her for her excellence in the kitchen, I would for her character. I used to think she and Logan were cute, but after what she's taken on in the past years, her integrity makes Logan seem like a degenerate.

Shay has a large cake box in her hands. "Special delivery!" she says brightly.

I guess, like the rest of us, she didn't nearly drown in a gravy boat last night.

"Come on in, sweetie. Oh!" Mom rushes to her small table and clears her own toast and coffee out of the way for the cake box. "Just here."

Shay puts down the box, and I stand to hug her, too, holding the duvet off the floor with one hand. I haven't seen her nearly enough since coming back to the Canyon. But she has every excuse to be busy since becoming a mom. I still can't believe what happened to the Mendez family. Shay's reaction to tragedy put her right up there in the pantheon of women I admire. She took on the world.

Yeah. Logan doesn't deserve her.

"How are you?" I ask.

"Business is crazy." She hesitates for a beat but wears a strange smirk. "But you...." She twirls her finger in the air in front of me, pointing at me like I'm the plat du jour and she'll take a slice of me. "You have been reeeeeally good."

Everything about the way Shay is smiling at me is weird. First of all, I have been the total opposite of good, and she's ogling me like I just won the lottery. Second, she's making goo-goo eyes or something.

"Why are you looking at me like that?" I pull the duvet up around my middle a bit higher.

"Becaaaause..." She draws out the word, waiting for me to interject.

But I'm not sure what she's expecting me to say.

"Because yoooou..." She waits another beat for me to complete her sentence. "And Ashton?" She's beaming ear to ear now.

Meanwhile, my jaw falls to the floor. It's not the response she expected, and her eyebrows pinch together instantly.

"Oh..." She flicks her eyes back and forth between me and my mom. "Are you and Ashton not...?"

I glare at my mom.

She puts her hands up innocently. "I don't know what she's talking about."

Mom didn't tell her? Monica? I know there's some evidence out there but it's not the kind of news Shay probably reads. Ashton said it was on fan sites and even I don't read those anymore.

Shay is embarrassed. "Sorry, Jolie... I overstepped. I just thought..." It seems like she's going to drop it but then picks the conversation back up again. "So you're not dating? I was just happy for you, that's all, not prying exactly. I just knew, you know, when we were younger..."

When Shay dated Logan, she was always so nice to me, and I confided in her, the least secret-secret in Starlight Canyon, that I then wanted to marry Ashton Dane.

I don't want to make her feel awkward. But I have to deny it. Even though I have no idea where Ashton and I stand right now, I made a commitment. "Why do you think we're together?"

Shay has the most beautiful, flawless tawny skin, but blotches of crimson dot her cheeks now. "No reason."

I tilt my head to the side, urging her to cough it up.

She mumbles while pushing hair behind her ear. "Puck bunny news dot com."

"A puck bunny fan site?" I blurt.

The blush creeps down her neck.

"Sorry, not judging, I'm just surprised," I say. "One—because I haven't read those sites since college and..." *Shay does?* I guess she still has a thing for hockey boys even more than I do. "Sorry, I... but what made you think we were together?"

"There was a picture of you and Ashton. On there and..." She mumbles again. "A couple other fan sites."

She fumbles around in the purse slung over her shoulder, giving me a few sheepish glances while she pulls something up on her cell. She leans in next to me, showing me a photo of Ashton and... me. "This is you, right? If not, he's only just gone and searched the world for your twin."

My misery has been so thick I haven't bothered to search for the photo of us that ended up online. *The Blackhawk Ice Rink*. There was nobody there. Ashton bought every ticket on sale to give us privacy. It was deserted apart from a couple of employees... one of which clearly didn't realize the point of buying a place out.

She takes her phone back and considers the picture closely again. "I swore that was you." She's apologetic and confused. She offers a kind smile. "But you're so much prettier."

During our conversation, my mom has gone to do something in her bedroom and now peeks her head out. "Sorry to interrupt you ladies, but Jolie, I need you to drive me to the Superstore for a few more balloons. Mon just texted it looks empty around the buffet table." She's saving me.

Shay drops her phone back into her handbag and appears as fine with ditching the conversation as I am. "Enjoy."

Mom says, "I wish you could come, sweetie."

"Yeah, I appreciate the invitation. But Antonio has soccer practice."

"The day after Thanksgiving?" I'm surprised.

"His coach is very serious. And so are the parents. It's like a cult, and they talk on the sidelines about whether the kid is good enough for the team or not all the time. Like it's the pros or something. Anyway, he can't miss it. Have to show that commitment."

"He's four," I say but wonder if I sound like I know nothing about kids now. "It's soccer for four-year-olds."

"Almost five, if you ask him. But after his uncle came to visit from Mexico, Antonio is mad about *football*." She makes air quotations. "He makes me call it football now. That's what they call the sport everywhere but here."

"Well, you'll be missed." My mom's words politely urge Shay to leave.

"Have fun tonight." She heads to the door but hitches her thumb toward the cake box. "There's a card taped to the box for Ron."

"I'll make sure he gets it."

When the front door clicks shut behind Shay, I bury my face in my hands.

Mom still doesn't get everything. "It *was* you in the picture? Please tell me it was you in the picture."

I nod, head still hung. My heart crackles all over again seeing how happy we were just days ago. How hopeful I was... before I knew.

My mom ushers me and my big mushy duvet back into her bedroom, and we sit on the edge of her bed. "I still think you should come. Don't let this fester."

"I can't be there all day. I'm not going to bring drama to Ron's party."

"Come toward the end. The boys have a string of away games starting again on Saturday. You can't leave it 'til then, Jolie."

She's right. I don't even want to. From the moment Ashton left my house, I wanted to run back to him, take it all back, change my mind, tell him I'm sorry... but each time I told myself that, I was reminded of Fletcher. Of Monica. Of everyone in this town and all over the country knowing the Danes' business. It's big.

But like my mom says, if Ashton is the one, nothing is bigger than us.

Bone-chilling dread sends a shiver down my spine. I was the one who suggested we can't hurt Fletcher. What if Ashton has had time to think more and now he agrees with me? What then? Do we carry on a secret relationship forever? Or worse... will Ashton decide it's better we are apart? "What if he doesn't want me back?"

"I have no idea what has transpired between you two but what have I always said?" She hugs me tight. "I'll catch you, sweetie."

Chapter Twenty-Five

Ashton

I LOVE MY DAD. And when I watch him step foot onto the linoleum floor of this basement he created as a sanctuary for his two boys, and see his surprise and the tear in the corner of his eye, I'm so grateful he's still with us. But an hour later, the music grates on me. I have no interest in making conversation. And the beer I'm holding is still three quarters full and warm because I've mostly spent my time concentrating on the stairs, the world spinning around me.

Several hours into my dad's birthday party, the amount of balloons and confetti popper shred made our cavernous basement recreation room look like a soft play area you could fall down in and not get hurt. Color, smiles, laughter, and music fill the air, but none of it infuses me with the least bit of light.

I watch the stairs all goddamn day and bite my tongue from asking the Hunters present if Jolie is coming. I don't bring her up, but I swear Sam keeps looking at me funny like she's either assessing me as the whodunnit in a game of Clue or she knows something she shouldn't. She doesn't seem the type to be checking out those puck bunny sites, but she knows enough teenage girls, her daughter included, and if just one person in this town reads that blog, it won't take long for news to spread.

Then, I'll have to relive losing Jolie all over again as every granny I cross paths with, and every old classmate at Sly's, asks if she and I are together. The mere thought of my mouth forming the word 'no' makes my heart pang with wanting and regret.

The one person I could ask straight is Logan, who doesn't know for sure. I make him text her, and she answers him: *Probably later*.

Later.

Every minute that passes seems like it should be later because even though she told me we had to end it, my life doesn't feel normal without her, especially not here in Starlight Canyon. It's like the party takes place in slow motion time lapse, and between every frame, my eyes are on the stairs leading out of our basement, seeing her appear with that wild smile on her face.

What have I done? Why did I let myself walk away? Now that the shock of Chloe's arrival and Jolie's words have worn off, I kick myself for ever leaving her house that night. I should have fought even harder.

I want to fight now.

"Achy Breaky Heart" comes on. My parents pushed our pool tables and lounge sofas along the walls so there would be a makeshift dance floor. Guests flock to it to do a line dance. Maybe this is my chance to make an exit.

But Joy Hunter comes to stop me. "You're not going to dance, cowboy?" She does a step ball change, trying to bring a smile to my face.

I give her a meaningless, polite, thin-lipped grin which is all I can muster. "I'm tired. Just one of those days." I drink my beer, and it tastes like piss.

She threads her arm through mine and stands alongside me. I've known Joy for as long as I can remember knowing people. She took care of me for two days while I had chicken pox and my parents were calving. She would bring me the same hot chocolate any morning she drove Logan and I to practice. I was close to her.

Close enough for me to read between the lines when she starts talking.

"Jolie stayed over with me the past two nights. I get the impression she's pretty beat up about something."

I'm frozen, not only with the fact that Joy just basically told me she knows about us in other words, but also thinking about Joey being so upset she can't be alone. Though I'm glad she decided not to be, I would rather her be in my bed. In *my* arms.

Joy stares out at everyone dancing but continues talking. "Good news is today I think I knocked some sense into her."

I simply listen.

"She had this strange notion that relationships are easy. I don't know where she got that from, but they sure as hell aren't." She squeezes my arm tightly with hers. "I got through to her. She's not as stubborn as people think. Just...

a volcano. She explodes like thunder but she sure is worth the show."

My God, that woman is a show. Jolie has always loved living. She has sunflowers for eyes and fireworks in her soul. "Yeah. She's... special." I have to keep it curt or I'll get choked up thinking about her.

Joy talking about her now is making my mouth dry. Is this code for me and Jolie actually getting a chance to talk? I hoped for it. I've known Joey for a long, long time, and one thing I know is she can be volatile. I want to let Joy's not-so-subliminal messages give me hope.

We stare at my cousins and aunts and friends of the Canyon, dancing in a line. Laughing. Missing steps.

I put my beer down on the table behind me. "Sorry, Joy, I'm going to head up to my room. I think I ate too much yesterday and just need to lie down."

"Okay, sweetie." She pats my arm. "You feel better now."

"Thanks." I turn to leave.

But she calls my name. "Ashton?"

"Yeah?"

"You know that thing fathers do when they show their daughter's boyfriend their shotgun?"

Age-old story. I lift my brows with an affirmative.

She smiles, reminiscent of her tough, sassy daughter. "Jolie's dad isn't here. And I don't have a shotgun. But... you know what I'm saying." She cocks an eyebrow. "Don't you, dear?"

I know exactly what she's saying. Hurt Jolie, and Joy will come running with torches and pitchforks. But I've already hurt Joey. And a lot more people will hurt, too, so even though deep down I know Joy is well-meaning and has given us her blessing, the story is thicker than she knows.

Up in my room, I have a hockey puck in my hand that I toss up an inch and catch. Over and over again. It's a meditative movement that sometimes helps me zone out when I'm stressed. The weight of the puck, the soft slap of it in my palm, can sometimes be soothing. But not today. The music winds its way up two floors to my room, and it's pissing me off. I grip the puck and pull out my phone to look at property listings within an hour of the Canyon again to pass time until I can leave the house without anyone noticing and knock down Jolie Hunter's goddamn front door.

We need to talk.

"Knock, knock." My mom eases my door open. "Hey. Fletch just arrived downstairs, so it's time to sing 'Happy Birthday' and cut the cake. You should come down."

I don't say anything. I can hardly look my mom in the face at this point. I managed on Thanksgiving to act normal, having a big dose of booze, but now I'm sober, and anger simmers beneath the surface, because for the past thirty minutes, the main question running through my head is— why should *I* have to be the one to tell my brother?

My mom did this. She was the one who strayed. Who made the mistake, albeit the best mistake of her life because I don't know anyone who doesn't love Fletch. But... fuck...

She considers me for a moment before saying, "I thought Jolie would be here by now."

And that's when I pop. "No, Mom, Jolie isn't coming tonight." I'm seething.

"I..." Obviously, she's had some sort of talk behind my back with Joy Hunter because she brings the same optimistic banter to the situation. "I thought you two were getting along really well these days?"

I glare silently at the puck in my hand so I don't send disrespect in my mom's direction.

"Ashton? Did something happen with Jolie?"

"No, Mom." I put the puck on the bed and push myself up to face her. "It's more about what *didn't* happen with Jolie that's the problem."

"You two have been together and…" She shakes her head back and forth, asking for me to finish her sentence.

"And a secret from thirteen years ago broke us apart."

She looks confused. Unlike me, I'm guessing she hasn't been thinking about this on a daily basis.

"Do you want to know why I let Chloe paint me like a jerk with the press? Why did I give her more than half my money even though she doesn't need it? Or deserve it for that matter?"

Dread is painted all over my mom's face. But she has no idea. No idea just how bad this is about to get. I am shaking from the inside out.

"Chloe knows about Fletcher."

The penny still hasn't dropped, because she's buried her secret six feet under. Her gaze tells me she has no clue what Chloe could know about perfect boy Fletcher. She'd never imagine my ex-wife could know about something that was hidden long before I even met her. I feel like screaming. Shouting. Yelling at my mom for bringing this on me. Logan was right. It's my responsibility to make a decision now, but Jolie was right, too. My mom should have never done this to me. To my dad. To any of us.

I wish she'd put it all together, but she still stares at me, waiting for me to put her out of her misery.

I speak cold, hard words, my jaw tightens, and I say all I need to for my mom to understand. "I guess Chloe must have needed a tie."

"A tie?" Confusion sparks in my mom's eyes.

I watch her carefully, as slowly, the questions drain and her brown eyes fill with terror and the answer to her question.

"That's right. Chloe knows everything. And when I said I wanted a divorce, she made the incorrect assumption that I'd go to the press and talk about her affair. I wouldn't have. But she made sure that would never happen. She hung our family's secret over my head and said if I ever leaked the reasons for our split and put anything other than irreconcilable differences on our paperwork, she would have a story of her own."

My mom claps a mortified hand over her mouth. "But then she told everyone you cheated?" Shame coats her words. "Why?"

"Because she *could*, Mom. She did it because she could. Because when you mess up and don't own up, you lose your power. You lose your right to speak. To move on. And to fall in love ever again... and that, Mom. *That's* why Jolie isn't here."

I know Mom doesn't understand everything, but she understands enough.

Still, as I'm finally able to unload a conversation I've carried around with me for over a decade, I'm not done putting down the most vulnerable one of all. It's a selfish thought. It's a weak thought. But I've felt it many times nonetheless. "You chose one son over another asking me to keep your secret. And that I could understand. Fletcher's life would be vastly different, and in your eyes, mine would go relatively unchanged. It wasn't right, and yet, a part of me can reach in deep and understand why you asked me to keep quiet."

Mom's eyes mist over, but she's a stoic woman who holds it together until I say the next words.

"Yeah. I understand how me hanging on to the truth about Fletcher seemed the lesser of two evils. But you chose to protect Fletcher even though it put a burden on me. I love my brother. I don't want him hurting any more than you do. But what's really bad is you choosing yourself because you never once admitted this whole thing is about you, too."

She comes to her own defense. "I should never have put this on you but I wasn't thinking about me, Ashton. I saved those papers to protect your brother. I could have just put your dad's name on the birth certificate and been done with it. It was legal and binding to do that, and nobody would have had to know. But I worried that not having access to his real dad could one day be a mistake. What if Fletch got sick with some disease and needed... I don't know... a kidney or something? I tried to do the right thing by keeping in contact with—" She stops herself short of saying his name. "It would have been *more* selfish to have never told you, your dad, *or* Fletcher about his real father."

And just then, her gaze slides over my shoulder, and horror paints her features. I spin quickly, and there he is, a sick, almost nauseated expression on his face.

Fletcher.

"Sweetie..."

"My real father?" he says, as confused as he is disbelieving. "What the hell does that mean? My real father?"

I'm too stunned to speak. Even though my plan was to ensure my mom and dad told Fletch the truth or else I would, him thinking he's coming home to a happy family affair and finding me and Mom coming to blows over this would have been the last way I would have planned to deal with it.

My mom races over to his side and grabs his arm which he quickly pulls away.

"Tell me what the hell is going on here."

I try in vain. "We can talk about this later. Let's go celebrate with Dad."

"Dad? As in the man who raised me or this other father you're talking about?" He's angry. "No, Ashton. I need to know what the hell you two were talking about here. I heard my name. I heard—" He hangs his head then peers up from under pinched eyebrows. "Tell me."

The strain of holding in years of secrecy drains out of my mom's body. A soul-stirring calm fills her eyes, and she says to me, without taking her gaze off my brother, "Go on down, Ashton. Light the candles and sing 'Happy Birthday.'"

Even though it really is my mom's story to tell, right now, seeing her like this, full of shame and heartache, I want to step in and save her from this moment. I want to tell him for her, because I know she's going to cry. *He's* probably going to cry.

But instead, I do what needs to be done. There's a house full of people downstairs and a beautiful, caring man who cheated death down there celebrating his second chance at life. That's where I'm needed. Before I leave, I wrap my arms around Fletcher's frozen body and pat his back with silent affection.

I'm almost out the doorway. My mom stops me.
"Ashton."
I turn. "Yeah?"
"When you're done with the cake, go find Jolie."

Chapter Twenty-Six

Ashton

Joy, Colt, and I light the candles as quickly as we can. With sixty, we need all hands on deck so the first doesn't burn down before the last is lit. We manage to get the last one done, and Colt shakes the match out—it clearly burnt his fingertip a little, but he is still the first to burst into loud song. The DJ turns the music down, and everyone joins in.

"Happy birthday to you..."

God, I can't wait to get to Joey.

"Happy birthday to you..."

All I can think about is her, and that's when I see a pair

of cowboy boots appear at the bottom of the stairs like I manifested them, because even without the rest of her, I know it's my woman. Next, I see her thighs in tight jeans, and her perfect, womanly waistline and full breasts appear in the space, striking me like only the sight of Jolie can.

Hope sparks around me like static electricity. *She came...*

I watch her puffy strawberry lips join in song.

"Happy birthday to Roooooooon, happy birthday to you."

She claps like the rest of the guests, and our eyes lock across the room. My hands make noise, but it's as though my mind and my heart are totally disconnected from everything but Jolie's eyes. She stares back at me, and it's the first time I can't read her thoughts.

But once I get her alone, I'll stop at nothing to convince Joey we belong together. The past couple of days have been the darkest I've ever known, and I don't plan on living without her light ever again.

Joy pats my arm. "Pass me that knife, sweetie."

She cuts the cake, and Colt and I help by putting pieces on paper plates with silver number sixties on them. Eve and Sam come up to fetch them from us and pass them out to everyone.

Jolie has made her way over near the bar and takes a piece of cake from Eve. Sam gives one to a young rancher named Weston from town who sometimes sells to my parents. He beams at Jolie, clearly happier than a pig in shit to be next to such a fine woman.

It's not going to be easy to get her alone.

I keep slicing through the milk chocolate and carrot cake until about fifty slices have been handed out. Mom and Fletcher haven't come down yet. I give my dad a bear hug, pat him on the back.

This whole thing is a whirlwind of emotion. Mom and Fletch are still upstairs, Dad is oblivious and bouncing around the place with joy and laughter, and Jolie arrived before I got a chance to talk to her. To top it off, she's doing a mighty good job of pretending to enjoy Weston's company. If adrenaline wasn't already surging, it is now.

Attempting to be discreet, I stare out of my peripheral vision until my eyes hurt, darting my gaze in their direction for brief confirmation that he is, in fact, flirting with her. It might be nothing, but he tips a finger at the person manning the bar, and next thing I know, Jolie is sipping a beer. She seems so relaxed. Like nothing has happened, just having a fun time with her beer and a bud. Maybe she stands by her decision. Maybe she's already over it. A painful concoction of rejection and anger pulses through my veins.

And I've never been one to watch from rink side.

As far as I'm concerned, Weston is much too comfortable next to the girl I still and will always consider mine. I don't want to be a dick. I don't have any right to storm over with a tempest brewing under my skin and an urge to send Weston packing.

But I do it anyway. Even though this isn't the time or place to hash things out, I am not watching some guy with body language and a dimple like Weston's offer to get my girl a drink at an open bar. I have no idea if that's what's happening, but I imagine it all the same, because jealousy has a vivid imagination.

I sidle up next to the two of them and gaze down at Jolie, my voice is darker and more accusatory than I'd like it to be. "How's that beer?"

She stares at me for a beat, searching my face for the deep, hidden meaning behind my question, and by the way she straightens her spine, I think she found it.

"Good."

Weston doesn't pick up on the tension between us. "Jolie said she needed to take the edge off, so I offered to help with that."

Weston doesn't realize how close he is to being slugged.

I haven't taken my gaze off Jolie. "I thought you liked bourbon?"

And that's when she makes the first move. "Bourbon just makes me sad now."

I dive into her eyes and hang on to the meaning in her words. "It makes me sad, too."

Weston glances between the two of us and finally gets the picture. "I'll leave you to it."

I stop him with a hand on his chest. "No. You stay." I grab Jolie's hand, and surprise fills her eyes. "We'll be leaving."

Making my way toward the laundry room off the side of our rec room, I lead Joey by the hand, shove her inside with only a few people watching, and close the door behind us.

"What are you doing?" She leans against the washing machine, placing her hands on the top, which pushes her breasts out invitingly. The clean sweet smell of laundry is the exact same scent of Bird's Eye.

I want to smash my lips against hers and kiss her into oblivion and tell her this is all over now. That enough is enough and we're meant to be together and she's not leaving this room without being my girl.

"I hope Logan didn't see you holding my hand," she says, a hint of sadness in her words.

"Logan knows."

Her lips part in surprise.

"He knows everything. He knows I'm in love with you. He knows I don't want this to be over... I don't want this to be over, Joey." My heart thunders against my ribcage. "I fucked up. Big time."

She shakes her head. "Your mom did."

"Yes, she did, but I mean I should have told you about everything. I honestly need you to believe me when I say it wasn't because I don't trust you. I really, really do. I trust you with my life, Joey. I trust you with my heart. You're in my soul; it's like you love me from the inside out. Nobody's ever given me that. It's the way I want to love you, too, and I let you down."

I clutch her hand and place it on my heart where I hope she can feel it beating in there just for her. "I let Chloe hurt you. That's on me. I need you to forgive me. It's always been you, Joey." I close the space between us and take her curvy hips in my palms to tug her into me. "I just got lost along the way."

I want to melt into her. I want the floor to drop out and we float like magical lovers in some star-filled universe with no beginning, no end, and no problems. But we still have a lot to get through. And that's okay. Because from the sound of it, Joey is ready to do this together, and with her and me on the same side, I can't believe a single world where we don't win.

She peers up at me. "What about Chloe? Do you still want to tell Fletcher, or do we hide until she forgets about it?"

"Fletcher knows."

She gasps audibly. "What?"

"I decided to give my mom a chance to tell him. So I told her about all that went on between me and Chloe and the blackmail... we argued..." I stop for a moment, thinking of my mom. Thinking of those two having the hardest conversation of both their lives right now just upstairs.

"Mom and I were talking about it all when Fletcher walked into my room."

"Oh my God." Her gaze is genuinely torn. "How is he? Or even both of them actually. Shit, Ashton, this is... huge."

I love what I see in her face right now. It's a deep connection to everything that is me. It's an empathy only a strong woman like Jolie can be capable of.

"I don't know exactly what happened. My mom sent me down here to host, and they're still upstairs talking. It wasn't how I wanted it to happen, but it's done now."

Music blares all around us, the flimsy door the only thing between us and chaos.

Joey's gaze is on the door, but it doesn't look like she plans on leaving. "Keeping secrets must be painful. Maybe that's why I struggle to do it. It's hurtful to keep the truth inside."

I take a risk and grab her hand, even though a couple of days ago it wasn't mine to have anymore. "That's what I love so much about you, Joey. I can believe what you say. I can believe in you. I'm so sorry I ever made you feel any other way..."

She bites her lip, and the corners of her mouth turn down. "Ashton, you aren't the only one who has something to apologize for. I fucked up, too. I was scared and shocked and so confused with Chloe showing up. I... fell apart."

I think about her mom's words. "No, Joey. You exploded. Like the volcano that you are."

Her gaze is grateful. There is no better feeling than being seen, and I know Jolie. Whether she's decided to stick by that explosive night or not, her reaction would have been the same.

She draws her lips into a thin line. "I did explode. It's a bad habit."

She's softer now, and I squeeze my hands around her hips because it feels right. "It's authentic. There's nothing more attractive to me than a woman who knows how to express herself."

"Really?" Her eyes brim with tears. "Even though that's a beautiful thing to say, you didn't deserve that, Pup. I know I was extreme, but at the time I was sick with all the things I discovered. I was sick with Chloe's words, sick with worry for Fletcher and you... saying I'm a volcano is putting it nicely. I basically threw up all over you. I'm sorry, too, and I wish I could take it all back." A tear trickles down her cheek. "I wish I could change that day but I can't."

"Don't apologize Joey..."

"I have to. I did the wrong thing. I ran away when you needed me most. What kind of woman is that? Not the woman I wanted to be for you. Not the woman I..." She lowers her gaze, and hair falls over her eyes. "Not the woman I *still* want to be for you."

I place my hands on top of the washing machine and cage her in, connecting my whole body to hers. I smooth some of her moonbeam hair off her ear, exposing her elegant neck. Leaning in, I breathe in all her earthy perfume and whisper, "We're going to make it?"

She reaches on her tiptoes to speak into my neck, her words quiet but powerful. "Ashton, we're inevitable."

My body melts against her, and I take her into my arms. Our lips press together, and I glide my tongue inside her mouth. Our tongues swirl; the taste of us is sweeter than ever before. It's honest. It's pure of heart. It's forever. Being with her stills the tsunami of thoughts that drag my sanity out to sea. Kissing her is like being in the eye of my turbulent life. Together, we're safe while a storm whips around us.

At this moment, it's like the world outside has failed to exist. I grow thick in my pants and grab her ass, hoisting her up on the washing machine. She wraps her legs around my middle, and I'd give anything to have her now and stay connected where everything is already as it should be.

We kiss hard. I bury my face in her neck and devour her until her breath is shaky. She's rocking her core into me and my pants are tight with wanting. I shove my fingers up her shirt and take her full breast in my hand. Holding her is everything. But I'm moving at a hundred miles an hour, because while touching her satiates one need, it ignites another.

She mewls quietly, and I unbutton my pants, filthy thoughts of making up for two days without her race through my mind. But suddenly, the door to the laundry room cracks open.

We both flinch, but before we need to dive into the pile of ironing and hide, the door gets slammed back shut, and Logan's voice vibrates right through the thin wood.

"There's nothing in there for you, little man."

Jolie's head drops to my shoulder, and she giggles. "Never in a million years did I think my big brother would guard the door for us."

"Me neither."

I push my stiff dick down into my pants and do up the zipper. Jolie wiggles her bra back into place and fixes her hair. There's a lifetime of this prepared for us, but it doesn't start right now.

I help her down to the floor and kiss her softly. "I love you, Jolie Hunter." I groan against her lips. My cock still pushes painfully against my zipper, and my woman just smells so fucking good. "I love you so much I really want to take you up to my room and show every part of your body just how in love I am."

She combs her fingers through my hair. "But we need to get back to the party."

I let out a sharp breath. "We do."

I rest my forehead on hers, enjoying the warmth when the cold realization leaves my lips. "Fletch is going to be so mad at me. Maybe he'll never forgive me."

"It's going to be okay. It might be bad *before* it's okay, but I just know in my gut, it's a permanent change but it's not permanent damage."

"I hope you're right." I don't let go of her right away. I need to hold her for a moment longer. I need to pray with gratitude for this moment so the universe gives us a million more moments like this one. Redemption. A chance to grow stronger in our love. I've never before felt the way I do now about Jolie. She's walking through fire with me.

I pull her close, gliding my hand down her head, shoulders, her spine, all the while urging her body closer to mine, securing us together as close as possible. We urge our bodies against one another in an embrace like none before. Like we're pressing flowers between us to make something both alive and eternal at the same time. That's how true love is.

It's so mind-blowing, it actually seems impossible.

And I have it now. With the very woman who also seemed impossible all those years. Jolie has no shame in her love for me and never has, even when it was unrequited; Jolie didn't hide it. The bridge of my nose stings wondering how I got so lucky.

Only a soulmate could turn your life around the way she has from tragic to hopeful. Because when she says everything is going to be all right. I believe her.

The party is still going strong. Music fills the space, aunties dance with the young ones, holding their hands and twirling them around. Eve and Sam are there, and it appears Eve is trying to teach Sam a dance. I'm guessing something from TikTok. The bar in the corner is a watering hole for Colt, Logan, and Weston, who's still drinking beer there. I dart my eyes around the room, and my gaze snags on my mom. The corners of her mouth are tucked in, and her eyes are vacant.

No Fletcher.

Joey spots Mom at the same time and rubs my arm. "Go on upstairs."

I toss her a grateful smile. I take the steps up two by two until I'm on the second floor and find his door closed. I knock. There's no answer, but I open the door anyway.

Just like mine, our parents left Fletcher's room untouched. It's a carbon copy of my own apart from his poster of Tom Brady replacing my Gretzky. And instead of a hockey puck, he tosses a football up and catches it over and over to ease his mind.

"Hey," I say, not yet entering the room.

"Come in," he invites me, but it's not particularly friendly.

His voice is flat and lifeless, and I hate that this has drained him. Fletcher is always full of life and fun.

I sit on the bottom of the bed, head hung. "I'm sorry."

"Me, too," he says. "Me, too, because nobody should have to feel the way I do right now."

"Would you have wanted to know a long time ago?" It occurs to me he might wish he was still blissfully ignorant.

"Or maybe never? I guess that's something someone in my position can't know."

He tosses the football thoughtfully, but it reveals no wisdom. "I don't know."

We sit in silence for what feels like a good two minutes, but it's clear neither of us are leaving. We're just two men, searching for words. There aren't enough apologies in the world to excuse me from keeping this from him and breaking the trust between us. But what's more important to me now than all of that is making sure my brother knows he's *ours*.

He stares into space as I talk, twirling his football in his hand.

"Fletch, the man who raised you is your father. I am your brother, and even though you might be considering disowning her at the moment, Mom will always love you more than life itself. Where you come from isn't nearly as important as where you belong."

His gaze flicks to mine. It's deep and meaningful, and I'm not sure my brother and I have ever looked at one another like this before. He's still silent, but something tells me he needs my words more than he wants to say his own.

My words are so meaningful they nearly burst my heart when they leave my lips. "I'll be here for you. Always. I'm here for you."

He nods a few times, staring at me carefully, then averts his gaze to the wall in front of him again. "Thank you."

"If it were up to me, we'd talk about this for a while." I wish I could get him talking, venting, anything.

"Yeah... I'm not really ready for that. I don't want to say things I don't mean or that I'll regret. I need to process this, you know? I'm angry. I'm sad. I just... I can't even articulate what's going through my mind right now and I've learned it's best to say nothing when that's the case."

I wish so hard we could talk all night until he and I are totally right. Until I get his forgiveness. But sometimes suffering is the way to cement change, and in this instance, it's my penance. Fletcher needs time. So time is what I'll give him.

I stand. "I love you. Just want you to know that in case I haven't said it enough."

He gazes at me, and there's a glint of lightness in his eyes. "I don't think you've ever said it."

Can that be true? How could it be when I mean it from the pits of my gut? "Well... I said it now."

His nod is like some sort of confirmation. I turn to leave.

"Hey," he stops me. "Mom told me about Jolie and Chloe."

"Yeah, you couldn't write this shit."

"Well... I need you to get the girl. No matter what happens to me, you go get your girl. I don't want you living in secret because of me. Because, well... I love you, too."

A lump forms in my throat, because only now do I realize Fletch is right. We've never really used these words before. Where we're from, vulnerability in men is a very recent development. In our house, we let each other know how we felt by sharing a last piece of cake or punching the guy who talks bad about the other. This?

I feel horrible for thinking it, but it's true. Hearing my brother tell me he loves me, knowing Jolie is my ride or die... all this ache is causing tiny fractures in my heart, and when they repair, I know it will be bigger than it was before.

My lips pull up in a grateful half-smile.

His face mirrors mine, and something warm fills his

eyes. "At least one good thing needs to come of this. You're lucky she still likes you now that you're old."

I blow a laugh out of my nose. "I really am."

I leave the room and shut the door behind me. My back hits the oak, and my chin falls to my chest. It's done now.

I just hope the truth really does set us all free.

Chapter Twenty-Seven

Jolie

WHEN ASHTON RETURNS to the party, Fletcher isn't behind him. My heart aches for the Danes. It's not good what Monica did. I'll never be able to excuse it, and at the same time, how confusing it must be for your deepest regret to have brought about one of your deepest loves.

Ashton and I wait until everyone is too drunk to notice us leaving together. I say goodbye to my mom without drawing attention to myself, and Ashton gives his dad the kind of hug he doesn't now understand. Then he gives his mom the kind she terribly needs.

We head back to my place, and straight after taking off our shoes, pad silently upstairs, knowing without words; we are both spent. Every sinew of my body is exhausted from a couple of days of pure adrenaline and emotion. By the expression on Ashton's face as he drops his overnight bag by my bedroom door, wanders deeper into my room, and lets his huge frame fall mindlessly on the bed, he's just as done.

I head into the bathroom to brush my teeth, and when I open the medicine cabinet, I dream about how his razor and Cool Water cologne would look in here. He still hasn't found a place in the Canyon. There's not much available in such a small town at any given time.

"You can keep some things here if you want. If it's easier for you since you only have a little bit of time home whenever you're back. It saves you from running back and forth to Moon Ridge."

He waits a beat. Was my offer too forward? Maybe he's still thinking we should lie low a little?

Finally, he says, "I was hoping you'd ask me to move in."

My heart flutters, and I gaze at my delighted face in the mirror, but my words are still full of sass. "Don't you know it's rude to invite yourself?"

"Don't ask. Don't get."

I'm doing a silent happy dance when he adds, "I'll find us someplace perfect at some point, Joey. Somewhere that we can make our own."

I head back into the bedroom and enjoy his long body sprawled out facedown on my bed. If Ashton and I move somewhere else, this place might end up empty. The thought saddens me. I know my dad would have wanted it to be full of joy and laughter and even wild, boisterous arguments. "I'd be happy to live here if you would. I mean, it's a big house with plenty of room for..." *Too early to mention the five kids I always thought we'd have?* "...for a big tall lug like you."

He laughs into the pillow.

I breathe in his body on my bed, on his belly, all strong frame and thick thighs and tight buns on my duvet, and it's the first time in two days I find a thoughtless, natural smile on my face again. He's here now. With me. Just like I've always dreamed. He's motionless, and I wonder how long it will take him to fall asleep tonight, if I should leave him be.

"Are you staring at my ass, Joey?" His voice is muffled in the pillow.

I giggle. "How did you guess?"

"Because you've always been a pervert." He pats the bed next to him. "Get yours right here."

I shove my jeans down and peel off my top, because Ashton is right about one thing, I do have a bit of a perverted streak, and the man seems a bit too tired to be disrobing me—nothing like giving him a head start.

When he rolls onto his side, his eyes brighten at the sight of my bare skin. "You want to play, do you?"

I shrug, as if bashful. I'm not. Of course, I want this sexy man stuffed inside me. I've been dying to finish what we started in the laundry room.

He tips his chin, all cocky like he was in high school. "Get naked, Hunter."

"You're going to make me do *all* the work?"

He smooths a hand over my bare tummy and darts his tongue over his bottom lip. "Show me what's on offer."

I unclip my bra and toss it to the floor. "What about these?" I roll my nipple between my fingers, and it's meant to entice him, but instantly I'm the one heavy below.

He takes off his shirt, and those pecs are making me lose it.

"What else you got?" he asks, pushing himself up to sit against my headboard. "Take off those panties. Show me how you like to be touched."

I hold my breast in my hand and circle my nipple, teasing him. "I need motivation."

His nostrils flare at the sight of it. "Oh yeah?" He shoves down his pants, boxers along with them, and tosses them to the floor. His erection stands thick and long , and he grabs it pumping it a few times. "This any good?"

"Exactly what I had in mind." I climb up his long legs.

"Show me first, Joey. I leave tomorrow and I need to see you." He jerks himself methodically. "I want to see what you do to yourself when I'm not here."

I wiggle out of my panties and sit between his slightly open legs with my feet on either side of his hips. "You like watching? And you say I'm the pervert."

"Spread those thighs."

I do as he says.

"Open wide, Joey. Show me."

I stretch my thighs as wide as they'll let me and expose myself, lips plump and already glistening, overstuffed with my desperate clit.

"Good girl. So ready. Are you always so ready like that?"

"For you."

"Spread yourself with your fingers."

I take two fingers and hold myself open. His eyes are so wicked and heated, they set fire to my seam.

"Circle your finger round that pretty clit until it's standing up high. I want it pointing right at me."

Did he just say that? The thought of my clit standing at attention is so damn hot my fingers stroke furiously. "God, Ashton."

A wicked grin tugs at the corner of his mouth. "Are you praying already?" He still rubs his hand along his shaft. "Dip a finger inside."

I plunge my middle finger inside, still massaging with my index finger and watch his own thick ones around his hard cock and want them inside me instead. Desire drips right down my ass and pools on the bedsheet.

"Another finger, Joey. Fill yourself up and touch that clit harder for me."

I do as he says, and in order to contain myself, my eyes flutter shut.

"Eyes on me," he commands.

His words have my nipples hard, my skin sizzling, and my finger bearing down with just a little more pressure than before. I drive my fingers in and out, imagining it's that dick in his manly hand.

"You see me?" he growls. "This is what I'll look like every night without you. I'll be holding on to my dick, dreaming of when I can sink it inside your pussy and feel your slick insides, tight around me."

I'm so close, I touch myself faster. Harder. "Do it then."

"Come for me first. I want to see it."

"Ah..." I moan, my clit pulses, wetness trickles down my fingers, and I unravel as my orgasm pounds through my veins.

"Good girl. Keep going." His hand works furiously up and down his shaft and he bites his lip.

I watch him like he told me to and etch the sight of him into my mind. Tomorrow, he'll be gone, which is exactly why I want him between my legs now. My entire core is wet for him right down to the tops of my thighs. He's still holding on tightly to that thick cock of his when I shuffle up the length of his body, my knees on either side of him. My pussy lips are spread wide, swollen and ready to sit down on that dick of his and have him fill me up.

When I'm angled perfectly over that steel shaft lying on his belly, he holds my hips steady and glides my pussy lips along his cock. His dick is nestled between my folds, and the ripples of his veins rub over my sensitive nub sending a shiver of ecstasy up my spine.

His fingers sink into my flesh, directing me, stopping me from going too fast. I ease off him, lift, showing him where to put it. I fondle his balls from behind.

"I need you inside me, Ashton."

He handles his cock, pointing it right at me. He positions it at my entrance, teasing it in circles. "Sit on me."

I'm about to ride him bare, and the thought of him releasing inside me is so damn hot I'm eager. I'm on the pill, but we've always used condoms. This time, I don't want to. There are no consequences but good ones.

We watch together as I lower myself down on his bare cock—I need to breathe and focus on relaxing to grant him entrance. I ease down halfway and then take myself up again, enjoying the sight of my cum all over his dick before doing this slowly, over and over again, one more inch at a time until his hips are in the cradle of mine and his shaft bottoms out inside me.

My insides grasp around him, tightening like a vise, and the pulse in his cock pounds inside me. Every ripple of his taut skin gives me pleasure, and I rise and fall over my man. My thighs shake, and I brace myself with my hands on his muscular pecs. My breasts bounce to his every move. I swear I could cry because he feels so perfect inside me.

His hands tighten around my hips, and he forces me up and down his length, harder, faster. His eyebrows furrow in concentration, and it doesn't seem humanly possible but he grows inside me, he bottoms out. I take a deep breath to take him in as he drives me up and down, harder, his sharp hipbones slamming against my inner thighs. My tits are bouncing... this man is making me come from the inside out.

I moan. "Mmm..."

"That's it, baby girl. Squeeze me. Let that pussy throb all over me."

My insides are rippling and spasming, making my thighs tremble, but the strength in his hands keeps me moving up and down over his cock.

Wetness pours out of me and right down his balls, encouraging him to thrust wildly. Finally, he releases, his hot cum spills inside me, fierce like molten lava, and I collapse my chest against his, my nipples scraping his skin. He reaches his fingers around and smooths them along my pussy lips, his dick still inside me, and the sensation is enough to make me weep.

He pulls his fingers away, and I ease myself off him and lie by his side, my core still thrumming.

That was everything. He rode me bare. My God, I never want to go back from here. And he never mentioned a condom...

I point out what to me is obvious but maybe for him, a tired mistake. "We didn't use a condom."

"No..." he says, unalarmed.

I reassure him even though he seems unfazed. "I'm on the pill."

"Okay."

I think for a minute. He's so relaxed about it, and I get the impression he wasn't even going to bring it up before the boo-boo. "You didn't know I was on the pill before we did it, though."

His body is heavy with relaxation. My head is on his chest, and I'm listening to the slowing of his heartbeat.

He caresses my arm. "What will be will be. I'm too old to not be trying."

Not trying? As in for a kid? I'm doing my second happy dance inside my head. And then I pretend to be practical, even though really I'm not, but I just need to be sure he's lucid. "We hardly just got back together, though. Like a couple hours ago."

He nestles me closer. "What are you saying, woman? We've always been together."

Just need to be clear. "So you weren't worried about knocking me up?"

"Quite the opposite. I figured you knew what you were doing, too, making the decision for yourself. If you're up for it, I am. Like I said, I'm getting old."

His commitment is blinding. My body bubbles with an odd but beautiful feeling I've never had before. Like I've entered some new era of love... achieved a new level, because this guy is saying he wants me to be his baby mama.

But all too quickly, I know how much we still have ahead of us. Fletcher only just found out and... Chloe. God, if she was hysterical over the thought of me and Ashton dating, what would she do to us if I got pregnant?

I trace my finger on the skin of his chest. "You have no idea how much I like the sound of that but... maybe we should still be extra careful? Until everything is smoothed out?"

He kisses the top of my head. "If we have to go through hell, we're going to do it like we own the damn place."

Chapter Twenty-Eight

Jolie

AFTER THREE WEEKS OF LONG-DISTANCE, I'm so insanely in love with Ashton Dane that I want to run off and get married and sail into the sunset, but I decide it's better to lie low. Our families know everything, and even though he has most of his stuff moved in with me, we keep PDA to a minimum in public, both in Starlight Canyon and elsewhere.

It's not right, and it isn't what Ashton wants. He told me we shouldn't make ourselves small for the sake of another—especially a person who's blackmailing him and holding his family to ransom. Though Fletcher has decided to go forward and announce this news so he doesn't end up in the same predicament his brother was, I just need time. I revel in our privacy for those three weeks, just me and the love of my life, savoring every single moment when he's home with me.

But when the day comes in his schedule to play his old team, the Los Angeles Raptors, he proposes a night away together and says he wants me to meet some of his friends from the team he played with for so many years. It's hard to deny him this.

I'm doubtful, because all I can think about is in Los Angeles we'll run into his hideous ex.

But he's adamant.

We're staying in a picture perfect, beautiful cliff-top hotel in Malibu, far away from the hustle and bustle of Hollywood. We spend the day hiking Escondido Falls and meandering through sage and ancient oaks, enjoying a waterfall the winter rains have made magnificent. We find a bench and eat fish tacos while staring at the ocean. Though I've seen oceans before, for this girl from a landlocked state, it never fails to draw a deep sense of awe. I can see why Ashton didn't think it was too bad here, and he plans the perfect vacation for me by wrapping up the day with a surf lesson. I thought I'd do better with my balance from horse riding but I only got up once.

Our night in the Kobu Malibu was filled with the kind of mind-blowing, relaxing sex that only happens when two people are using a rented bed. Ashton was right... We needed this night away, because it sure has given me ideas for our bedroom at home. I revel in being treated like a queen to room service, in-room couples massage, and my boyfriend enduring my favorite Christmas rom-com.

I never want to leave the room. And the next morning, what Ashton has to tell me has me wanting to leave even less.

Our suite has an enormous hot tub, and before we have to go to breakfast with his buddies and their wives, I insist on using this before we do. My feet hug Ashton's hips and his perch on either side of the gold-rimmed bubble bath.

He takes one of my feet in his hands and massages it. "Let's talk about today."

I let my head fall back and my eyes close, taking in the bliss of his fingers kneading into my feet. "Mmm…" I put my other foot between his legs, gently caressing his dick. "Second couples massage in two days? You must think I'm special…"

I stroke gently up and down, and he thickens under my touch. My eyes are still closed, and the scent of whatever herb is in the hotel bubble bath is divine.

His voice is low and considered. "I need to talk to you about something. Something we need to do today."

I thought all we have to do today is eat breakfast with his old teammates and wives, and I'd take a walk on the beach while he goes to pregame practice. I level my face with him, eyes remaining closed, because I don't want to overfill my senses with anything but his talented fingers and the smell of this room. "God, you have strong fingers, Pup…"

"I'm glad you like it…" Somehow, his words hang in the air just like I left his proposition about today hanging.

When I open my eyes, he's staring at me seriously, and I don't get the impression he's concentrating on my arch.

I lift an eyebrow lazily. "Are you about to ruin my inner serenity?"

His lips draw into a thin line.

Uh-oh. How could anyone possibly have a problem in a

tub like this? But he does. The mood between us has always been visible, and he needs to talk.

I wiggle my toes near his dick. "There's something telling me I might be using this foot for something other than your pleasure in a minute. Why do I feel like you're about to tell me bad news?"

He laughs lightly but still lifts my foot away from his nuts and places it to the side of his hip, then resumes my massage.

I can't be manipulated with reflexology. "Spit it out, Dane."

His brown eyes are deep and dead serious and take no prisoners with their announcement. "We should see Chloe today."

Yanking my foot out of his hands, I draw my knees into my chest and rest my chin on them. Chloe? Why the hell would I want to see her? I was worried about running into her, and now Ashton proposes we set up an actual reunion? "You and I have very different ideas of what a vacation means. I'll pass on that tour, thanks."

He doesn't respond immediately.

"Is that why you brought me to LA? I thought we were meeting your old Raptors buddies and their wives for break-fast today, not ambushing Jolie for a second time."

"It's not an ambush."

"What do you call a surprise attack?"

"First, we are meeting my friends today, it wasn't a ploy to get you here. But I told Chloe to come to the hotel this morning. Before they get here."

The water splashes around me like an open ocean swell. I can't get out of this tub fast enough. What the hell? I wrap a towel around myself. "That's not cool."

"No. It's not cool." He gets out and dresses himself in a

terry cloth robe off a nearby hook, his wrists hanging out of the sleeves. "It's not cool. Not fun. Not the stuff vacations are made of."

He states the obvious while I brace myself on the bathroom counter and stare at my fuzzy reflection in the steamed-up mirror.

His arms snake around my waist, and he kisses my neck. "It won't be fun, but this story needs an end. You don't have to come with me to see her. I can end this once and for all on my own and text you when she's gone, but I think we should do this together."

I don't know. On the one hand, Ashton is very annoying for putting this event in our otherwise perfect schedule. On the other hand, he's probably right. Closure is always a good thing.

But I shake my head. "I took two days off plucking ticks and expressing anal glands for this? Your idea of vacation makes work seem very attractive, Ashton." I would rather do any putrid vet job than see that woman again.

He leans over me with his giant arm to wipe the steam off the mirror. In the reflection is his soulful gaze and his boyish lips ready to tell me to be reasonable like he always does. Like I need.

"Joey, you see that man behind you?"

Our gazes meet on the glass, and I purse my lips in defiance, because every time he speaks, somehow I easily give him his way, he's so irresistible.

"That man in the mirror loves you so damn much it hurts him to keep it a secret. It hurts him to hide you. He wants to scream from the rooftops and jump up and down on Oprah's couch, wild with his love, and only one thing stands in his way."

I lower my eyes. I don't want his hypnotic gaze to

change my mind like only he can. I want to keep pretending Chloe doesn't exist.

He tips my chin back so our gazes meet in the mirror. "Baby girl, you deserve more. You deserve better. *We* deserve something at least resembling normal. So I'm going down there to find some closure and tell Chloe it's done once and for all. I'll meet her alone, but I sure as hell would love my woman by my side. United. A team." He pulls my butt against him. "Remember? We walk through hell like we own the damn place?"

"Ashton..." My lungs release the tension I've held since having my foot in his hand. "Can't we just forget her?"

"Will you, though? Really? And how can I let what she did to you go unanswered?"

I swallow hard. He's right. Pretending didn't make her go away.

Ashton rests his chin on the top of my head. "I get that you've needed time to process. But Fletcher already told his PR and agent, and they have plans to release a story themselves. Chloe doesn't actually have anything on us anymore. She needs to know that. She needs to know it's over. And that I love you. That you're everything to me. That I'm never even fucking looking in her direction again once the conversation is over. I never got to stick up for you."

I say the words but I don't mean them. "I don't need you sticking up for me." *I love him sticking up for me.* It's probably what made me fall for him in the first place.

"I'm your man. I like sticking up for you." He flashes a coy smile. "I get off on it. You're mine, Jolie Hunter. All mine, and I want everyone to know it."

I stare at myself in the mirror, knowing this will either be very good or very bad. I cross my arms and take his hands in mine. "I'm going to need a mimosa or something after."

"As many as you want, baby."

"Okay." I let out a loud sigh. "Let's do this. So what did you tell her?"

"I told her to meet me at the bar at eight-thirty."

"We're having breakfast with everyone at eight forty-five, though."

He counts the words on his fingers. "Fuck. Off. Forever." He holds up three fingers. "What do you think that took? Five seconds?"

I grab his fingers and push them down with a smile.

He pulls me into his embrace. "I'm not interested in a long, drawn out-conversation. I don't want to talk about the hockey stick incident. I don't want to engage in some sort of burn contest. I just want her to know you're mine, that she can't hurt us or ever break us apart. And... to never speak to either one of us again."

Half an hour later, we're dressed and heading to the hotel bar where he told Chloe he'd meet her. Since he wasn't sure I wanted to join him, she's not expecting me. But it doesn't matter. I don't really intend to say anything. I can't really trust my tongue around that woman anyway. Standing by Ashton and showing her we're united is all I care about. I already know the kinds of things she's capable of saying, and all the way down the elevator, I pump myself up to take her slander like a stoic champ.

She doesn't deserve anything from me anymore.

I see her before she sees me. She sits with her back impossibly straight, almost as if she feels like people are watching her. As it's the hotel bar and it's too early for normal people to drink, she's the only one there apart from the lone bartender. Her talons are long, manicured and shiny when she picks up a champagne flute and drinks from her red lips on a face full of makeup. Chloe wasn't nearly as done up when she came to see me in Starlight Canyon. She dressed up for the occasion, and the green-eyed monster whispers she's still hoping to impress my boyfriend.

She catches Ashton's eye and begins to smile, but when her gaze slips down Ashton's arm to where I'm holding his hand, her grin fades into oblivion. As we approach, her features become more and more hardened, her jaw so stiff it could crack.

She speaks to Ashton but looks right at me. "You didn't tell me you'd be bringing *this* with you today."

He kisses the top of my head, and it sends a reassuring wave of love through me. "I bring *her* with me everywhere now, Chloe."

She somehow sits taller. "Didn't you see the sign outside? No class. No style. No service."

Is she referring to me? I grit my teeth.

"Well then, how did *you* get in?" Ashton retorts, walking straight into the tit-for-tat trap I did when she arrived in that white Jeep at Bird's Eye.

His jaw tics, but he holds steady.

Chloe laughs as though they've both just made a joke. "So you came here to show off your pet, did you?"

My hand is balmy now but I already told Ashton I won't embarrass either one of us in a hotel lobby, and I made him promise he wouldn't either. I'm counting on him to finish this. And soon, because it will be so cringe for his friends to walk in on this conversation.

He clears his throat and bites his lip, shaking his head with a wicked, irritated smile on his lips like he has a really good comeback. But he holds it back, and when he gazes at her again, he says, "We don't have much time to talk, so I'm going to dive right in. We came here to tell you that you don't have a leash on us anymore. Fletcher knows everything, and his interview has already been paid for by ESPN. I don't think they'll pay much for your version anymore. You know, the one where you snuck through my parents' house and found private documents you had no business accessing? It will be fun to explain how you know everything. I can just see that conversation when the reporter does due diligence."

She cocks her eyebrow. "Oh, you're so cute, Ashton. As if that's all I have on you." She wiggles her finger as if scribbling something ugly between us. "This little thing you have going on just feeds the narrative. Ashton Dane—the unfaithful husband running off with high school sweetheart, paying his ex-wife to keep quiet."

"How do you live with yourself?" I blurt. *I've done well to only say that.*

Ashton pulls me into his big, strong arm, his side warm and comforting. "Chloe, the only opinion I care about now is Jolie's. If the world thinks I'm Satan's spawn, I just don't give a shit, because this woman here is the only one I have to prove any loyalty to. The important thing you need to know is I no longer have any to you. Do what you want with the press. Cry your sad story from the rooftops. Talk to whoever you like as long as it isn't me or Jolie. Contact me—or her—again and I'll take legal action. I'm serious. This is over."

She stands and she's almost my height in her five-inch stilettos. "Oh, you're threatening me? That's lush. You think you can control me, Ashton?" She looks like a wind up car pulling back over and over to let loose on us. "How dare you?"

Just when I think I'd better tug on Ashton's arm to just

get us the hell out of here, a hand claps down on Ashton's back.

"Dane-sy!"

Chloe's gaze tracks behind Ashton's shoulder and lands on the man who's greeted Ashton—a handsome, scruffy-haired center I recognize as Andrew Christensen from the LA Raptors—one of the friends we've come here to meet. Next to him is his gorgeous wife, smiling with flat lips because, well, this is awkward. She must know who Chloe is.

Andrew comes straight at me with open arms. "And you must be his better half? Jolie?" He wraps burly arms around me with a hug. "So nice to finally meet you. This guy speaks the world of you. You're the *exact* kind of woman I thought Dane should end up with."

I can't help but dart my eyes at Chloe whose face is a special shade of red.

Andrew doesn't acknowledge Chloe and points to his wife. "This is my wife, Gabs."

She shakes my hand, and the four of us have now made something of a circle in greeting. Chloe is very much outside of it. In fact, Ashton's back is to Chloe, whose mouth is parted like smoke should be blowing out of it.

Andrew peers at his watch. "We don't have a lot of time this morning before pregame. Let's grab that table." He finally greets Chloe. Well, sort of. His eyebrows furrow in confusion. "Are you coming to breakfast?"

She throws a hand on her hip. "No, Andrew. I am not."

"Thank God." He gazes at me with a twinkle in his eye and gives me a wink. "I'd rather poke my eyes out."

Chapter Twenty-Nine

Ashton

LOGAN and I are facedown on the massage tables, side by side. My calves need some work, and him? Always with the hamstring. Massages should feel good, but these kinds don't, and I'm happy to distract myself from the bone-grinding pressure on my skin by telling Logan what happened at Kobu this morning.

His cheek is squashed, and his speech comes out funny between misshapen lips. "I fucking love Christensen. I'm going to send him a bottle of Moët or something. That is hilarious."

"He's a beer guy. But yeah, Chloe was pretty bent out of shape. I'm glad Jolie and I stood our ground without losing it. But he's a fucking saint for saying what I was thinking."

He nods. "I just hope she doesn't come after you two again."

"Honestly, bro?" I lift myself onto my elbows. "I really don't care at this point. Joey and I are solid, and Fletcher decided to carve out his own destiny on this one."

"He's a strong man."

"Yeah, but that's little brother shit, too. If there's one thing he can't tolerate, it's being controlled."

"Sounds like Dash, too." Logan closes his eyes, like the masseuse just hit a hard spot.

"Pzzt. Sounds like you."

He lifts his eyebrows lazily, his body jostling around gently while the therapist digs into his hamstrings. "You're so obsessed with me."

"Obsessed with you playing well, to be exact."

His eyes shoot open. "I didn't..." He glances around to see who's listening then talks through gritted teeth. "I didn't drink in Vegas."

"Two nights there is enough to not need a drink. The air is thick and bad for your lungs, jet lag sets in because you can't tell if it's night or day half the time in the casinos. You need to start lying low or Coach will demote you to second line."

He shudders. "To quote my hero, Christensen—I'd rather poke my eyes out."

My therapist is done, and I sit up. "Maybe he'll even drop you to third."

His expression is appalled. "There's no need. Why do you always have to take it so far? So negative."

His therapist pulls his pushed-up shorts back down, and we throw on some slides to head back toward the lockers.

"I know Coach hates it. This is my second season with him grilling my ass, but what am I supposed to do? It's the endorsements and stuff."

"I don't know anyone who has to be in Vegas as much as you, apart from strippers and magicians."

He laughs. "Look, I'm being a good boy."

We sit, both leaning against a locker and putting our feet up on a chair, waiting for the coaches to all come in and do a briefing. There's one of those momentary lulls, the ones where the world goes quiet, like the whole universe pauses on an inhale. And that's when Logan's wisdom becomes clear. There's no time like the present.

I drop the news. News that will affect him almost as much as me. "I'm going to retire after next season."

Logan's head snaps in my direction, his face something between confused and mortified. "What?"

I speak low and quiet. "I want to be with Joey. I want to be in the Canyon. I want... well, I want things that eighty-plus games a year and constant aches and pains aren't a good trade for anymore." I stare at him seriously. "But most of all, I want to go out on top."

His Adam's apple works its way up and down his neck, and it's rare to see Logan quite so speechless.

"Don't mention it to anybody. I already talked to my agent about it, and he said we need to be careful about the timing of the announcement. But... well," I smile, "I already used my get-out-of-jail-free card with you, so it's not like I'll keep it from my best friend."

Logan finally breathes and stares at the floor like some sort of reality has set in. "Fuuuuck."

"Fuck is right. I never thought the day would come."

His gaze flickers up, and there's a sadness in it. "One more season after this?"

I put my hand on his shoulder. "We got a chance. Let's make it count."

———

The deafening roar of the crowd echoes in my ears as I skate forward, the cold, hard ice beneath me feeling both familiar and foreign. No matter how many times a man performs in a shoot-out, it feels like the first. It all comes down to this. The weight of expectation, the pressure, and the stakes bear down on me when I glide myself out to the center of the rink.

I raise my gaze to the box where Jolie has been jumping around like a wild woman with Gabs and Iris all night. The three of them shared high fives, celebration hugs, and from the look of it when they dance and mouth the songs on the loudspeaker, quite a lot of beer. It warms me to no end that my few friends outside of Starlight Canyon embrace my woman, especially on an occasion where they're cheering for opposing teams.

But right now, Joey is still, concentrating on the ice, her fingers clasped, hands folded in front of her mouth in anticipation of what might happen here. How I'll perform. Our eyes lock even across the vast distance. She lowers her hands, and a smile that could melt the ice reaches me. She turns around and points to the name on the back of her jersey. *Dane.* It's the first time she's worn it, though I bought it for her a while ago. It was the right thing to meet with Chloe. Now we're free. Now we're public. And the whole world knows that that small-town queen is mine.

She blows me a kiss, and I feel it bone-deep, taking it

with me to the puck. It's time to concentrate now. Time to do my job.

The opposing goalie, masked and commanding, stares me down from the net. I take a deep breath, trying to silence the noise around me, the jeering meant to put me off by the Raptors fans, who just a couple of years ago would have been barking like Great Danes for me. Humans are fickle. Apart from Jolie. I still can't believe that woman has been steady all my life.

I let out another breath, calming myself. The tension in the arena is suffocating, and each heartbeat reverberates through my chest.

The referee's whistle pierces the air, signaling the start of my solitary attack on the goal. I pick up speed, the puck dancing on my stick. With a quick feint, I try to outsmart the goalie. The puck leaves my stick, a swift shot to the top corner, and it's in. I glance back up at my girl, jumping up and down on her own. Gabs and Iris are clapping politely. They wouldn't normally, but they do it to make my girlfriend comfortable. They must really like her.

I skate back to the bench, and Logan is up. He hasn't been himself all game, but only I know him that well. He's been playing fine but without his usual finesse. The punchy boyish fire that he manages to hold onto, even in his mid-thirties, is absent tonight. But Logan's unique gift in hockey, and in life, is staying calm under pressure. As such, since we were knee-high, he's always been a closer.

We need this goal just to tie it up again and keep this game going. Every goal is etched on my bones this season, I want that cup win more than ever. For Jolie. For me. For Logan.

I stand at the edge of the rink, gripping the cold metal of the boards, my breath visible in the frigid air. The tension in the arena is thick, hanging like a heavy fog. The shoot-out is the deciding moment: will we play on for a win, or will this be our second loss this season?

The whistle blows, and my heart pounds when I watch him skate toward the goalie, the puck on the blade of his stick. Time seems to slow down, each stride like a bass drum in my chest. Logan is agile, his movement unpredictable, strong but somehow graceful.

He dekes left, then right, trying to outmaneuver the goalie. Finally, he pulls back his stick and in his signature play goes for the top-left corner. The goalie reacts with lightning reflexes, stretching out to make a sprawling save. The shot is blocked, and a collective gasp echoes through the arena, followed immediately by a deafening roar of victory.

Logan skates back to the bench, head bowed, shoulders slumped, a posture I'm not used to seeing on him. Though he rarely misses, when he does, he doesn't usually display the disappointed defeat most players do. Logan typically gets mad. Instead, disappointment is etched on his face, and my heart pangs for him. We made it this far together, fought hard in every shift, and now I know... all he can think about is our conversation in the locker room.

We'll regroup. He'll come to terms with it. And hopefully, he'll do what he has to do for us to finally, after all these years in the NHL, make that dream of two little boys on a small-town pond come true. This year or the next, we have to be holding that Stanley Cup up together.

But right now, much as I shouldn't be thinking it, I just want to be back in that hotel room holding my Joey.

Chapter Thirty

Jolie

THE SCORPIONS HAVE three days free in the schedule, and Ashton is back home. He's waiting there for me, hopefully with something to eat, because I am starving after a busy shift at Starlight Vets.

I've silently thanked Colt's intuition a thousand times over for not helping me start my own practice and jumping into the stress of being both a vet and a business owner. Having the freedom of being a consultant has allowed me more leeway over my own schedule, and I've been able to watch my brother and Ashton at a few away games, even taking my mom to Boston and Montreal for a few cold, wintry getaways. And of course now, when my gorgeous boyfriend has a few days off, I can take time off, too.

Voicing my boundaries has gone a long way toward helping me enjoy the profession. But it wasn't a silver bullet, and I also decided to have a once-a-month session with Colt's therapist. She opened doors to new ways of looking at my relationship with death, and I know that exploring this will eventually help me make peace with the things I need to do in my job. I've never felt more supported in my life.

Ashton offered to take me away during this break, but I know how much he needs downtime and being away from the fast pace. I'm fine with it, too, because the past few months have been like living a thousand lives. I want to get back to living one. I still have dreams of traveling, and that safari is still on my mind, but if I had to choose one life, it would have always been the one I'm coming home to right now.

I turn the knob to my unlocked door, and as I push it open, I hear a kid's voice whisper, "Shh. She's coming!"

I'd recognize the raspy little boy anywhere. Mrs. Mason finally took me up on that offer to babysit and is out with my mom at her book club tonight. I pretend to be surprised at seeing nobody.

"Ashton? Gareth? Anybody home?" I sense a rustling behind a floor-length curtain just next to me. I drop my keys and cell on the console table. "So strange. I thought they'd be here."

Suddenly, Ashton jumps out from behind the curtain and takes my arms behind my back, holding me captive.

"Oh my God!" I feign fear and pretend to struggle to get out of Ashton's clutches. "Let go of me, you beast!"

Gareth jumps out from behind my armchair with a lasso in his hand, holding it like the most menacing weapon in the world. "Give us your candy!" he demands in his most wicked voice.

I wrestle my shoulders as if trying to break free and defy the little boy. "I don't have any candy, you thief."

He sashays a few feet closer with the sass of Billy the Kid and repeats his demand. "Give us your candy or you get the rope!"

He twirls it around, and though he's doing a pretty nice job, I dart my eyes around quickly to make sure Ashton has put away anything that could be broken. It's all clear. He's going to make a good daddy.

"Never!" I shout. "I'll never give it up. These Twizzlers belong to me!"

Ashton pretends to grip me harder. "So you *do* have candy." He commands Gareth, "Give her the rope."

Gareth circles the rope several times, making pretty good work of it, then releases it in my direction but knocks my cell off the table and hits me in the hip instead of entrapping me.

I slide my arms out of Ashton's grip and chase my attacker with fingers outstretched like I'm going to get him. "Ha! Ha! You're mine now!"

Ashton, Gareth, and I chase each other in circles until I'm not sure who is chasing whom, but I do eventually catch up with the firecracker and give him a tickle on the couch.

"You think you can steal from me? I know every trick in the book, mister."

His mischievous giggle fills the space with warm joy. "I give up! I give up!" His words ring out through laughter.

I stop tickling him and step back. "That'll teach you."

Gareth covers his mouth, and his body shakes as he laughs into his palm.

I walk over to Ashton and grab his cheeks on either side and squeeze them. "And you…"

His voice comes out of his now-puffy lips all muffled. "We got pizzas in the oven."

Gareth turns around. "Oh. They must be done."

"Come on, squirt." Ashton gestures for Gareth to help in the kitchen. "We don't want this woman to get hangry."

Gareth runs to his side, and they head into the kitchen.

"She might eat all our Twizzlers."

I watch Ashton help Gareth understand how to safely get things out of the oven. He tells him to first have an appropriate place for the hot pan, and they put a trivet on the counter. Ashton throws a soft pair of oven mitts at Gareth's face who laughs and picks them off the floor, then shoves them on his tiny hands.

Gareth looks up at Ashton like he's the coolest guy in the world. Something dramatic sweeps through me watching Ashton take the pan out of the oven with a boy who has no father. No father just like me. My heart pangs for my own again. I can't really untangle the complex, knotted rope of feelings in my chest, but I'm glad Ashton's here for him, and his heart of gold makes me fall in love with him all over again. Ashton Dane is a hockey legend with a few short days off, and here he is, planning robberies and making pizza with a little boy from his hometown.

We sit at my dining table, and Gareth makes an effort to slice the pizza, but he's so frenzied, the pizza cutter goes everywhere.

Ashton takes his hand and guides it. "You have to concentrate on this. Line it up."

Gareth's tongue sticks out when he tries to make a

straight line over the pizza and its very wobbly contents. "My mom makes this look easy."

"I bet your mom makes a lot of things look easy, my man." Ashton takes a slice from the pie and puts it on a plate. "Here's a life lesson—appreciate your mom. She's always working harder for you than you think."

Gareth slides the first plate toward him, and Ashton slides it back with his big finger.

"Uh-uh. Ladies first. Lesson number two—good manners go a long way."

Gareth crinkles his nose. "I thought cowboys were supposed to be rough and tough?"

"Trust me. It's plenty tough to be a gentleman sometimes."

Ashton's lessons are cute, but this kid needs some food.

I pick up the plate and give it to Gareth. "Go on, little man."

"Thank you." He takes the plate, licking his lips.

Ashton and I share a lingering glance, and we communicate silently. I tilt my head and give him a smile, telling him how cute Gareth is. He reads my expression perfectly, darts his eyes to Gareth, and nods. And then he mouths *I love you.*

<hr>

After dinner, I take Gareth in the living room to find a movie on Netflix. He ponders the decision like it's bigger than it is, and finally he chooses *Nativity* 3, and I head into the kitchen to help Ashton with the popcorn. Ashton finishes putting the last plate in the dishwasher and starts it up. I pour kernels into a saucepan next to him and put the lid on, waiting.

From here, we can see Gareth's carrot top sticking out just above the cushions of the sofa. We stare out at him for a moment in silence when Ashton wraps his arms around my waist and says, "I want one of those."

Reminiscence tugs at the corners of my lips when he repeats the words we shared back in the Moon Ridge Ranch arena during Western skills class all that time ago. "Oh yeah?" I stare up at him meaningfully. "Me, too."

He glances over at the lounge to check Gareth isn't watching. The coast is clear, so Ashton lowers himself to my lips, grabs my breast, and circles his thumb over my nipple that stands at immediate attention at his touch. He rubs his leg against my core and massages me just hard enough for me to grow heavy. His words tumble into my mouth. "How much do you want one, Joey?"

I breathe him in. "I want one enough to stop taking the pill now if you said so." The kiss is growing toward something unstoppable, so I peel myself back because there's a kid in the other room.

He shrugs. "I already said so a while ago. Stop anytime."

"You're serious?"

"Dead."

He pushes against me, his body completely aligned with mine, and I check to see Gareth's eyes are still glued to the TV then tilt my head back to give Ashton access to my neck. Just one more kiss won't hurt.

He leans over and takes a nibble, growing thick in his pants. "I cannot wait to have you later."

He dives into my eyes with a desire I've never seen before.

"So you'll stop?" He insists.

"When?"

"Now. Just don't take any more." He pulls my hips into

him. "I'm ready to do everything with you, Joey. Ready right"—his lips are warm and soft—"now. I want more than one and I don't want people thinking I'm our kids' grandpa."

I don't even know what I feel. I never thought deciding to try for a baby would feel so natural, but then, it's Ashton. "Okay. I won't take it anymore."

His hands make my hips dance and sway. "We can start trying tonight."

"It won't happen today."

"Practice. We'll need lots of practice." He takes a hunk of my neck into his mouth and gives me one big, ravenous kiss, sending tingles down my spine, then pulls away, quickly putting space between us. He sinks his teeth into his bottom lip and squeezes his fists, staring at me like I'm the hottest thing he's ever seen. "I am going to be senseless tonight thinking about knocking you up, baby girl."

"Aren't you supposed to make an honest woman out of me first?" I say coyly.

He threads his fingers through mine, and his words consume me in the best possible way. "You're already an honest woman, Joey." He tips up my chin. "You're my today and every single one of my tomorrows. You'll be Mrs. Dane soon enough. When I ask, you better say yes."

I flutter my eyelashes. "We'll see."

A kernel pops against the lid, disturbing our moment and reminding me Gareth is waiting. He's probably gone through all the licorice by now. I shake the pan, and Ashton slides in behind me one last time, holding me in his safe, strong arms. He breathes in my hair like he does and moans gently against the shell of my ear.

"I'm so damn in love with you."

The kernels pop like crazy now, and Ashton glides his

hands down to my tummy. "Can't wait to put a bun in this oven."

His words wash through me from top down like some sort of elixir for eternal life. Because that's how I feel about Ashton, he's as ever present as the beating of my very own heart. He's the first boy I ever loved and he'll be the very last, too.

But the one thing I learned along the way is that Ashton was actually right back on prom night, suggesting I might have been ever so slightly delusional about my love for him. Happily ever after isn't a magical fairy tale. It's a choice. Still, even going through hell to get here, choosing Ashton is the easiest thing I've ever done. He loves me without restriction and demands. He trusts me without fear and accepts me for who I am. I'm not just in love.

I'm content.

And I can't wait to start writing the rest of our love story.

Epilogue

Ashton

FOUR MONTHS LATER

I LIE on the bed in our bedroom at Bird's Eye, reading about playoffs and stats on the players who made it to the Stanley Cup final. The Scorpions did not. We had an amazing run, a super season to be sure, but again, got knocked out just before the end. I wish we would have gotten farther. Given my impending retirement, I do feel the pressure for next season. I want so damn badly to achieve that childhood dream with Logan on the ice.

Joey pops her head, but nothing else, through the doorframe. "Whatcha doing?"

"Just looking at predictions for the Cup. Maybe I'll have Logan drop a bet for me in Vegas for laughs."

"Oh."

The smile on her face is something new, and I can't read her. She still hasn't stepped into the room.

I narrow my eyes. "What are you up to?"

"Just..." She changes her voice to be sultry. "Do you remember when you brought that stick home? For..." She cocks an eyebrow. "Fun?"

I lick my lips, hoping she'll be coming into the room naked in a minute. "How could I forget?"

"Would you believe it? I found a stick we can have even more fun with."

Instantly, I'm thick in my boxers.

She pushes open the door, and there she is in a little pair of panties and matching bra. Her arms are behind her, and I try to get a glimpse of what she has in her hand, but it doesn't seem like she could fully hide a hockey stick. Has she been to that sex shop out of town?

She keeps her arms hidden and crawls onto the bed on her knees, shuffling until she's right next to me, still kneeling. I rub my hand over her soft, feminine hip.

"Are you going to show me what you got for us?"

A moment of nerves spreads across her face. How could she possibly be concerned about me and a sex toy? Jesus, we've used her vibrators a million times. But this is different. Very different. When she pulls her hands from hiding to reveal what's hidden behind her back, it's a stick all right. A pregnancy test to be exact.

She beams, and her cheeks bloom. "Look what I got you."

My jaw goes slack. "Wait..." I push myself up and take the test from her. *Oh my God...* "You're pregnant?"

"So says the stick." She's shuddering with happiness.

I grab her in my arms and instantly swing her down onto the bed. I throw my body over hers in an enormous embrace. She's warm and womanly and everything in my arms.

"I'm going to be a dad." I peel myself off her and put my hand on her belly. "Joey... you have a Joey."

She bites her lip, her cheeks round with sheer joy. "I know. Are you excited?"

"Of course I'm excited. Are you excited?"

"Kind of freak-out excited, but yeah... so happy."

I press my lips into hers with a kiss that says a whole lot more than I love you. My woman is the wildest, most pure magic in the world, and now she's creating, right there in her gorgeous belly, a whole new universe for us to share.

Breathing her in, I devour her and slide my tongue inside her soft, delicious minty mouth and murmur, "I love you so much."

"Mmmm... I love you, too, Pup."

I can't help myself. She's never been so damn sexy. I unclasp her bra, and her breasts spill out. I take her nipple in my mouth and I'm ravenous with desire. I never thought Joey could be any hotter than she already is, but goddamn, the thought of my kid growing inside her is turning me manic.

I'm uncontrollable. I shove down her panties, followed by my boxers, and our bodies melt into one. She drapes her leg over mine, and my dick forces against her. There is nothing slow about what's happening. There are no words for how I feel, so all I can do is show her, be inside her, connect to her in the deepest possible way and make love to this woman. The mother of my soon-to-be child.

I run my dick up and down along her seam, wetting myself with her juices, and she wraps her hand around my cock to slide me inside. She's never felt so good. Her hot, swollen pussy is tight around my dick, and I ease in and out of her and bury my face in her neck.

"You're so sexy like this. All glowing... fuck, Joey..." Her insides clamp down. "I'm going to take such good care of you."

She gasps. "Pup... Jesus, babe, you're deep." She writhes underneath me, riding in sync to the punishing rhythm I've set. "You don't think your monster dick can hurt it?"

"Shit." I slow down, steady myself the best I can, but when I stare into her eyes, it isn't easy. I'm hard as fuck sharing the most special thing in the world with my woman. I thrust more carefully, but it doesn't matter that I'm not going strong... Staring into the eyes of my soulmate, my body responds naturally. My balls tighten and my muscles go taut... "Fuck." My release is involuntary, raw, pure with the most manly urge in the world.

She pinches her nipple and bites her lip. "Ahhh," she moans, letting go around me. Her pussy flutters and pulses around my cock. "Oh my God."

My hips rock more carefully. I steady myself to watch euphoria wash over her features. I thought my premature release would let her down, but she's humping me wildly and soaking the sheets.

We slow down and lie next to each other.

I run my fingers along the length of her arm and breathe her in. "Sorry, baby girl. I couldn't control myself."

She wipes her forehead as if she's been sweating. "Pregnant lady kink unlocked," she jokes.

"Yeah... guess I have a thing for breeding." I'm not even joking. For being so brief, that was the hottest sex I've ever had. "But I should have serviced you first."

"Are you kidding? I'm like, seriously feeling it down there. Maybe there's already extra blood flow or something."

She turns her face to me, and I stare into the gorgeous green eyes I hope she gives our baby.

"Maybe I have a baby daddy kink."

I kiss her nose. "I never thought anything could be hotter than that hockey stick."

<hr>

We wait until our fourteen-week scan to tell anyone. I feel positive as hell that if any two people are fertile and having a big strapping baby, it's me and Jolie, but I get her wanting to keep it private. She told me about her sister-in-law, Sam, and that even though Jolie is still young and we both feel healthy, it doesn't mean anything.

She wants all the proof. All the info in the world, and I should have known she'd have a great conversation with the sonographer, given that Jolie herself is pretty good at detecting fur babies. When the sonographer confirms a baby boy, we both cry. We're not criers, but I'm glad we know how to let it flow when the moment is worth it.

All the way home we talk about hockey skates and miniature ponies and that we can't get a cat yet but maybe a dog. We're in big-time nesting mode by the time we reach the couch. We stare at the photos we got from our scan. Something primitive happens to two people when they are about to become parents, something chemical that causes that instant bond, because I can't take my eyes off the blobs. They're the most amazing, gorgeous blobs in the world.

Jolie rubs her still-flat tummy. "Wow."

I put my hand over hers. "Since we can tell people now. Are you still up for what we discussed... since it's a boy?"

She nods gently. "Of course."

I grab my phone off the coffee table and get straight to FaceTime. Jolie and I have talked about this only once before, but it was a dead serious conversation. Fletcher is the first person we decided we would tell if we ever got pregnant.

The real end of the Chloe drama in my mind wasn't when Jolie and I confronted her in Malibu. It was when my brother braved making a PR statement. His agent and agency are among the most reputable in the country, and ended up making the statement public in a way only his truest fans noticed. Somehow, the talented people he works with made it a private public affair positioned as a niche special interest story that wasn't big news. But by not keeping it secret, Fletcher took away Chloe's leverage for all of us. My brother making that decision set us all free.

The video call rings, and eventually, my brother answers from what appears to be a poolside but he's wearing a polo. We're both post-season now.

"Yo..." He pops on a baseball cap to cover his eyes.

"Hey. Where are you?"

"Cabo."

I want to blurt out everything but don't want to be interrupted. "Do you have a minute?"

"Always for you. What's up?"

Jolie pokes her head into the frame. "Hey, Fletch."

"Hey, trouble."

Jolie glances at me briefly then back at Fletch. "So, we're calling you first about something really important."

Fletcher goes from sitting back casually in his chair to upright. "Yeah..."

She continues, "Because you are the whole reason Ashton and I are even together..." She fumbles on her words.

"That's not true. You two would have always ended up together, but I never mind taking credit for a good thing." He flashes her his dimple.

She smiles back. "It's true. But we wouldn't be where we are right now if you didn't, you know, have balls."

He throws his head back with a laugh. "I'll take that as a compliment."

"So we wanted you to know first that"—she gazes at me intensely and the impact of her words strikes me as if I'm hearing it for the first time—"we're having a baby."

Fletcher erupts in laughter and sounds of surprise and joy and exclamation points. "Damn! That's... Shit, I'm... I couldn't be happier for you two. You... I'm..." He stumbles over what to say but finally swipes a hand down his face and beams at the screen. "I'm going to be an uncle." He shakes his head, and our gazes meet on screen. "You're going to be a dad, bro."

I nod. "About damn time."

"It is about damn time." He's smiling ear to ear.

Jolie wraps her arm around me and leans in even closer. "And we already know it's a boy."

"A boy!" Fletcher shouts then glances around him, clearly in some public place maybe his volume isn't appropriate. "Hell yeah. I need to move back to the Canyon and make a quarterback out of him."

"Hockey," I correct.

"Football."

I scratch my head. "I'm not sure there's room in the NFL for two Fletchers."

He shakes his head. "What do you mean?"

Jolie hugs me and gazes at the screen. "We want to name him after you."

"What?" His jaw goes slack. "Seriously? Are you?"

The smile on his face is everything I hoped it would be.

"Guys... no... this feels like the biggest deal."

He places his two hands in prayer position over his mouth, and I watch the disbelief, awe, and joy dance in my brother's deep-brown eyes.

"I love you, bro." These words have now become commonplace between me and my brother, but they still feel significant as the first time I said them. "I hope our son becomes a man as great as you one day."

His eyes grow glassy. "With you two as parents, he'll be better." He takes his cap off, combs his fingers through his hair, and places the hat back on his head, smoothing it against his scalp. "Wow. I'll be damned." He talks to himself more than to us. "I'm going to be an uncle. To Fletcher junior."

All I see next is a hand clapping down on Fletcher's shoulder. He talks to the person off screen. "Yeah, be right there."

I excuse him. "You go. Play golf or whatever you got going on down there."

"I want you to send me those photos. The creepy, modern art ones people get with scans. Of all the things I've achieved, I think having someone name a kid after me is pretty up there. I want to show people pictures of my nephew." Before he hangs up he points a finger at us. "Who's playing football. All right, gotta go, but I love you both. Congratulations and..." He gives us a thin-lipped smile. "Thank you. This made my day."

We hang up, and I gaze at my woman.

"It's official." I put my hand on her tummy. "We name this kid Fletcher and we will have a lunatic on our hands."

She laughs. "Thank goodness. We can't be having a boring kid." She kisses me.

"And he's playing hockey."

"Pup..." She glows. "That goes without saying."

THANKS SO MUCH FOR READING MY STORY!

If you enjoyed BOURBON BREAKAWAY and want to see what happens with Jolie and Ashton. Join my newsletter and receive their beautiful Extended Epilogue. https://Book Hip.com/GANHQMQ

And if you have the hots for Logan now, his book is next! Shay and Logan are coming your way in Perfect Playbook. Order here—>https://geni.us/perfectplaybook

Here's the blurb for their second chance, single mom, marriage of convenience!

PERFECT PLAYBOOK

LOGAN

I heard of Shay Mendez before I met her. She baked. Was reportedly grumpy. Loved her big family. And had sinful curves she kept most men away from with her moody gaze.

We had little in common, except for the most important thing...

At college, Shay and I locked eyes in a grief support group. Both away from Starlight Canyon, she was the anchor I badly needed to keep me from floating away into darkness. My first girlfriend was my polar opposite, but everything I ever wanted. Guess she didn't feel the same.

After years in the NHL and her becoming a single mom, I run into Shay in Vegas of all places. A thousand teardrops, a dozen shots and two wedding rings later, we wake up in the morning married. Much like back in college, Shay and I have a lot to offer one another.

That morning in Vegas we write the perfect playbook for our fake marriage, orchestrating it right through the final buzzer. But I won't let it end the way she thinks it does.

This time, *I win*.

https://geni.us/perfectplaybook

Acknowledgments

Charmaine Aviguetero, I would have never put this book out in its glory without you! You helped shape this from start to finish with your patient voice notes and enthusiasm. You are the most awesome book bestie, PA and alpha reader a woman could ask for. I'm so grateful!

I also want to thank my fabulous beta readers! Caroline Palmier of @love.andedits and Tabitha from probablyalovestory. Having you ladies in my corner has been amazing... you helped me have confidence in a time I feel very little! This means so much. Your highlight are the sunshine in my day.

To all my ARC readers and those who support me on social media, I see you. This journey I'm on is propelled by your jet fuel and I never for a minute think I couldn't do it without you. I'm so so grateful for being able to live my dreams because of you.

Lastly, I always have to send grace to my family and friends who show interest in my author career even if they have no clue what I'm talking about. They love me for the spicy, sassy lady that I am. I live in a world without shame and I know I'm one of the lucky ones. Thank you so so much.

Also by Sienna Judd

STARLIGHT CANYON SERIES

Thirteen Candles

Mustang Valley

Perfect Playbook

About the Author

Sienna Judd is a small town, contemporary romance author who lives for all the spice and book boyfriends who are book husband material.

Sienna is an American girl married to her Prince Charming. She lives with her husband, three children, pony, dogs, guineas pigs and countless other animals on a small farm England. She thinks kitchens are for dancing, is everybody's hype girl and might be known for talking too loudly.

Like every respectable woman she also loves drinking champagne and eating half of every chocolate in a truffles box.

Her spirit animal is a butterfly.

www.ingramcontent.com/pod-product-compliance
Lightning Source LLC
Chambersburg PA
CBHW021239190726
48289CB00005B/1400